D1824420

Lincolnshire born Paul Warwick graduated with a degree in Geology before undertaking further studies in Information Technology.

He is married to Elaine and they live in Berkshire where he runs his own business and computer consultancy.

Paul has always enjoyed listening to a wide cross section of music and is an avid reader of modern fiction, particularly the fantasy genre, and now presents his first novel in a series telling the epic drama of a world where humanity is locked in conflict with another monstrous species, who have also evolved to contest for dominance.

THE MARCH
OF THE BAND

Paul Warwick

The March Of The Band

Vanguard Press

VANGUARD PAPERBACK

© Copyright 2003
Paul Warwick

The right of Paul Warwick to be identified as author of
this work has been asserted by him in accordance with the
Copyright, Designs and Patents Act 1988

All Rights Reserved

No reproduction, copy or transmission of this publication
may be made without written permission.
No paragraph of this publication may be reproduced,
copied or transmitted save with the written permission or in
accordance with the provisions
of the Copyright Act 1956 (as amended).

Any person who does any unauthorised act in relation to
this publication may be liable to criminal
prosecution and civil claims for damage.

A CIP catalogue record for this title is
available from the British Library
ISBN 1 843860 47 3

Vanguard Press is an imprint of
Pegasus Elliot MacKenzie Publishers Ltd.
www.pegasuspublishers.com

First Published in 2003

Vanguard Press
Sheraton House Castle Park
Cambridge England

Printed & Bound in Great Britain

Dedication

For my lovely wife Elaine and
joyous new baby son, Nathan.

With thanks for your support to Mum and Dad,
Chris, Simon and the Haires –
Joe, Margaret and Philip.

Thanks to Dad, Michael and Chris
for the proof reading.

Extra special thanks to David Dry and Thomas for
your help with the extraordinary art work.

And to all future readers – please visit
www.themarchoftheband.com
for maps, illustration and extras to compliment the
book.

Chapter One

The bar tender surveyed the busy club looking for the conspirators on his list. His alert gaze travelled constantly over the cosmopolitan crowd. Representing all corners and cultures of the planet, the customers packed the bar celebrating shared companionship and continued existence. Troops just back from the battle front were mixing with those due to leave, all drinking in raucous abandon to those who had died before and who would follow after, The fluid mass of bodies offered quite a surveillance challenge.

A thousand years was a long time to be at war, but for this pressured nation every season when the front held and every month that people weren't desperate refugees were reasons to celebrate. And here in one of the freest towns this was the hottest club. The music loud, the beat pounding and the dancing and romancing in full swing. The waiters and waitresses were getting into their routine as the place filled, working to keep people refreshed, and moving through to the tables and more private booths thereby relieving the pressure on the bar. Outside the queue at the entrance was building up in the fresh night air.

Mandibles, the bartender, had been allocated the senior slot on the front bar in the staff roster. Dressed conservatively in tailored black trousers and a grey shirt under a black waistcoat he sported, as always, his trademark necklace of polished teeth, mandible bone and carapace, souvenirs of a distinguished military career. The well tailored outfit flattered his powerful physique. He looked calm and professional even though beneath his tough exterior he worried about his ability to juggle the drinks and remember the orders that a professional barman would find easy. Still, he rather enjoyed the challenge of keeping so many people refreshed. It made a change from the usual work of a soldier. Stationed at the middle of the main bar he had a more junior bartender working on either side of his position under the centre of the pyramidal bar. Fashioned from lovingly polished light teak the bar fixture's ornamental roof matched the peak of the room's tight, green-black walls. Taking the ceiling to its tight apex, the naturally dark colours of the stone offered a mystery of shadows and the accompanying lighting added subtly to the atmosphere, offering a carefully calculated hint of claustrophobia that ensured the atmosphere in the club was close and intimate.

At the time when humankind had been 'Shattered' and forced to flee to the northern continent, society had been reformed. The constant battle for survival required extreme social reform and unlimited consumption of alcohol had become a thing of the past. People needed to be alert and as fit as possible to continue the struggle. Brewing techniques in the newly formed United Nation of Peoples had changed and a thousand years later society fully embraced these advancements. As part of weekly wages, therefore, a person was allocated a number of strength-based refreshment tokens. The most popular beverage that Mandibles was serving that night was the successor to beer, termed Nu Brew, it had the taste characteristics of a light ale but was almost totally free of alcohol. Refreshing fruit-based cocktails and such were also favourites that he was regularly asked to provide. Whilst beer and spirits remained available their token premium had such a heavy impact on an individual's weekly allowance that it was only very seldom that they were requested.

Mandibles needed all his wits about him to ensure that the one hundred customers at the bar were being served correctly. Each customer had an account stick set up, their tokens marked as spent as they used them; they could either have their total tally managed directly by the bar staff or choose to pass them over separately with each purchase. This facility, typified the high level of service that the club management was offering but made each shift taxing for the staff. On top of this, Mandibles also had overall responsibility for spotting certain individuals and reporting on whom they spoke and consorted with and ensuring that the table staff had them seated in the special, monitored booths. Still, life was never dull working the bar compared with cleaning or working the doors and time rushed by whenever he worked the head slot in the main bar rotation.

Fully open now for six months, the club was finally established as the number one spot in town, and despite his seniority, even military rank would not have been sufficient to keep Mandibles as head barman should he not be up to the job. As it was though, his quiet confident demeanour and quick intelligence made Mandibles a natural and he soon became a noted feature of the club's success. When teased about his new reputation by the other staff Mandibles often thought that, given the nasty attributes of some of the villains he had been asked to inform on, it was unlikely that popularity would offer much protection. Even in a military society, the majority of the club's patrons would have been surprised at the amount of weaponry available to the staff below the working side of the counter the club was taking no chances. A fashionable club by all appearances Mandibles, above all, knew that below the surface it was so much more.

*****

Several hundred leagues away an equivalent party was also underway. Deep in the plains of the central heartlands though, this was a much less glamorous affair: The venue a huge domed pavilion of waterproofed canvas. Payment was a single entrance fee and once in all the drinks and food were complimentary. Not that there was much choice, but the standard was pretty good. Certainly there was no alcohol available, with fruit punch or water the limit of the choice. What it lacked in adult sophistication though this party made up for in energy and enthusiasm, for this was the Central Plains Youth Militia's quarterly dance. An event now in its second year and increasing dramatically in popularity. From all over the region students would spend the run-up attempting to avoid trouble so that their superiors would authorise the attendance passes required to travel to the venue. For one afternoon then, and all through the night to the following dawn, the hottest bands would play and the teens could dance and party as hard as they liked.

Now as they approached Midst-night one of the hottest acts was just starting up. This group was possibly the one that could claim the most influence in transforming what previously had just been one of the many local events of its type. Several cadets from Master Smee's War Band camp had formed a smaller group, or Beat Combine as they termed it, and performed a set lasting a day-part[1] that had picked up so much of a reputation that other camps and training facilities had started to request tickets in such numbers that soon only a regionally organised event had the scope to fulfil the demand. The organisers had found that the atmosphere was extremely buoyant and in times of hardship, they felt that the benefits of greater unity and good-humoured revelry easily justified the complex logistics of organising the event.

The Beat Combine, which although fronted by the angelic sounding, and indeed looking, female singer Amelia, received the most profound praise for the pulsating beats provided by the rhythm section, Antonio on the bass box and Blue Boy on the drums.

As the lights rose during the 'intro' section to their first number – the lighting effects provided by one of the nearby engineering schools and their experimentation with linseed oil lamps and mirrors – the band came into focus. Amelia pale and stunning her voice part was yet to come in but the front row of the crowd were waving frantically at her and trying to copy her undulating dance as she dazzled and entranced with her gentle grace. Lacy was the other female member and played the wind instruments, Antonio was on beat box with Remus on the lutes, harps and other strings. But at this point it was the drums that were king and the rotating pools of light soon came to centre on the drummer. Considerably younger than the other Combine musicians, Blue Boy was certainly one of the most distinctive members. In a nation formed from the desperate refugee

---

[1] The nation measures time in years, months, weeks and days. Each day is divided into twenty 'day-parts' or more simply 'parts' each equivalent to a period of 90 minutes. Each day-part is divided into 100 mini parts or 'minis' or more commonly, fractions of a half, quarter, fifth, eigth or tenth part. Thus when a trooper speaks of a part in English this would possibly read as an hour, and a tenth would equate to ten minutes.

migrations of all the displaced cultures and populated from the remains of humanity, Blue Boy stood out, for he was, as his name suggested, not from the human branch of the master species, Homanid, but from their close cousins the Rainbow Folk. Blue Boy was clearly one of the Blue People, his skin tinted blue and becoming more deeply pigmented with age, as was common of all the Rainbow Folk as they grew towards adulthood.

Not only was it his colour but also physical appearance that marked him as somewhat different. Of the Rainbow Folk the males of the Blues and the Greens both tended towards similar physical traits: heavily developed musculature and great strength combined in a frame that was almost as broad as tall. As the drum beat tightened and the pace of the song increased the working of Blue Boy's muscles certainly stood out, and the particular Blue Folk heritage was definitely seen. Where the Green folk would grow to great size, providing strength and speed, the Blues remained more compact but with highly developed reflexes capable of performing great feats of gymnastics and athleticism.

The opening song was written to whip the crowd into a frenzied, dancing mass as with each round of the song the tempo increased and soon Blue Boy's arms became a blur as he subtly infused the rapid notes with a variety of swaying and pulsating beats, keeping the rhythm exciting, yet danceable.

*****

Back in Buccaneer Town the music was also pulsing and Jeffers Star was in his element, sliding gracefully between tables, seeing and being seen. As one of the North's most celebrated fixers, not to mention youngest, he was the man to know and as host and owner of the club and he was never more at ease. And what a club! Where else for the price of a weeks wages, or more – depending on appetite, could a group mix business and pleasure with a man so well connected, or simply enjoy the club and party. Other fixers were as well known, but Jeffers had that added something special. Certainly he made himself the most available and, despite the implied cost, you would certainly meet him in luxurious surroundings. The new band he had contracted was establishing themselves. He had picked them for their ease at creating subtle new takes on musical themes and leading popular fashion. The arranger, a young talented girl, whose service had faltered with a war band that had suffered almost total casualties a couple of campaign seasons before, and being too young for her own Mastership, found the club position a convenient residency in between postings.

The waiters and waitresses also provided an enviable mixture of excellent service and attractive deportment, firmly backed up by the ever-so-polite bouncers in a policy of 'look but don't touch'. It was said that for the last two seasons of campaigning, Jeffers had fixed upwards of two out of three of the independent contracts. The campaigns had been so successful that this season his patronage would prove itself as useful as a major placing in competition at one of the larger recruitment Fayres. What made this circumstance even more interesting was that Jeffers had yet to take his place in rotation on the selection panel as the chairperson.

The North had seen fixing as a trade as far back as local records existed, certainly for most of the recent millennium. When the United Nation of Peoples was formed after the 'Shattering' of the lost continents, the traditional practice of levying towns and strongholds proved unworkable. The new towns consisted only of mixed-race groups and family wealth to fund expedition parties was nonexistent. Consequently any standing army had to be formed of repeat-cycle militia conscription with the participation of all citizens, starting as cadets in a compulsory youth academy system.

Forming the core of the army in this way initially alleviated certain financial issues, however, as time passed and commerce became re-established the army put in place financial plans for the funding of fighting companies. These teams, or crews, of combatants fitting somewhere between the old historical method of the levied towns and simply paid mercenaries. Each crew had a leader and in order to be eligible to be such, a known soldier would be licensed. Once licensed this man or woman could form his or her own company and would then be responsible for training it to a certain standard. These groups would be paid a small standing fee to allow basic subsistence and then additional funds could be earned by enlisting for a variety of duties. Thus men and women who found civilian life dull could contribute to the war effort once they had completed their compulsory service, as, perhaps, a sport or in search of wealth or glory.

From the army's perspective, it was more manageable if the regular forces controlled all planning and execution of all campaigns, if not all the combatants. Licensed fixers of suitable qualification were tasked to fill gaps in manpower, with contracts awarded to suitable companies. A panel of qualified veterans sat on both licensing committees. The Board of War Control had the job of choosing which soldiers were suitable to lead teams and pick the very few fortunate enough to become fixers. To be a fixer required something special, not least the ability to relate to all manner of people. Those individuals chosen often turned out to be not only the most formidable talents in all of the Nation but also the biggest rogues.

*****

Lauren stood propped at the bar, foot tapping in time to the music. 'This club is good,' she thought, glad that she had made the effort to squeeze into a pair of finely cut moleskin leggings, a sleeveless vest and shirt top cut just short of too revealing. She could fit right in at this club, have some fun, flirt, and maybe meet someone. 'No, too close that! Well, maybe a careful fling.' Perhaps she could find some muscle, just about to ship out, no worry of complication. 'Wait!' Lauren caught herself, she hadn't wangled this posting to come here and waste time on fun, flirting and casual sex. She was here because her friend and colleague was dead and she had come to investigate. That was why she was out this night: or any night; to find answers. Chloe's mysterious reports had sounded much too real for her subsequent death to be anything other than suspicious.

It had taken a good amount of string pulling to cut short her commission at the training school and get assigned as the new Militia commander, Chloe's former post. Not to mention the disapproval these actions had received from her father who disapproved of anybody pulling strings, especially somebody as visible as his own daughter. In fact he had seemed even more reluctant than usual and, whilst there was no way he would know details of her friends misfortune, there seemed to be something extra about it that was causing him concern.

Stubborn as Lauren was, this protective parental display only served to make her more determined. Today she had been in the position for exactly three weeks. 'Difficult weeks at that.' Chloe had made the command sound so easy, but then she had had front line serving experience and a real reputation to offset her command. Lauren, however, was finding that away from the High Fort her father's name simply proved a hindrance, everyone assuming that he had eased his precious daughter into a position of command without much responsibility and out of danger.

Tonight though, she felt she had dealt with the main trouble maker and after the fight, high on the adrenaline rush of success and victory, she had changed into a provocative outfit and set out for the up-and-coming club that everybody was talking about. Now she had arrived she liked it, and she could see why everybody did. That didn't mean, though, that she knew what she was going to do. Several times already she had caught herself making eye contact with a handsome man, undressing her with his eyes, or turning so that he would get a better view or see her profile caught better in the light. The club used coloured glass and cleverly driven paper shades to move the lights and blend bright and soft colours moving over the walls of the club. This activity, though likely to attract conversation from admirers, wasn't going to lead her to meeting someone with interesting information. She wished now that she had waited before visiting the club, inviting one of her female colleagues. Still done was done and all things considered she concluded that bartenders were a source of local knowledge. She lent forward to order another mild drink and start a conversation.

Unfortunately Lauren had waited too long. Just after she had asked for her drink the band began their main set and the volume rose dramatically. Still, having decided on this plan she stubbornly chose to persist and was bellowing a general question into the bartender's ear. Leaning back the bartender gave her a considering look and shook his head miming lack of hearing. Lauren was used to men stopping to take in her profile, and wearing her light brown hair back in a simple pony tail as she was helped set off her eyes and face. In this case she got the impression that the barman's gaze was more professional than personal. Whatever he saw or decided about her he soon smiled reassuringly, as if in recognition of an old acquaintance. He then reached beneath the bar and pulled out a small, carved, blue wooden token. Handing it to her he pointed over her head where, looking up, she could see a dimly lit balcony bar. He then pointed to the token and at a door off to the side and mimed a knocking action.

Intrigued, Lauren took his advice, the token and the drink and squeezing through the throng rapped hard at the door. It was opened quickly by a smartly dressed young doorman who looked at her quizzically. She waved the token under his nose and pointed back at the bartender. The doorman nodded his understanding and beckoned her in, closing the door and bolting it behind her.

Suddenly the volume of the music was reduced to a murmur and Lauren felt a shiver of concern, realising that out of the common bar her safety was no longer assured by potential witnesses. Now she could be in harms way entering the door with what could have been a 'please murder me' token was a bit hasty. Still, she was here now. With one tough but still unarmed man Lauren decided that as she could certainly look after herself she might as well play out her hand.

Looking up she saw the tall doorman was smiling gently at her as if in encouragement. "Sorry to disturb you but I was just chatting to the bartender when the band struck up," Lauren started. "I didn't catch his last words but he handed me the token and pointed me this way."

"I see, my lady, well Mandi always is a generous fellow. No doubt he was explaining the club memberships to you and felt you would welcome a temporary members pass for the evening, when you were unfortunately interrupted."

"Well, actually, no sir, although I might well be interested. We were just chatting casually," she added honestly, biting her lip almost immediately the guileless words were uttered.

"Ah, I see. Well, no matter, the offer is still there should you so wish. The Night Fort club strives for the highest standards of service," the doorman replied smiling, clearly pleased to offer what the bartender had not.

"Mmm, yes, I certainly would appreciate experiencing the membership tonight then," Lauren blurted.

"Very good, madam, let me show you the way. I must say that you are most fortunate this evening. The duty host tonight is actually the facilities manager, and the evenings that he is in charge often have the best food and service of any. Some consider him as a partner in the club. No doubt he will be able to explain any questions you might have," her guide informed her as they reached the top of the spiral staircase. "Ah, here you are, this is the private members' balcony bar. If you would kindly wait here someone will be right with you.

He guided her away from a long and opulently stocked, beautifully polished bar of lacquered walnut and into a glass fronted cubicle. Here not only did Lauren have a splendid view of the stage on which the musicians were performing, but could also hear, via what she assumed must be a series of cleverly hidden grills, the music from below quite clearly.

"Ah, good evening Madam. I am Taverner, your host tonight." Lauren almost jumped at the sound of the voice suddenly over her shoulder. "Welcome to the balcony members' bar at the Night Fort club. On behalf of Mister Jeffers Star and myself I bid you sincere welcome." The music was not so loud, that, she should have heard the waiter approach. Turning quickly to face her self-announced host, she withdrew the waiter thought. The dapper man facing her exuded a feeling of warmth and hospitality beyond that of a mere functionary.

"My colleague informs me that our bartender downstairs has directed you up here, in a perhaps unsolicited manner. My apologies for his presumption; I do hope though that you will accept our hospitality here as a freely given gift and disregard any idea that we are struggling to sell you a membership." Taverner smiled benignly at the young woman, enjoying the opportunity to play his role to the maximum for someone used to the polished ways of the High Fort.

"Well, thank you for your kind words, sir. In fact a membership may be just the thing, though I admit I would have a number of questions before seriously considering the prospect," Lauren replied thoughtfully. "Perhaps a fresh drink would be in order and if you could spare a few moments of your time I would ask you to provide me with some information. Not only about your club but also the town as I am newly arrived here. I have been in Buccaneer Town just three weeks today," Lauren boldly informed her host.

"Why, madam, it would be a pleasure. We ourselves are only recently opened and we find our members attend less regularly between feast days. Moreover the members bar itself is somewhat more exclusive and strives for the best in service, for every guest up here a member of staff is always available to provide personally for his or her own needs."

The host then indicated that Lauren might follow him by gently taking her arm and leading her to the furthest end of the bar. As they proceeded they passed a number of similar, but more discrete, alcoves, all with splendid stage views and faint whispers of the music. Motioning her to a comfortable padded stool, at the end of the bar her host backtracked and reappeared shortly on the business side of the counter.

"Firstly, madam, I must apologise for not introducing myself more completely before. My name, as you know, is Taverner. Piker. Tonight's members' entry assistant may have mentioned that I am in charge of hosting Mister Star's excellent club facilities," Taverner began carefully, playing his role of a quaint, if stuffy, serving man. "Our establishment is appropriately licensed by the council of Admirals to supply fine foods, beverages and musical entertainment as laid out in the United Peoples' social charter," Lauren's host continued grandly, with an encompassing flourish of his arm in the direction of the lower bar which, whilst theatrical, he deemed a fitting addition to the description of such an opulent entertainment venue. "This we do in three ways. We host a general bar for the provision of the musical entertainment, beverages and light refreshment foods. This is open at certain times throughout the majority of the day. All members of the public are invited, although of course there are some conditions as to the nature of the attire of our guests and appropriate standard of behaviour, so as not to inconvenience the other guests or affect the levels of hospitality that we can supply."

"Secondly," Taverner continued, miming the carrying of tray, "There is the general restaurant. This too is open to all members of the community, although booking is almost always required. Thirdly we offer our patrons the ability to subscribe to this club under a private membership scheme. There are a range of options available, allowing each membership to be personal and individually affordable, although obviously certain standards are costly to meet. Generally though, the membership, which by the very nature of the service offered, is limited. Membership can therefore involve the use of certain other socially based club facilities, including this private bar, private function rooms, private dinning rooms or reserved parts of the general restaurant, complete management of a members drink credits and so on and so forth. This bar itself is a fine illustration of the kind of enhanced service we offer. No doubt you spotted the various alcoves we passed to reach our current position. Well, you may have noticed that each receives a slightly louder volume of the music. Thus at the first alcove the music is but a background murmur, like the gentle trickle of a stream nearby one might say. Here, however, if I pause in my discourse momentarily, you will be able to enjoy the music clearly This allows you the companionship of the bartender but still providing entertainment when he is called away to perform his duties." Thus, finished with his grand introduction, the dapper fellow simply concluded with a smile leaving Lauren free to respond as she wished.

"Well, Mister Taverner, I must say that your facilities from your description, and certainly from what I have seen, are most impressive. As a resident of High Fort until recently I can confirm that I know not of any establishment to which I might attribute a greater attention to detail." Lauren paused, "Although having a rough idea of club membership costs I would guess that the expense of a full subscription here must be extreme indeed," She said cheekily, matching his flowery speech with a slight smile to indicate that bargaining might commence.

*****

Stonebrow stood, arms crossed, to the rear of the pavilion. The Combine were just getting better and better and he was excited, despite himself, to hear some of his students perform so well. Master Smee's music camp was responsible for organising the event and so a good number of the camp seniors were dotted around the site. With the war continuing, the Militia was always on a state of alert and one of Stonebrow's responsibilities tonight was security. Every cadet was required to travel armed, but at a dance the carrying of weapons, of course, proved dangerous, so one of the security's key exercises was to collect up all the weapons and hold them at various known locations so that they could be distributed at a moments notice. The event's presiding supervisors, musicians themselves from Smee's camp, moved around armed. Stonebrow eased his sword, strapped tightly to his back, down to rest more easily against his shoulder. He had elected to do tent duty, but even here at the back the dancers were packed happily and sweatily together. He looked up to the security platform where he signalled for a report; the hand talk came back that both the internal and external security teams had recently reported all clear and that the long-range scouts were reporting routinely.

*****

Mandibles took a brief rest sitting in the stool-chair in the bar alcove. This session's junior, Barney, was well able to do a few moments on his own in the centre position. The juniors rotated twice as often as the senior staff. Mandibles needed the break to make his notes. Several of the names on the key surveillance list had been in this evening, and a couple of new names could be added to the list of their connections. Worryingly, one was a member of the local police, the Marine Patrol, and any involvement in the operation by members of the town's own law enforcement department would only lead to trouble with the operation that Mandibles was being asked to organise.

*****

Lauren had cornered Mister Taverner's sole attention for well over half a part, and he continued to answer her questions with no sign of impatience. "Well, the community here is fairly

23

cosmopolitan, what with the Admiralty deeded with possession rather than the military council. We mainly deal with the quartermaster function you understand, although here it is a bit different. We have a rotating contract awarded on behalf of the Admiralty to the town's Master Baker." He seemed quite at ease standing at the bar, performing small routine tasks as he talked confidently to the club's potential member.

"Master Baker Pearson has that role now and, since he landed the job, he has had all kinds of worries. The most recent being the seafood plague this last season. Plenty of folk have gone down with poisoning from eating bad sea staples. Precious few survived I can say. Many of the contracted harvesters and bed farmers have seen their businesses go under or have moved away. Fortunately the baker has invested his fortune heavily and the town is getting by," Taverner told Lauren who found herself more and more on the end of an almost military briefing and needing to ask very few, if any, questions.

Without waiting for comment her host continued. "Still life goes on and we manage to make do at the local markets and have some food imported. Luck with us, the club has not yet had any problems. It wouldn't do our burgeoning reputation any good either so we're keeping a close eye on the whole situation I can tell you. May I ask what line you are in, Madam?" Taverner finally asked the young girl carefully, believing it was time to move the conversation on and allow him to address things the girl was not aware he knew.

"Well, yes, Mister Taverner, I am the new Provost Captain of the Militia Honour detachment to the Free Admiralty State of Buccaneer Town and its holdings," Lauren replied, not bothering to the give the more workable version of her official title. Mister Taverner seemed like a man for expansive description.

"Ah yes, then you must be Miss Marshall. Sorry to have bored you with all this detail. You would have been briefed on most of it I am sure," Taverner offered, looking most uncomfortable.

"Oh no, in fact I hadn't heard much about the effects of the food problems. We'd just been told about a few minor health issues and to be careful of bad seafood generally. I suppose that the admiralty would want to keep a pretty tight lid on such affairs," Lauren reassured him gently, patting his immaculately kept hands.

"I must say our condolences on the death of your colleague, the previous commander. She was a nice lady, although we only saw her here occasionally. Would you like some more coffee?" he asked. Lauren watched as a staff colleague discreetly conferred with her host. "It seems that you are our last guest in this area tonight. "Time seems to have raced away," Taverner commented in what could have been a very subtle move to close the bar. "I hope you have enjoyed our hospitality."

*****

Another half part later Lauren left the club its newest member, feeling buoyant. Club membership seemed an easy way of securing reliable sources of gossip, if not information, and her careful use of a family allowance certainly gave her the means. She would be careful to test snippets of information with members of her own command so as to be sure it was not just a case of bar staff with wagging tongues and over active imaginations.

Lauren positively trotted up the cobbled street back to the Militia compound. In fact she was so happy that she completely failed to notice a suspicious looking fellow detach himself from the shadows and follow her up the street. He was fairly cautious but had to struggle to keep up with her fast trot. 'Curse the ultra fit warrior class,' he thought. The sooner the word is passed down for the bitch's removal the happier he would be. Still, at least it wasn't raining and as he knew her destination if he didn't keep up it wouldn't matter much. Finally he rounded a bend just in time to see the guardroom door slam shut.

Safely back home he thought. Soon she'll be nicely tucked up; and his instructions were to keep surveillance until relieved in the morning. Well, with not a huge time till dawn and her abed there was no way he was wasting sleep on that. So he scuttled away to report and request a replacement. As he drifted away, the third quiet individual to enter the street froze statue-still in an unlit side street.

"Ah, already the plot accelerates. Our little dove has

another admirer, one with pretty poor training as well. Let's see where this brute takes me. Forgive me, my dove, for I must forsake care of you for a few brief moments now," the shadowed figure whispered to himself, crouched in the filth behind a water barrel as his competitor passed casually by.

*****

The Marshall turned back to his aide, a funny, bright-eyed, plump little man with a shiny, pink face and thin limp hair brushed close against his skull. Wearing a thin matching jacket and waistcoat, pockets full of ancient pens and pencils and unusual, thinly-striped trousers, the Marshall's gaze was drawn frequently to the sigil embroidered on his lapel of some obscure specialist training school. On the aide's middle fingers of his only remaining hand sat a jewelled finger guard and, on inspection the only sign of his former position, the wings of a butterfly.

"A lawyer you have made of me, Marshall. The greatest duellist of this age I was," the plump man, snapped puffing up his chest for drama. "Well you saw him on the steps preaching his poison yourself. You'd have thought him less down-at-heel than that, I'd wager," the aide fumed. "Now you will leave it to me to bring the Church to heel. How do you propose I do that? At least my former profession will have prepared me for the show down. Vesper is a potent man. Don't count on me having succeeded on your return."

Eying his assistant with a curious half smile the Marshall turned to one of the guards standing in the shadows. "Captain Spence, go fetch me the Knight Bishops now," he bellowed in a voice like gravel. "Make it polite and give them, say, a tenth part to prepare."

Turning back to his chamberlain the Marshall continued. "Never believe that I have over estimated you Jonas. You served me well in the West, and I am grateful. But whilst we are at war quality men will never have an easy time." The Marshall paced out through the open window shutters, gently motioning aside the guard and gesturing to Jonas to join him.

"Knight Bishop Vesper, more than many others,

understands the forthcoming campaign." In a lowered voice pitched not to carry he continued, "He will get his expressed wish this season, far more in fact than he could have dared to hope. Should the Nation survive though, I doubt that he will receive what he is expecting."

Moments later a guard called out, "The Knight Bishops Vesper, and Starfire, High Marshall."

"Thank you, Captain Spence, that will be all. Withdraw your men to secure the outer doors," the Marshall replied and gesturing for the Bishops to seat themselves at the table, accepted his Captain's salute as the guards discreetly withdrew from the hall.

"Your Graces, I have presumed upon your time at such short notice only due to utmost urgency. Lunch has been prepared. Perhaps you will forgive my presumption when you learn the reason for my summons." Saying this, the Marshall seated himself at the head of the small table.

"The Nation stands but to serve the Marshall in this time of conflict," answered Bishop Starfire, the words uttered piously enough but the twinkle in his eye conveying his amusement at the attempted diplomacy. "Speak freely, Marshall, and please don't waste your time with politeness'."

"Well enough then. I would first like to introduce my new chamberlain, Sir Ewgene 'Jonas' Candwell. Bishop Vesper may be aware that he formerly occupied the position of Knight Provost to our garrison in the Emrate of Shae."

"Why, yes, Marshall," breathed Bishop Vesper. "I do know something of your Sir Ewgene, we have heard many rumours of his difficulties in that region. At one time I recall that he was actually declared outlaw by the Emir and spent nearly a year as a bandit partisan, dearly costing us the support of that particular Emrate. We also heard afterwards that a great number of Reptoids and some human confederates turned up dead in a hidden cave complex, not long after the Emir died suddenly in his bed. His cousin and successor, I believe, pardoned our provost over the charges which I recall were something to do with smuggling." The bishop tailed off as a number of waiters entered the hall and delivered a simple lunch of fruits, meats and cheeses, together with water and juices, before withdrawing again discreetly.

"As always, my Bishop, you are perfectly informed," the Marshall rumbled. "Now, to business as you said, Starfire. Ewgene is the new war chamberlain and he faces a stiff task in keeping the High Fort running during this season's campaign. My former bodyguard and chamberlain, Carstairs, plus a number of his command have retired from service, and placing themselves on the enders register are disappearing from the view of the world. His services in providing the bodyguard of the High Marshall have moved to Captain Spence and we have reformed the command from the remainder of my guard and every member of staff and students at the High Valley Combat Training School." The Marshall paused to rise and refill his guests' goblets.

"Vesper, the reason you have been asked to sow seeds of discord with your sermons, you may have guessed, is because not only will I and my new guard be taking the field this year but also with the permission of the Church we will, as you have been preaching, also be declaring this season's campaign a crusade."

"Marshall, his Grace and myself have of course discussed this matter and based on your information that the cursed Roke…" and at this point Bishop Starfire cast an enquiring look at Sir Ewgene, "may be plotting something major we are, of course, entirely in support of your action. It would, though, comfort us if you could further explain the nature of this threat and indicate the possible size of your expedition, and maybe reveal its time scale."

"Bishop, you need not be shy with detail around Sir Ewgene, although I admit I have kept my new chamberlain in the dark concerning the preachings of our esteemed Bishop Confessor. My apologies for the subterfuge," the Marshall finished as he turned to his new aide.

"My friends, one of the main reasons for this season's unusual campaign will be that I have confirmed intelligence that within the next three calendar years the Horde proposes to mount a full invasion against our Nation. I therefore expect that by the year's end the call up will be full and by that I mean every able bodied individual, whether civilian, army or church soldier, we will all be at war." At this bombshell Bishop Vesper drew in a chilling hiss of breath, Bishop Starfire gulped loudly and Sir Ewgene began alternately to worry at his tufted goatee and right ear lobe.

"High Marshall, your pardon for failing to provide you with such intelligence," Bishop Vesper replied immediately. "If what you say is true then surely a crisis faces us of a size unseen since the Shattering. If you believe that only an entire call up will suffice then you must have details that the Horde and their vile pet, Roke are capable of mounting an unprecedented and sustained invasion. Tell us, do the Roke are really have the Naval capability that would allow such a thing?"

"Truly they do, I have sacrificed scores of our best people to gather intelligence to that end. Whilst they still lag behind our developments by centuries they have indeed a basic navy, of such size that our own fleets will be hard pressed to stop their advance." The Marshall passed each of his officers a piece of parchment. "Whilst we have suffered little during this past storm season the north-eastern shores of the Battle Lands and the Lost Continent have been subject to a number of big blows. This disrupted the Roke patrols enough for us to slip several survey teams through. Although we only managed to extract a couple they had penetrated some new facilities and reported the kinds of troop and craft numbers that you see before you."

Bishop Starfire turned to his fellow cleric, his parchment crumpled as he subconsciously clenched his fist.

"This goes way beyond a simple campaign. I must hasten to raise the crusade call. May the Battle God protect us all!"

Chapter Two

By mid-morning the club kitchens were already hectic. The employees could use a large, tabled alcove, set aside from the main preparation area where at any time day or night they could expect meals and drinks to be provided. Generally it was frowned upon to eat or drink in any area where guests had access and the kitchen refectory was their own reserved place. Not that all the employees together would fit, but certainly as many as those in one shift could have on break time at once.

Barf was sitting at the far end of the room, away from the other occupants who were playing cards. His knees propped up on the bench, under his chin. He was picking at a tray of steamed gammon and staring reflectively into the distance. Sophie, the eldest of Star's two wards, had informed Mandibles that Barf was back, complaining that the usually boisterous prankster was no fun at all that morning. Mandibles gave him the nod and Barf lifted his food tray and the two ambled to a more discrete supervisor's alcove, where they huddled together in quiet conversation. For the next few moments Mandibles sat asking quiet questions and several times Barf could be seen tracing crude maps through his breakfast to illustrate the routes his quarry had taken. Mandibles quickly ended their discussion and indicating that Barf should catch a bit of quick sleep before his early evening shift he hurried off through the club to make further hasty arrangements.

'Certainly the girl Lauren needs sorting,' Mandibles thought to himself as he rushed up through the club, two steps at a time along the main stairs to the restaurant. Suddenly it was all he could do not to go tumbling back down as his foot slid out from underneath him in a pool of water. Arms flailing, he quickly caught himself on the banister and moving more carefully rounded the last bend to find, as he suspected, Liam. The boy, at six years of age, two years younger than his sister

Sophie, had acquired one of the wheeled mop-buckets and was trying to remove the soapy scum from its surface by scooping water out with a cup. The boy seemed obsessed with water; it wasn't the first time, nor would it be the last, that his complete disregard for spillage would cause problems.

"Come on there, Liam, lad," Mandibles muttered kindly. "It's almost time for the restaurant to open and you don't want our guests hurting themselves or getting their feet wet." Saying that, Mandibles put his fingers to his mouth and gave a piercing whistle of two short and one long blasts. Immediately booted feet could be heard running and Piker and Lawrence rounded the corner. Lawrence took one look and doubled back to fetch some cloths, whilst Piker simply swooped down and scooped the little boy up and, pulling an awfully funny face, spun him around in the air before also speeding off back where he'd come from. Mandibles shrugged inwardly at the bouncer's antics and moved to the upper stairway staff booth where, with a series of coded tugs, he sent a message down the wire to the booth by the Restaurant doors, indicating that all guests should be kept below for an extra tenth part.

By the time he returned to the top of the stairs Lawrence had vanished the bucket and was almost finished with the mop up. Mandibles and Laurence then hurried on to the main dining room. Here there was no sign of Liam or Piker, and Mandibles, assumed that they had spirited out through a rear staff stairwell. Looking up from checking the place settings Taverner raised a quizzical eyebrow and, receiving a non committal shrug from Mandibles, he returned without a pause to a place setting that obviously had attracted his attention. With his measuring ruler he adjusted a wine glass an almost imperceptible distance. With a sigh of satisfaction he waved Lawrence to his position by the door, and Mandibles away out the back, with almost the same motion that caused the ruler in his hand to disappear into a pocket in his jacket.

Taverner moved smoothly to the door to greet the first arriving diners and supervise his young assistant. Switching back in mid-stride Mandibles snatched the cloth that Lawrence was waving frantically behind his back and smoothly sped away out of sight as the young waiter began collecting the guests' hats and cloaks. "Hah, another busy day at the club," Mandibles muttered as he tried to recall what business he had been about before the watery excitement. Star's kids were great but they always managed mischief, it required every staff member to keep their wits about them. Still kids would be kids, and so would young Piker given half the chance. Mandibles made a mental note to check the roster later and ensure Piker hadn't goofed off somewhere with the boy for some foolery.

*****

By the middle of the morning the event began to wind up. Those cadets with less stamina were sparked out, some had managed to return to their tents but others had simply crashed out in a convenient space and were littered around the site, sleeping or resting for the coming exertions and journey home.

Once the event finished the afternoon would see most of the attendees giving their services for the clearing of the site. In fact tickets were distributed solely on the basis that the revellers would also form part of the ground staff, as required by the organisers.

This time, however, the event was completed in an unusual manner. Instead of the final act, usually very mellow in nature or featuring gentle, popular songs for a bit of a sing along, a booming drum beat began to roll out. Rather than more music this was a call for a general assembly and one which all were required to attend. Certain functionaries such as guards, lookouts and scouts were, of course, required simply to pick up a briefing as soon as their position or duties allowed them. The rest of the camp dragged itself up wearily and made for the general marshalling position.

This particular drum signal did not include a call for general arms and thus, with no need to visit weapon collection points the whole assembly was completed in pretty quick time, no recruit wanting their unit to be recorded as the last to muster.

The reason for the call soon became evident when the youngsters spotted a lady, wearing the mauve and crimson uniform of an official herald, standing next to Stonebrow at the top of the gently rising slope. Clearly an official announcement was due to be made. As the event marshals signalled to the officers that the roll call was complete, horns and trumpets rang out giving the call for a full-season campaign. The woman's voice carried far above the crowd.

"Hear and attend as I announce the Marshall's word. In this season of the year one thousand two since the formation of our state, the United Nation of Peoples, I declare a full expedition will be sent against the evil of the Horde. This expedition will also be the one hundred and eleventh Crusade and a levying call is being sent out across all the surrounding nations, not just Human but also Homanid, in a combined effort to throw off the threat of Reptoid attacks." The lady paused to allow this to sink in.

"The call up will therefore consist of the usual standing army commitments, independent companies will also be invited to compete at Fayres and there will be a requirement for all academy camps to be placed on full alert. This season will be a watershed in our campaign and the Marshall requires that I particularly convey the Nation's determination at this time."

Something of a break from the expected, the final words were almost lost as an uncharacteristic murmur greeted the news that the academies themselves would be put on alert, especially for the first Crusade within living memory. Squad commanders were quick, however, to restore discipline and not a few of the youngsters would spend some less pleasant time on report duties to make recompense. The herald moved off quickly, swapping a formal salute with Stonebrow, the senior commanding officer on site. Unlike the commanders of the free companies the War Bands carried full military status and therefore military rank at all times.

Clearly displeased by the lack of discipline Stonebrow's commands themselves were rapidly barked out. The troops were commanded to have the site cleared within a single day-part and that this would be done in full operational mode with hand signals, and vocal exchange only when strictly necessary.

Bristling silence surrounded his progress around the site as he oversaw the work. Cadets all over the camp laboured furiously, everyone seeking to avoid a tongue lashing from the normally laid-back young warrior. Even the effusive

Magnificent Bart, technically his senior, seemed subdued under his intense gaze. A dozen cadets were singled out for additional reprimand and loaded up with heavy packs and sent off to do laps of the campsite followed by latrine duty. Soon all the other companies had been dispatched and only those with members under discipline, and the band contingents remained.

Only when the last celebrants and the band's own youth squads set off at a jog alongside their kit wagons did Bart fail to keep a straight face and, letting out a guffaw, slapped Stonebrow heartily on the back. "You can be much too serious, Stonebrow. I'm not sure a few cadets won't have nightmares over your tongue lashings today. I thought your name came from being rock headed and stubborn not from those stony gazes you've been dishing out."

"Leave it out Bart, those greeners have bloody sloppy discipline. By the Battler, if they do end up at the front in that state we'll ship four from five back in bags within the week." With a slight grin, though, he surveyed the site. "Still, a pretty good time for camp clearance. Might even be back before dusk, if we drive our own scallys on quick enough."

Riding up to the rearguard Bart instructed, "Knuckles, take that worn out nag under your fat arse and check the sprats have got enough wide scouts going. Give a nudge to any loose fish."

Again Bart chuckled. "Man, though, Stoney, was the boy good or what. Whew-ee he's just going to get better and better. Two more years for us to work with them. You've got to talk the old man into an extra extension for Lacy. Man, two more years and even I'll be dancing. Might even be I'll write some songs for the combine, maybe even sing with them."

"Steady on, Bart, we've got two full seasons in between, anything could happen. You've seen how much traffic the boss is getting. There are some big things coming and I'm sure the integrity of one of the kids' fun bands will be far from the Master's main attention. Still you are right, they were pretty special this year. What do you make of the academy alert?" Stonebrow reflected.

"Pah, that, I'll bet in the early years that happened all the time. You know the Marshall's fascination with the past. I'll bet he is just restarting some academy alert routine to get the cadets used to service life." Bart nudged his splendid mount and nightfall began to prance playfully. "After such a light storm season we are all champing at the bit," he chuckled.

*****

Blue Boy began his day early. Up at dawn, an eighth part stretch and then Marvellous would send him off for a competitive run against one of the other musicians. That day, two days after his return from the dance, it was the slender figure of Split, who thrashed him soundly, as always, over the three league steeplechase course. Then back to Marv who had him up and down the climbing wall six times before a quick wrestle and tenth part of manic weapons drill with whoever was the first person past the circle. Then breakfast before studies.

At some time in the recent past Band Leader Smee had detected a lack in Blue Boy's progress and now had him studying separately from the normal classes. Often it was vocal style with Honeygold or intricate lute or harp finger work with the enigmatic, dark skinned Starling. After that particular breakfast it was breath control with the Magnificent Bart. Bart was a huge man, balding and twice Golden Voice winner. He always pushed Blue Boy to match his massive lung capacity and the lesson went on right through lunch, but the lad didn't mind because that afternoon, whilst the rest of the cadets had their usual theory classes, Blue Boy had rest and recuperation. Rest, though, these days was more often than not facilitated by being given archaic books on etiquette and tales of distant lands from which he was expected to derive musical, martial and sometimes even courtly material.

Bart was often telling him that a musician was, above all, expected to play at court, and some courts were a maze of etiquette and correct behaviour. Also, whilst every musician in camp was skilled in the reading of music, Blue Boy was now expected to scribe summations of what he had learnt in a neat hand for Master Smee, to ensure he attained the correct standard.

To be fair, Master Smee almost always managed to find some time in the day to help his 'unorthodox' student and Blue Boy was often given permission to leave camp grounds by

Marvellous to spend time helping his friend Moffet. Although a good few years older than Blue Boy, Moffet was a local country lad. A bit simple, he lived a few leagues further along the road, and suffering from almost crippling shyness he spoke only very rarely. However he managed a smallholding, growing all kinds of vegetables, that supplied much of the camp's food needs. Moffet was quite tall but carried himself in a hunched, awkward manner, as if trying to curl himself inwards and hide away from the world. His face always sported a frightening expression suggestive of ruined facial muscles. This combination gave him a dispensation from active service, providing he worked to supply the camp, where he traded his produce for whatever else he needed.

Mostly, all Moffet wanted was an occasional meat supper and permission to hear the musicians play. This was the only time when the wild, panic stricken look would leave his face and his slightly unfocused eyes gazed intently into the distance. Whilst an expert snaring animals in his homemade traps, Moffet was terrible at maintaining anything else. That was where his friendship with Blue Boy proved a winner. His largest problem was with his wagon. Pretty bad at driving the thing, Moffet almost always needed some kind of repairs doing on it. It was a twenty league round trip to the camp and he travelled a fair bit in it. Once a week Blue Boy tried to look it over. Moffet did have an elder brother, who chose to campaign almost constantly, although always visiting Moffet and the camp whenever he could. When at home he would spend a couple of days leave, ensuring that the smallholding's house and fences got a bit of routine maintenance.

Master Smee always greeted Scandrett warmly and they often spent time closeted away discussing, Blue Boy assumed, the arrangement concerning Moffet's dispensation. Scandrett, though, only managed a few days at home every year and the smallholding did require a fair bit of maintenance, especially the fences and the wire nets sunk below ground to deter burrowing rodents from attacking the vegetables. Master Smee had encouraged Blue Boy from an early age to help with the running of the place. He stated that taking a stake in the running of the smallholding made excellent sense and, further more, it would use up some of Blue Boy's boundless energy.

Blue Boy had grown quite fond of the shy man. Not pushing his company on Moffet he soon found that friendship did not necessarily require a lot of conversation. As Blue Boy grew older and his skin pigment became more evident, he had become more aware of his own differences, and whilst only the camp's younger children mentioned it he felt a similarity to the isolated Moffet. Blue Boy had also recently grown into a unique stature. Never going to be tall his frame, however, seemed to grow sideways to the point where his shoulder breadth and arm reach far exceeded his height, and this possibly set him apart more.

Bart finally released Blue Boy, who hurrying to a timetabled lesson, managed a rare feat of being early and found himself leaning back in his chair waiting for another lesson on the social history of his adoptive homeland. At an early age he had attempted to embrace a people clearly not his own, using learning about its history as an attempt to fit in. As he had grown up though, he had come to the view that communication skill was the real basis for developing relationships and, therefore, creating an environment in which he would be accepted. Despite confiding this to Master Smee, his schooling had become more and more separate from the majority of cadets, and he now found that social history was the only subject where he didn't have special individual tutors. Many times he had questioned his elders as to the reasons why he couldn't participate in group activities like campaign tactics, horse or animal husbandry or weapons practice. Their answers were many and varied but none ever rang quite true.

Mister Kyan was not a dull man though. He taught possibly one in five social history classes and as he walked in Blue Boy was relieved. More often than not this instructor focused his social history discussion on the basis of the nation's state religion. Whilst people were accepted privately practicing a variety of derivations and religious off shoots, provided of course that they were in accordance with the social charter, all peoples resident in the Nation were required to also adhere to the Nation's particular Battle God doctrine.

Blue Boy had been interested to hear that all the other

nations were also bound by the Battle God's Rules of Life. He had also lapped up, as all youngsters did, the stories and legends concerning the God's enforcement of his own rules.

The most universally popular legend and because of its dramatic nature, Blue Boy's own personal favourite, was about one of the nation's monastic groups. Commonly told as the legend of the Order Of Distance Battle, this story involved a group of several hundred battle scholars who petitioned for, and were granted, the use of a small deserted coastal island as their monastic retreat. 15 leagues from the nation's coast, back in the middle centuries, they laboured for twenty years to raise a formidable keep. The Great Battery it was called and it was famous for its huge internal ranges where new ballistae and spring-loaded weapons could be tested under controlled conditions. For ten years the long and often secretive work continued, until in triumph they announced the forthcoming mainland demonstration of superior ballistic technology. Two days after the announcement the Great Battery, and in fact most of the island disintegrated in a huge conflagration heard the full 15 leagues away on the main land.

Such a cloud of dust was produced that not only was it many day-parts before patrol ships could safely approach, but also the mess this episode produced meant that it was many, many months before mainland laundries stopped cursing the event. The patrol ships, on finally approaching the island, found only a single stack of rock remaining above the sea and clearly visible was the God's Sigil of Deterrence embossed deep into the stone.

Blue Boy, taking this story to heart was, therefore, not only proud but also careful to keep the full and entire Law of Life memorised by rote. A difficult feat, he knew that many other cadets often found just the Law of Obeyance difficult enough to recite.

The laws of life:

You may quarry iron, ferrous materials and clay and with these you may furnish tools and weapons;

Wood and other materials may be cultivated, cut and

collected from trees and plants. You may use what you can grow or collect or shear but you must distil nothing other than beverages nor shall you burn anything other than what grows, may be dried, siphoned from the ground or broken open by force of an arm;

You may not, on pain of death, use or explore exploding powders or blend sulphurous materials carrying the stench of hell;

The breeze may propel you or you may journey by the strength of your limbs or those of living creatures harnessed, or by means of wheels and pulleys driven in the allowed manner;

You may fight with arm or fire or physically propelled devices;

The power of the mind is a sacred thing;

If you live your lives and fight well according to these rules you will gain victory over your foes and gain the Battle God's blessing;

Those who break these rules will be destroyed.

Snapping back to attention, Blue Boy mentally berated himself for day dreaming and risking missing the crucial starting point of today's lecture. He soon found he was quite safe though, as the usual pre-class business was still under way. In this case the quality of previous written submissions was the key topic, especially the lack of quality apparent in some particular cases. Most classes were, by their very nature, practical but social study sessions required students to produce presentable pieces of work and were often shorter.

When pushed Stonebrow had admitted that many students in the standard military academies were excused the effort required to learn writing. He had even admitted that many would also leave with only the most basic ability at reading. Basic numbers, counting, time keeping and command phrases plus the shortened Laws of Life seemed about the limit, as far as Blue Boy was able to ascertain. The music academies, his mentor went on to explain, almost always required much higher literacy skills. Song words, reading music and writing it, all these activities, as Stonebrow was fond of saying, often echoing. Master Smee's own words, were related and essential.

39

A bit disappointed but less so than he had expected, Blue Boy soon realised that as Mister Kyan was recapping the basic religious fundamentals on this occasion he would not be speaking of the specific legends concerning the Battle God. No, today his discourse would be concerning the fundamentals of the religion in the nation's daily life, particularly with respect to the War Church. Many of the students around the room could be seen to display the same disappointment that Blue Boy had been experiencing. Now, though, Blue Boy was pleased because the church had many historical and even contemporary figures who were almost as interesting as the Battle God. In fact he remembered that the last session had left him with unposed questions in abundance.

That session had included mention of the famous Dove family, a clan that had almost survived the Shattering. Living out in the marsh plains of the great delta they had thrived in numbers. The most recent story had centred around the storming of Rooks Point in the Battle Lands to rescue a relative from execution. As far as Mister Kyan's brief mention had indicated, a small number of close family, together with a larger group of retainers and more distant family had breached a wall position long held by the Horde's corrupted slave race, the Roke. Whilst the story did not end particularly successfully the few that had survived had been hailed as great warriors and been held as shining examples of citizenry. The nation had itself then been shocked when these individuals had begun to shun the public view en-mass, and several had even taken monastic vows in order to disappear from public view.

Snapping his attention back to the present before he lost the thread of the lesson Blue Boy was soon caught up again as the tutor threaded his way through the surrounding social issues.

Being a martial state the farming union suppliers were headed and controlled by the Quartermaster General. His task was not only to manage the supply of all commercial and non-commercial food within the Nation but also certain production for exchange with neighbours to the south and west. Merchants existed under the specific regulation of the areas in which they traded, and could import certain luxury goods for internal trade in the United Nation. These imports were again managed by the

Quartermaster General's office and the scope of the products limited to minor luxury goods, things like perfumes, art and other life enhancing goods.

Mister Kyan went on to suggest that the northern population by its very practical nature, whilst being delighted with a bit of extravagance, took the same robust and careful view with purchases that they did with the standard Heavenly Laws. Trade also occurred in a more diplomatic way with the Rainbow Folk and the Caballeros and Desert Kingdoms which having themselves equivalent but non military organizations were somewhat more focused on trade. Being different from the north's fusion of different ethnic origins, but still united with a common enemy, Blue Boy could detect few serious problems with essential trade.

*****

Master Smee looked out across his people with pride. In the 16 years since his appointment as Band Master he had built up not only his reputation but also, physically, the whole camp. To have a band named 'War Band' in crusade year was a lifetime achievement for any Band Master. Despite his outward display of pride he also felt somewhat sad. Being the major war band almost always involved dangerous action and within the year he expected to hear news that a significant number of the troops he sent would be dead or maimed. Master Smee was well aware how extremely his people were to be tested in this company and he felt additional guilt because he would not be sharing in the danger. Despite the pride that the High Marshall's faith in giving the band the most dangerous and vital missions gave him, Master Smee still felt torn over the secret way he would be sending even his most trusted friends into the field, without knowing the full story or at least giving them some kind of choice.

Master Smee considered all those who lived in and around his camp as band members, for each contributed in some way or another. As band leader he owed them a great debt for helping build his dream and he always worked to ensure that he gave back all he could in return. This was not yet the time to start announcements and instead he spoke for half a day-part on honour and how the camp as a whole had worked to great achievement, how proud he was not just of their award winning music or the skills at arms, but also more practical matters such as how well they could eat, how clean the camp was, how healthy the animals were and how well behaved the children. He joked about the cadets and the old timers together and tried generally to impart his own enthusiastic view of the camp. Finally he went on to talk about the period running up to the campaign, that they, as a command, would undertake some pre-emptive exercises to sharpen them in case of call up and also that the news of the crusade should not be allowed to unsettle or redirect the camp's overall progress and improvement.

*****

Lauren looked at the note suspiciously. It was sealed with wax and addressed solely with her first name. The duty guard had found it slipped under the gate at the start of dawn watch, which pretty much meant it could have been delivered at any time during the night. She had only received it after returning from early drill at the practice yard and still wearing her under gloves, she took it to the window seat in her room and checked it carefully. Following certain unwritten rules she checked firstly for hidden needles or other sharps, calling to mind the episode in recent months of the death of a provincial provost caused by a poisoned package. Lauren searched around for a light gauze face pad to lay over the note and carefully used a glass fruit bowl cover to further enclose the letter whilst awkwardly slicing open the covering. No powder or sinister vapours emerged, even with the opening inverted, and back in the open she carefully drew out the single sheet of paper.

It was a simple note, not so much written as printed out carefully, to avoid any clues from handwriting, in a style similar to a child learning letters. Dated the previous day Lauren was surprised when it began with a coded introduction similar to that used by the secret cell she had formed. On further inspection it matched the definition for what Chloe would have designated had she set up her own cell locally. This both encouraged Lauren and made her wary. She did not know whether Chloe had been captured and questioned prior to her death. She also felt exposed because either she wasn't known specifically to the enemy and it was purely coincidence that as Chloe's replacement this new note had been addressed to her, or had Chloe broken the rules and revealed the members of one cell to another. Finally deciding to assume the best and be very careful she settled back to consider the body of the note. It read:

Message to control, further investigation into link over removal of guards shows leads to gaming house on Third Street, Firebird House. Clientel mainly local based, some female entertainment inferences, popular with guardsmen and chancers alike. 3 from 6, at least, regular visitors with other three more casual and not confirmed over dates. Suggest extreme caution. Contact One-Three-Fifty-four. End.

Well, the writing of the report also matched exactly with the secret syntax that the girls had designed and surely even under duress Chloe would have detailed an error in syntax that would have warned her friends. On this basis Lauren decided to treat the informant as reliable. Not having the handling agreement she was unable to respond but simply placed blue flowers in her window a sign of business as usual, she had been tempted by green, 'we must meet' but suspected that her source might be more useful if left undisturbed. Lauren therefore decided to memorise and destroy the note for safety's sake and was just crushing the remnants of the burnt paper into a sloppy wet paste in her washbasin when she heard footsteps on the stairs followed by a loud rapping on her door.

"Excuse the interruption, Ma'am, but you have been sent a priority request from the admiral's office to attend him with all possible speed. I have had Silencer saddled and he will be waiting for you by the gate momentarily."

"My thanks, sergeant, I will be with you shortly. Can you and another act as outriders for me if this is an official occasion?" Lauren called back at the still closed door.

"Certainly, Ma'am, the preparations are under way. I'll see you down stairs," and the sound of footsteps receded.

Moments later in standard operational dress uniform, effectively just a change of jacket, Lauren and her two escorts were trotting through the streets nearing the admiral's complex and their destination. Leaving the horses and her escorts in the outer courtyard she was hurried by an aide through several security points into a large briefing room deep in the heart of the complex. There she was surprised to find no fewer than three of the current active admirals, four of the most recently retired and a small number of other senior staff, most of whom she did not recognise. The admiral currently presiding over Buccaneer Town motioned her to a well placed seat.

"Ah, Lauren, thank you for joining us," Admiral Pentak welcomed the militia commander. "We felt it would be only good manners to include you in this briefing and to jointly pay our respects to our brother service. As you can see, though, this meeting carries the highest classification and that is one of the reasons we have called you here at such short notice. We are just concluding our business but you should know that the Marshall has announced not only a campaign but a crusade this year. On top of that, we can inform you that the navies will be moving to total mobilisation and every one of our facilities, including Buccaneer Town, will therefore come immediately to a high alert status. We felt you should know this so that you can brief your troops. We will of course appreciate your fullest cooperation," beamed the stout old man.

"Of course, Sir," was Lauren's immediate reply.

Without a pause to allow further questions the admiral turned in a semi-circle saying, "Thank you ladies and gentlemen, please be about your business." Lauren and the officers filed out in turn, leaving the room empty but for Buccaneer Town's own, Admiral. "Well my mysterious friend I am sure you have learned little new today," he said into the empty air, once the doors closed behind them. "Do you have anything you could add for my benefit?"

"Why, Admiral," a softly spoken voice replied, "of course you receive my fullest intelligence." The voice tried to sooth him. "I have little new to add but I can confirm that the plans we discussed last week have been fully implemented. All additional evidence confirms that the matter is at least as serious as we thought. We are now certain that Lauren Marshall's predecessor was murdered and that a number of the deaths from food poisons were murder as well. Lauren seems to be conducting her own private and unauthorised investigation, which in this case is proving useful in stirring the nest. She has, of course, been allocated extra, discrete protection."

When it was clear that the voice hidden behind the walls had paused the Admiral asked, "Do you consider that this threat will target the chain of command, especially in light of the war announcements?"

"Yes, I do, Admiral, though not in direct response to these recent campaign developments. In your operating manual for emergencies, could you consider scenarios eight and nine and inform me of your preference, the usual letter drop will be fine. In addition to those plans, I have sketched out an extra scenario which I believe will be useful for our plans and have left it on your desk. If we are finished I ask your permission to withdraw."

"Certainly, Mister Ghost, certainly," muttered the admiral as he stumped off to his office and its apparent scant privacy. "Oh to be back at sea," could be heard as he threw open the soundproofed doors.

*****

Greenleaf Tom sat back in the rickety old chair wincing at the distressed creaking it made. He had completed the first day of his inspection at Holding Seven-Seven-Two Central Plains. As usual the holding was going to make the minimum quota in all respects, in fact an amount of the crops could be diverted to the central supply. He was well pleased. This was the eighth season he had inspected Moffet and he had never had a complaint yet. Almost dusk and still the fellow wasn't back. Tom sipped his water and waited.

This year he had a number of new techniques to discuss with Moffet and also some options he might try with crop rotation. He had also dispatched an informal request to the area commander at the nearest camp and expected Moffet to have extra additional company this evening. Not that Tom had any real concerns that Moffet couldn't implement their decisions. Agriculturally he had as much inherent talent as any farmer Tom had ever met, it was just that Moffet didn't ever really appear to take part in the discussions.

As dusk finally fell two figures appeared silently at the farm gates and called out a greeting. Tom was reasonably sure that they had already circled the building and knew the score exactly. None of Smee's command ever seemed to take chances.

"It's me, Tom," he called out. "Moffet's not back yet but come on in."

"Blue Boy and Stonebrow," they replied politely. Tom had deliberately left out mentioning his assistant Sizell who was working with Moffet at the furthest reaches of the holding checking soil quality amongst other things. A quiet woman herself, Sizell liked inspecting Moffet and Tom suspected that the two of them had spent the whole afternoon in happy silence.

The tall, hard figure of Stonebrow eased gracefully up the steps and Tom, who now had the cabin lanterns lit, clasped his arm in a firm greeting grip. Stonebrow flipped the string from his hunting bow and stood it with his quiver and long sword in the corner. Retaining only a heavy-bladed belt sword that was leg strapped he sat down next to Tom and motioned acceptance to the offer of some water. Still a man of few words Tom thought.

Stonebrow made a gentle cooing noise and his companion then also entered the cabin. Careful men, Tom approved. This second lad also had a smooth motion but with him you could see it was all through effort. His slightly bowed powerful legs gave him a naturally rolling gait. He unstrapped a harness with a large back-slung axe and twin blades crossed over at the front. From the shape of the sheaths they looked to Tom like nothing so much as common kitchen cleavers. Obviously the lad had progressed much this last season as it was unusual for cadets to be personally fitted by a camp armourer. Tom said as much to Stonebrow.

"Tom the boy is progressing well. Smee himself made the award. Blue fetch out one of your cutters for Tom," said Stonebrow. Leaning back he watched Tom carefully as he inspected the still-sheathed blade. It was, in fact, a heavy cleaver though with the first three inches of the back of the blade sharpened around a gentle reverse curve.

It was the weight that impressed Tom most. Raising a look

at the boy he asked, "Heavy juice filed for armour?"

"Yes sir," the boy beamed. "Designed them myself."

"Oh he did at that Tom, and you should see them at work. Pretty nasty." With a gesture from Stonebrow it took Tom two hands to re-sheath the blade and then slide it over to the musician. Stonebrow himself unsheathed the blade and indicated that the boy should re-fix scabbard and battle harness. When this was done he used two hands to toss the blade in the air before the boy, who not only caught it as if it were a table knife but also had the other out in a smooth draw, blurring the air with a complex pattern of two-handed knife moves.

Blue Boy carefully finished the practice movements and quietly re-sheathed his blades. As he began to unhook his battle harness he paused for a fraction and said, "Hello Sizell, hello Moffet."

Stonebrow couldn't help beaming with pride and his normally calm expression flashed into a grin. Whilst he had been aware of the couple's approach for a while, and sure that Tom has also known, he was pleased that his display hadn't distracted Blue Boy's attention from other details.

He could see also that Tom was impressed. Stonebrow was so pleased he even went so far as to roguishly kiss the shy lady's hand in greeting, which made her blush prettily. Moffet was washing noisily in the trough outside and soon stumped up the steps. His distressed facial expression, whilst wary, remained reasonably calm once he saw that only the four were in the room. He sat down next to Blue Boy tapping him twice lightly on the shoulder in welcome. Stonebrow had yet to work out any of their personal code other than this greeting and it was something of a mystery to him how the two friends communicated further, although having watched them work he was sure that they had organised something.

Tom poured them water and they got down to business straight away. "Moffet I am certainly pleased with the progress. It looks as if the extra fields you now share with Grimble have surely achieved extra yield and I am marking thirty bushes of surplus for wagon transport to central plain store one. Root crops are also on target for area needs with perhaps a mixed cart of extra produce every second week for rapid transport to the coast.

Do you agree you can manage that?"

Moffet sat staring into the air for a few moments and it was impossible to tell if he had even heard what Tom had said. Abruptly he gently placed his hand on the table, three fingers extended, snatching it back rapidly as if embarrassed not to agree.

"OK, every three weeks, lad." Tom laughed. "Sizell, were you able to sample enough soils? The manure programme is, as you know, in its second season, do you think that the new rotation will be effective here?"

"Oh yes, Tom. This holding is still probably the lowest risk we have for trying the new methods. Moffet has been so successful and the sunken wire fences also look to reduce vermin losses greatly."

Business over, Sizell, Moffet and Blue Boy got down to the evening chores and Tom inquired politely if Stonebrow would accompany him to take a breath of air.

"Stonebrow, look I have always got on well with Smee and all his camp but this trip I don't have time to visit him. I need some advice, will you hear me?"

"Of course, Tom, anything you say will remain strictly between ourselves you have my warriors word," Stonebrow replied gravely.

"It's the lass," Tom started. "You know she is well past sponsorship age but I still feel responsible. She makes me so proud. There is no doubt she will be a better agro than ever I have." Tom paused before plunging right on. "Whilst her enlistment as a full time agro discounts her from much combat service she still has to serve one season. The extension awarded by her contribution expires soon. Frankly, Stonebrow, I am worried. Although she has worked hard to gain combat skills she shows little aptitude. Smee and others have afforded what extra practice you could, but I fear that the regular draft would dump her front line in a fortress and that would be the needless end of all her skill. Have you any ideas?"

Stonebrow clapped the worried man on the shoulder and guided him away from the cabin, strolling slowly, lost in thought. "I cannot dismiss those worries, Tom, for I fear you have the right of it." Stonebrow paused gently. "The luck of the draft pick cannot be discounted though and don't forget the

Battle God's blessing as well. As you know my own tours were quiet but even so bad luck placed me in harms way and the Battle God's luck pulled me through."

Stonebrow considered further. "My advice now is this. Sizell's spirit is strong and her link to the land is great. I feel that the comfort of dirt underneath her boots would count in her favour more than any amount more technical skill. Therefore, as you suggest, a fort or marine posting would be undesirable."

Committing himself Stonebrow went on, "I also know for a fact that she has been rejected from ranger selection, and that cannot be reversed. The most effective solution I can see would be one of the reclamation squads. Mostly they work land or sea and if you don't have the sea talents then that is an unlikely posting. The problem is once inland; whilst the combat is generally finished before they deploy, if it does kick off again it can be messy, very messy. Certainly her talents would put forward a good case. I know a couple of crews who might need recruits and it would count as the full service."

Tom stood looking thoughtful. "Well, Stonebrow, I didn't think of that. Initially the thought of sending her to the pickers is not good, but your description revealed the merits and I've heard the packs stick together pretty good once they accept you. I will speak with her now and let you know if she would like help to pursue it further. Many thanks, my friend."

Early the next morning Sizell splashed the dish water deliberately on Blue Boy. "Hey, Size, its good to see you," Blue Boy laughed. "What's our duty today?"

"Well, you scally, we've got some outer fields to test for the results of the manure cycle. Plus I want to see the state of the hedgerows along those fields now shared with Grimble." Sizell clutched her spear and the two companions set off. Today Moffet was going with Tom, and Stonebrow had left as soon as Knuckles arrived with the horses, to make a patrol of the area and set his young protégé a few scouting tests.

Being a plainsman Blue Boy knew that Stonebrow's attention to detail when on patrol was second to none. He didn't envy Knuckles the sore back he would have by the time he had been on and off his horse, bending down examining spore a couple of hundred times over the next few day-parts.

Suddenly Sizell darted off at a ground eating pace, and Blue Boy was hard pushed to keep up with her. Blue Boy knew she fretted over her ability with weapons, but crikey could she run. After a couple of miles she slowed and allowed him to catch her. Puffing gently Blue Boy gasped, "Hey, did Stonebrow put you up to that?"

"No, Blue, I just wanted to beat you one last time," she whispered, more to herself than him.

"What's the matter, Size. Why so sad?" Blue Boy demanded.

"Oh, it's just my last time inspecting you. My call-up papers have arrived and this time there is no extension. You know how hopeless I am with weapons. There's no way that I'll survive the front. I don't think I'll ever see any of you again."

Blue Boy bit his lip in frustration and searched his heart for something to say.

"Blue, its not that I'm a coward. I want to do my part, its just, well you know how I love this life and no matter how hard I work I can never get enough. It's great to be able to feed all the troops and feel like I'm really contributing to the war effort, the best I can. With my spear at the front all I will be able to do is fall over my feet and get killed, or worse get someone else killed."

"Oh, Size, I'd swap with you if I could. But you know the rules, I couldn't even if I was old enough." Blue Boy kicked disconsolately at the dirt.

"No Blue, don't let us be upset on our last day together. Give me a shoulder ride to the furthest field, I bet you can't make it all the way. I've put on weight you know." Sizell sprang to get Blue Boy in an ineffective headlock and quickly climbed onto his broad shoulders. Looking ridiculous he sped away, her long legs almost reaching the floor due to his squat build. He carried her easily all the way. In doing so though he missed the silent tears streaming gently down her face, just as she had, intended.

Chapter Three

The mist deepened as Sophie and Changworth made their way back from the market. Changworth always agreed that earliest was best, especially when Taverner was organising the roster. Although Chang never seemed to help old Millie in the kitchens he was always the one who went down to the docks in the early morning to secure the club the pick of the stalls. Recently Sophie, always an early riser, had discovered that the bustle of the market was an interesting way to start the day. As long as she remained within calling distance Chang allowed her to browse to her hearts content and she was soon able to chat to her favourite traders about the produce in quite a knowledgeable way. Most of the dock guards she knew by name, but recently, fewer old faces seemed to be around. Changworth suggested that the presiding admiral was trying some new rotation when Sophie mentioned it, but she had heard tales of frequent illness and knew that at least one had died soon after being stricken.

The illness was why Sophie assumed Taverner sent Chang to pick the food, Chang seemed such a sensible chap and he would pick only good food, she was sure. Sensible or not though, he wasn't so severe that she couldn't talk him into a shoulder ride or roundabout spin, in fact all the club employees were like family to her and she was as happy as she had ever been. Silly Uncle Jeffers, Barf, Old Millie, Piker and Lawrence, there was always some fun to be found, not that most of them didn't always seem able to get some chores out of her as well. Mandibles had said that it was so much fun because they had all learned to love life and always made the most of things. Sophie also knew that that was why the club would be such a success. Maybe Uncle Jeffers would let her help run it with him when she was older.

Through the mist she hurried that morning, hand firmly clasped in Chang's and he with a tray of large shrimps and steak on thin wood skewers, one of Sophie's favourites, balanced on his shoulder. Teak's stall was one of the best and about the only place that the club bought ready prepared food. Sophie loved stopping there and although Chang never seemed able to remember that, it was amazing how often they ended up buying the old chap's food.

As they ambled back up the hill they passed Master Baker Pearson's refectory. He was having an unusually large delivery for that time of the morning and many wagons were being unloaded by a party of men, clearly in a hurry. Few appeared to be regulars at the club although one called out a greeting to Changworth. The number one doorman at the hottest new club was a good person to know around Buccaneer Town, and with his chiselled features and shoulder length blond hair, fairly easy to spot too.

Back home by the fire they sipped hot cocoa and dried off. Taverner had already sorted through the market tray and Sophie had spied him separating a couple of skewers from the club's stock, for quality testing, as he called it, around the time of the youngsters lunch.

Changworth had joked that Baker Pearson was feeling the pressure of their business, needing to start earlier and bring in extra help. Taverner replied that yes, the Master Baker did look to be the major competition, but Sophie didn't think that he looked too concerned. After a few moments further reflection he did however suggest that if competition was about to get hectic maybe they should review their roster, and asked Changworth to supervise the other doormen and make sure that the morning reorganisation of stock in the cellar progressed thoroughly. Taverner was a stickler for rearranging stock everyday and when Sophie had asked why, he claimed that the secret of a well run club or restaurant was organisation and easy access to the staples. The danger from the large heavy barrels kept her from participating and, miming swimming, Taverner led Sophie, who was carefully carrying an extra cup of cocoa, upstairs to Liam, who no doubt would be making a mess with the water in the wash basin in their room.

*****

On that same morning Lauren was also out in the mist, heavily cloaked, and braced on top of an old hut across from the right hand side of the dock front. The position on the roof of the old drying shed allowed her to keep an eye on the businesses over a wide part of the docks. Unable to attend her surveillance activities every morning due to the duties of her command, she carried on regardless, keeping up all the investigation she could. Having spent several early mornings in this position she was, however, acquainted with the bouncer from the nightclub and the little girl and their food gathering routine. She smiled as the little girl skipped by hand-in-hand with the tough, serious man and then returned her attention to surveillance. Following the lead of the poisonings her investigation had been drawn to the Master Baker and the amount of business he seemed to be conducting. Although in his official position for a couple of years, as far as Lauren could tell the dockside compound she was watching was only a recently acquired venture, sold to him by a near bankrupt fishing business in the grip of the shoal poisoning that was ravaging the local economy. Indeed he was becoming her prime suspect. Every time she watched she counted his catch increase. She knew that the remaining fishermen holding out were unable to catch from the polluted banks and turning to less well stocked waters, were struggling to bring in even moderate catches. The other part of Master Baker's mystery was how he was returning a profit, a necessary evil for the quasi quartermaster in this haven of free trade that the admirals worked to maintain. Even with his ample catch, the sceptical population was not exactly going out of its way to consume fish due to the recent cases of food poisoning. Lauren could not detect any sign of increased tannery activity or other secondary industry to exploit the returning catches.

Official gossip suggested that he had hired the extra men to treat the polluted banks in some way and Lauren was sure that she had seen some kind of pump mechanism unloaded. Still, time was passing and what contact that she had with her counterpart in the Marine Patrol only served to emphasise that their routine continued as normal, checking for smuggling of alcohol, random checks to catch spies and the like, all being pursued normally with the Baker's enterprises inspected as often as any other comparable trader. More and more the sporadic and seemingly random, but not uncommon, outbreaks of poisoning suggested that perhaps her friend's death might indeed have been an accidental coincidence. After all, Chloe had been drowned, so there was no real link so far at all.

Lauren would have been less sure though, if the older fisher folk had shown any confidence at all in the activities of the Baker's boats. They seemed equally at a loss when she discreetly asked them to explain. Therefore, whenever she could she was out and about, ostensibly making such rounds as appropriate to her post of militia commander, but actually trying to turn up anything strange or interesting. Most of the time though, she felt as if she was wasting her efforts, for whilst she had a suspect and a number of strange unanswered questions, there was absolutely no link to her friend who had drowned, only the promise of some huge conspiracy by one of the town's leading citizens and officials. A scandal apparently undetected by the local authorities in a location where secret facilities, and therefore security was commonplace.

*****

Mandibles sat with his back to the restaurant door and moved the mirrored jug, so that the reflective surface gave him a view of the entrance, and then he set into the plate that Millie had given him. Quite where Jeffers had found this cook he had no idea, but whilst termed 'Old Millie', she was flowering into stunning looks in her mid forties and could cook up the most sumptuous food. Mandibles was always clamouring to be the tester for her cooking and today he had a large plate of beef strips in a black bean sauce. It tasted divine. He stirred his plate using the fork to pick tenderly through the moist vegetables, savouring each taste in turn, whilst mentally congratulating himself on agreeing to join the team at the club. 'Changworth matey,' he thought, 'you're not all bad.' This lady, Millie, didn't seem to be attached either. Maybe he would think about slowing things down and possibly even settling down, after all he got on great with the kids and Piker had turned out all right. As a parent he had probably missed out although stranger things had happened. Still, Millie was probably too old anyway, but they could sponsor a couple of ward kids just as Jeffers was doing with Sophie and Liam.

Taverner came in quietly and shrugged in indifference at Mandibles, who had clearly disturbed place settings at the window table with his flouting of the rules. He began to re-measure all the other settings in the room with his measuring rod. For a butler turned restaurant partner Mandibles always thought that Taverner moved a bit too well, often turning sharply within confined spaces and never seemingly off balance. 'Still, a lifetime of carrying loaded trays and setting places at table to the nearest nail width would probably do that to a person.'

With heavy prompting Jeffers had told Mandibles that Taverner had served his time over seas and even seconded for a short time in the Northern Army, but now was exempted from standard service provided he did the occasional piece of translation, being fluent in certain southern trade languages and corresponding dialects. There was something about Taverner though, even in this building full of secrets, that troubled Mandibles and he still couldn't put his finger on it.

Down in the kitchen Millie was experimenting with large game fish, so far she felt that she had failed to improve on mildly spiced fish steamed with fruit or vegetables. She had tried a variety of fish and spice combinations but remained unconvinced. Now an untried marlin-like fish offered her a texture that she liked and after a half part of steaming its flavour was good. She had also prepared some fruit by roasting it with hickory wood in an open pan, which gave the apples and pears a smoky, woody tang.

Now in the final stage of matching the two, Millie was reluctant to proceed as she felt that something about the combination of the fish and fruit still lay slightly beyond her grasp and she was reluctant to continue solely with trial and error, especially as Changworth had told her that the fish could only be obtained in small quantities at great cost.

She was pleased when Mandibles walked in with empty plate and guilty expression, looking around to see if anybody else would catch him having eaten in the restaurant, and Millie insisted that he put off his other chores to help her. Mandibles agreed, "Only if you protect me from Jeffers though. Jokes aside how can I help?

"Oh, you need not fear anyone when you are under my protection," she agreed with a sly wink. "Except possibly if I tell Barf you've been eating above ground in the restaurant again."

*****

"Blue Boy, I was interested to read your last work on the place of religion in the war. Your points on whether the army was created to pursue our freedom as promised in the religion, or whether the religion was a creation of the military government to ensure social cooperation, have proven a lively topic. Master Smee and I have discussed it at length, at one point I believe we both even agreed simply to throw you in the brig. Anyway we feel that you should be encouraged to balance your controversial views in your own way." Mister Kyan paused dramatically, carefully studying Blue Boy's reaction to his challenging comments.

"We therefore feel that you should be given further dispensation to finish a special piece of work. This week I will present to you three historic volumes concerning the Horde. Combined within these writings you will find perhaps the most comprehensive treatment of its history with respect to interaction with the human race. Many and disturbing are the excerpts on the origins of the Roke. We would like you to spend a full week exercising only at the start and end of the day and seeing only Marv. In effect, closeted away from the rest of the camp whilst analysing these works," Mister Kyan finished. Before Blue Boy, already used to being somewhat isolated from his fellow cadets, could complain the Master resumed his instruction. "You may discuss the topic only with myself and Stonebrow and you will present both the original work and this new presentation to a visitor we are expecting next week. Ask your questions quickly now boy, but consider this an order from our leader. On this task you have not a moment to waste. Nothing yet? Well, enough then. Let me begin with Turling's psychology of the Reptoid Horde."

Initially Blue Boy was well able to keep up with his tutor. The book started with a discourse on the anatomy of various Reptoids. Blue Boy, as many youngsters do, had a fascination with the odd and bizarre and at an early age had he learned of the semi-intelligent, giant, crab like Master Reptoids who often captained the Horde's war bands. He knew much of the green and purple Nasties and their differences in size and their lack of multiple stomachs. And, of course, there were the intelligent and yet fickle and vain Siblants who, roughly human in stature, possessed frightening attributes of speed and strength, putting them beyond the skills of all but the most talented humans. On an individual basis. Fortunately the Siblants cultivated a strange aloofness that prevented them from being particularly effective in groups. Stronger and quicker than a man they were the measure by which all great warriors were eventually gauged.

Egg-layers, Brown Crawlers, Twin Splitters, Four Jaw Raspers, Blue Boy could name as many as most experienced soldiers and he had studied long their theoretical weak points and could name instantly any special traits they might have. If they could spit acid bile, or secrete glue to patch their shells, Blue Boy would know. But this book did indeed seem to offer something new, it took the differences but didn't focus on strengths and weaknesses and how to kill the Reptoids, but on breeding habits and mating habits, cycles of hibernation almost even as far as to how their language would allow them to communicate.

When he mentioned this and asked how Turling could have survived to learn so much. Mister Kyan's answer shocked him to the core.

"Because, Blue Boy, Turling and ten generations of his ancestors lived in chosen slavery amongst the Roke with this work as their sole purpose. They willingly sacrificed their freedom and suffered great hardships to compile and smuggle out this text." For many moments Mister Kyan paused to allow these facts to sink in his student. Blue Boy found the Roke a bitter topic; brothers and sisters to the ancestors of the United Nation before the Shattering, but captured, forced into slavery and now generations later, so corrupted as to form a race apart. Willing allies of the Horde, the Roke were perverse and barbaric, often driven by addictive drugs or sickening religious cults.

Finally Mister Kyan continued, "Now let us consider this work entitled *The Migratory Evolution of the Reptilian Super Species*. This book was actually written over hundreds of years before the Shattering."

This news alone was enough to stun Blue Boy, however its contents revealed that when the work was actually started almost nothing was known of the Horde initially it just detailed vast packs of separate Reptoid species moving in a constant state of migration around what was known as the equatorial continent. As the book progressed it revealed how the authors had spotted certain tendencies for the packs to converge over varying periods and that following such convergence their expansion became much more deliberate. At the climax of the book, in the centuries before the Shattering, the authors were almost desperate for people to believe that these weren't simply a separate set of species but that they were being directed in consort. Re-reading certain sections it was evident from the narrative that the attacks weren't just becoming a bit more frequent and better reported as a result, but that human settlements were being obliterated as part of a deliberate plan. Regardless of these clear reports the tone of the chapters indicated that at the time this was obviously a little accepted fact. The last two hundred years up to the Shattering had seen the authors describe places on the southern-most continental edges, places now too dangerous for free humans to travel, where they alleged that camps had been set up and where humans were being bred and conditioned as slaves.

By the end of that book and the end of the third day, Blue Boy was both exhausted and delighted. Finally, many of the questions that he had built up over the years had a new focus and the complexity of his country's situation now seemed to fall more correctly into a bigger context rather than the social basis on which his past education had been based.

*****

When Lauren visited the gaming house she decided to play it safe just in case the note had been some kind of trap. She chose early afternoon when there was no approved gambling going on, but early bets were still being taken by the house gamblers on the coming weekend fixtures. The recreational games being played, both silk billiards and pressure billiards, also offered some side interest for those determined on making wagers. She ambled around picking up gossip, hearing snippets from around the room including;

"A greater number of new attacks could mean an unexpected phase of the war... Expedition fayres to be announced by the Marshall and a big new campaign... Smee likely to be the next war band... No news from Iron Isles is sinister... Light Storms that affected North ferocious further out... More rogue pirates preying on shipping... Roke crack down in Battle Lands with freelanders being killed or enslaved... A new master to be appointed... Death of Jake Dove, a hero of the Rooks Point rescue... Caballeros to name a new prince regent... Blue folk to resume trading... Rebellion amongst the legion at some work forts... Military trial of Roke spies... The alcohol ration to be increased... The war god strikes down some more desert people who have broken the holy law... Marshalls sent to defend the free landers captured and executed, could be Roke or other renegades... Increase in locust pests, blamed on Reptoid breeding and a deliberate plot."

Ordering a drink she finally asked the bartender if old Vee was in and expecting to find a man, she was told that "The old hag hadn't been seen for ages."

"If it's the healing of a tryst, a morning potion you want then you shouldn't dally, visit the old bag out of town," the bartender suggested. "I can provide a map in return for a tip," and duly drew her a rough plan with a charcoal tip. He was so pleased when she tipped him some cash that he poured her an extra shot in her drink, which she quickly downed, and hardly pausing headed straight out into the street. Checking the bar carefully the bartender popped to a room at the back and promptly relayed the whole conversation to a cloaked man who left quickly to follow the girl. One of the local gamblers eventually got up, having lost his pot and staggered off into the afternoon sunshine.

Bones had been particularly interested in the episode, especially the speed with which the news was passed on by the barman, and having waited to maintain his cover, pushed himself hard hurrying back to the Night Fort to report. Meanwhile Barf followed Lauren safely back to the Militia compound.

When Bone's report had been carefully considered by Taverner and Mandibles they dispatched Cat, one of the bar staff, to investigate and visit with the old woman. She was sent hurrying out of town on the premise of an unwanted pregnancy although it turned out the old woman was absent from her home in any case and a more extensive search was needed.

*****

Mandibles ignored Taverner's number clipped to the private practice training room door and walked straight in. The fellow was sitting cross legged in a relaxed position in the middle of the floor clearly doing breathing exercises. Mandibles strolled to a bench at the edge of the room and sat down. He looked to the far wall at the end of the hall where a human shaped target stood and getting up he walked past the apparently oblivious figure and inspected the dummy. He found that its head had been split by a long handled axe hanging haft down and eight throwing knives placed symmetrically, four down each side of the torso. 'The chap must have got fed up and walked down and stuck these in frustration. I wonder if he used a ruler?' Mandibles mused.

"You cannot know the answers to all your questions, Mandibles." Taverner's voice sounded in his ear. Mandibles stepped away from the man in surprise, annoyed that he had got so close. He glared at Taverner who just shrugged and carefully extracted and examined each of the blades before re-sheathing them in the bandolier he was wearing. "You didn't think I had thrown these did you?" Taverner asked with a slight grin. He was stripped to the waist and despite being trim he was less defined in the upper torso than Mandibles had expected from his sleek movement. "How may I help you at this late time?" the restaurant manager asked as he finally drew out the long handled axe.

Mandibles, realising how impolite he had been invading someone else's private training uninvited, bit his lip but carried on with a deliberately casual manner.

"Look, Taverner, I need to talk," Mandibles grunted stumping over to the wall bench to sit down.

"You come to the training room to talk," Taverner laughed. "I wonder what will happen if you ever visit the Oratory School in Las Skeene?" the restaurant manager jibed.

Already greatly frustrated Mandibles cursed and half rose at the joke, clearly not in the mood for humour.

"Stay yourself Major," Taverner offered showing Mandibles an empty pair of hands in a gentling motion. When Mandibles finally gave up glaring and returned to a sitting position, contenting himself with vigorous scrubbing of his hands through his hair as if to clear his head, Taverner continued. "What exactly is on your mind?"

"Look, Taverner, my contingent are soldiers, pure and simple. I don't think we are necessarily a good bet to act at being bar workers. For my part this extra intelligence work you have me doing – I can't make head nor tail of the information coming in. Each new thing I think I learn is contradicted by the next that we receive. At the moment I can't decide whether I have a good number of the Marine Patrol plus several town officials involved in a huge plot, or nothing at all. As hard as we try and investigate the former we just can't seem to get any hard evidence," Mandibles finished, giving Taverner an almost pleading look. "Isn't there somebody you can call in to look into this. I'm just sick of wondering if I am a puppet being played by a master or just a paranoid with a vivid imagination."

"What do your other officers – Barf, Chubby and Scars all say?" Taverner asked gently.

"Each seems plagued with the same doubts as myself, except perhaps Barf. He claims he hunts by instinct and that this whole town makes his hairs stand up and his bowels tighten. Mind, even he hasn't been able to observe whoever is controlling the watchers. Nor has he caught anybody doing any of the killing." Mandibles wet his lips and returned his penetrating gaze to Taverner. "Why have you set us to this but limited us to only two watchers ourselves? You have a sizeable number in your work team and if the fighting skills of the waitresses are any indication you have equivalent talent available to you."

"Mandibles, it is rude, I know, to answer a question with a question. You and your men are tough capable warriors – talented in many land and marine skills, as good as I could hope to find. Across the channel lies a continent, smaller than ours, one torn from our ancestors and now populated by huge numbers of our sworn enemies. For centuries we have fought back and forth over the battlements, walls and even the water. Do you not believe that one day the Horde will come against us again – they haven't been using all their resources for the fighting this past century? Rest assured that they are becoming more capable, more shrewd, and more able to act intelligently like us. I can assure you that in Buccaneer Town all resources are being used constructively. But there are many tasks and few suited to them, here and now. I am afraid that discovering who has penetrated the Marine Patrol, and why, has fallen to you and your men." Taverner paused his face a mask of worry. "Do not let your concerns stop you Mandibles, you are a tough brave warrior. Fight back, be strong and try not to be frustrated here amongst your allies for we do all work together. You could even speak to your boss, I know he is busy but his judgement is good and this matter is important."

*****

Outside in the fresh early morning air Barney, Justine and Scars were hard at work. Last night's crowd had been a bit untidy while queuing and Scars was jabbing at the ground with a spiked stick stabbing up the fruit peel that marked the line where the queue had been. Justine and Barney had split the flowers half and half. Justine was picking up the fruit peel, just like Scars, but from where those slightly tidier minded individuals had thought to stuff theirs in the troughs filled with flowers and shrubs. People on the whole were quite tidy, though, and the door men had already moved the waste bins provided each evening back to the outhouse for transport, by whoever was allocated cart duty, to the recycle dump outside of town. She soon had the beds clear of debris and began the process of dead heading some of the flowers, a bit of weeding and then polishing the brass edges of some of the chests now converted to ornamental garden pieces.

Once Justine had moved on to the next floral feature Barney would move to where she had been. His job was to use a ladder to reach the hanging baskets and, having checked the flowers, water both sets. He was most careful to water only where Justine had been, for once the baskets were dripping down onto the arrangement below he knew that she would default that bed to him and he would spend the next tenth with cold water dripping down the back of his neck, whilst she stood back in amusement, supervising.

Justine was one of the local waitresses employed by the club. Although there were girls who had come with the staff brought in with the Iron Island party the majority were local. Many of the shifts had waitresses all from the local town, but Justine worked a mixed shift. Not yet having served her first call-up she was one of the few who took the chance to brush up on her fighting skills by practicing with the others. Justine and her friend, Bella, had attached themselves to Barney's squad and Barf, having evaluated the ladies had set Barney and Bones to instruct them. Barney had soon learned that the girls were far from unskilled and wondered whether Barf had been making a subtle comment about his own capabilities. On second thoughts, he remembered that it was Barf and nothing he did was likely to be subtle.

This morning the squad were to be drilled by Changworth. Always working the door until late at night, Changworth and his room mate and backup man were a lot less visible than, say, Mandibles or Barf.

The number one doorman was a talent, no doubt. His classes were known to be hard on those who fell below his quiet standards. Justine was finished all too quickly, and flashing Barney a knowing grin, she hurried off with her tools and rubbish bin to get changed for practice. Barney watered the final basket and then carried the ladder in through the large maintenance bay doors at the rear of the club where he fixed it firmly to its wall bracket. He then raced to report to Scars, the senior member of the work team who, having collected all his fruit peel, was making his rounds and removing the slightest hint of weeds from the pavements and inspecting the exterior as a whole. He slapped Barney on the back, refusing his offer of further help and sent him in with a few moments to spare before his class. When Barney arrived dressed in a simple set of comfortable linen shirt and trousers he found the other students all already lined up in front of Changworth, who looked them over from a sitting position under the spear rack in the centre of the far wall.

The training hall was a large wooden floored cellar room with a high vaulted ceiling. Generally it contained rows of trestle tables where the wines were laid out and drinks made during the afternoon in preparation for the evening. In the mornings, though, it was laid out as a combat room and all restricted personnel were prohibited from entering whilst it was being 'tidied' from the night before. Eight men and three women were in the session. Bowing to his class Changworth stood up and without saying anything took a long-handled spear and, moving to the centre of the floor, shooed his students back to the walls. He proceeded to perform a series of complicated moves, once slowly and then again at high speed, finishing facing one way but then spinning to hurl his spear dead centre into a shield that Mandibles having silently entered the room now held. Speaking for the first time Changworth explained that he wanted each student to perform exactly the same moves and also experience the impact of the spear.

*****

Jungold was a taciturn man, quiet almost to the point of rudeness on occasion. The head wrangler, of the club he was one of those people who could relate more closely to the animals in his care than his work mates. Not that his stable hands Kint or Fitch were much better. The serving girls had picked them out as their current source of fun, but even they were forced to admit that the stables themselves were almost as scrupulously clean as the kitchens. Controlling the horses meant controlling the wagons and so those staff sent out to collect deliveries for the club down at the docks dealt with Jungold on a daily basis. With minimal politeness he handled the girls banter with a casual disdain and encouraged his staff to do the same, although under the constant barrage of flirting his young charges weren't always so restrained. Several times girls returned from the yard spluttering from a dunking in the troughs, satisfied, though, that the culprits would be nursing cuts and bruises for a number of days. Mandibles watched all this with amusement. All the different groups within the staff seemed to be bonding nicely.

The investigation within the town seemed stalled though. Either the briefing they had been given overstated what they were investigating or possibly the plot was on a much larger scale altogether. Mandibles had never found it this difficult to gather information in the past, even when operating in enemy territory. He agreed that certain deaths were too numerous for normal circumstances but the natural poison bloom in the local fish beds was an answer he couldn't disprove. Surely in a fishing community, such as this, there would be expert old timers who could disprove such a thing. The trouble probably came down to his being an outsider in the town. He could hardly expect local folk to open up about a conspiracy possibly run by local folk. His most interesting leads seemed to be coming from his technical people.

Chubby had been tasked with looking into the town's building records and somehow Taverner had got him night access to the architect's office. He had so far taken copious notes and moved on to the office in charge of imports and exports and the inventories down at the harbour master's office. Extracting all the appropriate covert building work done on the east side of town he was torn between the fact that either too much or too little other work had been done within the rest of the town in the last six months. Many imports of machinery were also listed and these just seemed to have vanished. He was due at the Chandlers office later today and Mandibles would be interested to learn the results. In the meantime his research pointed to the fact that officially the new fishing corporation appeared to have done a lot of construction with no record of the materials used; whilst everything had been correctly filed on their behalf the two sides seemed not to add up. Mandibles had therefore spoken to a couple of his lads and asked them to start a discrete survey of the corporation's properties, not just from a civil perspective but also as a military facility.

Perhaps Taverner was right. Although the boss was busy and had made it clear that Mandibles was being directly loaned to Taverner, and it wasn't their own command's problem, perhaps he should speak to him. That the other lads working the club were only being updated on a need to know basis didn't mean that something important happening in the town should be kept from the general.

Mandibles walked over to check the day's official staff roster. Lawrence or 'The Lad' as his father, Bones, always called him, was on restaurant duty as usual. He admitted to finding that work satisfying and that odd chap Taverner seemed pleased with him. Mandibles had also decided to add Barney more frequently to that area of the roster, although perhaps he had better discuss it with Taverner first. Scars was taking a rare turn above ground, being the cellar manager, in the members club bar this evening and Mandibles himself was on the members club door. Spillage and Piker would be running the main bar all night with Cat heading up the serving team including Justine, Mary, Barney and, it appeared, Fitch one of the stable hands. Changworth was as usual on the club door, and Chubby the door to the Restaurant. Expecting a big night both Bones and Millie would be running the kitchens with Kate, Marsha, Julie and Sprig, either in the kitchen or between the restaurant and the members' areas depending on numbers of guests.

*****

The music camp had to wait about a week before any further information was announced concerning the campaigning season. When it came, it was through semi-informal channels, with those officers in charge of the camp's various activities making the same announcement, at the same time, at the end of the morning. A rare occurrence, Marvellous had sent Blue Boy to help the farrier who, with the help of the camp's chief smith and armourer, Heat, was shoeing horses in the stable-like entrance to the secondary forge. Big Tar was a large, brusque man but a natural with horses. It was rumoured that at least two of his current students were approaching the completion of their training and that they would eventually take over the operational side of the camp's animal husbandry and that he would leave to serve out another tour.

It was Heat who actually recounted Master Smee's instructions to all the outbuilding based camp workers and, whilst on assignment, this also included Blue Boy. Blue Boy felt very at home in the forge and often volunteered to do chores in return for a bit of simple tuition. Late last fall he had spent two full weeks working with Heat in the armoury forge and that had resulted in his cutters, of which he was very proud.

Forty staff therefore gathered round, many heckling their leader, which even raised a smile from Big Tar although Blue Boy also caught him waving an admonishing finger at one of the youngest stable hands who appeared to be about to explode with mirth. The icy look soon had the child repentant. Big Tar was well respected by the camp seniors but he kept order in his own environment with a cultivated civility that in all the younger staff who did not know him well almost created a feeling of fear.

Heat quickly told his staff of the forthcoming meeting of the camp council. A set of manoeuvres would be used to finally decide who from each camp section would be sent, should the camp be selected for war. This pleased many of the assembled staff who felt that they were on the way to being over looked and, for a couple of parts, after they were dismissed to their duties, Blue Boy came across the buzz of excitement in all areas through which his chores took him.

*****

When Lauren heard she had received another note she was immediately suspicious. Her anxiety barely retreated on finding that it had been delivered by hand to the commander of the guard than it was back ten fold, because it was from Baker Pearson. Whilst Lauren had seen him a couple of times she had never paid too much attention to the realities of the person who had become her number one suspect. It was, after all, so much easier to plot and spy on a faceless organisation where people were like pieces on a game board rather than real people with real motivations. What had she done that had attracted his attention? It was weeks since she had arrived and any thoughts that he might now be greeting her in an official capacity were long gone. No, she had met him at the official welcome, albeit briefly and at a time when he was nothing more to her than the challenge of putting a name to a face. Now she would have to meet him at an awkward time. Even if he knew nothing of her activities or suspicions, would she manage to pass herself off casually? By all accounts he had achieved a lot in a short space of time, and there was no way she could discount him. Some people can smell secrets, her father had always said, when she had begged him to share some as a little girl. That the baker had found a clear evening in her round the clock duty schedule made her suspect that he had researched her routine before making an invitation, a thought which in itself caused her further anguish. Could it be that he had a source of intelligence within her own team?

Her movements recently had certainly been erratic and it wouldn't have taken much for somebody to have built up a pattern. Was she also being watched? She had tried to be careful and hadn't caught anyone following when the streets were empty. The only person she had recognised being at all out of place was that bouncer from the nightclub, and then he had just been waiting for one of his female colleagues to leave the baths. She decided to be more careful, but couldn't see how she could refuse the invitation without appearing rude and bring more attention down on herself. It was probably going to be a party with a guest list of some size anyway she decided. Most social functions maximised the guests to avoid any embarrassing episodes where a few individuals couldn't find anything in common. In fact it would probably be pretty easy, she decided, to mingle her way in with the other guests and have very little to do with her host at all. Having decided to make the most of the event she had hurried off to the baths with an evening dress bagged and under her arm, for pressing by the mistress of the bath house.

Whilst Lauren was sitting in a relaxing tub of hot water and scented salts, Mandibles received a frantic visit from Barf.

"By the Battler, Mandi, that girl is trouble. She's only going to have dinner with Pearson."

"Barf, where is she now?" Mandibles replied calmly.

"Tucked up in the tub at Madam Skillets place. I've sent Chaser down to keep an eye out."

"OK, let's see Taverner. Whatever we might decide could get a bit sticky." With that the two hurried up the back stairs to the top of the club where Taverner had his rooms. Pounding on his door soon had it open and found Taverner already immaculately dressed for his shift in the restaurant. He welcomed them in and bade them sit on a comfortable padded bench-chair along the wall of what must be his outer room. As Mandibles set the scene Barf quickly scoped the room and then Mandibles did the same once Barf was filling in the details. Taverner looked vaguely amused as they outlined the sudden invitation. He took stock for a moment before replying. "Well, I have no, information concerning further guests so we best assume it will be an intimate meal for two. Who will be eaten for supper though remains to be seen. Do we really think Lauren is as naive as she seems? Perhaps I have been remiss in assuming that the Marshall would have had her fully trained. Hmmm. Any immediate thoughts from you, Barf?"

"Well, he'd be pretty stupid to do anything so visibly and I can't see her making a particularly effective hostage, especially here in Buccaneer Town, except for upsetting her father and, let's face it, he isn't exactly known for sentiment when it comes to the matter of his governance. I think Pearson will be fishing or he's about to move. Best case, he tests his suspicions and she walks away. Worst case, he does her to stir up the pot. Therefore, either watch and see or kill him first," Barf added with a completely calm expression.

"Do you agree with your direct colleague Mandibles?" Taverner asked the senior man, equally as straight faced.

"Well, I'd probably pull him in and squeeze him. I don't think we are far short of enough evidence. I will admit, though, that I've had a couple of out-of-town crew weigh up either a snatch or what they do best – elimination. And I am, as we probably all are, beginning to realise he's going to be a tough nut to crack. That coach he travels in, well it's covertly armoured, and we think at least eight of his people would grade above an eight for combat skill. The buildings are all well secured and we have little or no intelligence from inside his camp. I'd put our chances pretty low for success either way, on his home territory."

"What, Mandi!" Barf scoffed. "Have we really classed him so hard? You make it sound as if he safer than Taverner sitting up here at the top of this club."

"Well, Taverner level with us. I think he is and I think you think so too."

"Good, Mandibles, good, but there are many questions in that one. What I suspect, and what I know and believe, are separate things. Geographically this town has great importance, it would be no great coincidence if two of the most complete intelligence facilities in the human territories were to have been set up here, each without specific knowledge of the other. If I said that I believe that our years of simply fighting the strength and numbers of the Roke are over, and that the Horde is becoming capable of fighting us in our own controlled and intelligent way, I would hope that would terrify even you Barf." Taverner paused, watching the two officers closely. "Yes, I believe that what Mandibles has said may be true and if not here now, then somewhere soon. Anyway, we digress, we have a duty to protect Lauren, even if only from herself. Barf, follow her as best you can and take one of the stable hands who knows the safe houses and vantage points. Tell him to take a full kit and choose any other runner between you. If she isn't out by eleven we'll go in. In the meantime I will try and arrange something official and believable to cut her evening short in a real and untraceable way. Barf, if things do get nasty be careful, Pearson could very well be their best man and our worst nightmare."

*****

Lauren left the bathing house just past sunset. Supplied by her bag she had been able to dress fully at the baths and saw no need to return to the barracks, especially as the invitation was an unofficial one. Although wearing a costly evening gown she had chosen conservatively and with a view to freedom of movement. For long moments she had been undecided about carrying a

70

concealed weapon and eventually chose one, not for its usefulness but more because it could be discreetly concealed.

The Baker had invited her to his dwelling situated down near the waterfront and it was a good distance to walk. She arrived quite quickly, her sense of disquiet adding a purpose to her steps. Soonest started soonest finished she had decided. The residence was simple and plain: completely walled around the perimeter a large iron-banded gate stood open, the welcoming glow of the lanterns inviting. She was greeted by a polite but little spoken doorman who bade her wait in a furnished outer chamber, decorated on one wall by a simple landscape drawn in earthy pastels of lush greens and browns.

The fellow was soon back and escorted her through a passage that wound its way between closed doors until it opened into a large central room laid out for dining with a lengthy table. It was set for only two guests at the end furthest from where she had entered. Realising she was the only guest she had taken several steps towards the table before noticing that the attendant was no longer beside her. Lauren turned around in time to see the doors close silently. Returning to face the table she walked towards the place settings and was about half way down its length when her host finally entered. He was a tall lithe man whom she remembered now from the welcoming party, because of the simplicity of his robes that night. Now, however, he was dressed in a similar but more ethnic fashion, still wearing little else but flowing robes. "My dear Lauren, I am so pleased you could come," he greeted her and clasped her arm in a firm warriors grip.

He gestured Lauren to take the place setting next to his at the head of the table and politely helped her with her chair. Firstly Lauren noticed his hands: his fingers were long but uneven where he appeared to have lost some fingertips, and lined with numbers of scars. As he sat down she noticed his eyes, a piercing, pale blue-green colour but with a slightly disconcerting milky shine. He looked her up and down carefully and began an evening of simple food and rapid small talk.

*****

The man at that time called Baker Pearson entered his private quarters after the dinner party and securing the door, turned around the room inspecting his little safeguards and markers that he used to ensure his privacy, before sinking into a chair. The girl, Lauren, had revealed much over the evening. It was clear to him now that she was more sophisticated than she appeared at first glance. That she had shown signs of discomfort in his presence, and shed doubt over his activities through the lines of her questioning he took for a veiled warning. But there was no way that the security services would have sent such a shallow and generally unconvincing player to follow up the previous accomplished operator. That the girl, Chloe, had died before talking had been a bitter disappointment and one for which a number of his employees had been required to recompense heavily.

He grew more reassured the more he thought. Yes, clearly Lauren operated on many levels. Perhaps tonight's meeting had even been cleverly manipulated by the girl, to manoeuvre him into making uncalculated moves. Still, the scale of the opposing operation also reassured him. His new, paid informant in the nightclub was able to confirm that rather than the club being involved as a whole, that those reported as providing her support were seeded by happenstance. The Baker had decided that these were operatives obviously dispatched from the High Fort intelligence service, cleverly taking up employment as cover with a recently expanding enterprise where employees could opt for flexible shift work. Signs, then, of an effective security operation, but whether routine, supporting Lauren, or specifically against him he was yet to be sure. He was glad, whichever, that he had located the expected opposition so easily.

Quite what Lauren's role in the operation was he still wasn't too sure. If it hadn't been for her visit to the gaming house and her obvious questions there, then he might have assumed her inquisitive nature was more in line with a green militia officer taking her honorary role in Buccaneer Town a bit too seriously. Plus, surely an intelligence operative would not become involved in the warehouse fights as she had.

Still, whatever her role, they had dined, on the finest that he could prepare, plain but perfect cuisine from another continent, another time, his secret dish had pleased him immensely. He had enjoyed the subterfuge, the knowledge of all he was doing and her pitiful attempts to monitor him. He had enjoyed the sense of caution and fear that she had tried to cover throughout the meal and he had enjoyed dining on his gruesome, special food right there in front of the daughter of the man described as the most powerful in the remaining human world. Oh, how he was delighted by the opportunities that this mission were presenting.

*****

Only when Lauren was safely back in her room did she breathe a sigh of relief. She had yet to come to a firm conclusion about the Master Baker but there was definitely something sinister about him regardless of her investigation. It wasn't that he had bullied or threatened her overtly in any way but she certainly felt that the invitation had nothing to do with social politeness. If he had been threatening her, the precise intimations had passed her by. The exact line of questioning had also been obscure but what she felt deep down was that his questions had been based on knowledge far beyond that of a caterer, no matter how grand. Possibly he had been trying to prove a link between herself and Chloe.

Thinking of her friend took Lauren back to a dinner party thrown by Chloe. It was at the end of that evening, emboldened by story telling and posturing, that the four of them had decided to form an intelligence ring with Lauren at its centre. How she was ashamed now: that on that evening the other girls had elected her leader for her latent abilities and, as they said, born leadership skills. Now here she was, one friend dead nearly three months and not only without an idea as to whether her friend had been murdered but also getting in deep with this enigmatic character the Baker. How foolish the four of them had been, just because they had lived a stones throw from the High Fort's intelligence centre and become overly romantic about tales of daring spies and adventures in far off places.

As her self pity grew stronger Lauren lay on her bed, regardless of the damage it might do to the shape of her gown. Just as the tears began to form, her inherent stubbornness kicked in and she sat bolt upright. Flying in the face of the naivety she now recognised, she mentally redoubled her commitment to the investigation. Taking up paper and pen she sketched out the town as per the official plan she had acquired, marking in people and places; she sat until dawn working and reworking links between events that had come to her notice. By the time she sat back she believed she had recognised the link and, doing her best to memorise her diagrams, burnt her notes thoroughly before making the best of tidying up for the day, eyes aching from tiredness but a little happier nonetheless.

Chapter Four

Finally Lauren managed to clear the official section of the dispatch box. There had been an unusual number of posthumous and meritorious mentions in the role of honour that would need to be posted, the fighting at the front was obviously escalating. Putting that parchment on one side she looked to see if anything personal had been forwarded. Personal post in official containers was about as far as her father would stretch his position's privilege, but today, however, Lauren found a letter from her academy friend, Kass, instead.

An outstanding student, Kass had graduated a year before Lauren, effected by an early transfer to a specialised engineering facility. There he had sped through four years of instruction in two and was now deployed on some vague special training exercise. Leaving a year early he had shared a party with Chloe, a year their senior, and though not privy to the girls' spy ring agreement he had been very supportive when Lauren suggested she might investigate their friend's death.

Despite all his early encouragement this was his first letter she had received since arriving in Buccaneer Town. She was greatly interested in why he had left her dangling so long. Having already cleared her desk of official matters she felt justified in wading straight into his letter. As usual he skirted the specific details of his assignment, although she knew that he was involved in projectile weapons and siege craft. Apparently his heavy involvement in recent exercises had prevented him from writing to his friends. He hinted that he had a new classification and that his mail was likely to be checked. As usual he didn't reveal exactly how he managed to misuse the dispatch service as he regularly did. Certainly his rank was not so high as to give him access to the box, nor did he ever mention powerful friends who would show a willingness to bend the rules. Nevertheless, she appreciated his efforts, as his letters usually arrived with all possible speed. Not that the inter-base postal service wasn't efficient, but wagon train and general sorting never proceeded as fast as the specially couriered dispatch boxes that travelled non stop if possible.

His letter went on to engaged Lauren's attention over his recent flirting, frequent reprimands for over sleeping and other general pleasantries and descriptions of the weather meant to replace any discussion of work which he seemed to be at non stop. Once the letter was finished and neatly folded all she could say for sure was that the weather had been good and that Kass seemed to be finding satisfaction in his work, whatever it was.

*****

Two days of frantic preparation later, the Band Camp manoeuvres took place, scheduled for the following three days and nights and all hosted in the nearby training areas around the central camp complex. The first two days were conducted to a standard format and allowed evaluation of the troops by having them repeat comparative exercises within equivalently qualified teams. It was almost the middle of the second night when several detachments were shaken awake and ordered to discreetly withdraw from the camp in a change from the programmed schedule. The remainder were roused noisily a tenth part after those selected were clear and force marched to one of the replica camps where the support personnel were started on complex maintenance tasks in a hurried and chaotic sequence. The fighting troops were briefed to defend the camp and prevent anybody penetrating the perimeter, but were offered almost no time to prepare as the separated attack force was unleashed almost immediately.

It was the ferocity of the attack that shocked the defenders. Officers who had up to that point been impartial observers donned the tabards of attackers and began to roughly clear the mock walls. With the dummy, padded weapons of a training exercise, permanent injuries were avoided, but the strength of the attack was soon revealed as a huge hole was physically smashed through the outer wall defences. The defenders were further surprised when several wagons were physically carried through the centre of the camp, the attackers forming a cordon around them and attempting to hold off the defenders who had by now spotted that the attackers had their own standard fixed firmly to one of the wagons. The fact that the defenders' own colours had been taken very early in the attack hadn't stopped the exercise and only added to the defenders resolve to win back some honour.

Blue Boy, who was fighting with the attackers under the command of Stonebrow, was shocked to be thrown right back over a wagon as he was tackled roughly by Big Tar and Heat simultaneously and was even more shocked when Big Tar followed through trying to wrestle him down. Despite the choke hold he was in, or possibly because it rendered him unable to move, he was forced to watch Heat and Stonebrow circling each other unarmed, the last two combatants contesting. He was even more surprised to see Stonebrow, one of the quickest fighters in the camp, take two heavy blows from Heat's fists, rolling with both before hammering his own return blow into the smith's solar plexus and dropping him to vomit noisily in the straw under foot. It was at that sight that the hold finally began to overwhelm him, and with his vision blurring Blue Boy began to drum his feet in a gesture of surrender.

By dawn both teams were back at the main camp. Instructions came to sit, which Blue Boy took as a sure sign that a lengthy briefing on the past few days would be forthcoming from Master Smee. Before Master Smee began though, he ordered the teams to form up in lines and sent each team to walk down the opposing line greeting and congratulating them. Heading the respective lines, Stonebrow, sporting a heavily blackened eye and swollen jaw, sportingly hugged the pale but smiling smith. Clearly neither harboured any ill will from the previous night's exercise and, following their lead the rest of the camp soon began to release their tensions. Whatever the Master's wishes Blue Boy was intent on retaining his grievances, especially as Big Tar had not released the hold, even on his submission, and had held him until he succumbed to unconsciousness and needed to be revived with a pail of water. The big man hadn't remained totally unscathed himself, with finger sized bruises around his throat from Blue-Boy's powerful hands and deep bloody wounds where the young drummer had torn at the forearm applying the wrestling hold.

Despite his protestations the farrier pulled him into a bear hug and gave him a broad smile as he moved on to ruffle the hair of one of the wind section whom he had also laid out, stone cold, many moments earlier in the defence and who, as a full band member, seemed overly ashamed at being humbled by a support team member.

Master Smee and Bart had definitely formed strong views about where bad blood was likely. As the lines passed, Blue Boy waited patiently with the others during frequent pauses for particular differences to be resolved. Blue Boy suspected that this was also a ruse tailored to prolong other, more, sensitive, exchanges, also relating to the previous evening. Once everybody had spoken to all the members of the other team the camp was ordered to reform in normal order. When seated once more Master Smee spoke for over three parts on his initial findings. Gradually, as the sun gained height and the day grew hot, he dismissed the camp, although in many cases Bart, Master Smee or other section leaders continued to debrief specific groups or individuals about additional issues.

About two parts later the camp received the federal messenger. In his official livery he rode up and after only a few scant moments closeted with Master Smee, or so Farnes, one of the camp runners, claimed later, the recall horn was sounded for another complete muster on the parade square. This was soon complete and Master Smee began a short speech with praise for the effectiveness that the camp was currently displaying. "I address you officially all too infrequently," he began, "but today I will have made up for this somewhat." He then went on to announce that this year he was delighted to confirm that War Band Smee had been announced as the official campaign musicians. He then went on to say that this was merely an official reflection of the honour that the band had already brought upon themselves, through their development and performance over the last couple of years, and in spite of the fact that they had not had the opportunity to play in front of the Marshall recently. He finished his announcement explaining that obviously his injury did not permit him to operate as a campaign leader and, therefore, he had decided to move sideways into a position of camp and technical director. He revealed that the band council had discussed the vacant position and that a new band leader and deputy had already been selected.

Blue Boy and the whole camp stood poised for his announcement, assuming the favourites to be Marvellous, who had stood in before, and the Magnificent Bart. Instead Master Smee went on to say that because an injection of youth was required for this crucial campaign, Stonebrow would be the band leader with Nathan Hurst, a popular man of much experience, the deputy. He also confirmed that the vote had been unanimous. The whole camp erupted in a barrage of cheering, drowning out his announcement that Bart would be running the camp as deputy, with responsibility for holding things ready for their return, or rebuilding the band should the Battle Spirit claim his comrades at the front.

Stonebrow was quick to step up and say a few words which passed Blue Boy and the majority of the cadets by in their excitement. Master Smee finally warned that the band was to prepare for departure to the central campaign fayre due to start three weeks hence and reminded them that the fayre site was four days travel away. Duties and rosters were to be announced by notice the next day. Smee and Stonebrow then retired for discussion with the messenger, allowing the camp an evening of reduced duties to celebrate the announcement.

Blue Boy had remembered the excitement caused in the camp from previous years' announcements and now this was doubly so because, for the first time in his experience, his own band had a role. Foremost on the agenda for discussion that night was who would stay and who would go. Some wagers were placed by the older cadets, with form based on which senior members had campaigned before and would, therefore, be likely to have responsibility for the development of the band's resources in the future. History was littered with stories of campaigns going astray, where band losses were almost total. Already Blue Boy's group of friends knew those announced earlier as leading the campaigners and that Bart, Smee and Split would be the main seniors to stay. Split and Smee being senior veterans and Bart as the next potential band leader for future seasons or should the band be called upon to send a second section to the campaign.

Early the next morning Blue Boy and Marv viewed the posters together and agreed that the listings were much as expected. Although some surprise names were up and Marv and Starling were named among the non-participating travelling line up, auxiliaries rather than full place band members. This led later in the day to rumours that the leaders anticipated high losses. When Marv was asked he replied this just signified that special duties or capabilities had been requested and thus the skill and experience of both could easily be explained. No doubt some of the unofficial camp commentators also held that because of the youth of the leaders the two might have been included as auxiliaries to act as special advisers, although that would not be consistent of Master Smee's reputation for directness.

*****

The schooling of Jeffers Star's wards, Sophie and Liam, was carried out in two parts. In the mid-mornings they attended the local ward school. Any child separated from his or her parents, the Nation termed 'wards' and whether it was temporary or permanent the use of the term was encouraged for all youngsters and the term 'orphan' actively discouraged. For two or three day-parts, at least three times per week, the children met the school's youngsters and were tutored by the teaching staff on various subjects – informative, practical or fun.

This was the minimum requirement that social law decreed for those up to ten years of age, before they were enrolled in the academy. The guardians, either of their own children or their wards, were then responsible for the other part of the young children's education. Depending on other duties, this was handled in a variety of ways from parental tuition to tutoring or even enrolment for more lessons at the ward school or another suitable facility.

Jeffers had always intended to employ tutors once he had passed on his basic understanding of matters educational. Then he had been moved to Buccaneer Town and the Night Fort. In his search he had found no one more capable than the steward he inherited with the club, Taverner. The two had discussed whether Taverner would help him with his search for the children's tutor and Taverner had suggested that he would be pleased to personally arrange further tuition but that he might utilise club staff, either off or performing lighter duties, to impart certain lessons.

Initially sceptical, Jeffers attended many of the lessons and was impressed with the varied knowledge that Taverner displayed and the hunger for learning that he seemed to spark in the children, in Liam's case even if it only lasted until he left the room. He was also impressed when Scars helped Liam build a working castle gate from wood, and of Sophie's blooming knowledge of commerce from her forays to the market with Changworth.

*****

As Lawrence made his way up the hill, walking back from the marketplace with Rosey, he quickly caught up with two female marines who were chatting loudly about the chariot races and one of their colleagues, Stibbings, who had reached this year's national poetry prize final. Unaware of being over heard one girl joked that if her companion was really serious about having a baby then Stibbings would make a good father, having brains, brawn and a great rear, but that her friend had also better stop binge drinking, especially if she wanted to avoid having the baby in the Legion.

Lawrence's interest in eaves dropping began to wane as talk moved to the campaign news, apparently reducing the number of pregnancy places by 15. Interest picked up again, though, when a third person joined the pair from a side street and the conversation soon confirmed him to be the aforementioned poet who was also walking back to quarters.

Stibbings apparently had been having bad stomach cramps and was doubtful that he could continue in his current position, especially as there was the campaign coming up. He asked if the girls thought he should have a chat with his captain and they discussed finding a replacement and whether he could or should gain a transfer to the enders. Finally, a fourth individual joined the long stretch up the hill and, being the captain, was drawn into the unofficial discussion, despite the poet's protestations. The captain reminded him that the results of the poetry competition should be announced around the time of the forthcoming fayres. He said he selfishly hoped the man would still be in the team at that time and that he would be upset once his long-standing friend transferred from the company.

Lawrence filed every word of their conversation to memory but tried not to show it, paying Rosey's banter as much heed as he could. The leading party finally stopped to split, with the female marines heading in the direction of the club, turning off the main street, and the men continuing up the hill to their quarters. As she turned, one girl flashed Lawrence a promising smile and Rosey dug her elbow savagely into his ribs when the marines eventually disappeared into their digs, slapping her arm in a crude gesture.

They continued in silence, Lawrence wondering why on earth Bones always seemed to run out of at least one herb for dishes he planned on those evenings when he relieved Millie of the main cook's shift. It wasn't as if the old bloke didn't go out and about during the day himself. Still, it gave Lawrence, known around the club by the nickname his father used, 'The Lad', time to himself. Quite often one of the waitress girls would also be about on an errand at the same time and it wasn't unusual for him to have company when he visited the market. Lawrence, whilst as boisterous as the next bloke was, he admitted, often very shy and quiet in the company of girls. Still, forced out on these errands the slender young man was soon able to forget his reservations and several of the girls he found really quite enchanting. None of course could compare to Millie, for whom he held a secret flame. No, these young girls were all right, but she was his love. Not that he would ever tell her, for a start everybody could see the chemistry between her and Mandibles, expecting it to break out in an affair at any time.

*****

Lauren trooped from the parade ground up Tone Hill to the

barracks. She had given the squad a thorough workout and was pretty pleased with their progress. Now that they were used to her youth and heritage they paid reasonable attention and returned a fairly normal level of backchat.

It was a difficult posting to expect too much, with the Northern Army presence in Buccaneer Town a token force, meant to be symbolic rather than effective. In centuries past the high command had ceded the town and its surroundings to the Council of Admirals who, as independents, garrisoned it with marines and their own military police, the Marine Patrol. Reporting directly to the high command they ran the area as they saw fit.

To be honest it was pretty much like any other town where the governing council would treat with the force commander. Certainly since their inception and initial conversion from piracy the Admirals had always proven good at what they were asked. Sharing the leadership of the associated land-based coastal defence force with the army, and together voting on yet another semi independent commander, they pretty much got on with running the fleet.

Recently, however, the nature of Buccaneer Town had changed. The fleet had in living memory opened two new facilities, both termed Docks of the Naval Reserve, man made and heavily fortified. One, a major harbour area, sat 100 leagues north and could dock sixty percent of the fleet in port at once. Fleet collateral had, therefore, never been better serviced and with rumours of another development under way, of equivalent size, to house the support personnel further south the strategic nature of Buccaneer Town, once the hub of the fleet, was in doubt. This had meant, though, that newly available dock space made for rare opportunities. Also, a flourishing entertainment trade for off duty navy staff, free from the seclusion of the new isolated facilities on multi day leave had, livened up the town itself.

Still, the demand for actual dock space at Buccaneer Town had fallen which resulted in only a moderate number of standing vessels. The unused docks had then been turned to other purposes, with the more northerly part converted into a more practical commercial port and a terminal for transporting off duty personnel to and from the newer, isolated bases. The southern district was highly classified and a discrete complex had arisen that was used by the fleet auxiliary as a special weapons and training facility. It was able to use normal shipping as a cover for the import, development and launch of new naval technology. To the common population this was presented as the Dump, a fenced off area for military equipment and bonded merchandise from the Iron Isles. Lauren's position, however, carried with it enough status to be briefed somewhat on the true nature of Buccaneer Town's activities. Two admirals were stationed in Buccaneer Town, one at each major base, two commanding the northern and southern fleets, one was based in the Iron Isles and one down at the combined admiralty command for the southern oceans, a liaison job with the navies of the other nations.

As Lauren crested the brow of the hill and looked out, she could appreciate the scale of the ship building hangars, lumber yards, pitch factories, forges, ballistic ranges, quartermaster stores, chandleries, rope winders and sail yards spread amongst the other businesses through the sprawl of the town. Just past the top of the hill she stopped at the female baths. Because her squad was so small one of the preceding officers had decommissioned their own bath block, converting it into a training room, and paid a retainer to two local bath houses for round the clock access. The baths had provided a set of lockers for the troops and, for the females, the Mistress of the house also further supported them by providing a laundry service. Shortly Lauren was back out on the street for the brisk walk, about a tenth day-part, to the barracks some few hundred metres over the next rise. As she passed back through the entrance she caught the eye of a fellow lounging idly against the wall, enjoying the view. He flashed a good long, gap-toothed leer at her and she recognised him as Barf, one of the staff at the up-and-coming club, the Night Fort. He was dressed in a not-too-smart khaki smock and trousers over scuffed boots.

As smart as Jeffers Star is, she thought, he doesn't manage to instil much of the same into his employees. Star himself might be a bit of a clothes stand, but he didn't half have a nice frame and a lithe way of moving. Perhaps she should try a new outfit and a night at the club, doubling the task and looking to pick up any new gossip at the same time.

*****

All morning and well into the afternoon Stonebrow, Bart and Starling, laboured out at the exercise range to prepare a further evening exercise. They had selected the most discrete venue and the number of senior cadets patrolling the obscured perimeter had been doubled for the next three days. Equipment needed to be selected and transported to the foundry where, behind closed doors, the smith made final preparations. Each of the selected team then spent some time at the stables where they chose two light, swift horses, a main one for the mission and a second choice should the first suffer injury. One of the wranglers had also been enrolled and once the selections were made her job was to enhance the horses' training and also keep them fit and ready.

The first night exercise was performed successfully, to strict instructions left by one of the Couriers. In fact three more night exercises had also to be planned by the weary trio and a second courier, who arrived the day after, actually involved himself in the final training sessions before leaving the next morning as if he had, instead, spent a comfortable night's sleep.

Over the four days Smee received a total of six more couriers, some arriving simultaneously from separate starting facilities. One man in particular occupied him constantly for fourteen parts with a couple of the other nominated seniors, and occasionally hauling Stonebrow back from his final preparations. This was the timing and planning stage, done separately by Smee and the others and then re-planned blindly by Stonebrow to confirm the set of tactics.

Firstly the resulting plans were presented separately to the courier and then again, together, ensuring that Stonebrow had considered all the options and could be flexible in his final planning when in the field. A second officer arrived whose sole purpose was to return the planning officer's reply to the high command, the first being in seclusion away with the two seniors for some rest. When the second courier left he was met further down the road by a heavy detachment of elite horsemen who gave him a comprehensive screen of protection until he boarded a ship for the High Fort.

Smee himself doubled and then tripled security, discreetly covered by arranging further short but intricate training for almost all the seniors and cadets alike.

*****

"Good to see you, Millie, how is everything progressing at that new club? Business good?"

.   "Oh fine, thank you, Mistress Skillet. Jeffers Star keeps us all very busy to provide what he calls 'the quality factor'," Millie replied. "Those flowers are lovely, did you do the arrangement yourself?" she asked, as spotting a large arrangement of purple blooms she bent to inhale their bouquet.

"Why, thank you, Millie, yes I did," the old lady answered with a smile. "It is nice to see them appreciated, so many young women these days are caught up in, how shall I say it, the adventure and romance of their military service, and forget the lovelier female pastimes. Mind, places like your club don't help any. I've never been busier with the alterations service. Can't say I approve of the fashions either, everything seems to be getting shorter and tighter and I am either fitting and refitting outfits to keep them skin tight, or trying to explain that once they, have been made smaller how difficult it is to enlarge them should the owner put on weight or muscle. And I can't say that part of my business is only required by lady customers these days either. You would laugh at the number of men who sneak along after dark or send along outfits, measurements and monies with female friends visiting the baths. In fact I suspect that there are a few women who make a business out of men paying them to attend my bath house as a guise for delivering alterations, I have taken on two new wards who can help with that work just this week." The old woman paused in her chatter. "Sorry dear I do go on. What can I do for you today? Unfortunately all the private bathing rooms are booked until this afternoon."

"Well in that case could you do me a quick facial if you have time, I have the rest of the morning off and there is some one I could bump into who is also free on our roster," Millie said looking unusually self conscious.

"I can always make a bit of room as long as you tell me all about him. Here, come into this small room and make yourself comfortable whilst I get Rose to sort out the water."

Mistress Skillet ushered her into a small, neat room with an old padded chair and a stool beside it and rushed off to fetch her materials. Millie looked around and smiled to see more flowers in a pretty pastel vase sitting on a small table next to a jug of drinking water, two glasses and what from a distance looked like a small book of poetry daintily illustrated. On the wall above the flowers hung a large embroidery depicting a view of a mountain meadow. The old lady certainly made every effort to provide her clients with an appropriately furnished female environment. Millie knew herself to be quite a good seamstress and maintained all her own outfits, although stopping short of altering the length or fit to follow the current fashions. She was glad indeed that she had not informed the owner of the bath house of this though, as had she known Millie may never have escaped again.

The old woman soon returned and, having carefully closed the door began to mix a face pack whilst flannels were soaking in the steaming water. Applying the first towel to Millie's face she leant in and with her lips close to Millie's ear whispered, "Before you tell me all about your gentleman, Millie, let me fill you in on some local topics." For the next eighth part, as she changed the cloths and applied the face pack, she leant in whispering her report.

*****

On the evening of the fourth day Stonebrow finally returned from the exercise yard satisfied that the group were near ready to execute their strange mission when under enemy fire in the field. He remained concerned at what certain other mission requirements demanded of himself, particularly the deep night exercises where precise instruction remained vague.

He was doubly pleased that after the day's exercise he had been able to report positively on the standard of the equipment he was to be sent with. Since his orders had been relayed, the armoury and fletching teams had been working shifts, producing much larger quantities of specific weapons than normally the camp ever consumed and therefore stocked. Random samples of the three main varieties of arrow had been tested throughout the day. Needle points with their steel tips for penetrating deep into armour or tough Reptoid carapace, stoppers with their bulbous tin bladders designed to collapse under impact trapping quantities of air, producing impressive concussive impact and finally, razor sharp leaf tips with wide heads to open up as much of the enemy as possible had all passed the accuracy and range checks.

The fire weapons had also been tested with success. The flame pumps came in two forms. The first with an integrated air and oil tank allowed the pressure from hand cranking to be preserved. Mounted on a back harness it would offer a twelfth part of trigger operated spurts before needing to be re-cranked. The second type, for mounting on some kind of platform, allowed the weapon to be fired and cranked at the same time with separate, larger, oil reservoirs giving much longer periods of continuous use. Finally, the aerodynamic, ovaloid porcelain hand lobs that could be thrown, spinning through the air with great accuracy could, of course, be filled with a variety of payloads including oil to smash on the target.

Stonebrow looked up to the conical roof on the west wall's gate tower and shrugging off his weariness trotted to the door and greeted the gatemen. And, using the top storey hatch, he slid himself carefully out onto the roof. Many were the times when he and Scandrett had sat together discreetly, watching the stars, even up to their most recent meeting. They mostly performed their debriefings sitting on the roof of one of the outer-meadow hay barns.

Whilst some people knew Master Smee to be active in the intelligence field, only a few had an idea as to exactly how far his network of informants operated or the importance that some of his activities could mean to the Nation. Raised from their early teens around the camp Stonebrow and Scandrett were known as firm friends, the local land worker and his odd brother being well liked in the area.

Many had been surprised when Scandrett opted for more tours of duty after fulfilling his service duties at a late age. Many attributed it to restlessness. Only Stonebrow, not only his friend but also his handler, had the complete picture of his full capabilities. Indeed, few people understood the amount of training that Scandrett had secretly been given whilst working as a teenager on his holding. Nor had his service been the standard battlefront infantry position about which he gossiped with the other land workers when he returned on leave. Far and wide he had ranged into the Battle Lands, sent to perform difficult tasks, greeted by his old friend on return only to be sent out into danger once more. Through all this, though, the pair had laboured hard to obscure the truth from Moffet. On Scandrett's last visit he had confided in Stonebrow. "However this one turns out Stoney, promise that you will look out for my brother. Behind his odd demeanour there is much depth, of that I am sure."

Scandrett continued, "He is certainly far clever than he looks. His strength is deceptive and I am certain that whilst he appears to show little interest, when he is shown something once he will be able to repeat it and even improve it straight away. I will admit to you, Stoney, that many times during my training I felt as if I was being followed. For all my skill and Smee's training I was never able to catch him at it, yes even today, but my instinct still tells me that it happens."

In recent times Stonebrow had considered this quite carefully. Since the meeting Stonebrow had twice found time to scout Moffet. Whilst he had been able to approach the man and observe his routine closely he had noticed nothing out of the ordinary. Quite whether he had remained undetected was another matter. Being a plains man from a tribe with much skill and some little original history, despite being displaced at an early age his scouting and field skills were considered very highly. Indeed, even now, many were the invitations that he received from the varied ranger academies.

Up until now, though, he had avoided dwelling on the subject, but about to leave on this exercise, he felt deep within himself a knowledge that it would be a long time, if ever, before he saw this, his home, again. He therefore resolved to conclude this matter by discussing it with Master Smee. He hoped that

Scandrett would have understood his breaking of their confidence. Before he approached Smee he resolved to question Blue Boy concerning his code for communicating with the lad. Perhaps that peculiar mystery would shed further light on the issue.

*****

The Admiral paced the depth of the room, "With the numbers of these ships, I cannot see how we can provide this level of transport and keep the movements secret." He reached down almost absently and plucked a goblet of juice from the table. "Pah!" He shouted, "for god's sake get this laced with rum will you," he called to the serving man. Bowing his head and hiding a smile Piker slipped back through he servants' door and headed off towards the cellar.

"The Marshall must have some mean plan in mind to require transport on this scale, and all manned and fitted for battle. If we floated all the fleet, both new and old, we could touch upon these numbers, but to have them fully manned and capable of giving a good fight, well, the men that would take, it's almost too much. Meaks, how many marines do we have that could sail and fight and be ready within a week?"

"Well sir, spread across the ships pretty thinly we could float and crew all the new battle wagons up at the shed. That would make about six thousand vessels including the roving fleet and all the available reserves."

"Six thousand! The amount of transport the Marshall has requested, even working at double pace would need nine and not six. What capacity and how soon can we bring on the schooners at shed Two?" the Admiral asked the facility commander.

"Shed Two! By the Battler, Admiral, that site has only been under construction for four months! Well, perhaps twenty of the advanced boats are coming up for sea trials, but they are the deep ocean craft, three times the draught of our current largest." Dark Keel offered, "We could bring those on and scrounge the rest, if we release the pickers flotilla that would add another thousand and that I feel might take us close enough."

"Good, good enough. Well then, my fellows, let's get all

these scoops and anymore that don't affect the coastal defences and make them sea worthy. Meaks, despatch the first battle wagons as instructed in these documents."

"Ah, good fellow, I hope this batch of juice was pressed longer ago, my thanks," the admiral addressed Piker as he quietly returned the pitcher, suitably laced for the towns governor.

*****

It was deep into the night as the cloaked figure made its way carefully up the stairs towards the Marshall's chambers, so far there had been no guards in evidence. The poor state of security both pleased and worried the stealthy warrior, for whilst it would allow him easier access to the Marshall's chambers it played on his mind that surely security would not be so lax. Had he simply failed to identify from where he was being observed and therefore also by whom?

Unbeknown to the intruder, had he returned immediately down the stairs, he would have found the captain of the Marshall's guard and another armoured figure. Resting lightly against the wall on either side of the bottom stair, talking away in sign language, apparently without a care in the world and fully aware of the passing of their mysterious guest.

Soon the cloaked man reached the Marshall's chambers and pushing open the door slid quickly but carefully into the outer room of the suite. Here there was a fire well banked for the night casting a pleasantly soft light over the walls. On the far side of the room light could be seen spilling under the door from a second room, which the intruder figured must be the bedroom. He closed the door silently behind him, appreciating the well oiled hinges.

"Welcome my friend," came the Marshall's rumbling voice from the tall-backed chair which obscured the sitting figure from the man at the door. "What news do you bring me from the cold regions of your kingdom?"

"Not good news," said the large black man as he freed his cloak and laid it on the table by the door. "I fear not just for the survival of my legions but also for the fate of Humankind, my

91

lord," the Commander of the Legions of the north said as he took a seat opposite the High Marshall, who at these words felt a chill run down his spine as if the warrior had brought the ice of the wastes clinging to his armour into the room with him.

As the two men began their meeting the ghostly concealed form of the Ethereal Watcher slipped through an open window moving stealthily and silently just into the range of their lowered voices, using its superior senses to absorb the whispered secrets without fear of detection.

Chapter Five

Blue Boy left the western gate of the camp deciding to practice his woodcraft and stealth skills by circling the perimeter and attempt to go undetected past the perimeter scouts. Not that he was often successful, and being caught usually delayed his journey because of the extra snippets of instruction forced on him in how to better proceed on his next attempt. No one ever seemed inclined to dissuade him from these attempts, though, and the delay in his arrival at Moffet's place, against the specifics of his orders, was never mentioned.

Deciding to spend up to a part he kept close to the outside of the town wall in the shadows where he attempted to identify any possible route by which he could climb the them. As usual, though, he found them in excellent repair with no handy cracks or crevices. Having failed before on this personal mission he had brought some heavy steel spikes, and when he judged his position to be immediately between the west and northern gates, and when the shadows from above indicated that the wall guard had passed, he attempted to hammer in the spikes and use them to lever himself up. Whilst he found it relatively easy and surprisingly quiet to get a significant portion of the spike into the wall, he discovered that the rock was so crumbly as to bear no weight whatsoever. He was also surprised when he hit a thread of metal with a further spike and discovered that the outer wall had a soft outer covering. He resolved to probe this discovery further without causing more visible damage to the walls, but soon gave up, wondering how he could ask the question without exposing himself to the standard response of 'Mind your own business!' He wondered whether in this case he might rest the depth of his new acquaintance with Big Tar, who Blue Boy suspected could be a fount of camp information, if only he addressed his questions correctly.

Having given up his idea of climbing the wall he cast aside

his worries about what would happen when the marks he had left were discovered and set off to the west of the camp. As it was he was caught some forty yards past the first rise, tripped by a set of bolas around his legs. Big Tar beamed down at him and motioned him to silence. Blue Boy was both relieved and concerned as the horse-husband freed his legs and motioned to follow, as he couldn't help but worry what was in store for him. The big, quiet man obviously harboured an inner violence and Blue Boy was under no illusion that his prestigious build was a match for the powerful veteran. Still, as Big Tar was his superior he had little choice but to follow the instructions. They headed directly to the nearest wooded area and then waited a short time before Big Tar led them off on a complicated looping, spiralling path, gradually widening outward towards where Blue Boy was headed. To his amazement only once did they come across a patrol, and then from behind, so they could hunker down behind some cover.

Soon they were safe beyond the patrols' normal boundaries and Big Tar produced two items from the pack he was carrying. "Thought I might accompany you today, Blue; you might also appreciate these. The first is a standard, thin camouflage cape, coloured for foliage. Your profile and colouring are all wrong for wandering around these parts and fatigues are often two slow to change, the cloak is a good tool for temporary actions of the sort that seem to entertain you. The second is a map of common routes that our patrols use, cross-referenced by individual and time. Whilst our patrols are pretty random you should also be able to learn something about the people. Next time you decide to play find out in advance which patrol is out, it's not too hard and could help you become more successful. Right, enough of the soft heart, now we've got a pretty tough pace in order to make Moffet's by when Marv told you, thanks to all your messing. So pick your feet up we're getting back on the road." With that Big Tar and Blue Boy ran all the way to Moffet's Homestead.

Allowing Blue Boy only moments to catch a bit of wind Big Tar bustled them out onto the holding in search of Moffet, who didn't seem disturbed at all to see Big Tar. He left Blue Boy with firm instructions to speed up Moffet's progress and get the vegetables harvested before sundown and returned towards the farm buildings. Blue Boy's confused expression was enough to amuse his friend who very uncharacteristically spoke, especially to answer an unasked question, "Wagon and Horses," signing that Blue Boy ought to work rather than spend time 'thought lost' as Moffet called it. Almost too tired to stand Blue Boy finally dragged himself back to the holding pushing a large barrow loaded with all kinds of root crops. Not only did Greenleaf Tom's visit report suggest that, correctly picked, the crops complemented each other, but also with careful timing it meant that through the harvesting of one complete field the camp was provided with a fair variety of supplies. Enough choice to keep even the precocious head cooks quiet. Big Tar was nowhere to be seen and there was no welcome lantern hanging in the cabin. This lapse in protocol had already caused Blue Boy, too tired to scout the cabin, to call out twice. He therefore sent Moffet up the nearest tree and proceeded, belatedly, to advance on the cabin drawing one of his cutters. He carefully passed two of the outhouses before ducking off the path behind the wagon shed, where lifting a hatch he attempted a silent entry. Halfway through the window, though, he froze as he felt the press of cold steel on his neck and suddenly rough hands grabbed his shoulders and levered him all the way through.

Big Tar pulled open his covered lantern and offered the boy a hand up. "Dinner time," he said, with no further comment on the hatch incident. He then called Moffet down out of the tree and led them towards the cabin where he uncovered two further lanterns to reveal that he had prepared a rich variety of food. Chastising Blue Boy for coming into the cabin unwashed he sent him back to the trough where Moffet was noisily finishing up. After the meal Big Tar sent the lads out to wash down the platters and scatter all the debris on the mulch patch before handing Moffet a bucket, an obvious invitation to visit the well.

"Look, Blue Boy, down at the camp everybody likes it that you try and practice what you are learning, and pretty good you seem at most things as well but, boy when it comes to stealth you stink. It is also about time that the instructors stopped being entertained by your attempts and sorted out your basic techniques before these bad habits become ingrained and can't be corrected. Blue Boy, sit with me and think about stealth. To you, a good indoctrinated musician it is probably all about sound. If you can hear something you know where it is. You are all filled up with good human knowledge. Let's see if we can reach some crafty animal cunning. Close your eyes, stand up, sit down. How did that feel? Could you actually listen as you were moving, could you place everything in the room with your eyes closed? Probably not. You need to follow your other senses more. Tomorrow ask Stonebrow to teach you something of meditation. Oh, and boy, don't mention me. It was Stonebrow's patrol we got past today, eh. And don't go scratching the wall any more! Bill will have a fit, it's a cement skin over metal springs, for strength against impacting projectiles, pretty clever stuff for building a fortress where there isn't any rock to quarry."

Rising early the next morning Blue Boy wasn't surprised that only he and Moffet were occupying the cabin. Inspection of the wagon showed it was in better repair than it had been for years, even though Big Tar had only had a couple of parts to work on it and carried no specific tools or materials. The horses were also well groomed, curried and fed. Blue Boy and Moffet, provided with such a useful head start, saw themselves on the road within a couple of parts of daybreak, needing only to clean the vegetables and load them into the wagon. With the cabin securely closed, up and the wagon swaying beneath them, they pushed on towards the camp.

The journey was long and familiar and happy. With Moffet silently concentrating on driving the wagon, Blue Boy found himself pondering Moffet's social position. Moffet's skills included trapping and training animals and gardening for supplies of fruit and vegetables and at these he was talented. However, his appearance and lack of speech and of more socially based skills left him classified as disabled. Still, with his long days of work and a little help with wagon maintenance each year he managed to produce larger crops of food than some of his neighbours. His other interest was to listen to the camp music as much as he could.

Blue Boy supposed Moffet's social role was typical of many individuals that the Nation organised separately, allowing official schemes for the disabled to give all types of partially active people a way to contribute. In some cases large houses, or even specially constructed camps or town suburbs had been created to provide good and easier working conditions.

Blue Boy had been surprised to hear that the former Prison Legion in particular welcomed disadvantaged folk, and there they were treated particularly well as equal volunteers. The Legion with its make up of 15 percent Militia troops on rotation, criminals, warders and the disadvantaged sections plus the short and long term volunteers who were often relatives of the staying guests, sounded a remarkable group of human settlements. Many of the volunteers were said to be people who had regularly failed to secure war company places, or were seeking something a bit different, even fame in some cases.

Life was, of course, that little bit harder serving out near the vastnesses of the polar cap and the cold tundra, but there was an honour to having served and a strong sense of bonding. All who served were marked with a different colour brand, though for the volunteers these markings were described as optional.

Trundling along slowly, with Blue Boy day dreaming of far away places, the pair completed their journey without mishap and arrived at the camp gates just before the sun reached its peak. Moffet would then camp out overnight, probably sleeping underneath the wagon, rather than take the bunk in the guest barracks that he was always offered, and then the two would set off back early in the morning Blue Boy expected another band member to accompany them as his trainer on the foot journey back, possibly even leaving Moffet to complete the final stages along a flat road that didn't tax even his erratic driving skills. Moffet was always excited to reach the camp, although until the music started, this just accentuated his look of wild terror. Master Smee always insisted that the camp children sit with Moffet during recitals, so that they could witness his blissful expression which helped lesson their fright at his usual contorted visage.

On that occasion however it was a sad affair. Master Smee limped straight out as soon as the pair arrived through the inner gates. "Blue Boy, never mind the wagon, the others will see to that, bring Moffet up to my study please." Stonebrow reached up to grab the reins and Marv, Split and Squeeler, one of the young trainees, started to unhitch the traces.

Master Smee's slow limping had only allowed him to reach his study door when Blue Boy and Moffet arrived and they found Starling and Bart already there. Master Smee looked disconcerted as he pulled out a padded box from the draw in his desk. Blue Boy's heart was already sinking as Smee clasped Moffet's hand and informed him that this was the medal sent to Moffet by the High Marshall himself.

"Moffet, my lad, I'm afraid the news is bad. Your brother, Scandrett, has been killed in action. Oh, lad! I am so sorry."

A pitiful whimper escaped Moffet's lips and his knees slowly started to buckle. The whimper became a wail and Bart suddenly stepped forwards to catch the young man as his bones seemed to turn to water. The wail became a shriek and Smee turned and grasped Blue Boy's shoulder before signing him to leave and close the door. As he turned to close it he glimpsed Bart laying the lad on Smee's bunk and Starling began singing in soothing tones attempting to calm the desolate man.

Food was taken up and it was several day-parts before first Bart and then Starling joined the others in the refectory. A mild sedative in a tonic and the soothing music had eventually calmed Moffet into slumber.

*****

Finally Lauren had managed to schedule four free parts together on the roster to allow her to visit the old woman. The crone seemed to live a couple of miles outside town, up into the southern hills, and Lauren figured that excessive caution would only serve to make her more conspicuous and she might as well head out of town during the day. Many would draw their own conclusions from a visit by a young woman to an old matron who was known, even in the male dominated gambling houses, to supply pregnancy relief. Perhaps bets were already being placed on her pregnancy status or lover. In fact, if her gaming house visit had been that memorable, the bets would possibly be on the length of time she might survive, probably just in days the way she was going.

Lauren felt the meeting with the Baker, whilst unnerving,

had at least sharpened her caution. She was now sure that she was being followed and even had an inkling that it wasn't just one group either. Perhaps her father had decided to take action after all.

Once off the main highway, the track she found herself following became quite rough and she was glad that she had dressed more for hard travel than for appearance. Once in the trees she made an attempt to detect if she was being followed; in this case she was fairly sure that she had been alone since leaving the town. Lauren, therefore, raced off using her running prowess to get to the cabin as quickly as possible. Figuring that if a tail had guessed the destination and fallen back she could reach her goal, gain the information and slip back through the rougher ground, next to the track, before anybody else turned up at the cabin. Perhaps she would even be able to gain a clear glimpse of today's shadow for inclusion in the profile that she was building up, her current plan being to gather enough information to dump it in the Admiral's lap and let him shoulder the final outcome. After all it was his town to control.

Within moments she had covered the distance and stood outside the hut. She knocked loudly at the door and hearing no reply tried the latch. It opened easily and despite a suggestion of lingering food smells the hearth was cold and spotless and there was no particular sign of recent habitation. She made a tentative show of searching further but, not wanting to disturb anything and reveal her visit, and not having time for a careful search, she decided to withdraw and at least salvage something by spying on her pursuers. She headed off to the left and took up position half a league back down the track.

A fifth part later she was snuggled into some long grass between two thorn bushes, a good place to observe, and because she had approached the position from behind absolutely none of the foliage in front had been disturbed. Lauren had spotted a couple of places where there were ancient tracks in the woods, away from the path, but this position was ideal. She lay watching the road and thinking back to her ranger instruction which she had to all intents abandoned to take up the search for Chloe's killer. It wasn't long before a couple of shifty looking characters passed by in front of her, moving carefully but not making any attempt to conceal their appearance. Lauren watched them carefully as they passed, noting the young lad with sandy hair and sparse stubble beard and his more serious companion who looked like nothing so much as a very dumb bear with an almost pointed snout-like face. Their cloaks were dark and serviceable but underneath there was no way of knowing quite what weapons they carried.

Several hundred spans further back from Lauren, high in a tree, Barf sat balanced on a thick bough keeping the trunk between himself and the track. There, if he leant round the trunk, he would just about be able to make out Lauren's feet. He, too, heard the men on the trail, but avoided looking down towards the road just in case his un-camouflaged pale face could be made out through the branches. He had decided not to use any face blacking in the woods so that he could move swiftly back into civilised areas without having to scrub-up. This was making him much more careful, having caught a good number of Roke on the basis of spotting skin tones amongst foliage on past missions.

Lauren was proving better in the woods than he would have thought, despite it being common knowledge that she had been working at the Ranger academy. Regardless of this, Barf, an old hand in the woods, wasn't having too much trouble tailing her. What was more interesting was that the men on the track had also sounded efficient, certainly more so than a number of the ones that Barf had scoped in town following Lauren. Only whispers of sound had given away their progress, but still enough to identify two individuals to Barf. As soon as they were gone Lauren was up and heading into town and Barf was obliged to follow her as she paralleled the path, ensuring that they had no more companions, before gradually rejoining the trail just before its junction with the main road. He hoped that the rest of his crew were performing properly as the stealth of what he assumed were the two men struck him more and more as the sign of professional operators. As he watched Lauren re-enter town, leaving her to be picked up by Lawrence, he wondered whether he should return to help the other surveillance teams, as back-up just in case. Mind, by this time they would be at the cabin and the cat would be out of the bag in any case. Instead

Barf decided to skirt round the town to re-enter by a different gate to the one Lauren and he had used to leave and by, which Lauren re-entered; a sensible move to prevent himself being recognised by anybody keeping the gate watched.

Meanwhile the two men following the trail separated just before reaching the clearing, leaving one standing quietly at the head of the trail to walk directly into sight. From the entrance of the clearing that man could just about make out the old woman moving around inside her cabin through what he knew to be the only window. 'I'm relegated to living outside of town in squalor and eliminating old women, how embarrassing!' The man thought as his partner silently circled the house, inspecting the close undergrowth with a deliberate display of caution. Signalling all clear just before he reached an angle from where he could be seen from the door, he sidled up to the cabin as the first man strolled casually up the path and rapped on the door.

"Come in," wheezed the voice of the old woman. The first man adjusted his cloak and stepped carefully through the door, doing his best to look pleasant. He was taken by how dark the cabin appeared and the dirt certainly seemed to have built up on the windows since the visit a week before, when they had found the old lady absent. Now the old bag was huddled in bed under a heap of blankets, barely visible at all, with a sleeping cap pulled down tight on her head.

"Greetings, good lady," the man said in an indistinct accent. "My name is Karl and I am on an urgent errand for a friend of mine, he was taken ill whilst having lunch at the Firebird House establishment. The bartender suggested that you might be able to offer him relief. His condition seems quite serious and it may be that he has eaten seafood recently it could be a case of bad staples. I am rather worried. Is there anything you can suggest?"

"Heh, he should be more careful what he eats and where he does it," croaked the old woman, with a noise that could have been a chuckle from her ruined throat. "Tell me of the symptoms, does his breath smell of anything in particular?" she croaked.

"Well, madam, could you accompany me back to town where we can discover whether you know anything interesting?" The fellow asked, realisation that this was going to be a considerable effort in his voice.

Whilst he was waiting for the old woman, who was shaking her head and muttering inaudibly, to answer his question his companion rapped three knocks for danger quietly on the front door. He turned quickly and ignoring the old lady stepped back out in the light to where his companion stood warily hand tucked into the front of his cloak.

As he stepped outside, Millie, who had donned the disguise of an old woman when her team had reported that Lauren had left the area but that the people following her were still intent on reaching the cabin, relaxed her grip on the trigger of the loaded arblast she held beneath the covers. With scant moments to spare she had avoided contact with the cottage's real owner, who seemed to be prowling the woods with her own mysterious rag-tag set of helpers, and made it inside the cabin.

What had alerted the two men was that up the track and into the clearing came six old chaps, miners from the look of it Karl thought. "Yo, Vee!" one of them bellowed at the top of his voice. "Vee, Jake's got the flux and needs to be purged and young Willie here has got the rot, in fact if you don't do something soon we will have to find him a new name after these forty years," the miner bawled, and he and his colleagues descended into laughter, all except the one who must be called Willie and another clutching his guts, who Karl took to be the flux-ridden Jake.

Deciding that circumstances would prove better at a later time Karl stepped back quickly into the cabin and said to the old woman, "Good lady, it looks as if you have further business, I will return again should my friend fail to improve."

"Good day to you, gentlemen," he said as he motioned his companion to move off down the track. "It sounds as if your needs are greater than ours," he muttered with a barely contained smirk, as the two men hurried off into the descending twilight gloom.

The miners stood and watched as the pair disappeared from view, standing in a loose fan around the door after which three stooped low and hurried to different edges of the clearing as the remainder took positions around the door, one stepping carefully in.

The leader and the one who had shouted out his friends' ailments raised an accusing finger, and pointing at the figure of the old woman in bed said, "We may have got rid of those unpleasant bastards but we don't like anyone impersonating our friend. Now get out of bed, whoever you are."

In the bed Millie pulled the covers even further up, almost to her eyes and for some moments the fellow at the door struggled to hear what she was saying, as she began croaking some kind of refusal, evidently worried or unsure as to how to proceed despite his firm demand.

From behind the chap came another high wavering voice, though this one precise and distinct. "Now then, Edmund, that is no way to speak to an elderly lady and certainly not me, if that is who it is," said the real old lady. "Although I doubt it, as I am most definitely me and she, therefore, cannot be. So as you are not me I think we had better know who you are and what you want, as perhaps my gruff friend first asked." Still Millie offered no answer. "Quick about it, dear, those scoundrels may soon be back with friends and we might just leave you here for them to kill," the old woman, who had appeared in the door, finished.

Even as the woman spoke the silence around the cabin was broken by a shrill bird call. "Oh, I don't think we need worry too much about them, although thank you for the help," said Millie as she finally threw off the bed covers and pulled the fruit peel that had distorted her features from her mouth. "Do you like the hair cap? I could leave it for you," The club operative asked irreverently. "Now tell your man to move his hand away from his weapon and we can continue at our leisure," she added, with a firm look and a waggle of her arblast.

The real old lady looked worried, "Edmund, check outside and tell me what you see." When there was no immediate reply she added. "Edmund, tell me."

"Well, Vee, I can see about a yard of steel and a stern man wearing camouflage with his finger to his lips. Ouch! Yep, it's steel all right," said Edmund backing into Vee as he was pushed back into the room by the sword at his throat.

Millie's darkly dressed and masked team-mate pushed Edmund fully into the cottage and reported to her without taking his eyes from the captives, "Boss, party one, two in number, have returned down the track and no more have been spotted. Uninvited party two, twelve in number, are being returned to outside the cabin. Party one appear to be competent professionals of the opposition, and we reckon they will be back. Party two appear to be better skilled and look as if they were professionals back at the dawn of time, all being similar in age to these two."

Millie paused to consider before answering Snibs. "Right, have teams two and three return to the far perimeter with four as support. Keep one and five handy, and be careful now darkness is falling. It's getting a bit like the teddy bears' picnic out here. We don't know who will turn up next, don't let us get caught out."

Millie motioned both the old timers to sit at the rickety table after Snibs had quickly but thoroughly removed the old man's weapons and gone outside. "Now then, Veronica, my name is Millie and as of now you are in a serious position. I warn you we are a fully approved intelligence team and you are slap-bang in the middle of our investigation. So, if you could explain your circumstances, we have some work to be attending to." Millie's words and manner, whilst stern, were clearly pitched to offer the old timers an easy way out.

Veronica moved into a chair pulled out in gentlemanly fashion by Edmund who, outmanoeuvred and bereft of his weapons, seemed to have lost all strength of purpose. "I haven't always been an old hag, Millie dear. I know poison and I know when people are given it. The first person I saw here in Buccaneer Town could have survived if he hadn't been dosed a second time. The second one was actually killed by his wife. That's when I knew it was big. When the Militia commander was killed I decided it was really big and kind of dropped out of sight."

"Veronica, can you tell me how you know so much?" Millie asked in a measured voice.

"Well, you know that young woman who tried to visit me earlier, she's Lauren Marshall, and I know that because for a time her father was taught by me when I worked for the previous boss. I've been dirt side and dosed more Roke scum with more nasty potions than you've had hot dinners. Used to be I lived here because I was semi-retired and useful, now I live here because I'm too old to run away, which is what most sensible folk would do if they suspected what I suspect about this town."

"What do you suspect, Veronica?" Millie asked, this time more impatience showing in her manner.

"Child, I suspect the town has the nastiest infection this continent has ever seen and it's because I can't prove it one way or another that I know it's true. Today is the third time they've sent people to kill me. You were lucky to have survived pretending to be me. I've been watching the cabin and it wasn't luck that Edmund came by with his cousins. But mark my words, this hut won't be standing too much later."

Veronica fell silent as Millie weighed these words. "Ok, then my next question is how do you still pull such strings?" the younger woman asked.

"Girl, look at those miners out there, they may be tough but you'll notice all the most useful ones are old, former operatives living in the hills in retirement."

"Well, then, I'd better see them all for a briefing and possible reactivation. I'm a bit troubled that I have not been informed about them, how can I be sure I can trust you?"

"We've been freelance for years, dropped off the active lists long since and finally forgotten when our original controller was moved suddenly to an action. She was killed, and without time or consideration for a handover. Since we are old we just remained dormant until I recently reactivated us, unofficially like, to avoid if not a premature, then certainly an untimely, demise. One of the guys has been watching the gambling house." Veronica paused then as if re-evaluating the commitment she had made to trust not just her own life but also her friends by sharing with Millie.

"Millie, I had been Military and not Admiralty and therefore uncertain as to whom to trust locally. I've also been unwilling to contact anybody out of town until recently, and was using Chloe Oak to feel out how the news might be taken. Her death also points to a militia traitor somewhere in that squad."

"Hmm, well, it doesn't put my performance or the all seeing, all knowing new security service in a good light when we don't know any more than you oldsters," Millie replied, coming close to acknowledging Veronica's story.

"Pah! And you don't even have records of our names," Veronica couldn't resist adding.

"Oh, I wouldn't be so sure of that Veronica Stubs," Taverner's gentle voice carried from the doorway. "I certainly won't ever be forgetting you and I hope you won't be forgetting your agreement with the boss."

Veronica jumped at the sound of his voice and Millie was interested to see the old woman spin and take in her partner. Veronica did not manage to conceal completely the look of surprise at whom she saw, or her visible pallor for the next few moments. Her voice was steady, however, as she answered, "And who might you be, good sir?" Showing a politeness that Millie had learned from her few short questions was uncharacteristic, she was convinced that Veronica was impressed or shocked, or may be both, to see Taverner standing before her.

"Ah, well perhaps I am mistaken, then, about the nature of our acquaintance, although I am sure we have met before," Taverner chided in his gentle way, inviting comments or questions in part but mainly, Millie had learnt, agreement. "I am Taverner."

"Oh, sorry, yes, Mister Taverner, I am sure we met briefly long ago but it took me some time to put the name and voice to the face. As you can see, time hasn't been as kind to me as it has to you. Are you working with this Millie on our town's problems?" Veronica replied carefully.

"I am here to assist the lady in any way I can. Tell me Vero, may I call you that, it was your nickname as I recall? Are there any other citizens with whom I may be acquainted here abouts."

"Well yes, err, Mister Taverner, possibly you came across Quick Light, outside at the top of the west slope watching the trail, who you might recall as Sparky Jack. He lives some 13 leagues west of here. Oh, and also Bob Steaks, known as Big Meat. He is a poor old chap now, being a bit older than myself. The rest of our unit is buried this side of the water or t'other." Veronica glanced back and forth between Millie and Taverner, hesitating over her next words. "I've a mind to move from here fast. Those scum will be back here pretty quick and not in a good mood for old ladies. May my rag-tags pull out and leave you to the pickings? We could disappear like, and the youngsters with us; they are all good kids, relations from the area who don't know much about this, just called in for numbers."

"Oh, you may, of course, Vero but consider yourself back on the semi-active list. Do you know Sam Salt over the ridge near Sheila Garr's smallholding?" The old girl nodded. "Good, please report to her for your duties. Millie will accompany you for a distance so please contribute anything you can. And take care of yourself Vero. It is not often I meet old comrades these days."

With that Taverner stepped out of the cabin and glanced quickly at the shadows cast by the moon to estimate the amount of time that had passed. Almost enough time to have reached town and back. He scribbled a few characters and waved Kint over from the head of the clearing. "Lad, see this as quick as possible to Sam Salt and then meet me back at the club. Top priority. Ok? Good, right, Snibs and Piker can you follow Millie and the oldsters out of the rear of the clearing. Cover up any tracks you can and in the unlikely event that they are followed please detain the pursuers, although avoid any contact if at all possible."

*****

"New kid huh?" Bar Ripper chuckled. "I ain't that pleasant girl. Could be you better off at the front. Still, I need a fifth for a crew now that Danglefoot got himself pin-cushioned at wall six." Bar Ripper walked quickly over to Sizell and pinched at the flesh of her forearm. "Girl, ours is a dirty business. We see all the bodies, one in three shifts we're simply on body collection. The others we still strip and handle 'em to reclaim the weapons. But if you've got the stomach and you're the type, it's a rare honour."

Bar Ripper walked over to lean on the far wall, "For us it only takes the agreement of two team leaders to raise an honour and we don't need no fancy flag rank. Between us we maybe do up to ten per season, more if a big one goes down, and it's often us, who apply for the honourable mentions and act the last friend

107

to those who are still dying. Many troops come to us and thank us, saying, 'Cheers lads, we know you'll treat us right if we are the last to go.' Each crew has a tracker, see, and over time we all get to read a site." Bar Ripper hauled on some strong gloves and fished out a freshly oiled pair for Sizell, "Put these on, girl, and we'll see what you've got." He gave her a bucket harness. "First fix that on without removing the gloves." She struggled for the first few clips and then managed it. Then Bar Ripper said, "Right, have it off and on again before my count is 50. One, two..." she was finished by 38. "Pretty good, doll." Then he walked out of the hangar to an area of broken masonry and debris.

He reached into a barrel filled with rain water and fished out several bars and stone rods and a couple of rusting swords. He then scattered them randomly over the debris area, which on inspection was about thirty spans across. Then loosening his breeches he proceeded to urinate over a substantial part of the whole lot. "Makes for a more realistic battle field you see. Command chain don't like me killing folks just for the testing. Study the area closely now, kid," he said over his shoulder. A few moments later he returned from the hangar and tied a blindfold tight around Sizell's head.

"OK, girlie, you've got a steady count of 200. Oi, Ferret, get your weasel-self over here and count for the girl," Bar Ripper bawled. "Don't want no stone in the basket only metal. Start now." A high whispery voice from the left began the count. "Tis a bit like night you see, we do quite a bit by night," Bar Ripper's voice carried as he walked back to the compound hut. Sizell wobbled over the debris in a stooping crouch.

Back in the command hut Tom and Ichanod sat waiting. Tom was counting against some notes he had made on a wax board. Ichanod could almost have been asleep. Bar Ripper booted him firmly in the shin to attract his attention. "You awake, brother?" Bar Ripper bellowed at him.

"Fine thanks, oaf," was the reply and sole acknowledgement.

"Well," Bar Ripper started. "Can't say as she's the most talented I've ever seen, but she certainly ain't the least. Our recruiting is supposed to be out of the book same as the rest of you." Bar Ripper swigged from a mug of suspicious looking fluid. "Damn Smee, and you Ichanod, and bloody favours. I ain't supporting no draft dodgers. If she's a worry at the front she'd be a worry for me. We are tight crews and we don't work right with single seasoners. Those we take are usually in for the long haul, there's a lot more skill to what we do than most understand." Bar Ripper paused.

"Green Man, you sure she's tough enough for squirming through guts? Trying to identify a boy with no face or a burned girl with her tits cut off and stuffed up her? We're the end of the road, the last testament to all our troops. Takes a certain kind of sicko to do the trawl." Bar Ripper leaned back against the wall and took another swig. "I've seen heroes after weeks of combat, Star, Fury…. They've all picked the short straw to help us in the past and I've seen them faint, puke, blub, fit and scream at the sky in rage, long after the battle was over. Just think of men like them. Is that what you want for her?" Taking Tom's silence for assent he hurried on. "Well, if she passes, which I think she will, if I know the Ferret and his counting, it'll be a two year contract though not just the one. We'll shuffle the teams and put her with Tiny, he'll keep her together."

He strode over to Ichanod and dragging the big man out of his seat waved a finger like an iron bar under his nose. "But I won't be having no further favours like this. No more whatever the past. Put that understanding to Smee, you hear. Say your goodbyes and see Schoolmammy on the way out for the draft papers. Tell her about your post routing but don't hold your breath, at least six squads including hers will be out by the end of the week. See ya." And finishing his mug of metal stripping alcohol Bar Ripper shucked on a filthy forge apron and disappeared through a sliding stone door into the interior, where the sound of hammering and swearing and blasts of intense heat veiled his departure.

"God, hand on my shoulder," whistled Tom as they strode out to into the sunlight. "What have I done to the girl?" Tom asked of no one in particular.

Over by the rubble Sizell had finished and was stretching to get the kinks out of her back. Ferret was poking about in the pannier examining what she had collected and, whistling an obscene tune he raised a thumb towards the compound office, the location Tom assumed housed the 'Schoolmammy'.

"Don't worry none, Tom," said Ichanod. "The Bar man he's rough as, OK, but he's at the top of his business. Your girl has got character and she'll do all right. Remember, you've a pretty sheltered life at the moment man it'll strengthen her character like. Don't fret none." Pointing over to a large windowless stone building Ichanod finished. "That is the reclamation armoury, pretty rare stuff comes in there and I promised some lads with weapons dockets I'd check for decent gear. See the lass and meet me at the office in a part." With that the big man ambled off, setting his hat at a jaunty angle and calling banter over to a couple of women unloading a cart. Tom shrugged and hurried over to Sizell, his heart falling as he approached saying his farewells.

A few day-parts later Sizell had settled into her bunk. Each crew stayed together rather than using the separate sex dormitories that she was used to. After a while a huge man strode in. "Hey, girl, I'm Tiny, and you're in my crew now. Let me introduce you to the rest of my low life."

*****

The door opened and a bell rang as a customer entered. The Chandler called out a welcome without looking up and finished writing out an order for his current customer. "Thank you, sir, we will bring this order round as soon as we have all the items assembled. Where are you moored?"

"Right at the end of quay six, it's the schooner," replied the young seaman, whose skin already looked to be baked hard by the elements.

"OK, sir, we'll be with you pretty soon," and with that he escorted the chap to the door. "Now, sir, let's discuss your business," the chandler directed at Mandibles.

"Could you possibly show me some of your anchorage equipment? I'm considering refitting a small sail boat."

"Certainly sir, if you could wait a few moments my assistant will be back from his lunch break and we can go to the equipment house to look at the gear, it's just out the back of the shop."

"No problem mate, I'll just browse around if that is all right?" Saying that, Mandibles walked over to a rack of ship fittings and began to sort through some tack, displaying a fair amount of expertise as he tied and retied some coils of rope onto the dummy eyelets.

"Sir, if you would come this way the Guv is ready for you," called a young pock-faced lad motioning Mandibles out the back through a curtained door way.

"Thanks son, pretty good stitching on those rope coils, did you do that?" Mandibles asked, flipping a coil onto the counter as he walked past.

"Why yes, sir, thank you, I've almost finished my prenticing."

"Good lad, very good," Mandibles chuckled as he strode through the doorway. He followed the corridor a couple of twists and turns and came out into a large stone-walled room. He looked around the room, the walls of which were lined with all manner of nautical equipment."

"Right then, Mandibles, you old scoundrel, I kind of expected a visit from you sooner," the Chandler said, rushing over to embrace his old friend.

"Well mate, I've been told to keep out of trouble so thought I'd better keep away from you, the original reprobate," Mandibles answered, good naturedly. "Anyways, the boss has told me to check over some of your stock. Do you have anything that might tempt us? You know what reluctant shoppers we can be."

"Ahh, well, if it's good quality wares you are looking for, then my chandlery is the best place to be. Now if you'll come down here, sir, I'll show you some great new kit." The Chandler winked, and walking over to a board of knotted ropes he flipped it back and upwards to reveal a rack of shining steel arblast.

Mandibles took a pair of soft cotton gloves from the Chandler and lifted one of the gleaming weapons easily from its padded resting place. The old quartermaster always liked to supply his weapons as if every recipient were headed for a parade and Mandibles was happy to indulge the reliable old chap. He balanced the crossbow, noting its strength and surprised to find that whilst the weapon was clearly strong and durable, the weight had been considerably reduced compared to the ones that Mandibles was used to.

"It's the weight ain't it Mandi?" The chandler moved in taking the weapon from Mandibles. The smaller man hefted it lightly even tossing it gently into the air. "The factory have taken the advances in rolling the steel that they've made with the new harp and applied it to the latest arblast design. If you like that you're gonna love the harp. Come down here." The old man motioned him down to the next section of nautical display and repeated the procedure of swinging out the panel. Mandibles followed closely. In this section lay just two weapons.

Superficially the harp looked like an overgrown arblast but with much bigger arms to provide the force of the bolt discharge. It was these larger arms, of the highest quality steel, that rang with a pure sound when they were released from tension. This led to the weapon's 'Harp' nickname. Instead of the weapon itself Mandibles gently and carefully picked up its projectile. Despite the added power the range of the weapon was below that of an arblast because of the bulk of what it discharged. Reptoids could often survive numbers of small and deep wounds but their physical make up reacted badly to large numbers of cuts, especially if inflicted regularly over a tight area. It had to do with fluid loss away from the membranous layer attached to the inside of the carapace. If numbers of the capillaries that supplied the fluid were cut then the membrane would go into shock, and fluid loss brought quick death to the otherwise hardy beasts.

The harp projectile was a mechanism with a passing resemblance to the spokes of the parasols that the ladies to the south used to protect themselves from the sun. Instead of spokes, though, the harp bolt had numbers of blades forced under tension. When the tip of the bolt hit its target the blades would be released and, springing forwards slice inwards shredding whatever it had hit. The bigger the harp the larger its bolts. Mandibles had seen mounted Roke brought down their horses cut in half by big harp and even a Red Master would be killed by a direct thorax strike. Harp and their construction often depended on the intended targets, in many cases harps were quite limited in range and crude. This tensioned bolt however was cleverly streamlined and Mandibles looked to the chandler with his eyebrows raised.

"Twenty to thirty percent greater range but still a class three impact with this you ruffian," the Chandler replied. "New from the factory. Changworth has been allocated two. Now, Mandi, give me your list and we can go over what you need. Possibly with a tipple in the back office?"

*****

"Right, Crowther, an early night for us, we will be up at dawn inspecting some of the engineers, but first a quick word with Carstairs before he leaves. Let us hurry along," commanded the Marshall, leaving little scope in his stride for delay or refusal. The little man followed on behind as did Candwell who spotted them from the stairs and, wanting a word with his counterpart, hurried along behind them.

"Stairs, my friend," cried the Marshall as he strode into the reception room.

"Lord Protector, kind of you to spare me a few moments," Carstairs replied in his cold aloof way.

"Nonsense, Stairs, apart from being one of the finest soldiers of this age you have been a great friend to me. I am sorry that I am sending you into such danger. Try and keep alive my friend, but remember that your action, though it may never be told, could be what saves the Nation. We need all the time that you can get us. May the Battler go with you," spoke the Marshall, face grave, yet daring enough to pat the dispassionate, older, man on the arm warmly.

"My friend, if he is there he won't be disappointed with the action, you have my word on that. Keep yourself and the nation safe while I am away. Now I had best go otherwise I will miss the rendezvous with the others. Tide waits for no man and all that. Fare you well, lord, and you, my brothers," he acknowledged his replacements, and with that Carstairs walked out of the High Fort into the night as if simply running an errand.

"I will miss you, old friend," the Marshall muttered under his breath.

"Sir, whatever he is doing is it wise to let a man like him

leave the High Fort at a time like this? I know it is bad form not to grant an old timer leave to join the enders, but in this case won't you reconsider?" said Candwell from the Marshall's side.

"Oh, stop that Candwell, you are as bad as Crowther. You'll not trick me into revealing anymore by playing along with the enders story; we all know I have sent him on a vital and ultra secret mission that even the high command haven't yet been informed of. In the coming weeks you will learn more but now let us drink a draught to my oldest friend, for the enders might have been a safer place."

"OK boss, but you can't blame an old dog for worrying a bone," Crowther said, winking conspiratorially at Candwell.

"Hm, well, just keep your mouths out of my secret stash of sweet meats. I am not entirely sure that all that desert intrigue has done your already inquisitive personality any good at, all Sir Ewgene, and Crowther certainly has no excuse," the Marshall berated them with mock anger as the three play-acted their way towards a drink, and away from the hurt that the Marshall clearly felt at the departure of his friend and mentor.

Chapter Six

"Pleased to meet you, Major Kass, I have heard good things about your progress. Can you demonstrate your current work?" the Marshall asked in his famous word-torrent style, greeting Kass warmly, gripping his arm firmly as if meeting an old comrade.

"Well, yes sir, we have completed the exercises on key stage one and my team are now working on two aspects of the main event. We will be responsible for targeting the long range, elevated bombasts on the open expanse betweens walls four and five. Here we have three sets of kit that combined should allow us to surprise the enemy with an accurate bombardment, without them understanding much about our capabilities beforehand," Kass summarised, assuming that he should match the Marshall's semi-formal approach.

Not being corrected on his tone Kass continued more confidently, "If you would walk this way, sir. We are using this quarry because the height approximates to buttress three of our allocated fort. Sir, if you use this lens you should be able to make out your aide down in the quarry," Kass handed a spy lens to his commander. "He has been given the task of picking us two random target positions and we will mark them with large red wooden figures. Once he has done this, which, yes, I think he has, my colleagues will surround them with a ring of similar shapes, at a distance of twenty spans, so you can see the weapon's effects. In the actual action there will be two weapons trained on each target point, slightly overlapping with the next pair, which will allow not four but six shots to be fired into roughly the same zone, on a rotating basis." Kass paused to see if the Marshall was following his description only to see that his commander had stopped and was drawing in the dirt with the point of his dagger.

"Do you mean like this, Major?" The Marshall asked as his

junior crouched down beside him.

"Yes, exactly sir, with the targeted areas like those loops you have drawn and overlapping here and here, and if these crosses here are the firing positions, this will fire and then this and then these two as well, all hitting their primary area. Whilst those four are reloading, the next sequence down will fire thus, as will the pair on the other side, causing minor damage and overlap here and here, which will certainly inconvenience anyone attempting to cross the first zone even if not as effectively as the primary weapons," Kass explained enthusiastically, pleased by the Marshall's understanding and interest in taking time to work the mechanism through with his drawing.

"Ingenious, Major, I commend you on the idea, but perhaps I had better see the weapons in action," the Marshall approved, but keeping any excitement that he felt out of his tone.

"Yes sir," Kass continued unperturbed. "The rotation we have discussed will mean the area can be hit 50 times per day part, which should effectively stop any Horde crossing a line 180 spans across, which is what we have been tasked. Your aide has been asked to pick places within that area cordoned off with yellow stakes, which represents halfway between walls four and five where the Horde has the largest mustering point if we attack out in a straight line, which I have been told is the plan. In effect, if we can clear the nearest half quickly our weapons can block direct approach by he Horde for enough time to allow us to dig into the area and possibly bring some weapons up capable of breaching wall five."

"Right, now to the workings of these weapons if that is all right, sir?" The Marshall nodded, hiding his amusement at the fact that the Major, barely 20, was briefing him as if he was the rawest recruit. "There are three steps. Firstly we use a calibration lens mechanism, which is built into the kit to pinpoint the location of the targets. If you look down this eyepiece, sir, you will see two loops. As I turn these knobs you will see the loops merge into one perfect circle, then these two ratchets move the circle and we do both until we have the target in the middle of the cross hairs." Kass performed the obviously complex series of twiddles and corrections carefully, allowing the Marshall to look periodically down the lens piece who felt that he had witnessed the core of setting the weapon.

"Once we have centred this – look now sir," Kass instructed, "we have the settings that we will apply to the bombast projector. Reading from the outside of the calibration mechanism the numbers are here, here and here on the target lens tubes and here on the elevation ratchet," the young major waited for the Marshall to grunt affirmation, "Also, knowing a few other details from the survey department helps us set up the projectors accurately. The crew will make the changes to the settings. OK sir, now we will repeat for the second weapon whilst crew one load a dye tracer. Would you like to perform this, sir?" Kass asked, and stepping back waited for a good eighth part while the Marshall struggled to calibrate the equipment, realising just how proficient Kass was to have made the complicated process look so easy before. Finally stepping back he invited Kass to check the settings.

Kass let out an impressed whistle, "Are you sure you don't want to transfer to our company sir, you have almost nailed it spot on?" He quickly proceeded to repeat the exercise, checking the adjustments looking at the second target point. "Good. Crew two if you could load a green smoke tracer. Crews report in."

"Crew one tracer ready," said the crew leader.

"Crew two tracer ready," rejoined the second crew.

"Crew one, ready as you are, fire by your count," Kass ordered. "Crew two, ready as you are fire on the Marshall's order." Before the Marshall could speak the crew leader of crew one counted down.

"Three, two, one, fire!" The smaller of the three catapults bucked and a projectile went spinning away. The Marshall followed it through its flight until it impacted in the quarry. He belatedly pulled out his lens to see that the area around the first red marker was now splattered with yellow dye, including a thin stripe on the figure itself.

"Crew one, load one block and one shredder," Kass ordered as soon as he checked the target sight with his lens.

"Sir, if you could order release for crew two," he reminded his superior politely.

"Yes, Major, crew two, fire!" barked the Marshall. The

second platform bucked and this time, rather than following the flight, the Marshall raised his lens to watch the target which suddenly was smashed from view. "Gods, Major, I think you actually hit the figure. Good shot!"

"Yes sir, now look back without your lens please," Kass replied cheerily, which the Marshall did to and saw a plume of green smoke rising from the second target's position.

"Now, Marshall, if you could quickly examine the figures around site one," Kass asked, anxious to hurry on with his demonstration.

"Yes Major, I have," replied the Marshall gruffly, irritated at all these instructions. Despite the rising excitement he was feeling that these weapons really might give him the edge he needed to avoid wasting the lives of thousands of his troops.

Kass, realising that perhaps this stage of the demonstration needed to be completed continued. "Crew One, fire by your count."

"Three, two, one, fire!" The two large weapons of the set fired almost simultaneously, the projectiles arcing to the area where a large plume of dust was raised.

"Sir, it might take some moments for the dust to settle, I suggest we travel down to the impact area to inspect the results, by which time you will be able to see the area clearly. Crews, good shooting, stand down and perform a resilience test."

As the Marshall, Kass and the bodyguards returned to the operations cabin and the tethered horses, Kass spoke on. "Marshall, our biggest problem has been manufacturing parts that last long enough to make them useful in combat. Almost all our weapons now have a number of usages for which they can be considered reliable. For our mission, you need cover for at least a full part, which means a very high number of discharges. By doubling up and having a number of reserves we believe we can execute our part of the plan, but it has been tough." By now they were heading down a steep path along the quarry wall.

Out in front Kass gave a hand signal to halt the party. "Marshall, this part of the track is in poor repair, I suggest we dismount and lead the horses."

The party trudged carefully down the uneven, winding track for an eighth part before Kass hauled himself back into the saddle, calling, "Right, we should be safe to ride again now." Finally Kass subsided into silence and one of the bodyguards nudged his companion as they reached the floor of the quarry and gave him a wink miming silence, as if he never expected Kass to stop talking. His companion just grinned before turning his gaze back to scanning the surroundings for any threats to his charge.

As the party rode the considerable distance away from the quarry walls they passed numbers of companies of troops performing a variety of training exercises. With the Marshall clearly an appreciative audience, Kass decided to point out some of the relevant highlights.

"Sir, down here you can see two more of my squads," Kass started up again, pointing off to his left. "They are working on the component barrier exercises for the assault. These particular cadets are from the final year of the academy seconded to our division. As you can see, each cadet has one component and a sturdy shield plus sundry frontline weapons. Each hurries up and engages their section of barrier protected by the shield of the preceding trooper. The troopers swap, each taking one turn on covering the next in line and the protective shield only being swapped and replaced if the out facing shield has sustained serious damage. The trooper then rushes on to the frontline for fighting or whatever." Kass's voice tailed off as the group pulled their horses to a halt a safe distance from the practice ground. Additional cadets and trainers were throwing rocks at the covering shield to make the practice more realistic.

After a few moments Kass continued his briefing, leading the group back down the line to where is was safe to dismount and inspect the barrier. "The fence sections, once locked, require specific tools to remove and separate them, although anyone with the knack can open sections quickly and reasonably quietly if required."

Kass then mounted and with the Marshall following close behind led the party out into a fenced off section of the quarry. As Kass rode through a gate one of the bodyguards, Garratt, stopped the Marshall saying, "Sir, this is a live firing section of the range which can be targeted by a large number of the weapons, we didn't bring enough men to cover all these weapons. Sir, I recommend that we don't go any further but watch from here."

"What about the final impact site, have we come all the way down here to turn back? You should have said sooner," the Marshall asked, irritated by the interruption and yet careful to acknowledge that his minder's concerns were real and valuable.

"No Sir, because of the distance to that point we ascertained that only the weapons we saw earlier can accurately target those positions and we left a couple of men at the top," the leader of his guards replied.

"Very well, Garratt. Major Kass, I have decided that we can watch this test from here. I take it that will suffice?" the Marshall told Kass firmly.

"Right sir, we can use the lens. Over here, sir, we have an anchored set of the segment fences, in this case tethered between two bombast blocks. We will demonstrate the degree of their strength by a direct hit from a heavy mangonel." Kass explained quickly, and picking up a flag the young engineer signalled to the crew and the weapon fired into the fence. In this case the dust cleared fairly soon and the group waited in silence to see that indeed the fence was still standing, if badly buckled.

"Marshall, we estimate that none of the Horde bigatrons will easily be able to remove the fence, although some could, of course, climb this particular barrier."

Kass guided the Marshall and his men back to the main track and continued his narrative as if a tour guide at a public attraction. "As we pass this cadre of troops on the left we can see cadets deploying rolls of tangle wire, by first dropping the weighted end and then using a powerful projectile thrower to carry the other end away from the wall, about 100 lengths. Whilst only of limited use a single roll will severely block normal Roke troops, and we reckon five rolls carefully placed will stop even a large beast for long enough to do it serious damage with projectiles."

Gently giving his horse its head, and calling across as the Marshall and his men did the same, Kass bellowed, "Now, sir, if we ride out freely into the quarry it will take about a tenth part to reach the impact site."

After the group had all reached the site, which had been

roped off by a couple of very young looking cadets, Kass and the Marshall were left comparatively alone, as the guards scouted the area and checked each of the new soldiers added to the party.

"May I ask a question, sir? We have manufactured stone based heavy component fencing and drilled in deploying it but must say that we can only work it with block and tackle, which is really not suited to battlefield service. Because of the length of time up to ten troopers would be exposed for long periods, and it makes the deployment of these a very dangerous occupation. Yet we are still drilling for emergency deployment, having been promised additional ways to handle these. Sir, can I ask if there really are other methods? Otherwise I would like to create something and, in the meantime, delay the deployment of that particular barrier type." Kass finished, mentally prepared for a direct rebuff.

"Major, please rest assured that there are indeed other ways for deploying the barriers, provided, of course, you techs have kept within the stipulated weight categories for each component," the Marshall chuckled.

"Oh, we have, sir, and once deployed these barriers are far better than even jointed masonry, I can promise you that, sir," Kass replied literally.

"Good, good, now where is the ring of figures?" The Marshall asked, gazing at the pitted landscape.

"Spread all around, sir. Can we dismount and put on these metal-soled outer boots? The remains of the weapon will shred your leather boots very thoroughly." Kass guided the Marshall under one of the ropes. "Look, here in the middle of the crater, this is the bombast block the second arm discharged, it acts as a crushing weapon, should any of the Horde be unlucky enough to be struck, but its main purpose is so that we can tether coils of tangle wire, or the fenced sections to it as a post. For each emplacement we will probably only fire a couple of these in the action."

Kass had pulled a bag from his saddle as they had dismounted, which one of the guards had, of course, checked. Now he opened it up, "Here is a model of the primary weapon we used at this location, sir. This is what the outside looks like: it is a smooth, large, porcelain pod. Now look at this side with the outer portion cut away. Inside we have an upside down spider-like arrangement of very fine, springy, steel arms, which when deployed has these rings holding the steel arms under great tension. As you can see, each arm has hundreds of heavy steel discs, filed razor sharp and carefully slotted into its grooves." Kass carefully passed the model over for the Marshall to inspect.

"The porcelain base is weighted with lead, which ensures that in flight the weapon levels and always impacts on the base. This central rod is then forced up, thus, and this releases the arms from tension. The impact and the tension shatter the porcelain which flies out in shards which, whilst being quite destructive, is nothing compared to the discs which are fired out in all directions at great velocity. As you can see, the figures we grouped around, which, incidentally, were all dressed in Roke leathers, have simply been cut to pieces. Here, careful with this. It was one of the disks, it looks as if it hit the stone bombast. Ah, here, further out, is another, one buried." Kass muttered, carefully probing at the dusty ground before extracting a more recognisable steel disc.

Handing it to the Marshall he continued, "That was our main problem, preventing great numbers from simply ploughing into the ground. For hard-stone areas we have a variant with steel balls, which bounce around kicking up stone shards and crushing everything rather than slicing. Both weapons have been tested on mail and plate armour; within this kind of radius Horde fatalities will be total." Kass stepped away, allowing the Marshall to wander the area and take his time, considering the potential of the weapon.

The Marshall returned to the group lost in thought. Kass was worried by his lack of positive feedback and continued, "Marshall, we can land 20 of these weapons on the targets regularly over a part and we have the stocks already prepared."

The Marshall seemed to read his concerns and asked, "Come on, Major, tell me what the 'but' is, there usually is one.

"After that the weapons begin to fail, probably down to ten percent active at the end of the second part. But for the first part I believe very little will be able to cross that line. One reason is that the Horde will not have the kit to prevent the after-shot debris from tearing their limbs badly as they cross the ground once the weapons have been discharged several times. We, on the other hand, have protective outer boots, metal and wooden mats and ground ploughs which in fractions of a part can re-open the ground for us."

The Marshall considered for moments longer and then finished, "Very, very impressive, Major. Your target section of the Bloody League could be the greatest drain on attack troops if we can't prevent the Horde from gathering in huge numbers. Your weapons look the ticket for giving us breathing space."

As the impressed Marshall turned back towards camp Kass piped up, "Sir, I have some further ideas if you have the time."

*****

"Gods, I never thought that engineer would stop with his ideas," the Marshall commented to his aide as they rode away from the engineering camp.

"Well sir, from what I could hear, they are worth every moment of earache," Crowther replied. "When you told me that we were going to unleash an attack with serious intentions of taking back the Battle Lands and to try and cross the 15 walls of the Bloody League, I just pictured it as suicidal. But with that kind of devious fire power to give us cover, I now think we might make it half way before we are neck deep in our own guts. Which is 100 times better than any odds I ever thought we would get."

*****

Life for Blue Boy went on as normal in the band for a while after the announcement about Moffet's brother. Many within the camp continued to salute Moffet with raised weapons as he passed during those days, especially as Moffet took to wearing his brother's medal around the camp. Then other news was released bringing a new focus. This was the announcement concerning the cadets who would be accompanying the band on campaign.

Blue Boy discovered his name at the bottom of the list. At first he thought it a mistake, or possibly a wind up by the other cadets, but as soon as he found Stonebrow his departure was confirmed.

Also a surprise was the number of the cadets who were included. Whilst only 17 were named, and most of these, predictably, the oldest cadets, it was still a shock that so many were being dispatched. The campaigning cadets always numbered a few potential talents to gain experience working amongst the regular support troops, serving with and servicing the running of the band's campaign on tasks, including animal husbandry, kit and mechanics, transport, camp security and medical provision. In this case, however, almost one third of the senior cadets had been named, including Rufus and Straws who already were almost considered junior musicians by the other cadets.

Blue Boy reacted quickly to the summons from Master Smee. As his commanding officer this was expected anyway. Despite his rank and reputation Smee paid close attention to the needs of his men and thus won their best efforts; their desire to serve coming from their belief in him.

Blue Boy's audience lasted the rest of the morning. They talked of many things, from the place of ownership and possessions and how a man's weapons fell into that category, to the loss of comrades and the importance of their memory. Master Smee particularly wanted to know how Blue Boy currently felt about being different. Finally, Master Smee reminded Blue Boy of all his commitments, especially the difference in commitment between a music cadet's oath to his band master and a soldier's oath to the Marshall. He emphasised how Boy Blue would be enrolled fully in service to the Northern Army, over and above being a citizen of the United Nation of Peoples.

Towards the end of the morning the band leader asked, "Blue, do you have any further questions?"

"Yes, sir. When the Reptoids drove so much of the human portion of the Homanid race from the occupied territories, across the Battle Lands and onto the Northern, continent it created this very different nation, compared to the other two surviving nations. We are even more different from the tribes of the hued folk. None of those other nations now seem particularly interested in fighting the Horde. How is it that the United Nation, and particularly the Northern Army, has been able to stand alone, fighting what is clearly a mighty foe, for so long?"

"A good question and one without a straight forward answer. The Horde, despite common opinion, has always shown a very canny attitude towards attacking the other nations and, whilst it has continued to probe them and refused to let them settle, there has never been a serious attack against the sovereignty of those nations. This explains the lack of interest from the other nations. What is less clear is that the other nations, some more than others, do actually support us; much, much more than is evident. They send some troops and large amounts of supplies as discreetly as possible to the Great Forts and are very positive towards us in terms of trade. For those nations do remember, perhaps better than we do, the powerful nations that the Horde trampled over in the Shattering, and the fear that the same will happen to them some day is not a small concern. We, as a nation, have also become skilled in the art of diplomacy, allowing this relationship to be always as favourable towards us as possible." Master Smee paused to pour them both fresh glasses of water.

"Finally, Blue Boy, we have powerful allies in the Iron Islanders, who whilst spread across their islands are quite numerous and are doughty warriors. Perhaps greatest and strangest of all is the Legion and the small ethnic tribes that still survive in that domain, for whilst it was started by the Northern Army it has grown strong and cemented strong roots with the peoples of those areas. It draws as much from those unmeasured resources as from the convicts and volunteers we send."

In many ways their talk was as frank and earnest as two squad mates sharing a mug, or a father and son discussing life.

Master Smee finished by stating how proud he was of Blue Boy and his progress and that one day the lad would make Band Master at least and maybe something more. He gave Blue Boy a coded word that would convey Smee's patronage, to be used in a number of emergency circumstances. As Blue Boy was leaving, the band leader pointed out that he should mind Marv's instructions, as if they came from himself. He instructed that mentor and student take their pick of the entire armoury before they left.

When Blue Boy returned to his billet, though, Marvellous had already acquired the weapons for Blue Boy, who was nonetheless pleased as all the sensible choices he would have made were there. Unsurprisingly Blue Boy was assigned to Marv's auxiliary squad, with Starling as second.

*****

A heavy rapping on the door caused all the patrons of the inn to pause and turn nervously towards the door. A wave of the doorman's hand indicated that the code was correct, and whilst this calmed the majority of the patrons many remained with hands on weapons loose in the sheath. A group of tonight's guards opened the inner door; once that was sealed they would proceed to check the newcomers. Arblast at the ready, the remainder of the guards formed a loose semi-circle around the door as bolt weapons were wound and arrows knocked around the rest of the room. This far into the Ragged Mounts safety was still patchy at best and as many settlements and meeting places had fallen to carelessness as to treachery.

Nobody in the Ragged Lands, the relatively free parts of the Battle Lands, survived long once they stopped taking precautions. Generally the Reptoids and their Roke resented any human habitation in the middle continent, especially ones that weren't strictly regulated. Thus, raids into the Ragged Lands were frequent, with bounties paid for confirmed kills of any new settler families. In such an expanse of inhospitable land, though, many pockets of settlers existed, mostly in constant migration. Supplies were smuggled in from the north. People were granted land rights and were somewhat encouraged by the military council who were desperate to maintain any human presence in the Lost Continents.

Smugglers and scavengers, moonshiners and bandits, these rough people would trade with both sides; the very population was a hotbed of espionage and double dealing. Tough people all, and careful from an early age, they went heavily armed, applied coded greetings and supported hidden meeting places such as this dive. A cave in the hills it had stood for as far as memory recalled, often deserted and always tainted with the stink of smoke and sweat and stale brew. With tunnel exits into an underground warren, and a concealed entrance with twin barred doors, folk could meet and trade, purchase booze and, for a while, share a bit of companionship and shut out the harsh reality of the fugitive life.

Whilst fugitives, many of the people present had chosen their way of life, whether to escape from the regimented order of the United Nation's social structures or as deserters, escaped prisoners, smugglers, militia agents or to defy the Horde. Whatever the reason, as a group, they survived and even flourished to an extent.

So everybody waited. Soon the return knock allowed the guards, plus two other men, into the smoky room. As they were recognised the men and women around the room turned back to their food, drinks and making out. The taller of the two men walked straight to the bar and enquired of the bartender. "Jake, we must see the Dogrell. Is he here?"

Jake looked at them thoughtfully and motioned his head to the far corner. He was concerned that whilst he recognised the two, he couldn't be sure that they weren't going to start some trouble, especially if they were actively looking for the Dogrell. Generally the bartender found that most people sought to avoid the brigand if they valued their health. As the man turned to head over, the bartender gripped the heavy iron bill that he kept below the bar and tugged at the man's sleeve. "Why?"

"Recent raid," said the man, "Reptoids about, and families slaughtered."

"Ah," Jake muttered. Then that would be the reason. Often areas were plagued by raids and the Raggers, if they couldn't shrug them off, would search for some bandit chief.

Stilt motioned his comrade and they moved through the makeshift tables where people sat on up-turned boxes, chests or the floor, until they reached the darkest, dingiest corner. The two men were part of a family group who had taken ship for the free lands when the father was on the run for smuggling raw brandy and needed to escape a legion sentence or worse. Now many of their family were dead. Others in the area had named Dogrell a likely source of aid, for whilst he was the worse kind of ruffian, people said his hatred of Reptoid and Roke meant he and his men would take almost any opportunity to kill some.

Here in the darkest, dirtiest corner sat a man in a ragged cloak, head and hands between his knees, his face hidden, looking down at the floor. By his side sat a bucket of raw spirit, slightly watered, with a grimy ladle. It had been mostly consumed judging by the stink in the air. Originally enough to keep ten men drunk all night.

"Dogrell?" Stilt asked. He got no reply. "Are you Dogrell?" he persisted. This time he thought he got a slight grunt. He shrugged and looking into the bucket he started to crouch down and reached for the ladle. As he was about to grasp the handle he looked up to motion his mate to join him for a taste; as the owner was obviously too far gone in his drink to offer sensible conversation or complaint. He looked down suddenly as his hand lost all ability to move. His wrist was caught firmly and painfully in the grip of a filthy, powerful hand. "Mine," rasped a voice.

"What?" muttered Stilt absently, as he strained to free himself from the vice-like grip.

"I said, 'the hooch is mine,' dung breath." Suddenly Stilt was dragged painfully to a standing position, as the figure uncoiled smoothly from his position, showing no effort or sign of strain, of dragging his large captive to his feet. Stilt was now placed squarely between the man and his mate. As Garth tried to move to a position to aid him, Stilt found himself roughly dragged back and forth to maintain his in between position as a human shield.

Still pretty much in the shadows, Stilt could make out little of Dogrell's features: a squarish jaw, a mass of matted hair and piercing blue eyes were about all.

"As you seem to have attracted my attention, you may as well tell me what business you are about so that then you can then get lost," Dogrell rasped. His voice was a low, worn, scrape, cracked even, and carried a convincing hint of threat.

Stilt hesitated, more from lack of a prepared speech than anything, but very soon the grip on his wrist began to tighten inexorably.

"OK! OK! We're Raggers from the eastern mass. Not been

128

there long, 'bout a season. Six of us, young to old. Garth and me we went for supplies, came back, folk dead and eaten. When we moved on found several other groups also gone and most other folk forted up. Weak Mike, who we bought our plot off, he said if we got here you'd sort it and that with Reptoids loose he weren't leaving his hole." Stilt paused, unable to tell if the grip had weakened any or if his arm had just gone numb up to the elbow. "We want revenge. You can have half our stash if you clear the beasts. We'll help."

"No, you won't!" Dogrell commanded. "Don't return till day after tomorrow. Bring the payment to the barkeep here, else you'll get a visit yourselves. Oh, and tell Weak Mike to grow some balls. I ain't his keeper."

The grip was released suddenly and Dogrell crouched down to gather up a long neatly fastened pack leaning unseen in the darkness.

"Get some water and finish the brew if you like lads. Drink to your folks," Dogrell rumbled as he eased past them, his tone now uncharacteristically light. "Just stay here like I said."

*****

Thirty leagues away and twenty into the eastern block, the dawn was just beginning to rise as the Reptoid pack leader settled down to eat. Three more small groups of the wretched humans had fallen to the pack during the night. With all these kills the beast was finding it surprisingly easy to control this pack. First Claw, as his society now named such leaders, was from one of the Horde's new conditioning camps. Genetically Siblants had never been disposed to work together or cooperate, but the new camp conditioning seemed to allow this. As a product of the camp though the beast was only barely aware of the changes wrought in himself and his pack members. Still, challenges to his command had been few and he had only needed a quick fight to warn off one of the other beasts.

As he crouched back to rock-munching on a bone the Second Claw hissed a warning to him. A human was approaching. Without looking up he hissed back, "Where from? The sentry should deal with it!"

129

"From the south First Claw. Directly past the place where Blood Talons should be."

'Worthless beast,' thought the First Claw as he rose up to sort out the issue. 'Must be eating rather than doing his duties.' The First Claw clambered the slope to where his second was crouched, looking out. Yes, definitely a human approaching, but moving strangely. No human he had ever killed had moved so smoothly or rapidly over rough terrain. This one could be more trouble than expected. First Claw let out a call to the rest of the pack, warning the other three sentries and calling the three remaining pack beasts to the flattened ride top.

Hardly pausing to skip around a boulder, the Dogrell smiled to himself as he heard the Siblant make its call. It was only recently that Siblants had begun to travel in packs, rather than singly, and he liked it. His hunting was becoming more rewarding now that the prey was more complex. Whilst the risk of hunting Siblant was great, especially when he travelled alone, he found that the combat and, therefore, the rush of success was too quick with a single foe, no matter how skilful. In fact, because the Siblants were so fast and dangerous the combat almost always needed to be too quick.

Recently, Dogrell hunted alone more and more. With no other humans around he could relax his careful control and allow his body to express itself to its maximum capacity. Twenty more yards, a couple of moments, and he would top the ridge and there he would meet his foes.

The First Claw saw the human top the ridge to the plateau at the far end from his grouping. With a gesture he moved Blood Eyes to a more forward position, hissing to the others to stay back and allow him the kill. The human barely slowed and began a strange skipping advance twisting and weaving hefting a puny spear and dodging side to side as he advanced. Suddenly the spear snaked out and the First Claw felt a stinging pain through its right shoulder. The human must have cast its spear and scored a lucky hit. Well good, instinctively the First Claw knew that it could easily survive any hit from a human spear and now the puny specimen would be seriously disadvantaged having lost what little protection the distance weapon had afforded it.

From the Dogrell's perspective things were progressing just as his rapidly formed plan had conceived. He had dropped his pack on topping the rise and with the coil of strong steel cable in his left hand he had used a skipping shuffle to judge the reflexes of the Siblant before casting the barbed spear which had sunk into the target, engaging its barbs, and with the short 'T' bar stopping it from passing too deeply into the beast. Coming abruptly to a stop Dogrell took a step back, and sliding his hands up the wire gave a powerful tug on the cable, still attached to the spear.

The First Claw was absolutely astounded as it was dragged off its feet. Never would it have thought that a human had the strength and it cursed its footing, assuming that loose material beneath its rear claws had given way. All annoyance turned quickly to fear and then to agony, as it looked up to see the human spring in quickly and place a well timed kick directly to the First Claw's head carapace.

Unknown to the First Claw, who was dying, its brain had been pierced by a myriad of fragments from his shattered head. The Dogrell was delighted, not only had his steel toe-capped boots proven to be an effective weapon but he could also see that the next closet Siblant had approached, from behind the body of the first.

Flicking a loop of the cable out over the beast's head Dogrell dived full length, away from its slashing claws, and rolling over his shoulder came to his feet some six lengths away. With a bunching of his muscles and a huge heave of his shoulders he snapped the cable taut and, with a loud pinging sound, the loop of steel wire tightened to just a fraction of the width of the entangled beast's neck, literally snapping its spinal arrangement and almost tearing the head clean off.

The third of the group was now attacking, and without further time to react Dogrell simply stepped into the beast's embrace, and drawing a stout knife plunged the blade deep into the breast of the Reptoid as it sought to drag its claws in close and crush the life from the man. Looping his right arm over the encircling appendage the Dogrell simply turned his back to the creature. With one arm linked and his left hand still pressing in on the blade, he kicked his feet up and away and allowed the whole weight of his body to drop onto the contact points. This had the effect of both twisting the beast down to its right, so that its balance gave way, and crashing appendage, first into the ground shattering the limb and then increasing pressure on the sharpened blade drawing it further through the beast's internal organs collapsing its air bladders in the upper chest cavity and thus inducing asphyxiation.

Finally Dogrell's plan began to falter. He had to struggle greatly to free himself from the grip of the dying Siblant who, although now having no thought for continuing its attack, would never again loosen the grip of its appendages. Dogrell knew that at least one more Siblant remained in the vicinity and that for every extra moment he remained in the embrace the chances of it reaching the scene and dispatching him with little difficulty increased.

With one final huge effort he levered himself free. Looking around, he was alone and jogging to the far end of the plateau he made out the Siblant speeding in the opposite direction away towards the flat lands. Clearly it had decided that any human who could dispatch three of its kind would be ready for a fourth and that it would get away while the going was good. Whilst Dogrell's lust for the kill was sated he couldn't throw off the idea that the Siblant was simply going to report what it had witnessed. Adding further to the Horde's knowledge was not something that he relished.

He decided therefore, to set off in pursuit. Quickly collecting his pack and extracting his weapons from the dead Siblants he set off after the beast at an easy but fast pace. He reckoned that the beast now had a tenth part head start. The beast itself, being also concerned that it should be free of pursuit, soon picked up the sounds of the human following. Normally the dramatically over-developed musculature of the Siblants ensured that they were capable of moving two or three times faster than a human on foot, over vast distances, and even capable on occasion of out distancing mounted troops for short periods.

This human, however, seemed not to follow any of the Siblant's limited understanding and, for one of its kind, it was in the rare position of being at a physical disadvantage.

Dogrell was running with all the freedom that his body

would allow, taking in great gasps of air to offset the massive labour of his lungs. From a distance he appeared to be taking huge bouncing strides. He knew he would suffer later as his muscles cramped and stiffened. Like any exercise that was not regularly practised, using his body to its full capacity often left him racked with the aches and pains of pulled muscles.

The gap between himself and the beast was closing, especially as the ground flattened for a way and he stopped needing to twist around and leap over boulders or gullies in the cracked landscape. The beast itself was now labouring entirely from fear. Suddenly it felt itself pulled up short as a hand reached in from behind and, dragging it to a stop, smashed a knife into its head and thorax joint, ending its life.

Four full parts later with the bodies of the Siblants discreetly buried and as many tracks swept away as he deemed prudent, the Dogrell finally slouched down into the corner of a greasy drinking den. All satisfaction was by now gone and he prepared to ease away the physical pains and post fight melancholy with a trough full of strong spirits and the welcome of drunken oblivion.

*****

Barney looked carefully round Jeffer's office. Not that he expected to see anything new or interesting, just that Spillage's conspiracy comments in the refectory had caught his imagination. Jeffer's was obviously a soldier, everything was quite neat and tidy and he had the usual trophies and trinkets placed around the room that he would expect for a distinguished campaigner. What Spillage had failed to consider in his conspiracy theory was that Star was not much older than either of them. Mid-thirties compared to late-twenties, many of those years spent campaigning. Who was to say that Jeffers lacked the basic wealth or position to be so established as to own rather than command the Night Fort.

"Well, Barney, what can I do for you? Is there a problem with the club?" Jeffers asked from the open door.

Barney suddenly felt a growing panic and sense of remorse. "No sir, I, well, I'm not sure what I am doing. This posting isn't as simple as front line duty. I think I have been letting the intelligence side of things, well, get on top of my imagination."

"I see, well have a seat. You've come to my office to check me out then. Juice?" Jeffers asked, motioning to a burnished jug and two matching goblets.

"Thanks, sir."

"I take it you haven't discussed this matter with your seniors?" Jeffers continued, still smiling.

"Err, no sir."

"OK, well you should learn to trust them more, but now you are here let me help you. Please don't call me 'sir;' Jeffers or Star, not sir."

"OK, Jeffers, it's just a stupid thing. Me and my mate, we did our weapons practice early today, got back to the refectory and started talking about how amazing this place is. I mean we only arrived to open the place six months ago and were told it had taken about eight months to build. Yet it is massive and complicated and so well organised. Surely it must have taken longer to build than that."

"Well, the building was complex but remember that it was a building conversion after all. Much work had already been done on the inside. Anyway, as interesting as the building is I can assure you that the engineering sections are capable of far more impressive feats than this place. Plus you haven't mentioned how this affects me, or your visit to my office. I mean, once it was built they put me in charge and unless you were hoping to see some plans I can't help you much. I'm more the expert in pulling buildings down than putting them up."

"Well, we were speculating about who actually runs the place you or Taverner. My mate sort of said that if I looked at your office and then Taverner's, well I'd know what he meant," Barney said, trying to be discrete. "Sorry sir, but when you came in my reason for seeing you escaped me. I suppose I was off next, with some made up excuse, to see Mister Taverner's room and, well, it all sounds so foolish now, sir."

"I see, well that is much more interesting. I agree that things look odd here, but remember, Barney, that much of being a soldier is about taking on your orders, trusting your officer and not wondering about things you don't know or can't change."

Jeffers leant back in his chair. "In answer to your question Taverner and I work together, rather than he for me as the public are told. In the same way your boss has his objectives, about which I must say I don't have a complete picture, so do I and so too does Mister Taverner. In any organisation there will always be communication issues like this. Let's resolve this a bit further, son. Take some more juice and bear with me for a moment." Jeffers then walked to his communications board and jangled a certain combination of wires. A few moments later Mandibles knocked formally and entered briskly.

"Take a seat Mandi, young Barney here has furnished me with information that leads me to believe that communication within the club is not running as smoothly as it should be. I have left it too long between briefings. I commend your man on the directness of his answers. It seems that the disparate and distinct natures of the operational side of this facility are not sufficiently clear to allow all duties to be performed smoothly. We need to organise more briefings for all staff members so that we can run as comfortably as possible. As I see it, Mandi, we have three streams of activity. Your people, who receive direct command from your secret boss. I am technically a civilian required to perform certain activities as a licensed, well fixer to put it bluntly. We both therefore need a liaison officer to fulfil our roles both with the admiralty, being based here in Buccs, and also with the Militia for our operations in a wider capacity. From my perspective Taverner performs that role for myself and to a certain degree for yourselves. Whether he is in any other way operational we shall now ask him, he should be here shortly." The three men sat for a few moments all looking thoughtful.

"Ah Taverner come in old chap. It would appear sir, that your cover is blown," Jeffers began with an open smile. "Our two functions would like to brief the staff," he waved at Mandibles and himself, "And it would be useful if we include something within the briefing that could bring an end to, err shall I say certain speculation concerning your activities."

"Ah, I see Mister Star, well certainly I would be pleased to help out. Basically I completed the preparations for the club on behalf of the Admiralty firstly and then yourself when you so kindly offered me a position. This now allows me to act as an intermediary for yourselves and also perform certain other duties for the militia communications service. For example message birds and the like. The few other employees who now work here but are based under my function also technically work for the militia."

At this point Mandibles made his first contribution to the discussion. "Taverner, does that include all the local staff?"

"Why of course, Mandibles, dear fellow, no disrespect to my esteemed colleague and property licensee but this facility is purely for the purpose of conducting military intelligence operations. Your own presence here is evidence of that. Quite what or how extensive the other operations currently ongoing are I am not at liberty to disclose, taking direct instruction from my superiors. However, needless to say, on a staffing basis almost the entire capacity of the facility is committed to your own current agenda. Perhaps it is time for your own briefings to be more thorough. If that is all, I have a number of tasks awaiting my attention in the restaurant. If I may?" Receiving no indication to the contrary Taverner gestured formally, "Thank you." The quiet man bowed slightly as Jeffers agreed his request with a wave of his hand.

"Well, I think that sums it up. Alas the secret of my own lack of personnel is out. Can I leave you to arrange the details of a department-wide briefing? Ask Taverner to present it with you if you will. Err, Mandi, have a chat with this young man and his mate if you would. Whilst I think this exchange of information was needed, perhaps it could have exercised more formal channels and kept us officers on our toes. You may go, Barney, thank you for your frankness." Jeffers smiled as he waved the youngster out.

"OK, Mandi, no harm done, but this staging of your troop, well, it doesn't suit them all. Perhaps you could discuss it with your mysterious boss and help out the younger chaps. Last week's vetting exercise gave us a clean bill of health, but gossip and rumour won't help us. Don't look so surprised, I've seen you and Barf appraising Taverner as if he arrives every day on a magic carpet."

Chapter Seven

It was mid morning before Mandibles and Millie could arrange a general meeting in the main bar. The children were safely outside tending the horses with Jungold.

"OK everybody, we've got a number of announcements today. Firstly, the investigation that Mandibles has been heading up is now getting results. Consequently we are permanently setting our alert at level two," Millie announced in a surprisingly powerful voice. "Secondly, as a result of this we could be seeing some combat action." Millie looked over at Changworth, paused and rubbed her forehead. "And finally, because of the potential seriousness of these unfolding events, Jeffers has decided to move his wards away from the club. Jeffers himself is off on secondment to the Fayre in the central plains and will be taking the children with him."

Millie hurried on to finish her speech, "Personally I will miss the little tykes and thought you might like to know that they'll be departing in four days time."

Piker suddenly jumped to his feet, "Hey, boss!" he called to nobody in particular, "can we throw the kidders a farewell party? I'm sure some of the guys and girls will throw in a bit of off duty to get things ready."

"Err, yes, Piker, but where do you propose to hold this party?" Mandibles asked.

"Well, sir, I thought as we live in a club we could sort something on the main bar. Can you fix it for us, sir?"

"What do you reckon, Millie?" Mandibles asked his opposite number.

"Only because Piker asked so nicely, now, if you will all pipe down maybe Mandibles can deliver his part of the briefing," she finished, glaring down at Piker with a bizarre kind of deaths-head grin that actually sent shivers up his spine.

Mandibles, reminded of the serious nature of his news, soon

lost his smirk and continued. "I can confirm that we have successfully located an enemy facility in this town. This facility appears to have been operating for some months and whilst we have not yet identified its purpose or exact size and capabilities, we are aware that it has killed a number of citizens and has operatives in many local departments. We suspect that the poison bloom itself has been staged or certainly exploited, at the very least."

"What about the alert level, Mandi?" Barf asked from the back. "Do the teams outside the club need to go armed?"

"Yes, Barf, I know you've all had knives and we need you to continue to conceal whatever you take. Arrange with everybody suitable levels of disguised weaponry, any combat harness you can work into your outfits would probably be best."

"Any further questions before my final point?" Mandibles asked, casting his gaze around the hall. "No! Well, OK then, so who is volunteering for the party prep?"

"I'll help," called Snibs.

"And me," echoed Barney.

"Me too," cried Lawrence and Bones, father and son almost together, echoed by pretty much every other staff member.

"Right, we need costume banners, special food. Hey, Bones, you are in charge of the food." Bones nodded happily in reply to Mandibles directive.

"Hey, boss, I think we should invite the other kids from the ward school," Piker shouted across the hubbub.

"Right, Mister, you've earnt it. Oy! Pipe down everyone!" Mandibles bellowed in his best parade ground voice. "Mister Piker will be the party co-ordinator."

*****

Time with the children suddenly seemed more important and age won out that afternoon, with Bones taking Sophie to the training park to pick flowers. Barf, Liam and Piker were also out, visiting the docks on an errand for Taverner and seeing a ship that had docked recently, a new style of huge, deep, trade galley. Bones and Sophia were going to watch Barney training round the steeplechase circuit. He had been thinking of trying the event in the Autumn games. Bones was a frequent spectator at the track anyhow, mainly for the trackside gambling that occurred there but also because Sophie enjoyed the flowers.

As they strolled in the sunshine they were surprised to see Jeffers and Changworth working-out on the bags. Jeffers, whilst having a tough reputation, was almost never seen training, even before his dispute-settling fights in the warehouse. Changworth, however, seemed to be instructing Jeffers in some punching exercises. Seeing their comrades approaching they stopped their exercise and soon Jeffers and Bones wandered off, engaged in banter about recent and future wagers. Sophie tagged behind waiting for Changworth to pack up his exercise kit and they trailed behind as they headed towards the viewing area by the athletics track.

Sophie knew that Jeffers and Bones were always very careful when it came to their pre-wager preparation. Stopping, short Changworth plopped himself down in the sun next to Sophia and with careful politeness suggested a different way for wearing her flower necklace. Scrabbling in his pack he produced a small oilcloth-wrapped package which he offered to her as a gift. She quickly opened the ties to discover a small illustrated book on flowers. Diving straight in she quizzed him hard on the subject and he smiled as he relayed what he knew of the answers, apparently not much according to the little girl.

As the sun reached its peak Jeffers and Bones waved off the last of the wager takers and declared it time for lunch. Instead of heading back to the club they walked over to the nearby parade square and the field kitchen there. Changworth handed over their civilian payment and they were soon tucking into bowls of light stew and trenchers of bread.

"You watch your change when you come here," Bones joked, "That cook is a right scally!" he proclaimed, winking broadly at the stallholder, who, playing along, started to protest his innocence before flashing a smile, notable for teeth lacking rather than showing. "Pah!" exclaimed Bones, "No wonder he always does stew, can't chew nuthin' else."

Out on the parade ground Sophie spotted a female warrior shouting at a group of troops. "Who is that lady, Chang?" she asked.

"That's Lauren Marshall, the High Marshall's daughter, Sophie. She is in charge of the militia command here in Buccaneer town. Do you remember how I explained about the town and the navy?"

"Oh, Chang, you know I always remember. Why is she angry with the men and women?"

"Hmm, Sophie, I think it is because she expects them to do things how she says, and I don't think they have been." At that moment the group jogged over to the nearby benches where Lauren flashed Changworth a wave, before returning to the square, her troops now loaded down with big heavy battle shields.

"Chang, I think that lady likes you, she gave you a special wave, even Uncle Jeffers didn't get one." This comment received a grunt from the club owner, now pretending to snooze in the sun.

"Err, no, Sophie, she just comes to the club sometimes and wants me to remember to let her in."

"Well Chang," Sophie considered seriously, "that makes an awful lot of women in the town waving to you who want to come to the club. Are we doing really well, Uncle?" At which point Jeffers and Bones broke into laughter and Changworth turned a deep red, and calling her a scally, chased her around the square for tickle torture. When they returned the others were much more serious and Jeffers and Changworth walked away in quiet conversation. They were quick to return and announced that they must all hurry back to the club for afternoon chores.

Lauren's shield squad was practicing with six archers firing padded arrows to create authenticity as Sophie and the others passed. Around the parade ground there were areas surrounded by high chain-link fences, preventing the spectators from being injured by the training weapons. Walking away, Sophie pointed out the growing number of male spectators gathering to watch the lively and lithe commander working out with her troops. As Lauren took a place in the shield wall, a few brave whistles earnt fierce glares in return. Still, as Jeffers instructed the party to continue he turned back to watch, giving Sophie a guilty shrug.

Due to fair weather Jeffers had tried stretching his license by putting a few tables outside the club's main entrance with fruit punch and chilled light beer served from beneath an umbrella by a very well dressed Barf. As the group headed past through the main bar they stopped to chat with Barney, who was back at work polishing the bar to a high shine through the heavy layer of wax he had been rubbing in. Barney, hair still wet from the baths, was obviously glad for respite from Old Soak's taunting. The older man quickly began to harangue the spectators to agree with him that Barney, having two left feet, should default their bet over the championship steeplechase in advance.

Sophie asked Jeffers if she could help Taverner with folding the napkins in the restaurant. Jeffers indicated his agreement with a nod and a wink and she rushed off in delight, keen to show Uncle Tav her new book.

No matter what subject she learnt about Taverner always seemed able to add an extra snippet of knowledge. Now with her new book she hoped that some of the flowers would fall outside his knowledge. After all, she thought, Changworth had said there were over one hundred pages in the book and each with at least two pictures. Surely Uncle Tav wouldn't know all of them?

Of course he simply nodded and named each picture as she pointed to them. He even took a napkin and quickly folding it produced a distinctive tightly-cupped flower instructing her to search the book and show him the nearest match, which she did just as he finished the last table a third part later.

It wasn't until much later that evening when she was dropping off to sleep that she suddenly thought, 'I wonder if Uncle Tav didn't give Changworth that book in the first place.'

*****

Starling and Bart had drawn staff kitchen duty that day, pretty high odds on them both being selected at any one time, and for some reason this triggered unusual interest. For fun the whole camp made a special effort to be up for breakfast and Bart, dressed in a floppy chef's hat, and Starling, hair pulled back under a scarf, laboured with the two kitchen kids to produce a record 200 cooked breakfasts. Pretty much only a quarter of the health conscious camp would normally have had cooked food at breakfast but today the joke was on the high and mighty. Even Master Smee played along, going for seconds.

Blue Boy wished he could stay longer, some of the blokes had started wagering on the clean-up exercise and some just wanted to watch Starling's dark, lithe form. A bit interested in both, Blue Boy, however, was due at Mark Sleight's farm early enough to help with some fencing and to take Mark's weapon assessment. It was pretty much unheard of for a junior to take an assessment but technically Blue Boy already had enough grades and because Mark was a good lad, who was perfectly happy with Blue Boy he wouldn't take offence at a cadet being sent to measure his weapons ability.

Mark's farm was a generation holding. He was in his third solo year since his Pap had passed away when he was 15. Rumour had it that Smee would arrange stewardship for him during his service, a time at which he might sensibly have deeded it back to the nation. Many people, however, felt more comfortable with there being a significant number of individual land owners to share communal responsibility, rather than defaulting all the land-based issues to the Junta. Quite who would take on the job was a mystery and on occasion, despite his age Blue Boy liked to imagine it was himself. Certainly with all his experience he could do the vast majority of the farming work and before his selection had quite fancied himself as a farm custodian musician.

*****

Lauren rummaged in the storage locker at the base of her bed. Finally locating the padded undershirt she straightened and looked around her room. How cramped it seemed compared to the suite that she had occupied for so many years at the High Fort. She knew that she had been spoiled, not having to leave her home to attend the academy. In just how many other ways had she been spoilt she couldn't say.

The High Fort carried a name that more than described the position of its senior occupant. It was a massive building, just the keep itself dwarfing even the dock areas of Buccaneer Town. Apart from the battle platform atop the keep and the suites of command rooms and deployment hangars right at the top, the Marshall and his retinue had the highest residential floor, three down from the roof with the Marshall's rooms at the rear and Lauren's close by, moving forwards through the honour guard to the sub commanders and other Marshalls.

Both her apartments and her father's included an outer sitting room, which in her father's case also included an entrance hall running the length of the apartment and giving access to the main, corridor as well as direct access to the central and rear stair cases. Then there came the bedroom, dressing room and bathing areas.

Lauren walked to the window and looked out over Buccaneer Town. In the militia compound she had the best room and, she supposed, also the most defensible. That being said, in this case defensible meant on the third and highest storey of the office complex rather than the barracks and, as such, not overlooked by any other buildings. The militia complex being positioned near the top of the hill, and her window facing out over the bay, the view of the waters and the shipping was good. Not really being a marine person, though, Lauren much preferred the mountains. The highest levels of the High Fort had given truly stunning views, being at a height that looked out on the nearby mountains, up to the high peaks and down into the nearby mountain valleys.

Lauren returned to her bed and began to change. Being a military based civilisation almost all clothing was designed with practicality in mind. Even the fashions followed along practical lines, for women as well as men. Lauren found it easy to get good fitting and yet feminine battle gear, which had evolved over the years. Padded shirts to fit under battle harness, cut for a female figure, she had in abundance and only in her teenage years, when her stature seemed to change from day to day had she needed to worry about her gear not fitting.

Carstairs, who had acted as her private weapons tutor, had reminded her at the time, "How would you find things, Lauren, if you weren't continually presented with gear by outfitters striving to gain the patronage of the Marshall? Next time you think to complain to me or blame your gear think of the thousands of other girls going through the same thing, but with only the quarterly gear rotation and no money to have kit altered. Many of those kids may even go into battle with what you call ill fitting gear."

Whilst that had made Lauren pause to think, she remained aware that her performance at practice often mirrored how comfortable she felt and now was glad that she had been able to take advantage of the quality gear she was offered. If she remained trim then her current stock would last her years, short of losing it in a disastrous campaign, of course, and then she would probably have more considerable problems to worry about.

Dressed in padded shirt, soft underharness, light sleeveless mail shirt and heavy weapons harness over the top, together with soft but thick leather fighting breaches and sturdy steel toe capped, heavy soled, laced boots, Lauren was quickly dressed in an outfit that could double either for daily training or light combat fatigues. Her one concession to her position was to have had a light over-jacket made in the same style as her official dress jacket, but which would fit comfortably, provided the weather was cool, and smartly over her other kit.

Generally Carstairs had been an invaluable instructor, although she now wondered whether his aloof manner, and the fact that her father had only been able to afford her scant attention, had obscured much of life from her. The fact that Carstairs had also commanded the honour guard had also meant that many of the troopers given to protect her father, and to a degree herself, had also followed his cold demeanour. Certainly it was only during later years in the academy with her three female friends and Kass that she could remember thinking of herself as other than a loner. Still, whatever issues there may have been with Carstairs as an instructor in social development, he had more than made up for it with the skills he had given her in combat. She knew he had followed exactly the guidelines that her father had set in addition to the standard academy training, but only she and Carstairs were aware that she had proven talented enough to have taken half the time to reach the prescribed skills; after which Carstairs had taught her obscure and deadly methods, all the time focusing on her ability to conceal these skills. In some lessons he had taught her six or seven different styles for each of a number of moves and then drilled her in changing smoothly through the moves, swapping styles and leaving her with the ability of unpredictability which, he claimed, was a most significant weapon in battle. Eventually, after six years even Carstairs, a known conservative, had warmly praised her skills in an awkward moment when he caught her alone before she graduated and left for the ranger camp.

*****

As Jeffers took his seat on the panel he reflected on the current champion. A blisteringly quick youth with an unorthodox style focused around whipping cuts, but effective nonetheless in a tournament environment. Jeffers supposed it was a deliberate attempt to conceal the source of the individuals training.

Recently a couple of his staff had approached him and suggested that he should lift the ban on the club staff accepting challenges, especially as he frequently used the ring to settle points of dispute or negotiation. Still, the imported staff seemed to take it all in their stride, and acting as the bouncers they were the ones most subject to turning aside insults or challenges.

Anyhow, now Jeffers had accepted the post on the panel his fighting days would be over and he would need to find something other than the occasional grudge or celebrity fights to keep him sharp.

In the Buccaneer Town warehouse grudge-fights, padded armour was worn and the full sized weapons were of realistically weighted wood. All outer garments being light in colour and the weapons treated with a solid dye, the marks made by the weapons were used by the judges in decision making. Despite this attempt at safety, the contests were contact sports, usually a fight would end only with one opponent somewhat injured. In order to fulfil tradition and bend the non duelling law, the fighters all went masked and although known people could settle scores in the ring, once a tournament fighter's identity became common knowledge they were expected to retire from the ring.

Buccaneer Town's fights had semi-official support by including a governing body of thinly veiled officials. They served as a panel to assist the referee but could participate actively, so that the fights remained suitably controlled. Now Jeffers was on this panel.

By taking his seat this first time he was agreeing to abide by the archaic rules that had been delivered along with his invitation. Despite his general reputation as somebody motivated by self-advancement, Jeffers only enjoyed a fairly small subset of his duties as a fixer. This sort of formalised self-congratulation was generally the sort of thing he tried to avoid after all, this panel was really just some closed-circle club. Looking around he passed smiling greetings and nods to various civilians and a couple of token military sorts, the kind of soldiers who occupied their medium rank desk jobs for the majority of their lives until something or someone pricked their conscience over real contributory service.

As Jeffers expected the meeting was a dry selection of meeting minutes washed down with an average wine that would have had Taverner in fits. The following gossip session at least allowed him to mingle, and as he practised his socialising he sifted the surrounding conversations for a hint of gossip that he might feed to Taverner, the information terrier, or Millie the Mastiff, one worrying at conspiracy the other inclined to smash it open.

As usual, though, with citizens of medium importance, little of interest was being discussed. Occasionally the Baker and his rebuff of the panel's invitation was mentioned with much tutting and head shaking. Looking around Jeffers was sure that the elected quartermaster wasn't losing much sleep about spurning what, in most circumstances, would have been a position of valued social status. Although, whilst Jeffers himself held the concept in low esteem, it was interesting that the Baker had felt secure enough to rebut the offer which was sure to have closed a number of commercial opportunities.

Making a mental note to discuss this back at the club Jeffers returned his attention to a waiter with a tray of savoury snacks. He walked to the walls of the opulently converted room where a half-decent display of antique weaponry had been arranged.

*****

When the news had been broken that Blue Boy was leaving the camp for the campaign he had been overjoyed at the prospect of seeing some action. Despite being the youngest cadet by two years he felt the choice was vindicated by his capabilities. In fact, nobody in particular seemed to have found any issue with his inclusion, especially Marvellous, who seemed to be taking it for granted.

It was only when Stonebrow had taken him aside soon after the lists were posted and advised him to make a plan for visiting those who would remain in the camp, and not leave his good byes until the last moment, when they would all flash by, did he really stop to appreciate what he was losing.

Not only would he leave behind the only home he could remember but also all the people in the camp who were what really made it home. As soon as he managed to free some time he headed off to visit Split. She had left him a message that he should visit her in her room, the senior camp musicians being given private rooms in a block in the bailey. Split's room was on the third floor of five, and the second above the ground to have grenulated arrow slits as windows. As direct as she was, her room looked out over the gate house, and this position of entry and exit had seemed entirely in keeping with her personality when Blue Boy had visited it before.

"Hi, Blue, how are you today?" Split asked as he entered the room, after she had replied to his polite knocking. "Excited about the campaign?"

"Yes, I can't wait. Well, actually, I am a bit sad today. It wasn't until I started making a list of all the people I need to visit and say goodbye to that I realised who I would be leaving behind. Is that silly Split? Am I just being childish?"

"No Blue, our friends are part of us and anybody who doesn't find leaving their friends behind them sad has something missing in them," Split replied quietly.

"Split, thank you for all your help and for your patience with my archery. I know I haven't always been the perfect student."

"Don't worry so, young man. You have worked hard and developed what talents you have. Nobody could have asked for more and I for one am very proud to have taught you." Crossing the room the tall lady embraced him and he could smell the mint and lemon she used to wash her greying hair. "Now you get along and don't give Marv too much grief."

Blue Boy had to stop on the stairs and, out of sight, fought back the tears. He wondered whether these upsetting farewells were a good idea, but eventually carried, on composed once more, and hoping that the remainder would prove easier. With the camp so busy few people were able to spare him long but everybody had something kind to say or some advice to offer.

Blue Boy was able to spend more time with Honeygold as he had a lesson booked with her in the schedule. He was a bit surprised when he arrived at the practice room to find a note on the door telling him to attend her at the band hall itself. Each band camp, as Blue Boy understood, usually had a building constructed solely for the purpose of housing recitals and other performances. Master Smee's camp was no exception, and he had designed and constructed an ornate building of folded wood, which some band members claimed was of revolutionary design, far exceeding his other great achievements.

It was rare that the building was used by any but the senior musicians, or those on cleaning duties. The building was split into two main sections: the instrument display room, which doubled as a mini museum, and the concert hall itself. Honeygold was already waiting for him, perched delicately but rebelliously on one of the glass display cases. Famous for her natural flirtation she immediately embraced him to her spectacular body, and taking his hand led him into the concert hall.

"Do you remember my first performance here after I was drafted into the band, Blue? Oh, it was the best day of my life. I know you have been here forever, but outside the rest of the music world has great respect for Master Smee. To be granted a place in his band was like a dream come true and to be invited to perform a solo at the next concert, so soon after being accepted just topped the whole thing off. I had just been a junior in my previous band, you see, and not only did I have a full place but also the Master accorded me every respect," Honeygold almost danced and twirled as she relived her memories.

Turning back to her young pupil she directly faced him and

continued, "Wherever you go and whatever happens, Blue, always be grateful for the opportunities you have had here. But remember that the world is not always a fair place, so take care." She led him over to a music stand and said, "And now Blue, I want you to be the first person to perform with me the male part I have spent the last three years writing, which matches the first solo I sang in this hall. I suppose with you going I will have to make do with Bart for the actual performance," she said winking slyly. "Oh, and don't go letting Marv give you too much grief."

His voice raw from the demands of his singing lesson, Blue Boy finally emerged into the late afternoon sunshine and headed over to the maintenance yard out in the town. Here the senior stonesmith and joiner, Bill, had his workshops. Officially Bill was part of the maintenance facility working hand in hand with Heat, the smith, to keep the camp in good condition. Blue Boy knew him best, though, because he shared the position of bow master with Split and was the artisan who actually made the majority of the bows for the camp.

As a young lad Blue Boy had found the art of bowmanship the most difficult to learn and Bill had taken him under his wing, working to get Blue Boy to control his strength when drawing the bow so that he could develop a smooth draw and clean release. Although never going to be an expert, Blue Boy was nonetheless grateful for the help and patience that Bill had provided.

"Hey, Blue, skiving again aye? Get yourself inside the shop. Little Bill needs a hand moving some of the stock," Bill shouted across as he mounted his horse and sped off on some errand. Resigning himself to the chore, Blue Boy rushed in to where Little Bill, actually six and a half spans of muscle, was moving a fresh load of timber to the drying racks. Wiping the sweat from his brow he looked at Blue Boy, who just shrugged, and indicated a pile of timber and a rack and let the powerful boy get about the task.

Little Bill was actually a few years older than Bill and had suffered a nasty wound to his jaw serving on the front line. Bill returned just as the two were placing the last timber. Little Bill simply ruffled Blue Boy's hair before making his way out to wash up for the evening meal.

"Now, Blue, what can I do for you, broken another bow?" the joiner asked.

"No sir," Blue Boy replied politely, "I came to say my good byes now so they don't get rushed and I wanted to thank you for your help with my archery."

"No problem, lad. Now I will see you here next season and hey, make sure you give old Marv as much trouble as you can. It keeps him young."

*****

Millie climbed the steps up to the ward-school dormitory rooms. She waved across to Mister Trapes, who ran the half of the school for the older children, and knocked politely on the door.

Instead of a reply she heard a noise from above, "Pssssssssst." Careful not to look up she quietly said, "Who is up there?"

"S'me Stinky Pete, what do you want boss lady? The next briefing ain't for a couple more days and you shouldn't come here otherwise. It's difficult enough keeping Sour Grapes Trapes off our back as it is," said a small voice said from above.

"It's not official business Peter, get someone to let me in will you, otherwise Grapes will catch on," Millie hissed, smiling around at Mister Trapes who had started to walk over.

The small boy on the roof rapped some kind of pattern and suddenly the door opened. She waved over at the headmaster who seeing she had gained entrance, waved her encouragement to go in and went back to his duties. Inside she was greeted by all the occupants, grouped around the door obviously keen to find out the reason for her visit. All the kids knew of the agreement for acting as runners even though only a few were currently on the roster.

"Everybody, I've just left the infant's block and have come here with the same invitation," Millie started.

"Oh, it's about the party then," said Peter from the back of the room, sounding a bit disappointed that no new action was in the offing. "Millie, we have voted and most of us will be there. Can we draw lots for a reduced shift?"

"No need, Peter, it won't go on too late and the club lads

will be out and about," Millie answered. "See you all there then."

"Pah! Amateurs on our streets," Millie heard one of the little girls say as she walked out.

As Millie walked away from the ward school she reflected on the risks she had taken in recruiting the kids. Not only did they risk exposing her involvement in intelligence, as well as a definite link to other club employees, but also to the youngsters themselves should things actually turn nasty. Despite these concerns, which she had discussed at length with Taverner, he had still recommended they use this school, but they had made that the limit of their involvement.

Taverner assured her that such activities were actually quite common and she accepted that he had vetted the youngsters himself. Millie, therefore, accepted his quiet introduction to who he termed the ring leaders. Since then she had cultivated some of the older and more mischievous wards, providing them with dummy periods of day and night time extra curricula supervision where they could act as lookouts. This was possible by first finding suitable cadets and then positioning them with the headteacher as additional teaching resources, for which the over worked teaching staff were immensely grateful. The cadets then helped further as the wards' first line of control.

Thus the Night Fort with its extra, youthful, employees practised lookout techniques. The kids even using wire runs across key roof tops as a reliable way of discreetly sending information.

*****

Smee had already warned Moffet that one day Blue Boy would leave and come back to visit, as had Scandrett. He had, in fact, been careful to remind Moffet of this a number of times. Therefore, he could introduce the fact that this was going to happen and explained that Moffet should dress smartly and come to the leavers banquet to help cheer up Blue Boy. A special pre-banquet afternoon meal was arranged for Smee, Blue Boy and a few more, which was a bit reminiscent of Scandrett and Smee eating together. During the meal, which Blue Boy initially felt was too contrived, he began to really enjoy himself. Master Smee put it to Moffet that Blue Boy was feeling much better, and would now be able to partake in the music later. Moffet looked quite calm and pleased and went off together with Blue Boy and Merry, a tough female cadet with an infectious grin who was scheduled to fill Blue Boy's position for the farm maintenance.

They went on a tour of the music hall, trying a few instruments whilst no one was watching. Finally, Moffet presented Blue Boy with his brother's spare travelling gear done up neatly in a bundle with a couple of fishing lines, lures and some snares. Then rather than staying the night he simply got on his wagon and weaved his way off, waving briefly from the turn to the gatehouse.

The farewell dinner passed off as a noisy and good humoured event. Those band members staying behind provided the entertainment, with Judy, Fingers, Lythe Kyle, Taure and Starris all taking turns. It was true to say that the alcohol rationing was strained heavily but in most cases it was those staying behind who were the worst offenders.

As part of the entertainment, not only did Stallic, the camp's head chef, leave the kitchen but he also took a turn providing the entertainment, performing a quite impressive duet of a medley of popular songs.

The least popular item was a misjudged attempt at comic impressions of camp members by Call, from the maintenance team. Despite skitting Stonebrow, Heat and Master Smee the only impression that received anything other than derision was when he disappeared and reappeared with Bart wearing female costumes supposed to represent Honeygold and Split. Somehow it seemed that Call's ability at falsetto vocals had long been over looked, and when the cries for the two men to show off their legs were satisfied by a bizarre leg kicking dance routine it brought the house down.

Blue Boy ate heartily and thoroughly enjoyed the evening, forgetting all about it being his last night at home for he had never felt as comfortable within the camp. Quite who had arranged the seating plan Blue Boy was unsure as it seemed to follow no pattern that he could fathom. He was sat between

Honeygold and Bill, but on a table at the furthest end from the stage, which was usually where the honour table at which Bart and Master Smee, who were now at a table in the middle, usually sat.

Chapter Eight

The day before the children were due to leave, Piker lent forwards after lunch and, winking at Sophie, said, "Well, if the kids are leaving we should throw a party."

"Yes, please Uncle Jeffers, but we would need to invite all our friends. Can we please, we could use the club and I could be the hostess," Sophie announced, doing a twirl in an imaginary cocktail dress.

"Well, OK then," Jeffers replied distractedly.

"Oh, no!" groaned Mandibles, "All their friends means hundreds."

"OK, gentlemen, I think that it's an excellent idea. I will arrange the roster appropriately. Mister Jeffers, a word if I may," Taverner pronounced, dismissing the gathering with a wave.

"With some small work and closing the club for the afternoon we can put on a splendid party," Taverner pronounced as he led Jeffers Star from the hall.

Piker span Liam around in the air. "Cool! Guys I think we should have costumes and I'm off to see Seamstress Sian and see if I can get her to spare some time from Star's wardrobe." The precipitous lad then rushed out of the room.

"His name certainly does not come from avoiding his social commitments, it must just be his work," called Snibs to his retreating back. The older man, casting a nonchalant glance around the room, hesitated before rushing after him calling for him to wait up, to the great amusement of the remaining staff, who themselves gradually began to disperse.

"Where is Snibs?" asked Taverner, as he re-entered the main bar. "That scoundrel is supposed to be setting up the terrace bar. Pah, I do not know why Mister Jeffers tolerates such a group of lack lustre's," he muttered to no one in particular and scooted off again on some further errand.

Mandibles heaved a sigh, "Come on kids, let's go and see if

we can help with the terrace bar then. If we do a good job Snibs will owe you a favour, and it's always good to have someone like him in your debt."

When the kids had left and only a few of the senior staff remained in the main bar Bones turned to Changworth, "It looks like it's going to get rough if Jeffers is about to ship the youngsters off. Are we going to see something heavy, Chang? I wouldn't want any nasty surprises to shuffle me off this mortal coil sudden like. Once you reach your half century, action doesn't come as easy as it did before."

"OK old timer. I can tell you this. The investigations point to more than a small raid, in fact I will go as far as suggesting quite a nasty conspiracy might be going on here. So I want you all to keep an eye out for each other. Whilst it is not exactly likely to become an active tour, view it more like a shift down the mines back home, with careful precaution every step of the way."

"Right oh, Boss... er, Chang." Turning to Lawrence the aged soldier said, "Come on Lad I need to do some of those loosening exercises and then we can get tonight's bar food under way. Possibly best if we also check bow case three, you do the steel and I'll do the yew."

*****

As the band marched through the countryside the rolling hills, typical of the area around Camp Smee, gradually gave way to more a regular, if sloping, landscape. This change more than anything reminded Blue Boy of how much he was leaving behind, even if, he had been along this way several times in the past.

Looking around the party Blue Boy could tell from the expression of many of the other party members, and not just cadets, that they were coming to the same kind of view. Definitely the excitement of being named the War Band was rubbing off, and the reality of forthcoming action was sinking in. Nathan Hurst, acting commander, was running the journey as a defensive march with outriders and although everyone was supplied with two mounts and many spares for the wagons, he was ensuring that the band members were practised at getting off and walking or trotting the horses in rotation. The band were used to travelling this way and well able to keep up a good pace without over tiring the horses, but in this silent mode the whole exercise seemed much more serious.

Finally, even Nathan tired of the melancholy atmosphere and started up a marching song, Within a few bars all of the main party had shaken the feeling loose and were singing along, even the non musicians, many of whom, with no musical ability, made up in effort and volume what they lacked in ability. For the rest of the morning this effusive singing carried on, one popular song after another, some with solo voices but mainly belted out by one and all.

Well familiar with the songs and comfortable on his choice of horse as well as on foot, for short distances, Blue Boy turned his ever restless attention to the surrounding countryside. As the afternoon came on the road was more and more often joined by farm tracks, many of the farm buildings only being a stones throw from the road. Blue Boy knew they had long since passed the point where the farms had ceased to be managed under the authority of Smee's camp. They had become part of the general supply operation, keeping only what they needed and sending the remaining, and majority, share direct to the central store facilities. Greenleaf Tom, Blue Boy supposed, if you had to give the supervisory function a face and through him to the Quartermaster general.

Thinking about Tom also led Blue Boy to wonder how Sizell was getting on. Ichanod, who was travelling with the group supervising one section of the outriders, had kindly informed him that she had been accepted at one of the main Central Plain's associated 'National Reclamation Camps', as they were officially termed. Ichanod had laughed when Blue Boy had asked what her new colleagues were like and whether they would look after her. Ichanod had left him with the simple answer, "I think you have more to worry about looking after yourself."

Despite being disappointed with the lack of detail and unable to pursue the question any further with the temperamental horn player, Blue Boy had been able to coax Stonebrow into revealing that the facility where Sizell was enrolled was run by Ichanod's brother, and from that Blue Boy drew a degree of comfort.

Despite the well tended farm areas Blue Boy was surprised that on a number of occasions the road narrowed as it travelled through quite thick areas of wood land. Whilst the hedgerows here were no worse tended and trimmed than along the majority of the road, that the woodland had not been cut back further seemed strange to Blue Boy. When he was finally able to prise Stonebrow away from the courier, later on in the afternoon, he put this observation to the band leader.

"Come now, Blue, did Mister Kyan not describe the two official bodies who regulate the roads outside of towns and official facilities?" Stonebrow replied, clearly not going to give a direct answer.

"Well, yes, he did: the Agricultural Department and the Area Partisan Command," Blue Boy replied sullenly.

"And what do you deduce from that?" Stonebrow continued.

"That they are not always very good at it!" Blue Boy replied, suddenly resenting the work he was having to put in for what seemed like a straight forward question.

"Well, if that is all you can contribute to your own consideration then go and join the group on foot, and remain on foot until we reach this evening's camp or you have the answer. As commander of a band on war footing you need to contribute to my every request to your full abilities. Now get out of my sight."

"Yes Sir!" Blue Boy replied, suddenly realising that he had obviously not picked a good time to address the question or offer dissention or even indifference.

As it was late on in the day Blue Boy had little concern that he would be unable to keep up with the troupe. He reflected that the only reason that Stonebrow had been approachable was because he had taken over the driving of the wagon from Mable, the animal husband who had ridden off and was still no where to be seen. Stonebrow on the wagon had allowed Blue Boy to drop back through the band to ride alongside it. In fact not only could Blue Boy not see Mable, but Nathan Hurst seemed to be the only rider who had not returned from his turn with the outriders.

Blue Boy realised that anything could have happened, although if the animal husband was the only party member dispatched it pointed to some problem with Nathan's mount. Blue Boy resolved to keep an eye out for Nathan, Mable or the piebald horse. Meanwhile he thought more carefully about his question. Regarding the roads deliberately narrowed through the woods, it suddenly came to the young boy that although the partisans had recently been most known for managing out of town resources such as water, roads and policing issues, their primary directive was to organise defences in times of war. As no significant war or even battles had ever been staged on the northern continent since the formation of the nation, after the 'Shattering', the profile of such activities was understandably low and this bore consideration.

As dusk began to fall the troupe approached another wooded area, just after which it was determined that they would camp for the night. Blue Boy resolved to complete his tasks quickly and find some way of testing his suspicions that these narrowed roads were actually carefully contrived ambush points.

Once the troupe stopped to camp Blue Boy rushed to Marvellous for his orders. All the rest of the crew were assigned their usual tasks such as firewood collection, building sections of the simple stockade, meal preparation or tent pitching. When all the others were dispatched Marvellous turned to Blue Boy, his disappointment obvious. "As you can't seem to remain on a horse why don't you go and keep yourself at least acquainted with them and help Milton, who is standing in for Mable tonight. Don't return to your tent until he has dismissed you."

Blue Boy bit his lip in frustration because he had managed to disappoint both his best friends. He rushed off to find Milton, the former courier, now apparently assigned permanently to the troupe. He was busy picketing the horses on the furthest side of the camp, away from the road and not a great distance from the woods. Blue Boy was pleased because once he was dismissed he might be able to slip out that way and return through the woods to the road.

Milton greeted the news of his help with an utter lack of expression and allocated Blue Boy a picket of ten horses to settle, feed and check over. Nor did he show any surprise when Blue Boy returned in record time: He simply motioned the lad over to the picket, where he quickly checked a selection of the horses, and simply allocated him another picket, apparently finding nothing worthy of comment.

If anything, Blue Boy finished these even more quickly and had to wait while he suffered an almost exact repeat of the first inspection. Finally, when Blue Boy had finished his fourth set, and when all the others on the same duty were absent, probably dismissed after only having done two or three, Milton indicated that he should stand at ease and then disappeared for a good tenth before returning.

"Right son, follow me," was all he said, and started off through the camp towards the road at a brisk pace. Blue Boy followed, intrigued, as they stopped first at a guard point where Milton appropriated a covered lantern. He led them straight to the outer-most guard point near the road, where he exchanged a bit of sign with the perimeter guard before leading Blue Boy through the darkness to the road. He marched the lad all the way through the darkness, making their way by the scant light of the moon until they were deep in the woods where he uncovered the lantern.

"Right, lad, two things, firstly you have one part with this lantern. I want you to spend that time making your way back to the camp. On the way you are to identify two other places where the surroundings are cut specifically to allow for a classic ambush position. What I will want you to explain to me is where the positions are, roughly, in paces. Start measuring from here back to the camp. You must also tell me what the classic ambush types are. Do you understand this op?" he finished dispassionately.

"Yes Sir," Blue Boy spoke up firmly.

"Good. Secondly, Master Smee has had you prepare a special piece of theoretical work. We will also ride together behind the troupe tomorrow afternoon when you will present it to me, both verbally and with the notes you have prepared. You may check this activity with Marvellous Martin when you return this evening. Do you understand the second Op?" Milton asked looking at Blue boy as if to measure his reply carefully.

"Yes Sir," Blue Boy answered firmly again.

Milton simply turned and walked back towards the camp and out of the lantern light. "Blue Boy, make sure you return the lantern to the road guard within a part," Milton's voice carried back softly.

*****

The party was scheduled to run for the three parts up to midday, with the children leaving early the next morning. Almost on the dot the whole ward school turned up, students and teachers. Sophie and Liam had been confined in the kitchens, helping prepare the buffet but unable to view the preparations in the main bar. Uncle Taverner had said it would spoil their surprise.

As soon as they were let in though, it was worth the wait. All the children were allowed to rush in together with the room was still dark. Entering from the opposite side Sophie and Liam reached the middle of the floor first. Suddenly all the lights started rotating on the stage. It seemed that Jeffers had managed to get all the cadets who took temporary work running the club's lighting to come in for the party and for a tenth part the band played and the lights flashed to enchant the children. Then, suddenly, all the coloured filters were removed and other lamps uncovered to light the club fully.

All the young children cheered and even the older ones, posturing and pretending to look tough, were taken a back by all the bunting and streamers arrayed around the club, completed by a banner above the bar saying 'Good Bye Sophie and Liam.'

At first it was the older children who were difficult, all huddling together and resisting Barf and Scars who were having to work hard trying to organise all the children into two teams for some race games. Finally everybody was ready and the running races were held which at last got things moving.

Once the children slowed down, tired, but not half as tired as Barf and Scars looked, Katie helped organise the children into sitting in a semi circle and then announced the next entertainment. "I proudly present to you the amazing Bones, conjuror extraordinaire."

Bones spent almost his entire act making coins disappear

and then pulling them from the children's ears, or pulling eggs from his mouth, at one point causing Lawrence to call out, "Does that mean less work travelling to the market for fresh eggs, Pops?" He finished his section by presenting the little girls with bunches of flowers pulled dramatically from thin air.

"They are up your sleeve," one of the older boys called out, only to be shushed by the rest of the audience.

Finally, his repertoire exhausted, he announced, "And now my apprentice magician the marvellous Snakey Pete!"

Suddenly, the majority of the lanterns were shuttered, plunging the room into a gentle gloom, and a few moments later a couple of focused beams returned picking out Pete in a magnificent purple robe, his arms extended like two huge soft wings. With a flourish he slid across the remaining distance of polished floor and went straight into his act.

"Now then, ladies and gentlemen and Liam, I would ask for quiet whilst I perform a very dangerous magic act. Here now is my lovely assistant, Cat, pushing on what looks like a couple of drinks trolleys, my amazing magic box!" he exclaimed, with a dramatic flourish to the end of the bar where Cat had appeared with a large box covered in red paper.

"Now children, excuse me young James, could you lend a hand?" The little boy jumped to his feet nodding vigorously. "Splendid. Now James, I would like you to climb up here; Barf, a chair if you would, please, for my assistant James."

Without even getting up Barf leaned to the nearest empty chair and tossed it feet first at the part-time apprentice magician in his velvet robe and purple felt hat, who caught the chair as it sped towards him, feet first, with a terse look at Barf.

"You see, James," he said, smiling back down at the small boy, "Even magicians can't get good staff."

"Now James, climb up here will you, you have an important job. Firstly, it is important that a lady is never allowed to climb into a box without a young gentleman there to hold her hand. Secondly, you keep holding her hand all the way through the magic just so you don't think I have made her completely disappear."

Pete turned to Cat, "Now, my lady, I have furnished you with a handsome companion, if you would climb into the box.

Look, children, just in case something goes wrong I will lay this sheet over the far end of the box. Here, in she goes; here come her feet under the cloth. Right Cat, are you comfortable?"

"Yes sir, Mister Magician," Cat simpered, playing her part.

"Good. James, are you comfortable? All right, you just nod away young man. Is Cat still a real lady? Another nod? Oh good. Now for the difficult part, I will take this saw and now, yes, I am going to cut our head waitress in half. Hey, if this goes wrong who thinks Barf would look good in a dress doing her job?" Pete asked the children.

"Noooooo," was their unanimous answer.

"Well, all right then, I had better not mess this up. Now I start sawing here, cut, cut. Does that tickle there, Cat? Hold on to James' hand if it does. Almost through. There now," Pete said, looking naughtily at the pile of sawdust under the trolley as the saw blade appeared from beneath the cloth. "Hey James don't go telling Mister Taverner that I messed up the floor with my magic. Right, another nod, I'll take that as a promise."

"Katie!" he called with a flourish. "Could I trouble you for my separators? Ah, thank you miss," he said, taking two pieces of wood with a dramatic bow to his helper. "James, hold onto Cat's hand tightly, this may tickle her a bit more."

He pushed the first piece through a slot in the box. "Did that hurt?" he asked Cat. "No, well I will push on quickly anyway," he shrugged cheekily to the children. "Now if I separate the two trolleys like this and spin this one round you can see that, look, here is where Cat's feet are beneath the cloth. You can see I have cut her in half."

"Ooooooooh," cried most of the children, except for one little girl who stood up and shouted, "Put her back together, I don't like it," and promptly bursting into tears.

Pete looked dramatically to the roof and with his hand flourished across his fore head moaned, "Everyone a critic." Katie came forward to comfort the girl.

"As you insist little lady," he said turning back. "And now if I push this back here, remove the wooden separators here and here, sprinkle a little magic powder here and here. Lady Cat if you would get up as I push you back together. I think... ahh... yes, she is whole again!" he shouted with high drama as Cat stepped down out of the box. Slamming the lid down quickly so that James, who was trying to look inside, had his view obstructed, Pete took one more pronounced bow and taking Cat's hand encouraged her to do the same. He hurriedly wheeled his props away to the loud applause of all the children and the adults watching.

"Thank you, Pete," Bones called after him. "Wasn't he good boys and girls? In fact he was so good we have had trouble finding an act good enough to compare. So with that in mind the management of the 'Night Fort club and Magic Party Centre' have booked for your enjoyment, well, yourselves, because now girls and boys, please find yourself a partner for Piker and Felicity's comedy dancing competition." So saying he stepped back and motioned to where Felicity entered pirouetting gracefully as the band stuck up.

From the other end of the hall Piker staggered in wearing a pair of huge boots with the laces tied together. He and Felicity then did a comedy dance routine, she graceful and he clumsy. Finally it ended to great applause, with Felicity daintily postured and Piker a heap of arms and legs on the floor.

"Now children, I think it is time to see if you can do better than Piker. The band will play you some songs and we will see which boy and which girl are our best dancers." Turning to the door she waited for a sign before continuing, "but first, before the music starts, let us introduce our celebrity guests. Firstly, allow me to present Jeffers, the big brown bear."

At which point Jeffers came in wearing a comedy bear suit, closely followed by Taverner who was disguised as a tree, with just a round hole for his face to show through.

"Mister Taverner as the Wise Oak Tree and finally, Miss Millie the famous desert Sultan."

"Sultana, one of the bigger girls called out laughing," as the applause started from the children for the costumed judges.

The three hurried over to the table and took their seats, all except Taverner whose trunk wouldn't bend, clearly a design issue that had been overlooked in the hurry to prepare the costumes.

For a good third the band played and the dancing competition saw many prizes awarded, only to have the final victor's dance interrupted when Barney and Chubby rushed out onto the floor, skidding along on their knees, dressed as a pantomime horse. This prolonged the dancing for a couple more songs as the pair in the horse suit struggled to dance their way through the children, dragging a good few in their wake who had decided that clinging to the horse costume or trying to climb on for a ride would be fun. Finally Piker and Felicity gave up trying to pull the laughing children off and it nearly ended in tears when Barney and Chubby finally lost their balance and went tumbling down in a pile of children. Fortunately though, the children landed on top of Chubby and not the other way round.

To end the party Snibs, helped by Sellwyn, set up a stall where he had coloured a whole variety of juice drinks with food colourants that he had bought down on the market. Each of the different glass jugs was labelled with a magical sounding name, all except the green one which was called 'Barfs stinky sock juice', and which for some reason didn't seem a popular choice. Having picked their drinks whilst tables were being laid out the remainder of the party was occupied with a noisy meal and even noisier food fight: nobody could work out afterwards whether it had been started by a seven-year-old boy or Snibs and Piker.

As the party drew to a close, and the ward children and their teachers thanked the staff and took their leave, Jeffers called the staff over.

"On behalf of Sophie and Liam I would like to thank everybody for the lovely party, except perhaps the person who put itching powder into my bear suit. But now the time has come. I am afraid now, sooner than expected, the children and I will be leaving. Jungold is fetching our horses around now. Please come over and say any farewells, for we leave within the quarter part."

Many hand shakes, hugs and tears later the children were mounted, both sitting in a deep saddle in front of Jeffers on his fine chestnut mare. Jeffers and the children waved to those staff members who had come to the town gate, before Jeffers put his heels to his horse which took off at a gentle canter down the road, away from the club and their home.

As the children rode up towards the road junction they met Kint coming back the other way. The children were surprised to see him and called out, but he just smiled and waved and Sophie caught him signing 'OK.' That she had been able to persuade Piker to teach her military signing was a secret she intended to keep from certain guardians and authority figures for as long a she could. She knew her next step would be to locate a new teacher, which might not be easy, but Piker had said that she would soon find some kind hearted solider who humoured children and had a fondness for secrets. After all, he had said, she had conned him into it.

Uncle Jeffers had already told them that they would be heading for River Ford, but when they reached the junction with the main road and the sign posts, rather than taking the road in any direction he cut across the junction and headed off the road and down a shallow bank. After a couple of moments Sophie felt that she could make out a faint path through the undergrowth which their horse seemed to be following. This led them to crest a rise where the trees thinned out to a grassy clearing and she spotted her favourite riding horse tethered near a neat little camp.

'So that was what Kint was up to,' she thought.

"Is that more to of Pete's magic Uncle Jeffers?" Liam asked innocently, waking from his doze. Truly her brother seemed to be able to sleep anywhere Sophie was discovering.

"No young man, it is some of my magic. Now if my guess is right then that pot over the fire should contain a tasty portion of stew. Who fancies one last scoff compliments of Millie?" Jeffers asked, sliding nimbly from the saddle and lifting the children down quickly.

*****

By the afternoon of the second day Blue Boy was more tired than he cared to admit. He had worked hard for the day-part after Milton had left him, but even by the light of the lantern he found it difficult to identify precise locations along the track for an ambush. He did however manage to find three places where he could envisage traps being staged.

The first, he felt, was where the trunks of two large trees were scored as if cables had been tied from one to another. The second was where a couple of dips on either side of the track seemed to be man made, forming extra cover for attackers to shelter and in one case the culvert seemed to cut back under the road and Blue Boy felt that he could have followed this tunnel a certain distance had time not been pressing. The final position was pretty much a guess and Blue Boy, desperate for a third, speculated that some of the larger trees near the entrance to the woods could possibly make a suitable platform for archery or missile weapons.

He had hurried back to hand over the lantern at roughly the right sort of time and then sought out Marv. Something about the old fellow's demeanour had informed Blue Boy that he was not yet entirely off the hook for offending a superior. Rather than asking all his new questions he had simply got Marv to confirm that Milton could request the second task. He had then taken himself off to the tent he shared, stopping at the cook fire where Knuckles had saved him a meal, albeit a somewhat dried up one.

He awoke early, as was his normal routine, and leaving the tent for a wash was only mildly surprised to find Milton sitting waiting for him.

"Get your wash, lad, and meet me at your horse in a tenth. Your packing will be taken care of," was all Milton could find to say as he hurried off into the pre-dawn mist that wove its way around the tents like cotton strands on a thistle bush.

Now late in the afternoon, back with Marv and his group, Blue Boy could relate his morning exploits to what Milton had shown him. They had mounted up in silence and instead of heading off towards the track, Milton had taken them away around the wooded area to the farthest side south of the road. Here he had shown Blue Boy lengths of concealed trenches prepared, apparently, for a pitched battle should a force be 'persuaded', as Milton put, it to leave the road. Getting their horses to cross the final trench that paralleled the road and blocked entrance to the woods looked impossible but Milton clearly had the knack. Dismounting and leading their horses down one way and then back another showed clearly that such an activity had been prepared for.

Once in the woods on a small track, Blue Boy had been shown a number of hides that could house an untold number of men and horses; whilst they were all in good order they were certainly all empty. Milton confided in Blue Boy that the partisans would be maintaining caches of long-life foods, equipment and weapons throughout the woods. He made no effort to show Blue Boy any of these hidden places, and the boy was left wondering whether he could have located these or not.

Slowly and carefully they made their way through these hidden paths, with Milton pointing out a variety of careful changes that the partisans had wrought amongst the trees, even to, the extent that they had wired saplings and, over patient years, encouraged the very plants and trees themselves to grow into specific shapes. A defensive garden Blue Boy decided with a new respect growing for the partisans and their forestry skills.

When they reached the road it took but a few moments for Blue Boy to relocate the places he had picked. He realise that Milton had greatly over simplified things by asking Blue Boy to pick three, the entire road side being a carefully controlled environment providing cover for anything from a single warrior to a whole battalion, depending on from which direction an enemy force approached.

"Are all the wooded areas that we have passed so far as well planned as this one Sir?" Blue Boy asked.

"Well lad, it depends on certain factors. I must say that this particular example is a bit extreme, and I would hazard a guess that a couple of generations ago much of this area was cut back and saplings planted with careful planning to create what you have just seen. As we continue we will see that this place has a particular significance."

Milton had hardly paused and soon they were back in the saddle. The area where the camp had been was now deserted and Milton took the opportunity to scout it. Most of the evidence had been removed: turf carefully relayed where fire pits had been, or the stakes that had surrounded the perimeter and Blue Boy felt that Milton was quite satisfied.

"That a camp was made is evident, but how many it contained would take somebody a good few parts to figure out and that is all I can ask. We must hurry to the river."

They mounted and cantered down the road at a moderate pace. Blue Boy had been interested to see that the road entered a culvert with the banks soon up to his shoulders as he rode. As they had rounded the final bend he recognised that they had reached the Plains Brooke River. Here Milton stopped and explained that to make reasonable time from the central plains up into the hills, towards Greeners Gap, this roadway was the best route. "The river is too shallow to be defensive and despite some simple efforts to make it more of a bottle neck for an advancing army, which I will show you soon it forms only one part of a defensive plan."

Moving carefully on foot, the horses hobbled on the roadside, Milton showed Blue Boy some of the changes made to the natural break of the river: bricking some of the banks to make it less convenient to enter or leave the water, making the bridge easy to remove and placing a number of defensive underground bunkers on both sides.

Blue Boy asked, "If there has never been a serious assault on us from across the water, why do we invest the considerable effort to prepare all these defences?"

"Well, I was hoping that your recent studies would go some way to answering that question. Let us sit here awhile and you can take a part sum-up what you have gleaned from those books," Milton replied in a quiet voice, plopping himself down on a grassy bank overlooking the river.

Blue Boy followed his lead and pulled a clutch of papers from a document roll that Master Smee had arranged for him to wear attached to the back of his battle harness, next to his axe. He had then taken not a part but almost two to present his summary of the works, and then another one answering Milton's quiet questions. It had become very clear that Milton was completely familiar with the three works. Several times he had challenged Blue Boys' inferences and had even taken the notes and crossed sections through with a charcoal.

"Well then, Blue," he finished, "from those works do you now doubt that there is a considerable, if concealed, intelligence working within the Horde. Certainly the Horde's numbers grow dramatically, far more than the numbers we kill each year. If you combine those two factors backed-up by historical precedent how long do you think it will be before the Horde finds a way to cross the water?"

"Milton, is it really that serious, are we doomed to suffer another Shattering?" Blue Boy asked disconsolately.

"Cheer up lad, knowing there is a problem puts us half way to solving it. All you have seen and learnt this morning is that there is a lot more planning in place for an invasion than is obviously on view. The same is also true for how we are planning to take the fight to the lands occupied by the Horde. Come, we have a good ride ahead if we are to catch up with the troupe before dusk."

It was well past the sun's peak when Milton had led them back to the horses. "Oh and Blue, let me hang onto your notes will you, I think you have the important bits locked away in your head now."

Several parts of hard riding and they had rejoined the troupe as the late afternoon was turning to dusk. They reached another stand of trees where this time the troupe had company.

Nathan Hurst's second-in-command, 'Charming' Dave Choker had apparently ridden on ahead and forewarned the old woman who had a cabin in a clearing just back from the road. Her home doubled as a kiosk where she could serve up food to passing companies and Blue Boy remembered fondly the fat old woman who lived there from when he had travelled to Riding Dale a couple of years before.

Soon the company were settled in. Instead of needing to cook separately Violet had been able to prepare large vats of stew and all the hungry troops needed to do was queue up and have her ladle out the staples and collect chunks of bread from Dave, who had been seconded by the formidable woman as kitchen help.

Tonight it was Blue Boys turn to pitch his tent on his own. He was informed by Marv that his own truculence had apparently been contagious, and that Knuckles had fallen foul of Nathan Hurst, who had needed to put down his usual mount after the poor beast had stumbled and cracked its fetlock in a rabbit hole. Despite their best efforts Mable and Nathan had been unable to splint it to ease its pain or allow it to be moved, and the tough decision had left Nathan uncharacteristically moody. Knuckles, never the most diplomatic individual, had opened his thin-lipped mouth once too often and now was digging the latrines for the entire camp.

*****

Although Jeffers was up early, the children, exhausted from the excitement of the party, the emotions of leaving and the rigours of the ride, slept quite late, which suited Jeffers well enough. A couple of parts past dawn he roused them, though, and showing them how to take a good wash in only very little water, soldier style he assured them, he let them start their day. He cooked a quick breakfast of hot oats with a spoonful of honey and together they quickly packed up camp.

Allowing Sophie to manage her own horse and with Liam riding in his saddle, they made the short trip back to the road where Jeffers winked at them and told them he had a surprise.

Soon noises could be heard from the opposite direction to River Ford and Sophie realised that whoever Jeffers was waiting for had arrived. Sophie thought the noise that the approaching horses were making sounded odd and, whilst she could make out numbers approaching, something sounded wrong. Finally, instead of horse she realised that a large number of people were running along the road. Within moments about one hundred troops turned up and the captain hurried over to Jeffers where he threw him a smart salute.

"Well, Captain Sombers, you have finally arrived somewhere on time, how does that make you feel?" Jeffers said in mock seriousness.

"Pretty good, you old fraud," the short but determined looking man replied. "How are you Star?" He turned to look at the children and to their surprise and Liam's amusement he threw Sophie a salute and said, "Eamon Sombers and company reporting for duty, mi'lady."

"I'm not a soldier, silly," Sophie giggled.

"Oh! Sorry there Miss, we are just a crew of simple spear fighters on our way to the fayre. Do you think your kind father might allow us to travel in your company?" Eamon asked her quietly as if Jeffers might not hear them.

"They can travel with us can't they, Uncle Jeffers?" Sophie asked quickly.

"If you wish so Sophie. But are you sure we can trust such a disreputable looking bunch of individuals?" Jeffers asked her in return, keeping a very straight face.

"Uncle Jeffers is right," Sophie muttered as she turned back to Eamon. "Captain Sombers, do you give us assurances of your good conduct and fine behaviour and swear not to cause us any strife, in the name of the Battler?" she asked carefully.

"I so swear, Sophie," Eamon replied without hesitation.

"Then it is a done deal," Jeffers concluded, and with that the troopers picked up their strange long bags, some needing to be carried between two people being over twelve spans in length, and began to jog along the road with Jeffers and Sophie gently riding alongside the road next to Eamon Sombers, who began to have a conversation with Jeffers in sign.

*****

Up early for their third day of travel, Dave was obviously keen to break free from the attentions of Violet, who seemed to consider him a 'nice piece of fluff'. He made his rounds early, instructing the band to travel with their instruments. Today the cadets and camp support staff would perform the out-riding so that the band could ride and play.

"It's time to practice our stuff," Dave bellowed as the band mounted up. "Camp tune to start and then marching order seven."

Steve Rumbles began the opening drum beat, his two drums fitted over the front on his saddle, and off the band went leaving the rest of the camp to load up the remaining wagons and catch up as they could. For the rest of the morning the band rode as a stately procession. Blue Boy had somehow been selected to drive the wagon that now contained Violet and her wares pitch kit which she was taking to set up at the fayre.

The morning sunshine beat down and the whole atmosphere of the procession became more one of determined purpose. Blue Boy wondered why the band had not played anything for the first two days. Violet was clearly enjoying the music, though, and was dressed all in velvet of various hues, a frock which Blue Boy assumed was one of her best. She treated her young driver as if he was a courtly courier escorting a royal lady to an important function, like the stories he had read in the ancient books on etiquette. This fiction was even more closely matched when Dave took his conducting out and began to ride around the band as the road began to cross a large plain of level grassland allowing the band to combine the music with a display of precision riding, crossing back and forth in complicated patterns in time with the music. When Dave happened to pass near Violet's wagon she would greet him with a delicately executed flourish of a wave, a very regal wave Blue Boy thought.

"This is much better Violet, the past two days have been so quiet and solemn. Especially the bosses." Blue Boy spoke his thoughts out loud.

"Oh, lad, that is pretty usual. All the leaders have served before and will have been briefed on what is expected of them. I suspect the bands suffer more than other companies at the start because they understand that not only is their purpose to undertake some of the most dangerous work but also, once in the field, to use their talents to boost the morale of the rest of the troops." Violet paused before continuing. "The announcement of the crusade means that many hundreds of thousands of troops will be deployed in a large offensive, some of the officers will doubtless have heavy responsibility. It takes a while to let the burden settle. I guess it only sinks in when the journey begins. But enough of that, don't they make a splendid sight? You must be very proud that one day you will be riding with the band. I heard tell that your dance went well recently. Are any of the other members of your ensemble in this troupe?" Violet asked genuinely.

"Only Antonio who plays the beat box. He is with the out riders today." Blue Boy replied thoughtfully.

"I'm sure you will all play together again, Blue. Oooo, look here comes that lovely Dave again, he is sooooo fine I'd like to get my hands on his booty," the large black mama purred.

Blue Boy just laughed and twitching the reins encouraged the wagon team to pick up pace and take his lady closer to her prey.

*****

It was about a part before dusk when Jeffers and Eamon called a halt to the day's travelling. They had only taken a couple of quick third-part rests throughout the day and when Sophie had asked Jeffers how far they had travelled he replied, "Oh, about 28 leagues, which with all the company on foot with full kit is really quite impressive. My compliments Captain Sombers," he said, raising his voice so that the words of his compliment carried. "Now Sombers let us see if you still camp like a bunch of Raggers," he continued, unable to resist the opportunity to stir the compact man doling out instructions to his junior officers.

Ignoring the comment, Eamon looked pretty competent as he strode around the campsite supervising his troops. About a third were women, although to Sophie they all looked pretty tough and unapproachable.

"Uncle Jeffers, we can help set up camp," Sophie told her guardian as he was rubbing down his horse.

"I know precious," he answered, "but tonight I think you ought just to sit back and watch them a bit. Check out how they work as a team and who it is safe to upset and who it isn't. Then tomorrow, when you do get chores, you will have been able to choose properly who you want to help."

"Oh, all right, as long as you answer some questions," Sophie insisted, "Like all the troops have one straight bag which, as they describe themselves as a spear company, would be their spears. However, some have similar, shorter, bags and others are carrying those long bags in pairs. Are they some kind of parts of a big tent or something?"

"Not quite, Sophie," Jeffers replied. "The short bags are rolls of javelins which are a kind of throwing spear, and the long bags contain a special type of pike which, again, whilst being similar to a spear isn't ever thrown. Eamon's company have people skilled in all kinds of equipment."

"Oh, I thought it might be something interesting," Sophie complained. She wasn't really much of a one for finding weapons interesting Jeffers remembered. 'I hope she shows more interest and some aptitude when it comes to her turn to serve,' Jeffers hoped, a small tingle of fear passing through him before he could fully dismiss the thought to the distant future, where it belonged.

Chapter Nine

For the whole next day Eamon Sombers and his men ran lightly, with Jeffers and the children riding moderately at their side.

Sophie could do little but marvel at the stamina these men and women were displaying, and also at the fact that some even sang or chattered away as they ran, almost as if they were just out for a stroll. Jeffers explained that the group were trained to travel specifically in this manner but agreed that watching them from horseback made the exercise look impressive.

The group of travellers passed through hill and valley along the well maintained road. Stopping whenever Eamon ordered his troops to rest they ate comfortably and the weather remained mild and pleasant as they travelled over the gently undulating countryside.

The only discomfort anybody suffered was that Liam found the entire exercise boring, and if either Sophie or Jeffers weren't working hard enough to keep him entertained he soon informed them noisily of the fact.

*****

Returning to look around the first spot he had picked, Blue Boy thought Marvellous seemed to have overlooked the perfect place to camp. Having re-examined his choice carefully he returned to where Marvellous had finally pitched their group about half a league further away from the centre of the camp.

"Marv, why didn't we camp at the first spot, it seemed perfect?" Blue Boy quizzed the old man as soon as they had some privacy.

"Come back with me," Marv curtly instructed his young charge Leading him by the arm back to the spot where they had been. "Young man, you are right. From every physical aspect this is a prime camping spot. Unfortunately we were not the first to notice this. Do you see that standard over there? The winged lion is a Griphon, and the leader of that team goes by the same name," Marv indicated as discreetly as he could. "Now during the day everything is quiet, but at night, once they have spent the day competing and the night drinking, this place will be so noisy that you'd be hard pushed to hear what I have just said. Ask around when the others arrive and see whether they would have fancied camping next to the Griphon's crew."

*****

"Stonebrow, what do you know about a crew run by the Griphon?" Blue Boy tried to ask subtly, as they worked on setting up the camp site area.

Stonebrow looked at him intently. "Well, the Griphon is recruiting here at this fayre, although I suspect you knew that. He himself is a seasoned campaigner used for dangerous, mainly land-based missions, and as such seems to be trusted and respected. He is known as a good commander and in battle he always puts himself in the van of his troops. At about six and a half feet tall and twenty sacks weight he is a massively powerful individual and in competition would be difficult to defeat in many, many categories. At a double innings though many taunt him as being past his prime and I suspect he drives himself all the harder for that fact, something that could be a considerable worry if I needed to trust his judgement. Off duty he is unbelievably raucous and his crew of men and women are all known as party animals. Why do you ask?" Stonebrow finished.

"Well, I just questioned Marv as to why we didn't camp next to the Griphon and he just suggested that I ask round."

"OK, lad, but avoiding that camp site was a narrow escape I can tell you. While we are on the subject, remind me what you know about fighting companies," Stonebrow asked.

"Hmm, well, each is formed by a captain who needs prior permission. He then receives any monies earned and then splits this amongst his people. There are some good stories about captains whose own men felt that they were being scammed. The captain is, of course, expected to provide group equipment and fund training. Err, hmm, depending on the mission the team may be accompanied by an army liaison officer who observes and forwards his set of opinions to the campaign leader. A squad may be bonus driven, depending on the size of their achievement, to encourage flexibility in campaign conditions. Past performance also determines at what level their subsistence payments are set. Cor that's bloody hot!" Blue Boy swore as craftily he tried to swipe a sausage from their cook fire whilst Stonebrow was occupied with stitching on his battle harness.

"None of that language now, Blue, please. You earned yourself the burn by pilfering, you little scally," Stonebrow chided gently. "Now on with your discussion, please you are doing acceptably so far."

"OK. Most people are expected to contribute over and above their two compulsory terms, certainly more the longer they live, on a voluntary basis, is that correct?" Receiving no acknowledgement he continued, "Therefore Marv, in his mid forties, would be expected to have voluntarily campaigned, what, possibly twice more? For the majority of the younger campaigners this usually involves the fighting companies I think, whilst old survivors finally register as an ender, which means that for the remainder of their lives they are subject to honourable service. Our tradition suggests that we would have failed to fulfil our personal responsibilities to the human race if we died of old age in our beds," Blue Boy finished thoughtfully.

*****

Sophie and Liam started to wander towards the stalls, attracted by the sounds and smells on offer. Before they got several yards, though, they both felt a smart tap on the shoulder. Eamon stood behind them, "Hey there! You can't start the fun until I can. Jeffers has urgent business though, so why don't you help us plan our camp and then I'll take you on a special tour. You'll meet more interesting people that way." Gaining reluctant nods of agreement Eamon continued, "Liam, I think you should help Clara pitching the feed shelters and settling down the horses. Sophie, you and I will lend Des Rudd a hand with the main marquee."

For the next parts time flew as Sophie helped the spearmen

mark out the position of their pitch. Each of the team of six working on the marquee made sure she saw the important parts of their task, and by the time they had finished she realised that she now knew pretty well how to pitch the Marquee, and also that the soldiers could have done the whole thing much quicker without her.

Eamon hurried over once he saw that the single biggest job was finished. "Right, time for the show. Clara will take Liam, and Sophie, you are with me, you can ride on our shoulders," the small man said, "and direct us where you want to go. We'll meet up at Corgi's kiosk about dusk, if not before," Eamon told Clara.

The two pairs of adult and child began to follow the neat but often winding pathways between the campsites towards the centre of the fayre. Sophie was excited to see the great mix of companies and it was interesting just to see the differences in the way each arranged their own pitch. The further they travelled the busier the pathways became until Sophie was no longer aware of Clara or her brother.

Gradually the campsites began to merge into more business oriented stalls, which delighted Sophie, with refreshment kiosks mixed with vendors of every conceivable type of product both military and civilian.

After a quarter part of leaving Sophie to her own thoughts, Eamon began talking. "Right then, Sophie, it is a great opportunity to see people this year, I can't remember a bigger Fayre. You'll like the first stop. Are Clara and Liam still with us?" Deciding to take a risk Sophie waved her clenched fist to sign 'no' or 'stop'.

Eamon laughed, "Right my girl, they've probably gone down to the lake to see the boats. I poached Clara from the boat service and she gets aboard anything that floats whenever she can."

The pair trotted on as the campsites became fewer and for a distance food stalls dominated. After a few moments more her tour guide pointed. "Look at this coloured pavilion over here. Here we have a full company of Hospitallers, it's rare we see so many at a Fayre and I've never seen them in full formal dress like this. Have you learned anything about the Knightly Orders?" Eamon asked.

Sophie waved some fingers at him.

"Ah, you need to use your fingers more to indicate the proportion of agreement or understanding, like this," the compact man demonstrated. "Well, I am sure you will stop me if you get bored. There are the two major orders, the Knights of the Church, or the Templars, and the Knights of Life, the Hospitallers. These we see here are the Hospitallers, although we might see some Templars later. Once you have joined an order you are a member for as long as you live. Both orders are known for their prowess in battle and have long and proud histories in our war against the Horde." Eamon stopped just short of the magnificent pavilion's coat of arms, stitched into the rear wall of the tent and guarded by a stern looking man with a battered face and gleaming armour, and gently lifted Sophie off his shoulders and down onto the ground.

"Perhaps we can find a Hospitaller to tell us more about their order. I only see them when I'm getting patched up and I try to keep that to a minimum."

Sombers trotted the little girl around the tent away from the rear where they had paused to admire the vibrant sigil and the gleaming guard.

"Excuse me, sir, this little lady is interested in hearing about your order. Any chance one of your company could spare us a short moment?" Eamon asked one of the impressively presented guards at the pavilion's well trodden opening.

"I will see what I can do for the lady, sir," the young man replied. Half turning to the opening called, "Brother Stream, can you spell me for a snatch?"

After a brief rustling of the entrance a figure emerged bowing his head to duck under the entrance flap. He was possibly the largest man that Sophie had ever seen.

"Thank you, brother," said the young guard. "Err, sir, may I say who is asking?"

"Certainly, I am Eamon Sombers."

"Eamon, he's huge," the little girl said tugging at Eamon's sleeve and pointing up at Brother Stream.

"Sophie, be polite now! Brother Stream may be up high but he can still hear a little shrimp like you down here. Instead we should congratulate the brave knight on his impressive stature. It is an honour for us to be granted this favour by Sir Stream, head captain of the Third Mission and sword bearer for General Lanos." Eamon turned to look up at the big knight, "My apologies, Sir Knight for this intrusion, had I been more circumspect rather than showing off to the girl I might have defeated my foolishness and realised that a military lecture was beneath your company."

"Nicely said Spearman, but worry not," boomed the knight, his gravel voice almost shaking Sophie in her boots. "We Hospitallers are pledged to offering all kinds of relief to the masses. The dispatches we received from the Second Mission a couple of seasons ago spoke very highly of your company and I would welcome the opportunity to stand beside you. In fact, are your company in good form for the Fayre? I would hate to stand my money beside you instead and find your reputation over stated by my excitable brothers in the Second."

"Sir, Knight, we are indeed in fine form, although this years competition will be most fierce. I am hoping for any of six placings, but I should warn you that we are already commissioned and are here for the fun."

"Very honest Sombers. My brother and I will keep that tit bit to ourselves," He said, grinning over at the other guard. "Ah, here comes Brother Gates," the big man finished as the tent flaps parted once more.

"If you would come this way, my lady." The young knight beckoned them through, winking at Sir Stream and Sombers. Within the marquee the decoration was even more ornate, with thick tapestry and velvets dividing a large communal area from a number of smaller compartments, sleeping quarters Sophie assumed.

They were led through rows of tables, where groups of knights were going about all manner of business, until they reached the far side where a middle aged man with long platted fair hair and a closely cropped beard sat sealing documents with wax. He was quickly on his feet delivering a courtly bow to Sophie, which she returned with a prim little curtsey, just as Uncle Tav had shown her. He then briskly saluted Sombers.

"Good to see you both, very good. I am Collie and will tell you some facts, a few tales and answer your questions for the time I can spare." He took the barest sign of agreement and plunged straight on. "OK, I shall begin with who you see here: we are the Third Mission. The Hospitallers are split into five Missions spread across many home bases, both small and large, in the Nation. We provide hospital facilities, the largest of which are based in the Great Forts, Grand North and Grand South over on the Battle Lands. We staff these facilities by rotating troops from the five missions. Soon we, the third, are scheduled to return to Grand North, and so please forgive my brothers here for our sloppy presentation as they may mistakenly still believe they are on leave," the fellow pitched loudly enough to carry to his nearest colleagues, who guffawed, glared or ignored him as they each saw fit.

"How does that sound, little lady?" the knight asked Sophie.

"It sounds as if you do a fine job, sir. How do your men keep their clothes so nice and clean?" Sophie asked with a girl's passion for order.

"Miss, you would not believe how much work we need to do that," the knight replied smiling. "We don't normally wear these uniforms, which are our best and finest. This year, you may have heard, the Marshall and the knightly orders have proclaimed a Crusade against our enemies. That is why we have brought a full company here to help celebrate and honour this, one of the greatest recruitment fayres." He paused briefly and then winked at Sophie continuing, "Also, dressing up like this we might impress a few people and gain ourselves some more brothers and sisters. How would you like to join us?" the gentle knight asked.

"Oh, sorry sir, I don't think Uncle Jeffers would agree to that, I am only eight," Sophie replied, looking shocked.

"Perhaps in a few years then," the knight replied with a sly smile. "Now I am afraid those gentlemen heading this way will require my time now. I hope I have been able to help," the knight finished, bowing formally.

"General, it has been an honour," Eamon replied, accepting the offered arm grip.

"Yes, thank you, err, General," Sophie said, curtsying in return to his bow.

As they left the tent Brother Stream stopped them, and kneeling smoothly he took Sophie's hand saying gallantly, "Call upon my services any time, little lady."

As they walked further on Sophie looked back to where the big knight was watching them go, and with a curiously thoughtful look he flashed her a salute before entering the tent.

*****

As Jeffers hurried through the lengthening shadows, the day almost done, towards the pitch that the fayre guard had directed him to, with news that somebody had a message for him, two figures detached themselves from the side of a nearby tent.

They stepped directly into his path and took what Jeffers saw as aggressive body postures in the faint dusk light. Surprised to be accosted at a recruitment fayre, where he was likely to know the majority of people, his hand found its own way to the hilt of his favoured hand-and-a-half sword resting at his hip belt.

"Now then boss, there won't be no need for that. We're just funning with you, man," one of the individuals called as Jeffers continued to stalk deliberately towards them.

"As I recall the last time I saw you 'funning' you lost a hand, mister," Jeffers called out in return as he stopped just short of the pair. Rather than being reassured by their comments his body looked to be tensing even more as, if to attack.

Suddenly the larger of the two started forward and he and Jeffers met in a crashing embrace.

"Claphand, how long has it been?" Jeffers asked as he finally managed to escape the embrace, and walked into the same from the next old comrade.

"And you, Mags? Time has not marred your looks," he told the disfigured woman. "Well, you aren't scared much worse than I remember. What are two old legion hands doing this far south?"

"It has been a long time, pup," Claphand answered with a strangely mellow voice for a big man. "As to what we's about, well, that is looking for you," the big dark skinned chap answered.

"The messengers you are expecting today, that's us lad,"

Mags added. "And I don't think we are exactly going to make your day. Come and share a brew with us and we will fill you in. We'll be accompanying you to the tent anyway and I don't think that the group will miss you for a few extra moments," the badly scarred woman offered.

The two legionnaires turned to walk on and Jeffers thoughtfully followed. "Look Jeffers, there ain't no easy way to say this. The boss is recalling you to serve with us and that isn't all. We have seen some weird stuff recently and things are going to change beyond the stacks, but I'll leave that to the boss to fill you in as soon as he arrives. He's round and abouts and you are to wait here at the Fayre site for him." Claphand paused but Jeffers made no comment. "In the meantime he has arranged for a possible home for the youngsters until this piece of business is concluded. He suggests that me and the lass take Sophie and Liam to stay with the Green Lady up at the lake."

"Whoa there friend, lets slow this right down," Jeffers said, stopping suddenly, causing the others to carry on a couple of paces before turning back to face him.

"I don't work for the boss man any more, I have one of my own," Jeffers spat out, feeling the pointlessness of his words almost as soon as they hit the air.

"Sorry Jeffers, but I guess this comes from yours as well. Fury was pretty sure he would get agreement from the Marshall," Mags answered.

"Still the double act," Jeffers sighed giving each a further piercing stare. When it was clear nothing else was forthcoming he decided, "Well now, we may as well head straight to the meeting, I seem to have lost my thirst for an old-time reunion, so to speak," Jeffers muttered glumly.

"Your choice Jeffers, but man, you ain't gonna believe whose going to be there." Claphand laughed, slapping him on the back with his stump.

"Why don't you just surprise me," Jeffers came back half heartedly.

As Claphand threw back the tent entrance and ushered the fixer through Jeffers began to see what he meant. The first person he spotted, sitting closest to the door on a campaign stool, was Marvellous Martin the famous swordsman and musician.

Jeffers had met him several times and liked the gruff old-timer, whom he nodded to politely. As they were sitting in a loose semi circle, clearly expecting him, Jeffers looked to the next person in sequence without hurrying. Whilst the light in the tent was fairly good Jeffers still needed a double take to recognise him though.

"I thought you were dead," was all he could say, offering his hand in a warriors grip.

"No Jeffers Star, fortunately for us the Heron is a most difficult man to kill," the next in turn answered for the old warrior who simply grunted. Jeffers turned to the man who had spoken, who was now standing although Jeffers couldn't recollect whether the fellow had been sitting or not when he had walked in the room. This man was of medium height but of powerful frame. "An honour, Master Calm," Jeffers said smoothly, offering his palm in the tradition greeting of the green plainsmen, an unspoken reference to his wife and hence the arrangement with the children.

"I am sure that now we will meet more frequently," Master Calm replied in response to his implied gesture.

The next individual in the group had the oldest appearance. Fingle Spires was also a master, but in his case from the class Armourer and Weapon Smith, truly it was unusual for the Fury's father to leave his workshop.

"Master Spires, please stay seated, truly Claphand wasn't exaggerating when he spoke of my surprise at the fellow attendees of the meeting," Jeffers said happily.

"Well, I hope that he hasn't been too free with his information," a voice hissed from the farthest corner of the tent which remained in darkness. That voice made Jeffer's hair stand on end and his hand subconsciously stray towards his weapon.

"Steady Jeffers, no need for that," came Master Calms voice soothingly.

"Err, sorry, no. No disrespect intended Master Kroll, my apologies," Jeffers said a bit too quickly for his own liking or pride.

"No matter Jeffers Star," said the giant warrior pushing his long arms forward into the light, two palms pressed together in a sign of peaceful greeting from another age and another continent.

Jeffers copied his motion and turned finally to the last member of the group. "And you, sir, must be Wayne Shield, commander of the Host Guard. Pleased to meet you," he said to the bulky armed warrior who stood alert beside his charge carrying the long footman's flail that symbolised the responsibility of the Host Guard.

"Likewise, Commander Star," came the voice, muffled by the warrior's helmet, its gaze never leaving the back of the tent where his charge was by now sitting again Jeffers assumed. It was not unusual for Master Kroll to travel to recruitment fares to judge the unarmed combat contests and for people to petition for his tuition or even apply to join the ranks of the Host Guard with their responsibility for his restraint. It was, however, very unusual for him not to be encircled by the Host Guard. But then, Jeffers supposed, if the combined presence in this tent wasn't sufficient guard then he simply didn't want to think about what might happen.

"May I, Fingle?" Master Calm asked the old armourer, whose tent it seemed to be.

"You may, my friend," the old chap replied graciously.

"Jeffers, we have asked you here today for many reasons. A great conflict is coming to our nation and you will be playing a significant part, as will all those gathered here I am sure. One thing that we want to offer you is our support." Master Calm stopped here to beam a smile round at those present.

"We have also been discussing a particular issue that together we have invested much time in, and which we hope you will participate in. If you will allow me to fill you in later on the specifics I would be grateful. I am sure you appreciate that not only do you see a great amount of talent assembled here today but also some of the most significant egos abroad in the United Nation of peoples at this time, if not ever." Master Calm chuckled at his own joke as did Marvellous who hooked a camp stool from behind him and passed it through for Jeffers to sit.

Bowing in recognition of the offer Jeffers took his ease and motioned apologetically for Master Calm to continue.

His smile unperturbed Calm continued, "We are well aware of this and whilst we are trying to compliment you by offering you our support we are also illustrating how important we consider the tasks that you will become involved in, for to each of us time is greatly valuable. We would urge you to view these endeavours in which we are involved as greatly serious. To us death is not the ultimate failure, whereas failing with our plans certainly is." Master Calm paused to allow the gravity of his words to sink in, his comments met by nods from several other individuals. "Simply put, we would appreciate your greatest efforts for we believe that your past accomplishments will be as nothing compared to what you may achieve in the future." With that oddly dramatic sentence Master Calm sat down his famously beatific expression somewhat sombre.

"Ah, now, Calm, my friend," Fingle said finally, rising to his feet, "It remains only for me to finish our peculiar little event. Whilst you may think that all I do is sit in my workshop unaware of the world and its passing, I will surprise you this day. I have come prepared, and for me prepared means, giving gifts as of course any good host should. I would say that I put a lot of thought into these items but, as I am an armourer and you are warriors, you may suspect that I have brought each of you a custom made weapon, and you would be right."

Turning to the rear of the tent he spoke into the darkness, "Master Kroll, my friend, could I impose upon you to light the lanterns near where you are sitting. I am afraid that I offered you the travelling cases as a seat my large friend." Sensing hesitation from his guest Fingle spoke reassuringly, "You need not worry, this tent is doubled lined, no shadow will be cast and you can still make a dramatic entrance tomorrow," The weapon smith finished with a wry chuckle.

"My thanks, Weapon Master," rasped the voice, as suddenly first one and then a second lantern came alight.

Jeffers caught himself staring at the seven-and-a-half span monster frame of Master Kroll. Mostly hominid, Master Kroll had appeared in Grand Fort North over a century ago, claiming to have escaped from captivity on the lost continent and asking for sanctuary within the human realms. He had spoken little of his past, and certainly not recently as far as anyone cared to let on. Rumour had it he was the result of bizarre Reptoid breeding programmes although he seemed equally disinterested in countering the other rumour, describing him just as a freak of nature.

Eventually he was transported to the north where he was kept imprisoned for a not inconsiderable period before finally loosing patience. Legend had it that he escaped as easily as walking out of the prison and appeared the next day hundreds of leagues away, insisting on an interview with the then incumbent High Marshall, who for some reason, amused by the ancient etiquette of the request, had spent some considerable period sequestered with the petitioner. What exactly was discussed was never revealed, but the agreement was taken up that Master Kroll could take up the life of a migratory teacher of unarmed combat. He was given the freedom of a large section of the north, the only condition being that he was to be followed and surrounded at all times by a heavily armed force of the Host Guard.

The final condition to his 'stay' in the north, as it was described, was a self, imposed declaration that he would never take up arms until the day when he began a quest to regain his home lands on the lost continent: a time when he would openly declare war on the Reptoids and their allies. He had decreed that within twelve weeks of that day he would march across the Battle Lands and take ship back to his home land and, whilst many people speculated, none who had ever met the impressive being would dispute that he could achieve such.

Since that agreement he had lived simply, taking between ten and one hundred students and training them excellently to perform dramatic feats of arms and valour. A bonus effect being that the Host Guard, always numbering 1000, who were there to guard him, and who were limited to short periods only of rotated service, were able to also engage in the training and had, in their own right, become a mighty force of troops. To them Master Kroll had introduced a weapon, which he called the 'footmans flail'. Despite never touching one he had instructed the host guard in techniques with it that made the steel-spike shaft, topped with a sharpened whip-like chain arrangement, into a devastating weapon especially when used against specific types of Reptoid.

Despite having seen Master Kroll several times in the past, with his grey mottled skin and enormous musculature not too dissimilar, in bulk at least, to a full grown green plainsman,

Jeffers just couldn't help but find him startling.

"Now my friends," Fingle spoke, bringing Jeffers back to the present. "If I may start with our most recent arrival, Mister Star. Jeffers, it is common knowledge that you favour a hand-and-a-half broad sword heavy and yet sharp. Marv, will you do the honours and open up box one? Thanks. Well Jeffers, I will admit that yours is not an original weapon. High Marshall Creatus, from the third century of the Nation, was once presented with a five-foot-two-handed long sword of great antiquity. Unfortunately the Marshall was killed in battle, a battle in which the tip of that impressive weapon was broken off. Since then the remains of the weapon have remained preserved in the royal armoury, such as that pile of junk is named. Our current Marshall, as we all know, looks both to the future and the past and he has given me free rein to reuse anything suitable within that collection. Now with the thicker section re-forged and given a new handle and new edge, I present to you your favoured weapon, may it serve you well."

Still wrapped in a light mix of silk and velvet cloths, Marv passed to Jeffers weapon with a plain and practical hilt work and a scabbard each decorated only with embossed stars, subtle and fine. Jeffers drew the blade a third and looked down on a very-dark blue steel that he could see, even in the poor light, carried a fine sharp edge.

"My thanks to you, Master Spires," was all he could find to say.

"Now to you, Marv. From the same collection, but requiring much less work, I present you what is called the guardian blade. It belonged, about two centuries ago to the commander of the honour guard, a valiant warrior, and in your present role, it is an apt gift. May it serve you as well as it did my great, great grandfather." Marv simply took his weapon and saluted the weapon maker.

"To you, Master Calm, I simply return some things that I have kept for you, I hope that you will forgive my presumption and that these will not serve you ill."

"Commander Shield, for you and your charge I have matching weapons, although on different scales. Sir, I realise that generally you fashion your own flails as part of the right of

187

ownership, but in this case you may forgive my presumption. If you would keep Master Kroll's until a time that is suitable I should be grateful."

"Your gift honours myself and my teacher," Wayne Shield answered, sketching a bow in the direction of the smith but still not taking his eyes away from his charge.

"And finally, Heron, my old friend, for you who was at one time famous for loosing quality weapons I have a battle axe of a new design, please hang on to it long enough to let me have some feedback." Fingle returned to his seat and, as if recalling his list of duties with the difficulty of his age, was already sitting down before turning back to Marvellous. "Marv, of the two boxes left please take the shorter one, it contains something for your charge. The longer one, leave that, it is just a present for my son had he been able to make this meeting."

"Now, if you don't mind, this old fellow would like a nightcap and some rest. Good luck to you all."

Chapter Ten

On the night of Lauren's final fight she prepared by dressing carefully. Her small clothes were all comfortable and designed to be worn in combat. Next a tight undershirt and breeches, with a fitted, sleeveless, mail shirt, heavy belt, upper and lower arm greaves with bars, a quilted over-jacket and right arm shoulder guard were all added carefully in turn. Even her boots had built-in greaves and mail ankle protectors. On her head she had a two piece, full-face helm and, together with her shield, was stylishly adorned with the sigil of a whip. The idea of the two-piece helm was that she could remove the face section to end her battle run at the conclusion of her final fight as champion. While many may have suspected, or known her to be the current tournament champion, the unmasking would be symbolic and ensure her retirement. After all, when the public knew her identity the full effect of the law would apply and neither herself, the organisers nor potential challengers could cause her to fight another tournament bout.

Lauren was always careful to eat lightly before fighting. She had exercised gently whilst putting on the gear so as to warm up and to ensure the correct fit. As all her kit was well worn in, the extra care she took might have been over the top, but her training had been explicit and given her a completely professional outlook.

Two parts after dusk, bundled in a cloak, Lauren flitted carefully through the streets, down the hill and into the middle of the dock district, east of the club and barracks. Arriving at the warehouse she went straight to the dressing room to deposit a short sword and meet with the referee and weapons master for weapons choice. The earlier bout, however, had been delayed. Waiting in the changing room on this, her sixth, fight seemed worse than any of the others. It wasn't that she was poorly prepared or that in standing down her identity would be revealed or even the fact that her scheduled opponent had withdrawn at the last moment and been replaced by the mystery winner of the previous event's newcomers competition.

She had taken the first fight as a way to discipline an unruly member of her squad and to gain her command's respect. Having entered anonymously she had found the excitement of the offer of a second fight too tempting and had continued her run to five, taking the previous champion in her fourth fight. The tension and pressure she felt now was almost painful, but it was more than the fight. It seemed to be, she decided, that the failure of resolving Chloe's death, and her lack of progress, was building up inside her like a great pressure, and the potent rush of tournament fighting was no longer sufficient as a pressure valve. Instead, tonight was just another distraction preventing her from resolving the mystery and doing something positive.

*****

Taverner, sitting in the stands, could almost feel Lauren's distraction as she came out for the warm-up. He disliked the fights intensely, but had visited once before after somebody had commented that the current champion fought in an unusual manner. It had taken him scant moments to identify the fighter as Lauren, and Barf, who had been tailing her and loosing her when she had reached the fight arena, (unfortunately because he was professional enough to be searching for her and not watching the competition bouts) had been sceptical when Taverner had informed him. He had never lost her in that way since though. On this occasion Taverner was ostensibly with the Admiral's party on a combined event, in part staged at the fight venue and in part held as an exclusive meal for the Admiral and a select few back at the club.

As the challenger came out, Taverner's eyes widened slightly. There was no doubt that this man was a product of the Horde's combat camps which trained and fought gladiators to the death in a 'reward and survival of the fittest' kind of arrangement. No, he was a regular arena fighter certainly and his warm up was precise, extreme and very, very professional. Taverner wondered what was distracting Lauren and whether she would notice.

In the end he felt that her distraction probably helped her and allowed all the training that she had received to pour out, untainted by nervy constraint, as her mind worked something else over.

Her luck also seemed to run to the challenger being new in town. For whilst she barely turned several early attacks, cruelly aimed to cripple her, but expertly and professionally delivered, he appeared never to have seen her fight. If he had then he wouldn't have walked into one of her unorthodox moves, but one which Taverner had heard a couple of the fight fans discuss. Anyway, he ducked low beneath what he thought was going to be a cut, only to walk straight into her mailed fist. By the time he regained consciousness her identity had been revealed and Lauren had taken the salute and hurried out the arena, apparently unaware that her opponent had been a ringer.

Taverner was relieved that whilst Lauren was a pretty poor spy her combat instructors had strengthened her natural abilities and forged her into a potent weapon.

He rode back to the club with the Admiral, who was commenting overly on the skill of Lauren keeping everybody guessing for so long. As they travelled Taverner pondered whether the attempt to injure Lauren indicated that the plot was speeding up or just that the opposition had tired of her meddling. Certainly the same thing could have been achieved more permanently and with fewer witnesses outside of the fights, so maybe secrecy was still required. Or was a warning being sent? Taverner felt that if only he could get some kind of firm clue as to the origin of the Roke spymaster, he would gain more insight. The introduction of tonight's specialist opponent demonstrated hidden resources but provided no further precise detail. Any effort to trace tonight's warrior would no doubt reveal little, especially as he would probably be found face down in the harbour on the morrow, if ever found at all. Failure, Taverner suspected, in the enemy camp was not likely to be taken particularly well.

*****

Halfway between dusk and midst-night, her fight over, Lauren hardly paused in the dressing room. Part way through the fight she had decided to penetrate the dockside facility. After the fight went as expected Lauren headed down to the docks. She left the warehouse and heading directly east soon reached the quay front; turning to the left she headed towards the Baker's compound in the northeast of Buccaneer Town. She made good time and soon arrived outside the fence, unaware that she had been spotted one time too many by the compound guards, who had recently received orders to lure her into a trap should she be detected.

Obedient to his orders, on receiving the news that Lauren had been identified, the compound commander arranged for one of his men to inspect the outer fence. Making it look as if he had been called back unexpectedly by a fellow guard, the appointed man left his gate unlatched and partially open as he hurried off into the compound.

Quick to spot this, and determined to finally investigate her suspicions, Lauren rushed through the gate and slipped into the shadows, just in time to avoid the returning guard who closed the gate quickly as if he had inspected it and found it still open.

Looking around the yard she saw that regular guards were patrolling most of the areas, but it seemed to Lauren that if she took the advantage, one of the closest warehouse patrols was thin enough to allow her to reach its interior.

*****

Arriving moments after Lauren, it still took Barf some significant time to reach a convenient roof top. Not simply being able to break a window he had to gain more stealthy access to a building which would provide him with a useful view.

As he slithered carefully to the edge of the roof to survey the scene he looked down in time to see Lauren slip through the gate. "Bloody sloppy guards," he murmured to himself and then, looking more carefully, drew in a sharp breath as he wondered whether it was sloppy or deliberate. Lauren passed cleanly through a large open space, conspicuous by the absence of patrols, whilst the rest of the yard was guarded like a fortress.

Before Barf could find a way to send Lauren a warning she was inside the warehouse and obscured from view. Racking his brains he decided he would follow her, using the same route. Taking one last look he realised that now the gate was as heavily guarded as all the others and the patrols had returned to that particular area. Was it just coincidence and had Lauren been lucky to find such a good opportunity or had she been lured into a trap?

Surely if it had been a trap, Barf thought, then the warehouse would have been quickly surrounded, but despite the returning patrols no effort seemed to be made to capture the intruder. Barf, therefore, determined simply to wait, hoping that Lauren was ghosting around an empty building looking for clues.

For a short time after she had entered the building Lauren was, indeed, ghosting. Suddenly her world went black as a heavy blow crashed into her left ear. She had been trained by the best, though, and even in the dark, from behind she had detected the motion at the last moment. Able to roll with the blow she came off much more lightly than the Master Baker had intended. Even so it did not prevent her from receiving a good whack and passing out.

Satisfied that she had received the full weight of his cosh the baker looked down at her prone form and bit back an urge to chuckle. Finally, despite his instructions, he had been able to enter the action, and he liked the way it felt.

"What good to have the perfectly trained warrior, if he was never used as a weapon?" the traitor said to himself. He then picked up the weight of the armoured female and slinging her over his shoulder as if she were a string of onions he jogged out through the rear doors and hurriedly crossed the yard to the boat scheduled for a visit to his controller. Tossing her in he instructed his men to bind her arms and legs and place her in an empty cage somewhere near the Marine Patrol officer.

*****

Meanwhile, up on the roof Barf had company. This meant that whilst the baker was crossing the yard Barf was distracted, although he was able to catch glimpses of the courtyard, enough to sense signs of serious movement. Hanging from his fingertips, having lowered himself over the edge of the flat roof at the first sound of the patrol, his toes balanced on the lintel above a window he held himself still whilst a team of Roke agents searched his rooftop. This initially allowed Barf to continue his surveillance. It was when he suddenly saw lanterns across on the roof opposite as well that, adjusting his grip, he pulled first his face up under the guttering and then the full weight of his outstretched legs until he was stretched horizontal. Keeping the length of his body parallel to the roof overhang he could hold on and not fall six stories to the cobbles below, remaining hidden in the darkness of the roof lip, his view mostly obstructed, until the patrols withdrew.

"Still as gymnastic as ever," he grunted to himself, some eighth later, as his cramping arms dragged the dead weight of his torso back over the lip and onto the flat part of the roof.

He wondered what had happened over in the compound whilst he had been playing hide and seek with the traitors. Security, if anything, seemed to be tightening, but there was still no audible or visible evidence of a search or any other kind of disturbance. In fact the only change to the scene was that a small fishing boat was just pulling away from the quayside, all quiet and peaceful like. Barf sighed at his impotence and settled down to watch, listen and wait.

*****

Lauren gradually came around and from the first glimmer of consciousness was careful not to betray any sign that she was awake. The world seemed to be moving gently around her until she realised she was on a boat which, whilst explaining the movement, didn't particularly reassure her.

'Where was the baker taking her?' she asked herself, for somehow she felt sure he was on the boat with her. She checked her predicament: arms and legs tied and her head sticking out of the top of a narrow, vertical, body-sized cage attached in a row of six. As her eyes adjusted she could make out that two other units seemed to be occupied by people, either unconscious themselves or drugged or even dead.

One of the prisoners appeared to be wearing the uniform of the Marine Patrol, an officer of the watch by the look of her. Well, help to escape was not an option Lauren decided. She would need to look out for herself. The ropes themselves she could manage with the sharpened edges on both her mailed gauntlets and boots, designed for just such an eventuality. But quite what she would do about the cage she didn't know. That could prove tricky.

Lauren was glad she had been careful not to move her head openly to look around, for she soon realised that the cage was in an open hold. After hearing some communication with the sea gate controllers she sensed they had passed out of Bucc harbour and were moving further out to sea. The tarp covering the hold was thrown back and through lidded eyes she saw the Master Baker climb out of the hold. Emerging smoothly from the dark corner in which he had been sitting, he was quickly on deck peering carefully down into the hold as if inspecting his catch.

As he stood there for a good while she felt her neck muscles begin to stiffen in her awkward posture. Eventually he turned about and quietly gave orders to moor the boat. No sooner had they done so than she heard a splash, as if somebody had been cast over the side, and for long moments she was unobserved and got to the business of loosening her bonds.

*****

When the baker had first been subjected to the presence of the Mind Squid, years earlier, he had associated entering the water with proximity to the creature and, therefore, fear. In those days, of course, he had been pumped full of the addictive drugs and therefore much less himself.

Recently though, the baker had begun to approach his encounters with the beast with more mixed emotions. In the same way that the blend of drugs he had been forcibly addicted too had begun to fade in effect, so the effects of the mind-tunnelling of the squid had become a more fluid experience. He was sure that the monster could detect something of the change and several weeks ago it had attempted to imprint a stronger

195

residual control on the baker's mind.

The baker with his secret regime of mental exercise was happy now, though, that he was able to enter and leave the sessions with this set of alien thoughts in place, but could tidy them away into an unused mental space on a day to day basis. His current theory being that the Mind Squid would consider him suitably restrained but, actually, away from the water the baker had his free will intact.

It was the compulsion of the summons, rather than its power or range, which were increasing, that the baker felt on the boat when it was tethered above the meeting point. That had faded. In fact the baker felt that he was much more able to penetrate the thoughts and knowledge supposedly hidden deep within the creature than the creature could now manage with him.

Not that the baker was necessarily preparing to betray his controller: the creature and its water-borne powers being the link to his homeland, still the only place that he felt truly comfortable. It was just that he had always felt that the process the mind creatures used felt so unnatural and intrusive that he had begun working on a way to adapt his mind to the process, the side effect being that he was becoming stronger at the expense of the creature's power over him.

As he swam down he felt the familiar warmth wash over his face as he opened his mind to the mental pictures and sensations from far away.

*****

For Lauren, working on her bonds, all too soon more shadows were cast over the open hold and a couple of crew members came into view, fastening what looked like a small derrick crane to the side of the vessel. This was soon finished and she heard more voices. One, the baker's, at first sounded oddly indistinct but soon became clearer. Suddenly crew members were sliding down into the hold attaching chains to the cage, which was unceremoniously drawn into the moonlight as fast as the crew could work the crank wheel.

As the six-person cage came out of the hold Lauren was

surprised to glimpse the baker, soaking wet, towelling his hair dry. He had an odd expression, half elation half distaste, on his face and she wondered what on earth was important enough to send him down into the cold water. As she rose level with and then past him she heard him murmur, "Farewell now, my lovely, soon all will be clear to us. Farewell."

Then the cage was over the side Only as the crew member knocked out the fixing bolt did she realise that they simply intended to drop the whole arrangement over the side and into the water. With one smooth motion the cage plunged through the water; it was all she could do to remember to take a deep breath and wait for the disturbed water to settle. The cage did not have far to descend and soon came to a halt, still upright although completely submerged, and close enough to the surface for Lauren to make out the ship through the moonlight. The nearby sea floor was similarly littered with the debris of other cage episodes.

Hoping she could not, in turn be, seen from above, already free of the ropes intended to keep her upright, she immediately bent into the cage to free herself from the other bindings and crouching down worked her arms free and then her legs.

Whether her bending down caused the creature not to see her she would never know, but first off it visited the non-uniformed captive at the far end of the cage. Things seemed to move in slow motion. Although Lauren was working frantically she still had time to see the creature flap its way gracefully through the water above the cages, and settle what she assumed was its head region over the face of its unfortunate victim. The contact did not last long and soon the creature moved closer to Lauren. As she finally freed her bonds it settled on the marine officer.

Closer now, she could see it had a strange cloak-like body that flapped it through the water, which though strange, was nowhere as scary as its head, which was much bigger than a human's. Despite having a domed forehead and a distinct pair of glowing green eyes, that was where normality ended, for where its nose might have been its face became a mass of green, blue and purple glowing tentacles that obscured, she supposed, its mouth region. As she saw the ruined face of the first victim she realised that the creature, and not drowning, would claim her life and she forced herself as far down into the cage as she could manage, her hands scrabbling around the sea floor for something of use to defend herself.

Whilst she was hunting with her hands she couldn't take her eyes off the creature and its hypnotic gaze, although later she tried in vain to convince herself that it was the woozy effects of being forced to hold in breath so long.

Almost in slow motion she saw its tentacles come towards the unfortunate woman officer's face, which seemed almost to come back to consciousness for those few instants before it became engulfed in the mass of tentacles. Closer up, Lauren saw a different reaction this time, the creature, which she subconsciously recorded as a squid, spent measurable moments clutching the human, whose body began to jerk in a most unpleasant manner. Then all too soon Lauren felt the creature's gaze turn to herself and its expression changed slightly as it looked down and found her fully conscious.

Lauren began to feel a longing, almost strong enough to force her to stand upright as the creature used its powers to command her to plunge her face into its hideous tentacles. Luck went Lauren's way, for as her hand found the flaky iron of an old boat hook, a possible weapon, she regained some composure. By now her lungs were bursting and she felt close to blacking out, as she realised in horror that the hook was firmly trapped under the heavy cage. Lauren knew that by herself she had no chance of freeing the boat hook. In desperation she tore loose the metal plate that formed her left boot's shin guard, and surging upwards defiantly plunged her hand up to her forearm deep within the creature's mouth. What the metal plate damaged Lauren could only guess, but it must have been part of the damnable beast's brain for it seemed to loose its mental powers immediately. Convulsing its powerful body a few times the creature buffeted the cage right at the top, knocking it over onto its side, and smashing from her body what little breath Lauren retained. Further out Lauren's darkening vision saw the creature's body drop onto the cage and sea floor, dead a gout of air bubbles and thick blood that discolouring the water rising from it.

In her early stages of drowning Lauren pushed her hand out

through the cage almost as a spasm, trying to direct some of the bloody air into her mouth. Partially successful a few gulps later, now almost gagging on the metallic taste of the blood, she realised she had lost the boot plate, but her hand touched the boat hook which this time moved. Somewhere deep in her air starved brain she realised the hook was free from the weight of the cage.

*****

On board the boat moored above, the baker's patience finally gave out. He wasn't used to the Mind Squid taking long with its victims, for it had incredible power to tear information from a human mind when there was no need for the subject to survive the experience.

That the baker had neglected to feed Lauren the drugs, leaving her resistive to its commands, had meant that the creature was focusing its full powers on her. Trapped in its final preparations to merge with her mind as she surged upwards to stab it, the creature was not given the opportunity to communicate with the baker as its physical brain, and then mental powers, collapsed inwards as it haemorrhaged to death.

'Surely the creature would have identified the two female intelligence sources and started with them?' the baker thought. If so, then by now he would have been signalled back into the water. As the creature was dying the baker, who had already given the order to turn the boat and therefore missed the physical signs of the struggle, sent his own communication down through the water and assumed that the emptiness he found meant that creature had left for wherever it had made its lair.

Whilst he was surprised that Lauren had contained nothing of interest the baker was used to Reptoids showing little interest in human concepts, such as politeness. He simply ordered the crew to cast off the mooring, intending to follow his plans as previously confirmed; impatient to get the final operation under way, he ordered the boat to set sail.

*****

Dimly aware that the position of the boat was changing, somehow Lauren levered the metal bar into the nearest hinge of the cage, Its three spans of leverage, and her desperation managed to free the hinge enough for her to squeeze partly through. She thrashed her arms in vain, trying to wriggle towards the surface, more from reflex than awareness, desperate not to be abandoned out at sea, already half drowned. Suddenly she was stuck in the back, and turning to fight off some new predator she was buffeted again, wrapping her arms around the assailant as she had no way to escape. As the vessel, now under sail, began to move away the thing that had hit her, and which she had grabbed hold of defensively, turned out to be a trailing sea anchor that had been overlooked. Tightening her grip just in time, it pulled her like a stone from an unripe plum, all bruised flesh and torn skin but never the less free of the watery prison.

How Lauren dragged herself to the surface, and gulping in blasts of air and water in equal measures, managed to not only hold on but also pull herself close enough to the ship to grab a more suitable hull rope, she would never remember, but hold on until they returned to the dock she did.

*****

As the baker's boat returned to the harbour mouth Piker sat atop the club's highest level. He had the north and east to watch whilst Lawrence had the other side. Both were sitting back to the chimneystack. It was a quiet night and Piker was carefully honing his short sword, gentle stroke after gentle stroke, skilfully moving his gaze back and forth in time with the blade on the stone. As the night moved on and he became satisfied with the razor-sharp edge, he eased the blade into his shoulder sheath and pulled a leather roll from his belt. This contained a set of spearheads, fresh from the armourer, encased in soft baked clay and wrapped in waxed paper. He had brought up a shallow bowl and short, spear width stick and he began to unwrap a leaf shaped spearhead, quickly glancing down. Just as he had it clear and was cracking off the outer clay a faint horn blast came to him from the harbour. He glanced up and called softly to Lawrence; at the same time a nearby roof boy whistled that he had heard a call, and then whistled forwards a query to his next and closest companion, closer to the docks. Part of Piker's brief on starting at the club had been to work with Millie to organise a small network of roof based sentries who could pass intelligence quickly around the town.

Soon enough he and Lawrence had the group of ward kids well organised: making nests on key rooftops and by swapping shifts they kept up a continual watch. Piker then simply organised the rotation of staff, who manned the club's rooftop, to pass the watchers' information down into the club and attend periodic briefings from Millie. That night the news was from Barf and it appeared to be serious.

*****

The first full night of the fayre was always the biggest musical performance of the event. The band had planned its programme so that Blue Boy joined with them after the first interval to replace Mitch, who good naturedly had agreed to the young prodigy having a percussion slot for the second set.

Now midway through the third section, with Mitch back on drums, Blue Boy was still buzzing from the performance, now a little more convinced that he might be allowed to campaign with the band. He was sitting for the conclusion of the concert with Marvellous' friend, Heron, and two young lads. These boys had been competing in the combat trials. One lad, Trince by name, sported a bandaged, cut and bruised face. On the far side of the fire Blue Boy was introduced to a very tough looking yet mature lady who named herself Mother. The final two comrades, who Blue Boy had met briefly the previous evening, had shocked him into stunned silence. The smaller, jovial mannered chap was revealed as the legendary Master Calm; his juggling companion was revealed as none less than Fingle Spires, the Master Armourer and father of legendary Legion commander, Fury. Nonetheless, neither of these two erstwhiles displayed anything other than easy natured friendliness, and certainly none of the other companions appeared overly awed.

Blue Boy immediately took to re-assessing the rest of the campfire fellows for signs of celebrity. He noticed that the two young lads also displayed a degree of politeness and attentive conversation that revealed a certain lack of familiarity and he was glad that he was not alone in being new to such social circles.

The hillside above the performance area offered a most attractive setting and, as night settled in more fully, the sunset across the valley merged with the placement of the braziers to set off the band's position spectacularly. Away to the left down, the hill, Blue Boy could make out the campfires of the competition site and camping areas that surrounded the rocky outcrop for about seventy percent of its exposure. Most people, though, appeared to have made the short climb up the slope to where the bandstand and the viewing terraces occupied the hillside. The terraces, and indeed the area offset below where the stage was constructed appeared so well worn as to be natural phenomena, although Blue Boy suspected that they were so perfect a viewing gallery for the spectators that they had originally been engineered.

Looking out across the terraces, Boy Blue could see from the extent of the crowds, that the attraction of the band was, as many people claimed, as big a draw as the competition itself.

His attention brought back to his companions, Blue Boy was interested to see a shadow detach itself from the darkness next to Master Calm, who rose and gave the figure a small, neat bow: an act from a Master that only served to increase Blue Boy's attention. The figure was dressed in baggy, flowing robes that hung down in layers, each overlapping, and cleverly forming a tunic and trousers that billowed with each movement, rippling like somebody wearing a number of cloaks on a windy day. As the figure stepped into the firelight Blue Boy was shocked to see that the man, and it was only an assumption, had skin made up of swirling coloured patterns of blues and oranges and reds. Almost as if the figure could sense his interest 'he' made his way around the fire, pausing slightly to greet the other companions, until he stopped before Blue Boy, offering a bow and then a hand to ease Blue Boy to his feet. As he took the grip Blue Boy could feel that the stranger's arms were covered by long soft cotton gloves, dyed to match what appeared to be face paint.

"Blue Boy, I must commend you on your performance," an eerily soft voice told him. "It has been a pleasure finally to see you perform. I am sure that Smee's loss is Calm's gain. Good luck to you young man." Then the figure was gone, his gait almost smooth enough to be described as gliding over the ground.

"I see you have met Painted Stan," Master Spire's voice brought Blue Boy back to himself, causing him to realise that he had been staring off into the night where the figure had disappeared.

"Er... Sorry Master Spires. Who was that?" Blue Boy mumbled in embarrassment.

"It was Painted Stan, Blue Boy. Sit yourself down and I will tell you something of the Painted People." Master Fingle directed the cadet with a gesture to take a seat. "Back before the threat of the Horde, there were the humans, like myself, and the Rainbow Folk, like yourself. To be honest they didn't always get along. Humans by their very nature tend to aggressive behaviour, and if left unoccupied we tend to work our way into disagreement. There were, back then, a number of unpleasant, if minor on today's scale, conflicts, particularly between your own Blue People and certain human nations. If we describe the human antagonists back then as bad then there were also humans who were good, who honoured their relationships with the Rainbow Folk. One such group was the mountain hill tribes who went so far as to wear their faces painted in ritualistic coloured patterns to honour all the Rainbow Folk. These tribes remain today, and although spread in very small communities they live in harmony with their neighbours, be they Human or Homanid. Most commonly they are found living in the hills or mountains amongst the Greys. In short, the tribes always honour their military commitments and there is usually at least one of the Painted People fighting with the Army of the North. It is most common that the tribe whose turn it is will send a chieftain or a talented son or daughter. They are almost always hardy and competent fighters, and in this case Painted Stan is truly exceptional."

Master Fingle paused as if choosing the correct words. "The tribes' people are quiet and polite, bound by ancient codes of conduct. It is, therefore, most interesting that Painted Stan acts as the Giphon's lieutenant; a small island of calm in the stormy sea of ruffians that make up the rest of the company. Eight years Stan has fought for us and if he wasn't due to return to assume his status as tribe chieftain he would no doubt be a potential Master of the future. It is odd but fitting that he came to speak with you for he is something of an enigma, rarely leaving the Griphon's rabble except when he actually competes. He will be this fayre's champion for sure."

*****

When Barf had moved to avoid the sentry patrol he had missed Lauren being off-loaded onto the boat, but waiting and watching a couple of parts later he saw the boat return, lighter by the look of the displacement. After a further period of waiting he saw Lauren, through his spy lens, slip back over the side.

"War burns," he swore to himself. With the numerous sentries now visible around the compound she had little chance of remaining undetected. He also worried by her condition, it looked as if she had travelled a long distance in the water.

Running quickly to the farthest end of the rooftop he hung down and pilfered a street lantern from its bracket on the wall. Tampering with the wick he ensured that it would keep burning even after he had cracked the clay oil reservoir. Then he threw it in a long arc, out over the compound wall and into a heap of tarps, all well coated with fish oils from the decks of the trawlers which now sat gathering barnacles around the compounds' dock allocations.

Starting a decoy fire was risky, and after that he was committed, and so with hardly any hesitation pulled out a small hand-horn and let out a burst of coded notes that shrilled back from the docks into town.

Running to the door of his cabin the compound guard commander spotted the blazing tarps and the nearby wooden walls already ablaze and sent a message down into the cavern via a runner. He then ordered another guard to ring the alert bell and bustled out into the yard to deal with the horn blower arsonist.

The Master Baker sat below in the cavern and cursed as the news reached him of the disturbance. To avoid any action now might add risk to the offensive later, by allowing the remaining town defences to discover some of his planning. "Well a few parts extra to hold shouldn't affect the plan too badly," he announced to nobody in particular. Just after midst-night he gave hasty orders for the acceleration of the traitorous attack, some three day-parts earlier than planned.

Lauren made good use of the state of alert and activity within the compound. She began her escape through the confusion of the fire. As the compound commander and some eight men exited the compound to search for the fire starter in the surrounding buildings, little did they know that Barf had taken his diversion scheme much further, and behind the smoke and heat of the blaze had jumped to a jarring rest on top of the fence before heaving himself over.

As the fire-fighting guards began to arrive the smoke acted as a screen and many of the compound personnel were dead within moments from Barf's stealthy knives, their bodies heaved into the flames. Sweating in the heat he maintained a loose plan, to fight within the compound for an eighth and weaken the gate guard in the nearby area. Hopefully, Lauren would spot his interference, or just the opportunity, and escape through the exit with the fewest visible guards.

With the smoke sporadically billowing and clearing Barf needed to fight harder as the guards gradually became aware of one or more intruders inside the compound. He thought he gained an occasional glimpse of Lauren, stealthily creeping towards one of the exits.

Deciding to force her hand Barf picked up a sword and spear and stepped far enough out of the smoke to be seen. Bellowing, "Lauren this way!" he proceeded to cast the spear, which brought down a lantern further into the compound in a rain of burning oil. He proceeded to hack down the nearest few guards as they ran to attack him.

Lauren didn't need to be invited twice. She ran quickly past him, pausing only long enough to scoop up a weapon from a fallen guard, and unaware that the brave man was on his own and not part of a co-ordinated rescue effort, she sped to a gate and quickly dispatching the two remaining sentries was soon out on the street.

When Barf was sure she was some distance clear and out into an area that Snakey Pete, his backup, could clear for her, he decided to look to himself. Despite being singed and a bit bruised from the jump, and with palms and fingertips bleeding from the exertions on the roof, so far he had not been cut by the defenders. Deciding he would like to keep things that way he ducked back into the smoke and out of the same compound exit that Lauren had used.

Knowing Snakey would have grasped the basic essentials of his plan from the horn warning he had sent, he was surprised when several more healthy Roke guards appeared. Only after a furious fight was he able to get away any distance down the streets around the compound.

Dodging and weaving through the winding, narrow, dock front streets he could hear drums and calls back in the compound, and taking a breather he started looking for any sign of Lauren or his back-up. Roughly where he expected Pete's initial position to be, he snuck into an alley. Sprawled on the ground in a dark corner he could see a shape which as he moved closer came into focus as his comrade. Snakey Pete had clearly been dead for some time and lying face up, his open eyes staring at the sky, Barf could discern no wounds to his front despite the great pool of blood under him. Two other bodies lay close by, showing Pete hadn't been taken completely by surprise.

At the entrance to the alley Barf sensed some movement and three more potential assailants came into view. Rather than compound guards these men were dressed more professionally and approached Barf as if they had been waiting for him.

"You see, Clegg, I told you the flesh would return for his pup. What a sadly predictable end for someone the chief claims is dangerous. Why didn't you run home, flesh? You could have died in the warm then flesh!" the apparent leader of the warriors spat.

"You stabbed him in the back, or shot him down, you miserable cur," Barf returned. Seeing the wounds and the damage inflicted on Pete, with so few apparent casualties, Barf knew these men must be good or tricky and began to worry more for Lauren.

"Oh no, the flesh is angry with us Stegg," joked one of the other warriors as all three drew blackened blades. "Well, we had better hurry him to meet his friend again."

"Oh, save your wind scum bag!" Barf called, his voice irritated but controlled. "Let me see you put your money where your mouths are."

A tenth later Barf finished wiping the blood from his knives. 'They had been good, very, very good. No wonder Pete had lost,' Barf thought. He bent down and patted his comrade on the shoulder one last time, closed his eyes and lay his sword down on his chest in an honourable pose. "No shame, lad," he whispered.

Then he was up and running, for if this was the standard of Roke warriors roaming Buccaneer Town then, out in the dark, he needed to find Lauren before they found her.

After five more streets he began to catch the tail end of a party of brigands, only to become entangled in a series of brief but savage fights. He could hear further fighting up ahead but once the party became aware of him behind them they began to disregard their orders, fighting him instead. A fact which Barf hoped would allow Lauren more breathing space. As he fought he wondered at the numbers of warriors that had been sent out in such a short space of time.

Lauren, herself, had felt her hopes rise when, despite being chased by a group of ruffians, a couple of arblast-equipped night watch guards investigating the sounds of combat came upon her, a few streets from the compound. Lauren blurted out her troubles. They took her at face value and bravely stood and tried to face down the pack, shooting down two before all three of them became involved in a fight against a greater number of opponents.

The younger and more reckless of the watchmen threw himself into the mêlée, shouting that his companion should get the girl free; this released enough space for the other two to dash off in the opposite direction. Buoyed up by his notion of chivalry the watchman indeed held off the rabble for several moments, until he was shot in the belly by a close range arblast, and falling to the floor had his throat cut savagely.

Barf reached the scene of the commotion within moments and jumping over the four dead or dying Roke and the watchman ploughed into the back of the remaining rabble, causing half of the remaining ten to turn and fight.

Two streets further on Lauren and the watchman were again caught and, turning to fight the watchman, soon found that it was Lauren defending him and not the other way round. With a little more space he began bellowing over the commotion "Help! Woman attacked! Help!"

Quickly, several noble-minded towns people arrived to help defend her against the mob of assailants who, despite being attacked on two fronts, were being reinforced regularly from the dock area, a fact which both hindered Barf but also helped to carry him along in a sudden surge of bodies, out the other side to within lengths of where Lauren was fighting. However, as the locals pulled down two more ruffians others rushed them and soon the second watchman was stabbed and fell down dying, along with the few mostly unarmed towns folk. Through some furious action Barf made it to Lauren. Only defending against the pressure they began to back up enough so that when they suddenly turned to flee towards the club, hand-in-hand, the mob was slow to pursue them and they slipped the nearest few assailants and headed off again, running up the hill. Getting to within a couple of streets of the club Barf pulled out a whistle to report to the club, which was now close enough to hear his summons.

*****

At a half part past Midst-night the Collector looked out at the flotilla islands, which once constructed had worked brilliantly as the landing platform. The huge central vessel propelled into position by the Reptoid Bigatrons lay at anchor, with vast numbers of other purpose built craft chained to it, to provide a basic kind of floating quay across which further troops could easily clamber as vessels continued to arrive.

Twenty thousand of his troops now stood on the human shores with thousands more due to land over the next three days. The northern defences had been brushed aside like insects. With the holding force that was to be left behind, and with Buccaneer Town due to fall in the next few parts, the invasion of the last remaining human realm looked to hold. The Collector, a traitor to his own nation, decided to stick with the original plan, despite the fact that the second wave of his ships was reported delayed.

To the north the giant forms of the Bigatrons had disappeared into the darkness. With the nearest wall guards poisoned the huge beasts had been able to approach the walls free from the threat of fire. Using their huge bony tails they had beaten at the walls until their combined strength had smashed stones free, allowing them to tear down an opening through which they could proceed. Once through, the Collector had arranged for a Siblant to instruct the powerful but slow monsters that they were free to roam at will, their only instruction to do it northwards along the wall.

Within the part, and much further in land, standing in the ruins of the Defence Force relief camp the Collector became more confident still. The breaching of the wall and the spread of the troop deployment had occurred at a speed that surprised even him. He had, as planned, left only a token force at the breach to hold it until the next wave of troops landed. Now with a clear pathway inland ahead of him so the assault on Buccaneer Town to the south seemed only of low priority. Happily, early reports made it sound as if the troops tasked with that would also succeed.

Therefore, waiting only long enough to hear confirmation of the start of the town assault, the corrupted general set off, heading at speed for the central region. His intelligence indicated that the Marshall was in the middle of launching an assault of his own, a fact that could only help to spread the defence resources even thinner. Never before had the Horde been so close to taking the ripe northern land. The Collector would proceed by destroying key, central, military bases and then wait for a link up with the other forces when they finally arrived. Eventually he would fall on the High Fort, with such numbers behind him that it would never stand, and his revenge would be complete. Once the Northern Command's base was taken and occupied the surrounding area to the sea would become the prime staging ground for a full and massive Horde influx. With the numbers due to arrive, his follow up forces could not fail to batter the coastal forces into submission, and he would become a king amongst the Roke.

As he stood revelling in imagined future victories, looking back over the remnants of the coastal battlements, watching the van of his force move off into the interior, the Collector recalled his instructions from the Reptoid sub-leader who had set his orders the day that they embarked.

The First Claw had come to him in person, saying, "Your humans of the north are our greatest threat. They remember and know what it is like to be pushed. True, they are fewer in number than the other nations, but they are more prepared for our coming and have more spirit for the fight. There is more than we can see. In the same way that we have evolved for war, so has the north. The mixing of the strains of man is dangerous to us for you live closer to your legends. As we come into our power so may human spirit allow our threat to be countered. The War Leader opens my eyes and I, too, can see that the main danger are the northerners and the distant ones coloured blue, they, too, are dangerous to our plans." Much of the Reptoid rhetoric had washed over the Collector's drug fuelled conscious mind, but his powers of recollection remained perfect as always.

The beast had continued, "Before he sleeps the leader will visit the breeding pens once more. The next generation of children will bring terror to all human scum. Those more arrogant and less watchful distant nations will cower as the brood spreads. More terrible than those yet seen, the plains shall ring with our cries. Go, you Collector, and pay me the tribute that you owe."

Despite his petty pretensions of power the Collector subsequently missed the more important information. Immediately after he had departed the sub-leader was summoned for a rather one sided mind contact with the Horde Leader for further orders. Pictures and sensations had flowed across the link bombarding the First Claw with instructions and taking information from his mind, no need for phrased answers.

In essence the leader had said. "First Claw, return to Battle Lands and finalise release of the Infestor Imps, the Battle Lands must remain stable for their transport… Have we bred enough to strip clean the north within a cycle...? No... When the numbers match open the Mountain and let lose the trial batch beyond the wall... But have a care, ensure no breeders are sent, once free we could not contain the flow, they will not be stopped... First Claw, do you suspect the flesh have any concept yet of our plan...? Only limited investigation by the leader of the flesh... Good... We must not delay fleet, it must serve to distract their attention... Move all the occupying Roke garrisons forwards by most direct route... It will just look like strengthening support for major raid on the fortresses."

Pausing only for the briefest instant, so that the First Claw's mind would not be swamped with information, the message finished, "Roke must remain unaware of plan... even most conditioned human slaves would falter should they divine what we intend... next few weeks Roke traffic with lost continent must tail off... traffic diverted... cages are readied for the transport of imps...each a mature miniature Reptoid needing to eat twice its body weight of food per day... three weeks until breeding cycle... use conditioned Siblants for patrol... Push remaining Roke to Trade Town... abandon them... clear area except for the skeleton force remaining at the main Roke naval compound... chained slaves labouring under Siblant masters... easily controlled... transport the remaining breeders in a controlled way across the waters and into secured Battle Lands... wait for the northerners to turn their attention back to their embattled lands... When fleet has embarked send part of the imp plague... breeders as well secretly following on the back of the Collector's mission amongst them... push my hungry children through the front... have them feeding and breeding in north before cycle turns once more. Bring me news of victory when I awake... soon I wish to move my palace to the north."

*****

Barf's warning reached the club's other operatives so that by a half-part-past Midst everybody was active. The club team had a number of other conspirators under observation and the chaos that Lauren had caused dockside prompted those tasked with individual observation duties to be acting even as the Roke accelerated their plan.

At gate nine Sellwyn, an operative based outside of the club staff, quickly managed to warn the relief guard when he hurried to check their status and spotted a man delivering them food, recognising him as a suspect. He warned the guard with an appropriate code word and spoilt the poisoner's plans, especially as he panicked and guiltily drew a weapon. Some of the relief then rushed immediately to the guardhouse to find strangers standing over their poisoned comrades. A fierce but brief fight had the guardroom and gate house back under control.

Theirs was the first of many general poison alerts of the night that were carried around the town as the early, sporadic fighting began. Sellwyn continued to help with the relief guard and got them to keep up the Roke flags and middle portcullis, leaving the gate with the appearance of being open from both inside and outside, whilst actually acceptably secure. They needed to defend the inner gates when a party of Roke arrived with messages for the landing force further up the coast.

Sellwyn, a veteran of intrigue against the Roke, when serving in the Battle Lands, deciding to play the hero was allowed through the gate, donning both the garb of the poisoner and additional adornments off one of the messengers. He also took the dead man's horse and rode out in disguise.

Riding hard, Sellwyn had to detour around 2000 Roke foot soldiers, on the road and close to arriving at Buccaneer Town. The Roke commander believed Sellwyn's pretence and confirmed meeting a real runner, with information that traitors held the gate open having left immediately after the poisoners had tricked the original guards.

Sellwyn left them with this false belief and, worried by the size of the attack, was even more determined to cause as much chaos by deception as he could to the enemy plans.

As he rode hard to reach the main road junction, the foot soldiers arrived at Buccaneer Town, unaware of the reversal of fortune until the outer gates crashed down upon them, followed by some rapidly heated boiling water. Some gathered citizens, who the relief guard had called out, 200 or so, trained and primed to act as rampart defenders, had rushed to the walls. Grabbing their own weapons and opening watertight lockers on the ramparts to reveal arblasts, bows, spears, caltrops and porcelain hand lobs, they formed the main defence. Therefore, a further nasty surprise also greeted the next ranks of Roke, who still piling in behind those scalded and screaming in a crush at the outer gate, saw a third of their number killed outright, below the walls by the defenders above.

Sellwyn raced up the road and managed to ride as far as the main fork where he was stunned to meet an agitated Roke commander with another sizeable advance party, apparently one of many. Because Sellwyn felt that Buccaneer Town was now sufficiently alerted, and the nearest gate secured, he convinced the Roke that the gates were now closed and urged them to ride to the town to help force through the defences. In this way he hoped to tie up as many Roke at Buccaneer Town as possible and reduce the number that could proceed inland, and hopefully allow whatever ambushes that could be arranged to be more effective.

The suspicious Roke commander, unknown to Sellwyn, had already doubled the number he had been instructed to send to 2,000. Sending another four hundred men he ordered his sub-commander to take the 2,500 and head further inland, down the road. With 100 men as his personal guard he mounted his horse to find a higher officer to confirm his orders, back at a staging point closer to the coastal breach.

Sellwyn had initially planned to cut his losses and head back to town once he had sown some seeds of disinformation. Now he was aware of a massive invasion and he decided that the chance of seriously damaging a normally frail Roke command structure greatly out weighed his own personal danger.

Managing to disappear in the confusion, leaving with the 400 town reinforcements, he peeled off to follow the officer by faking horse trouble. Then, doubling back, he caught sight of the leader and followed him to see where and who he visited at the major staging camp.

Sellwyn's blood was pounding in his ears as he dodged the sentries. Taking a risk he entered the camp commander's tent to assassinate the leaders. With a pilfered arblast he shot down the most senior-looking Roke and swept his knives, out throwing one into the throat of another before wrestling the third down to the ground, his hand over the desperate, foul smelling Roke's mouth, muffling his cries for aid. Despite successfully killing all three ranking Roke officers, silently enough to escape immediate attention, he was unfortunately disturbed by further Roke entering the tent unexpectedly.

Despite taking a deep wound one of these managed to raise the alarm and Sellwyn was injured badly fighting his way past further guards. Fortunately for the brave warrior, small groups of local citizens, formed swiftly into groups of partisan fighters once news of the initial invasion had spread, were also sporadically attacking the camp. Staggering about, crying false about being injured by the "Northern scum," he managed to escape into the night and nearby woods before a Roke watch commander had the camp settled again.

No senior Roke officers remained alive in the camp and none of the others knew to report the splitting of the troops at the road's fork or that Buccaneer Town's rear gates were holding. Sellwyn, in bad danger from his wounds, was only saved when he accidentally staggered into one of the partisan raiding teams shortly after his escape amongst the trees. He was bleeding heavily and, with so few in the team in serious danger themselves, there was little that could be done at that time except help him hide and provide first aid and provisions. His vital information was, however passed on. Thanks to his efforts the partisans managed to take advantage of the Roke confusion and hold the road for some parts, allowing the north to make a strategy to retake the fork and push the reserve Roke back to the breach in the coastal wall.

*****

Back at Buccaneer Town, no later than a part after Sellwyn had left, the fighting for the gate continued with the bloodied Roke determined to force their way inside. Fighting inside the town had grown heavier as large numbers of renegades had emerged from the baker's hiding places around the town. Consequently few additional reinforcements had made it to the ramparts and the Roke and their ladders were slowly overwhelming the defences.

Despite the speed of the Horde invasion force breaking through the coastal defences, and the treachery within the town, the defence commanders still had access to speedy communication through the use of messenger birds. All combat units of any status within the area were, therefore, quickly brought into action. That included the Iron Island commandos who had been discreetly camped in the nearby quarry awaiting Changworth, to arrange their dispatch to the Battle Lands on a secret mission.

The Roke attackers were, therefore, unprepared for the 400 elite Iron men who rushed around outside the town to fall upon the remaining 1,700 Roke as they were caught mounting their ladder assault on the gate. With the 100 citizens still on the walls and partisan archers and foot soldiers arriving all the time, suddenly the odds were evened. The Roke were trapped with few rear defences, having expected only their own reinforcements, and were cracked and crushed against the walls quickly before they were able to push back. Soon all that remained as a concerted Roke force were several hundred attempting to retreat back down the road as a fighting square.

Roke losses in this engagement ran to nearly 1,700 men for 100 Iron Islanders and 120 northerners on the walls, incapacitated or dead. Road patrols and partisans were able to dole out a few horses, and mounted riders rushed passed the Roke survivors to create temporary roadblocks not far from the main road fork.

The remaining Iron men split their force, most pursuing the retreating Roke but substantial numbers also entered the town once they were satisfied the gates could be held. The Iron Men and townsfolk, down from the walls, started taking the fight back through the streets, circling to each gate house to ensure that none had fallen and clearing brigands away from any that were threatened.

Chapter Eleven

It didn't seem to matter how early Sophie woke, Eamon Sombers always seemed to be up and about, doing his rounds or cooking breakfast. She liked Uncle Jeffer's friend a lot, especially as the night before he had convinced her Uncle that the children be allowed to watch the first three sets performed by the band. Initially her Uncle had said they could only see one.

Sophie had been very impressed by the blue man who had played the drums in the second part, and had laughed at Eamon when he had explained that the drummer, despite being talented, was still very young and, therefore, was lucky to be allowed to play at any events at all. Jeffers had agreed with Eamon, "Sophie, the lad is only a few years older than yourself. Last night was the first night of the Central Plains fayre, probably the biggest annual music event short of playing at the High Fort."

Sophie still had misgivings about the merits of the band members but agreed with the event's popularity. Eamon had informed her that up to 10,000 people, or more, had been gathered on the hill side to hear the band perform.

When Sophie had finished her breakfast she started trying to coax some into Liam who, always excitable at the start of the day, was proving especially so, being over tired from staying awake late the night before. In this kind of mood she knew they would need to watch him carefully, for with or without Clara he might make a dash for the water and the boats.

The flap of Uncle Jeffers' tent flew back and her guardian stepped confidently out into the morning sunshine. Taking a sly look around he saw only his wards' and took the luxury of a large yawn and a stretch, playing to the children. Strolling over to the eating area he took his wards hands and led them up the slope away from the camp saying, "Hey kids, come and sit down over here. I need to talk to you about something important. You know the reason that I came here was for my job. Well, that was good because it meant that you guys could come along too. We enjoyed the journey together, didn't we? Even if that little chap Sombers and his friends tagged along spoiling the scenery."

Liam snorted and shook his head, brandishing his miniature spear fiercely. "Oh you liked him did you Liam? Well good for you. He's not a bad friend really so remember him because he will remember you. Anyway, the problem is that the work I came here to find, well, it turns out it means that I will have to travel on a very long journey and I won't be allowed to take you guys with me," Jeffers finished sadly.

"Sophie, what do you think about that?" her Uncle asked her carefully.

"Does it mean we will go back and live with Uncle Taverner at the club and wait for you there?" Sophie asked, clearly hoping for second best.

"No, I am afraid that will not be possible. One of the reasons that you came on this trip is that the club may not carry on for much longer. Taverner and I talked about what we would do if that happened and there is one suggestion that we agreed upon. There is a nice lady who lives out in the country who we think you might be able to stay with; we have asked her husband and he agrees that it is a good idea. Would you like to stay with her until Taverner or I can come and see you there?" Jeffers asked, looking fondly at each of the unhappy children and their downcast faces.

"Liam, do you think you can do that and be a good boy and look after your sister until I come back?" Jeffers finally asked, breaking the silence. Liam's nodded reply for some reason caused his sister to burst into tears.

"Now, Sophie, don't cry, please," Jeffers said as he picked her up for a cuddle.

After an eighth part Sophie was still crying. Jeffers spotted Eamon Sombers down the slope in the camp and let off a piercing whistle which caused the spearman, and a number of others, to look up where Jeffers motioned the spear commander up the slope with a couple of hand signals.

"Look Liam, Eamon is here. Would you like to go and play with him?" Jeffers suggested to the fidgety young boy.

"I want Clara," the young boy replied vigorously.

"My choice as well, lad, but wait and ask Eamon when he gets here," Jeffers chuckled.

As the short man crested the slope Jeffers smiled at him, but not with his eyes. "Hey, old man, you are getting slow. Don't think I will be finding you any more jobs if you can't keep up."

"Chance would be a fine thing, older chap," Eamon responded cheekily, looking at the children first and then Jeffers, questioningly.

"Can you occupy the lad, Sombers? I need a chat with this little princess," Jeffers replied, ignoring his friend's unasked query.

Eamon glanced at the little girl sobbing in his arms and smiled sympathetically, "Sure boss, but you promised me no more jobs and already another one."

He turned and knelt in front of Liam who was already tottering towards the edge of the slope, since Jeffers had let go of his hand when Eamon arrived. "And what would you like to do little man?" Eamon asked Liam kindly.

"Clara, I want Clara," the boy answered smiling.

"Oh, I see, it is like that is it," Eamon replied as he took his hand, sticking out his lip in mock rejection.

"Uncle Jeffers said he wanted her too," the little boy replied solemnly in response to Eamon's look of spurned hurt.

"Oh! I'll just bet your Uncle did," replied Eamon laughing as they started down the slope.

After the man and boy had walked out of hearing distance Jeffers stood up and took Sophie's hand, leading her further up the hill. They waded onwards as the grass got taller which, uncut, came almost to Sophie's waist. As they strolled Jeffers waited for Sophie to break the silence, but as time went on it became clear that she was simply going to vent her frustrations, beheading every daisy that crossed her path.

"Look, Sophie, we need to talk this through. You know that in the past we discussed how the ward system works. You also know that I promised your mother and father I would look after you if anything happened to them. Now, remember I told you that I had served my duty to the nation, several times over in fact, and that people who act as guardians for young children must have served their dues so that they will not normally be called for duty except in a crisis. Well, you know that Uncle Taverner and I have special jobs, the kind that mean that we can be called away, and that we have to go. Normally this wouldn't happen but in this case I must go."

"Yes Uncle J," the little girl answered, trying to work with him, especially as he was treating her more like an adult than a child.

"Well, I won't hide it from you, both Taverner and I have been called to do our jobs and they sound quite dangerous. I don't want to leave you but I promise that I will do everything I can to come back to you safely. Will you agree to go and stay with Lady Green? Oh, I forgot," he said craftily, "do you remember Claphand and Mags? Well, they will be going with you and staying for a while out with Lady Green as well. They arrived at the fayre late last night. You can see them later." As this appeared to cheer the girl slightly Jeffers pressed on. "It really will be quite exciting. Lady Green, as her name suggests, is one of the rainbow folk and before we go I will introduce you to her husband who is here at the Fayre. He is quite famous."

"I know, Uncle J, he is Master Calm, but he sounds kind of scary. I heard one story where he turns into a fish. Mind, if he is a nice fish Liam would like that."

*****

Further round the camp Marvellous was also juggling, telling Blue Boy his news like a hot potato and finally calling him to one side. "Blue Boy we need to talk privately, our orders have been confirmed. I need to talk to you about them. Come, walk with me for a while," Marv told his young protégé.

"What do you mean orders, Marv? Are the band being sent somewhere new?" the young teenager asked as they walked together out onto the hills.

"Well boy, that could be possible but I meant just for you and me. Our time with the band is, I am sad to say, over. We are being assigned to somebody new."

"Wait, Marv," Blue Boy interrupted. "You have easily completed enough service, even I know that and I am just a kid, not even a senior cadet."

"Well, son, I am afraid that for we two the usual rules do not apply." He saw the boy begin to turn away and promptly hurried on. "Blue, wait until I have finished before you make any snap judgements. A long time ago Master Smee was asked to take you in and teach you all he could, and he in turn asked the same of me. Well, that phase of your life is now over. I don't think the boss and I have done too bad a job, do you? No need to answer that now boy. What I am saying is that we were never actually intended to go to the front with the band."

"Well, where are we going?" Blue Boy asked cautiously, he could see that Marv was taking this very seriously and he tried hard to listen calmly.

"Blue, we are going with another master, one who will continue your training. We will be assigned to Master Calm," Marv told Blue Boy quietly. "He has not explained much to me as yet but I believe he intends to train you personally, in place of you attending the academy. It is a singular honour if he does, for he has never done this before."

Blue Boy walked a few paces further and Marv gave him time to work his thoughts through. "Will you be with me for the training, Marv?" Blue Boy finally asked cautiously.

"I will always be near Blue, certainly at the start. The training is solely for you though. Thank the Battler I am too old. Master Calm has also been asked to supervise the training of a special cadre of troops which will include Mother and the two lads you met last night. I will be permanently assigned to that group which will be carried out in parallel to your training. Master Calm has reassured me that the overlap will be significant."

"Well then, Marv it looks like more farewells and new challenges. Thank you for leaving the band for me. Can I walk alone for some while please?"

"See you back at the camp in a part," Marv replied, turning back to his own painful duty of leaving the band, his love of 30 years.

*****

220

Taverner stood quietly as Lauren reported to him. He could see that the evening's events had shaken her. That Lauren had immediately accepted his explanation of the club's operations and only given Millie's credentials scant attention showed him just how much. Insisting that she report immediately, Taverner had, however, kept her waiting whilst he and Millie quizzed Barf, who when dismissed immediately left for the main bar for orders to re-enter the action.

Then, still covered in the blood of friend and foe alike, Lauren had described her capture, the mind beast and how she forced her way back clinging to the boat on a careless loose rope, caught only moments after she surfaced, barely alive. The alert caused by Barf's diversion caused the boat's crew to disembark hastily. She raced through the telling of her running battle including an initial dash through the foul smelling tannery that Barf had missed. The help of the two watchmen and their death fighting beside her caused her much distress and she only mentioned casually her minor wound, gained next to Barf when almost at the club. Changworth's rescue Taverner already knew of and of how a couple of patrons had immediately moved to take up the fight for her, only to catch her fall as she fainted.

Whilst she was being revived with a large brandy, and Barf was composing himself and his report, Taverner had raised the facility's alert status to the maximum level. After a quick briefing Millie and Mandibles had disappeared to ensure the watchman's warning had been augmented and transmitted to the level of a full town alert. Taverner, therefore, had the luxury of comparing both reports in a very short space of time.

As soon as Millie returned he continued. "Thank you, Lauren," Taverner started, "Tonight you have been very brave and I know Buccaneer Town owes you a great debt. Millie here will provide you with anything you need, but you should understand that the club, as well as the town, is under siege. Numerous Roke reinforcements have arrived outside our doors." Lauren looked pensive, pacing the room, clearly distracted. Taverner looked to Millie, who just shrugged. "You need to consider how your command can be deployed as we suspect that fighting will spread throughout the town. We will send messages for you across the rooftops." Taverner paused for another brief moment but still no questions were forthcoming. "We will endeavour to support you in your command but it may be that you will have to fight here, with Millie or Changworth. Although it is barely a part-past-Midst we expect that fighting will continue within the town for some considerable time. The more Roke we can lure here and dispose of the better. That is our plan until we receive clearer intelligence. Until we begin to push out into the town we will not be able to help your return to your command. If you will excuse me now Lauren." He bowed politely, as if she were still a customer and he the restaurant manager.

Turning to his second in command, he continued "Millie, I suspect we will need to be able to get enough men to the dock front and check the town gates fairly soon. Attempted mass landings are to be resisted and town strongholds secured." So saying Taverner hurried off into the club, and as Millie headed in the opposite direction she made no move to stop Lauren from following her.

*****

Down on the dockside it was chaos. Four of the eight Roke vessels arriving in response to the Baker's hurried signals managed to force their way through the sea gates before they closed, with only one town ship able to slip through to protect the sea-facing side. The two patrol ships normally stationed off shore had been sunk by the attackers, and treachery within the harbour left the five remaining defence ships mostly ablaze, with crew members sickening from poison or fighting for their lives.

The special operations schooner that had made it sea side turned to harry the Roke who were now attacking the gate defences in an attempt to get in and land their troops. The schooner, out numbered, could only manage to prevent a concerted attack, causing two ships to turn and fight off its own attacks.

This, however, eased enough pressure off the defences. The Roke ships had the added threat that should all four turn to attack the local vessel the gate might open to release more defending ships. The walls being high they were unaware of the situation within the harbour or that this was a single ship, a pure fluke that it was manned and ready to sail at that time of night.

*****

Lauren and Barf had just raced past and Changworth was tackling the closest pursuit. He stepped back and ducked down just in time to avoid a crushing blow from the third man's axe. With a straight leg thrust out in front of him his move flowed as he crashed his booted foot, heel first, into the second assailant's knee, crushing the bone. He rolled smoothly back over his left shoulder bringing that same flailing leg whipping dangerously past the third man's face and forcing him to step back.

This move brought Changworth, deliberately, to the doorway where he tugged the recessed bell cord in a warning sequence. Crouched there he studied his assailants from the relative shelter of the doorframe. Suddenly he surged forwards to where the first man lay bleeding and planted a devastating kick to his throat ending his mumbled cursing permanently. From the frame Changworth had unclipped a short wooden baton and now armed he circled the limping knife man to get a clear position to deal with the axe wielder.

Seeing his two mates down the man was much more cautious, but the sight of a bouncer armed only with a short wooden club, against his heavy axe, was too much temptation and he unleashed a wild swing hoping to cut the interfering doorman in half. The chest high swing could only have missed by fractions, but as the axe sped past to the end of its arc Changworth simply ran his club down the length of the axe to tangle in the two handed grip; the axe man felt sudden pain and then darkness came as the bouncer used the heel of his hand to drive the fellow's nose straight up into his forehead.

The axe man dropped, twitching, to the ground as his ruptured brain gave in to the pressure. As the prime door keeper of the club it was not uncommon for Changworth to be out numbered, but usually it took a bit of time before steel was drawn, and then not often swords or axes. Stooping to pick up the axe he sliced it through the neck of the knife man limping over to try and stab him; holding it loosely in one hand he bent to free the man's dagger.

Walking back to the door Changworth could hear more booted feet running up the road. He rapped on the inner door and Spillage quickly drew back the grill plate.

"Three down and more on the way, have we got lock down?" Changworth asked.

"Problems in the restaurant guv, Mandi asks if we could divert any jokers in through the bar," Spillage replied.

"OK, get some people upstairs and then shut off the back and get this door open, no entry except to the bar. Is Barf available yet?" Spillage grunted an affirmative, concentrating on working the message wire. "Good. Then break open a tool locker for you and your squad, mail under padding for everyone," Changworth ordered.

As the door opened and his companion rushed off, Changworth stepped back into the street to see if the newcomers were friend or foe. Wearing the same green armbands as the other three he suspected foe as one youngster pointed at him screaming for his death. Strictly speaking, at that point he had fulfilled his role and he should have retreated behind the door first dropping the outer portcullis gate and once safely inside let them cool off. However, stepping further forwards he examined these opponents so vocally committed to taking his life. From a first glance they looked about the same low calibre as the others, but he knew from hard experience that it always paid to be that extra bit careful. Because of the overt fierceness of their cries he felt entitled to spare any concern for their well-being and have a little fun.

Mandibles called softly from the doorway, "Tav says the restaurant doors are still wedged open. I suggest you kill a couple quickly and toy with the others for a bit, then lead them in here. Its going full scale across town and the more we get in here the better. We're sending groups out the back way to check the town gates. Chubby will drop the port when we get enough in. Then we'll make the rest dead quick."

Changworth's attention was forced back to the mob as more shrieking thugs had got close enough to attack. Sending a readable body movement off to the left he encouraged two to step forward right into the path of his axe as he, in fact, stepped right and gutted one with the edge before reversing the controlled sweep and caving in the second man's face with a brutal jab of its blunt edge. 'Well that's your two Mandi' he thought. With plenty more arriving he decided to stay for a bit and picked one of the others who, hanging back, seemed to be directing the attack. Changworth dodged a new thrust and, stepping back, deftly sent the axe spinning away in a graceful horizontal arc, to crunch heavily into the helmeted face of his target, dropping the man to the floor like a sack.

Nobody appeared to notice the fall of the leader but Changworth didn't begrudge the loss of the axe too much. These toughs clearly weren't drilled in fighting as a team; skipping back from another sword thrust he allowed the point to pass his hip and sliding his hand over the out-thrust wrist twisted the limb back on itself forcing open the man's grip and allowing him to pluck the weapon way, even as he hammered his elbow into his assailants throat. In a blur of movement he was forward again, stabbing left and right to clear away the crush of attackers, who by now were arriving in sufficient numbers to cause real danger.

Fencing amateurishly with another swordsman he used the kind of ineffective sword play that got so many cadets killed at the front: crossing swords and the like until stepping back, suddenly his right leg came up to his chest and then stamped down through his opponents groin area, causing the chap to bellow in pain and slamming him back into his comrades. In this space Changworth turned and fled, careful to weave slightly and thus avoiding a couple of hastily fired quarrels. With a roar the pack charged after him and he was all the way into the bar before he heard Chubby's signal that the gate was down. He was also interested to hear the cellar alarm sounded a few moments later. It looked as if Chubby had augmented the plan and left a tempting cellar entrance open to split off a few more ruffians.

As he entered the bar Barf called him over to the main section, where a three-quarter-length gleaming broadsword was waiting for him. Holding out his left arm Barf quickly strapped him into a metal arm bar, or foregreave, as they termed it, whistling a bawdy tune in his tone deaf fashion. Leaning over the bar he could see that Barf was adequately prepared, although now that he was wearing his grubby, sleeveless poncho top it was difficult to know quite what the unconventional soldier was up to. Finally Barf pressed a small double arblast into his hands. Shrugging he pointed to the left and they both turned and shot down two men a piece as they entered the bar. A bow also sang twice from the other end of the room before a door slammed shut. As the mob staggered over their six dead colleagues they entered a room to find Changworth and the three remaining patrons ready and waiting. Twelve men piled out onto the bar floor and the defenders moved smoothly out to engage them. Changworth could see that the marines were used to fighting together and called out "Solo," which they acknowledged before advancing swiftly out away to the left. Now Changworth could make out Barf in the periphery of his vision standing on the bar top up to some mischief.

*****

Once Lauren's news had been relayed to Taverner he decided on a plan of action and, consulting with Changworth, dispatched more staff to work with the town defence and some to continue defending the club, which was now completely under attack.

As the morning entered its third day-part those dispatched into the town, dispersed to various points, discovered that although the poisoning alert had gone out a substantial number of the city watch and marine patrols had already been affected. The Fleet HQ and connected senior-staff quarters were also already under heavy attack and many fires had been set.

The one piece of good news was that the staff sent to help secure the Chandlery met little resistance and the equipment stores were broken open to good effect.

Down at the harbour the number of Roke vessels that had successfully made it into the harbour weren't getting on too well. Of the four, one was sinking, two were attempting to secure and reopen the sea gate's defences and only the fourth, and largest, had successfully docked already landing a significant number of Roke; the crew were working to disembark some more sinister Reptoid raiders.

*****

Piker rounded the corner at a run, charging the rear of the retreating Roke and running two through before they had a chance to turn. The last opponent turned swiftly and lunged for his throat and Piker had to drop his pike, deflecting the sword with his armoured gauntlet. Grabbing the Roke's sword arm he snapped it down and spiked him in the throat with his free hand's finger blades. Bending to gather his pike he looked up in time to see the massive shape of a Red Master scuttle round the corner. Piker had never served near 'red country' and it was his first encounter, though like all advanced academy students he had studied anatomy and tactics on the old enemy. Its dry tongue flicking the air for moisture and scent had clearly picked out the Ironlander as a target. The Red Master began to hiss grotesquely as it moved forward, rising up on its rear six legs to present the large pair and two smaller graspers ready for the fight.

It was now three day-parts past Midst-night. Moving towards the Fleet HQ in the southeast of Buccaneer Town, Piker knew that with all the fighting the town defences to the rear of his position were sparse and that these creatures could move at considerable speed when scuttling on all legs. Rather than retreating and being caught in a less convenient spot he decided to stand his ground and fight. Moving forwards, balanced lightly on the balls, of his feet, he made two calculated feints before dropping and skewering one of the larger rear limbs just above the equivalent of a knee joint.

Above and to his right a whistled call rang out telling Piker that allies were on a nearby rooftop. His elevated comrades further called that he should keep moving and that they would provide a limited amount of missile support. The circling continued for several moments, a stalemate as both human and Reptoid fenced for the best position, all the while the beast pushing him further and further back, ignoring several ragged flights of arrows. Suddenly Piker's unseen allies called out a further message. He should count down from ten and then attack as he could. The allotted moment came with a spear arcing over to plunge into the Red Master's face. As the beast shifted to defend this new direction Piker, forewarned, took his chance and sheared his pike up and through a flailing thorax appendage, tearing one of the major front claws on the left side almost completely off the big red's body. As the pike tore smoothly free he followed its upward swing and at the peak of its arc, just as it began to fall, he twisted smoothly and drove the head deep into the juncture of another of the Reptoid's rear legs.

With two rear legs punctured on the same side the Red Master was suddenly much more vulnerable and began squealing, hissing and shrieking unrelentingly. Piker, wincing at the ear splitting volume, was forced further back towards a corner by a sudden charge and finally it landed a great buffeting blow, numbing his arm and smashing off the but end of his pike as he rolled desperately to avoid the follow up. As he came up again he heard a three-whistle, blast warning of imminent danger, and shouts and screams could be heard from the rooftop above.

Whatever was going on up there, he was grateful for his comrades help, the remains of the spear and several arrows and wounds could be seen around the red beast's head carapace. Piker wondered how long he had been fighting the brute. Perhaps his wish to supply his former patron and friend Mandibles with such an impressive set of jaws had been ill advised. With these few quick thoughts he backed up a further few steps with the beast, though advancing, seemingly looking up at the rooftop. Piker was now backed as far into a corner as he could afford; if his next strike didn't gain him more freedom to move he would be in real trouble.

No sooner had he begun to lunge than the Reptoid attacked, batting his pike aside with its good fore claw, at the same time heaving forwards, dragging its wounded legs. Its main claw was coming back almost immediately, despite the wounded legs finally giving way. In a moment of cunning, rather than retreating Piker stepped forwards. First he impaled the base of a good leg, before reversing the thrust and driving the splintered remains of the butt end crushingly against one of the smaller arms on the wounded side, ending the move in a position crouched almost below the Reptoid's gut carapace.

It was this crazy move that saved his life, for suddenly a further number of Reptoids, known as Green Nasties, began dropping down around their bigger cousin. Green Nasties, or the green rock wall species, were something with which Piker had had plenty of experience. It also meant bad news for him. These small, quick, devils hunted in packs and a shivered pike was definitely not the equipment for fighting them, let alone crouched below a limping war master Reptoid in a rage of fury. Still, whilst he was down here Piker thought to make the most of the situation. The Nasties were unlikely to approach the enraged Master too closely and Piker could keep beneath the Master with moderate ease. Screwing his bigger hand spikes onto his gauntlet he began to pound his right fist with all his might into the belly carapace, while at the same time driving his shivered pike head deep into the front foreleg joint and keeping it wedged there.

From far away he could faintly hear human cries and he hoped he could hold on long enough for the beast to be pulled down. The Master was having great difficulty moving in any direction now a further leg was pinned, and seemed to be trying to sink down to crush him. Piker battered away relentlessly, though his numbed arm was now becoming weary. Looking up he could see that his spikes had forced a useful sized crack in the armoured belly plates above. Soon he would have a choice. To remove his pike from the leg would allow the beast certain movement but it could then be thrust into the Master's guts in a certain, if not, instant death blow.

Suddenly the Master started to heave itself upright and Piker saw several Nasties edge forwards. If the master had communicated its desire for his removal to them, then all other bets were off. He dragged the pike out of the leg wound and drove it deep into the Masters belly, causing the brute to somehow rear right, up squealing in anguish, its forelimbs thrashing and grasping at the pike, tearing the remaining protruding pike haft to shreds.

Piker was just in time to catch the first Nasty. Spiking it in the thorax joint he flipped it over in a neat move and stamped his left foot down into its face. At the same time as the first was being choked the second leapt at him and, unable to free his foot, which had slid into the grinding jaws he sank backwards screaming in pain as his ankle shattered. Despite the agonising pain the spring of the second beast and his twist back threw it off over his head where he could hear it crash over the coble stones, hopefully in some way injured. No time left, a third was rushing in now and with his first assailant rigid in death, Piker was still unable to free his foot. All he could do was lunge towards the third in a classic fencer's thrust, driving his finger spikes straight into the beast fierce maw. As it shredded mail and flesh from his arm he drove his fingers up through the softer membrane and grabbed hold of a good part of its brain matter. The pain was almost too much with the beast on his arm dead and falling forwards, dragging him down, its jaws locked upon him in rigour.

Piker knew this final misfortune signalled his end, for unable to move either leg or arm he was rooted to the spot as the dying master opened its ferocious mouth and keening savagely, smashed itself forwards onto him, trying to force the whole human into its mouth. Other town defenders were running into sight now and a couple saw Piker raise his free arm straight above his head, staring grimly forwards, whether in salute or to try and force the other hand into the master's brain and assure its death they would never know, as instants later he was crushed into final oblivion.

*****

Elsewhere in town two other club men had also been killed early on. The party that Changworth had finally lead out of the club became separated, Snibs leading his four companions across town to the southern-most gate. Changworth reached the harbour viewing tower, also in the south eastern district near the Fleet HQ, where survivors of the garrison there, who had escaped poisoning, had managed to hold on and he got an eye ball view of the progress of the harbour defence. Unknown to Changworth, at that time the town band and the sea cadets had taken small boats out to face the undocked enemy ships, attacking those trying to land men on the sea wall. In the moonlight it looked to Changworth as if the little boats were damaged or sinking, locked together with the closest enemy ship. He could also see the wall defenders setting light to the second enemy vessel, and although ragged it looked as if the defences would hold, from the seaward side of the wall at least.

Still a day-part away from dawn Changworth could hear, rather than see, the two other organised attacks that were in progress inside Buccaneer Town and so left the relative safety of the tower to lend assistance. One was where the enemy ships that had reached the docks had off loaded troops who were now fighting their way through the streets towards the Admiralty Fleet HQ, and the second where the traitors and troops smuggled in, comrades of those he had fought outside the club, were attacking the battery in numbers to get through to the sea wall and reopen the gates.

A limited chain of messengers allowed Changworth to learn that outside town there had been further skirmishes and that the local district militia had sent alerts of the landings further north. From the unassailed south message birds had summoned 100 riders from the southerly flat lands, the White Plains. Entering through a gate still held by loyal troops, the crucial reinforcements, were pushing in through the town, only to become fragmented on hitting the hard fighting around the Fleet HQ, which prevented any serious numbers from pushing the enemy through the town towards the docks.

Changworth had seen enough. With the Admiralty under attack and the Admiral absent he decided he had little choice but to raise his own standard and take charge of the town. Deciding to go round the areas of heaviest street fighting where, unknown to Changworth, Piker had already been killed, and back to the club to rally support, he found new scenes of fierce fighting. Since he had left the club building secured it looked as if the defences had been breached. Almost at the main bar door, Spillage joined the group at a run, searching for men to help at the southern gates, where the town was loosing heavily, blurting out the news of Piker's death and that he was being pursued.

"Cripes," muttered Changworth as large numbers of assailants rounded the corner, sweeping his men away from the club. He dropped to one knee and surged back up, stabbing a Roke warrior in the throat. Gushing blood the man fell back opening a gap that allowed Changworth to cast a captured dagger, end over end through the air, coming to rest buried in the chest of a renegade running in to join the mêlée. Stepping back

Changworth stooped to pick up a fallen axe and as an attacker stepped in to smash his skull Mandibles speared him in the throat before launching his weapon to impact in another approaching warrior.

Changworth was happy that his old ruse still worked and back on his feet he used the axe to smite a foe nearly clean in two. He was breathing heavily now, his reliance on his comrade and the knowledge that Mandibles had held his life in his hands, causing his adrenaline to rise. Training aside, Changworth knew deep down that when he was fighting alone he could always remain calm, his self-belief total. When he fought with his team, although he knew that as a group they were awesomely effective, he found that despite all the years he still lacked the ability to trust absolutely in anyone else. It was a secret he thought he had kept most of his life.

In the recent fighting with the tail of the Admiralty attackers Mandibles had shown his skill with javelins, scoring multiple hits within moments. Changworth was continually awed by his friend's blistering speed. Even with Mandibles in a rage having learned of his former ward, Piker's, death Changworth witnessed such skill it challenged his ability to visually take in what Mandibles was doing. Ducking and weaving he performed the most incredible moves so that Changworth could not work out whether they were accurately calculated risks or feats of madness that succeeded only because of luck.

Eventually battling past the club they too were split up, and with dawn faint on the horizon, Changworth was almost relieved when he found himself fighting amongst strangers and could forget any immediate concerns about his friends.

*****

Most of a part later, whilst Changworth fought on in the dawn's early light, despite feeling the beginnings of despair, around him the battle for Buccaneer Town had turned in his favour. The north-western section of town had held off the Roke assault and reinforced by the iron men the situation in that district had become stable if defensive. Eastwards, towards the harbour, despite occupation centred on the baker's dockside compound, and heavy fighting at the battery which defended the northern end of the sea wall, the sea defences had held by the narrowest margin. It was to the west, near the strategically less important club, and in the southeast at Fleet HQ where the landed Reptoids had spread, that the fight for control remained heated, although even the pair of gate houses successfully captured by the plotters offered the town little additional danger.

Through the night Changworth had picked up and lost so many comrades as he had struggled across town, that despite his experience he was doubting his ability to make a difference. Finally, with a few remaining, White Plain's men and assorted marines he was close to re-taking the most southerly gate. Finding Snibs he could only leave him bleeding, possibly to die from a punctured lung, a wound he had taken trying to reach the gate himself.

Seeing his commanding officer, caused the tough young man, Snibs to rail at his injury, and hearing that his armour was now available, despite bleeding heavily, had sent back for his second set. This was promptly furnished, now that Changworth had managed slowly to push the enemy forwards, leaving the areas behind him relatively safe for support activities. Snib's armour also contained a pouch of illegal drugs which would almost get a dead man to walk, but which also drained a body to its last. For him it was a certain death sentence but he wanted it anyway, for the moments of movement it could give him.

Temporarily invigorated, Snibs had slipped past his comrades as they methodically cleared the streets. He walked out into the final area still controlled by the Roke that Changworth was moving to clear. Fully armoured Snibs engaged a party of twelve Roke and with every movement and every blow they struck he cut one more to a total of eight. Even then he was standing as he died in front of Changworth, upright eyes raised to the open sky as he had wanted.

That was not the last tragedy. Within moments a final report returned from the retaken club. Upwards of 50 Roke bodies had been spread around the breached bar and restaurant entrances of the club when Changworth had despatched Lauren, Barf and Bones to cautiously enter the main bar. Here they found themselves alone and quickly reinforced the barriers at that nearest entrance, surprised to find the doors smashed and the light portcullis torn from its fittings.

They carefully checked the deserted ground floor only to encounter the enemy upstairs in the restaurant, temporarily cutting them off from their search for comrades. Retreating past the restaurant stairs into the terrace bar, already the scene of much bloodshed, they were forced further away from the restaurant. They found Spillage and Old Soak, sprawled across tables overturned for defence, dead amongst many attackers.

Barf had got pretty angry and using a table as a huge shield managed to block the restaurant door. Holding the Roke inside he directed the others to break open a bench-seat to reveal more weapons. With arblast, some light spears and a new bow for Bones the three took the battle more effectively to the Roke. In a brief respite Bones, covered them through an interior door and the three escaped further through the club into an area where the enemy couldn't get access. They found that the other lower areas had all been sealed successfully. A number of the waitresses were attending several wounded, including Chubby, who could only reveal that Barney was fighting up top having ordered the lower levels to be sealed off. Bones, Barf and Lauren took an iron grill up through the cellar and surprising the Roke guards at the ground floor restaurant entrance, finally cut them down and barricaded the club closed once again.

Now the remaining Roke were trapped inside and Bones and Chubby, whose leg was now bandaged up, left to hunt them down, being able to enter and exit the restaurant at will. Barf took Lauren down to the deep cellar armoury and they began to use the cellar hoists to send bundles of weapons up to the club girls. Team leaders throughout the town were quick to send staffers accompanied by groups of locals to a side entrance to re-equip. All poorly equipped because of the surprise of the attack. A couple of disabled veterans arrived from the chandlery and they took on the weapons dispersal.

In the early dawn light Barf, Major Bartrum Harlech, was the first club-based soldier to emerge fully clad in distinctive armour and carrying his general's standard, free from the need for secrecy now Changworth had announced his real identity. Lauren departed with a couple of locals to attempt entry to the

Militia compound to get her own armour. Barf, carrying the general's own armour, with maybe 30 armoured locals in support, was ready to leave to reinforce his commander when he heard the news he was to take along to his general.

Inside the club Barf had learnt that at the very start of the battle a clever Roke operative, posing as a customer eating in the restaurant, poised to attempt to enter the kitchen and poison the food, had disabled the main restaurant portcullis. Furthermore, as the fighting had started he had allowed full access to the stairs by jamming the second gate as it came down. This had concentrated the fight for the club in an around the restaurant. Barf had seen first hand the dead bodies scattered all over the place as he had help secure the doors before he left.

With the iron gates still unusable the club had been entered a second time, when the wooden restaurant doors had been forced. The attackers were only hampered at all because Chubby, the building technician, had used three clever screw arrangements to drop sections of dummy wall on groups of attackers forcing entry at the external doors.

At least another ten Roke were killed in the second battle for the restaurant and five more as the entrance and outside area were cleared when the three companions had been sent back in. This meant that in some places bodies were piled three high.

As Barf was about to leave for the second time, right when it looked as if the club was finally cleared and secured, news came down that three Roke, hiding amongst the bodies in the restaurant, had surprised Bones. Catching him across the face with a barbed whip, his chest speared by the other two he had gutted one and Chubby had shot down a second, before the third was stabbed by the bar girls as he tried to flee. Barf was told that in an emotional farewell the dying Bones had instructed Chubby and Melissa to say his goodbyes to his Ladd, Lawrence.

This was the news that Barf reported to Changworth as the general rose from closing Snib's dead eyes. Changworth's jumbled command was finishing clearing the enemy force from the southern-most gate, in the background. Their friend lying at his feet, Changworth told Barf that Piker's body had also been retrieved.

The news of the numbers of Reptoids still roaming the town quickly caused the pair to shake off their sorrow. Changworth looked up at his standard and passed an order that the rest of the troops fighting with him should go in rotation back to the club for full equipment. Once armoured he and Barf launched a more direct and savage attack on the Roke force. The two fully armoured northerners spread chaos in the Roke as they began cutting their way steadily through the inferior forces. They even encountered a number of Siblants and, showing a fearless display of teamwork, cut down each beast with ruthless efficiency, stopping only when Changworth had selected a forward command post.

Morning was well advanced and still the attack on the Fleet HQ, several streets south in the bottom-most corner of Buccaneer Town, needed to be broken. Survivors of the fighting provided information that the front of the building lay in ruins. Frequently these brave marines challenged Changworth with disheartening rumours that the Admiral had fled the town on horseback. As Changworth formulated his plan to secure the southeast, Barf was dispatched to the northeast to secure the traitor baker's compound. Changworth finalised his three-front plan by sending Mandibles to head the defence of the sea wall along with a visiting foreign military commander.

Only a short time after Barf had left the club Mandibles and six others, including Barney who, bereft of opponents, had slipped out to fight in the streets, had returned, later to leave in full armour and pretty soon the whole complement was fully armed and officially deployed having either returned or been taken kit.

*****

"Mister Jeffers, could I please talk some with you, sir. It is concerning the meeting you attended last evening. Perhaps we could stroll?" the compact man asked, his white smile appearing next to Jeffers out of the darkness.

"Why yes, of course, Master Calm, the weather is fine and the camp is proving a bit stuffy and overcrowded," Jeffers replied as casually as he could.

"Myster Jeffers, I would tell you of my plans for the young protégé I have agreed to take. In accordance with the law he will be trained under a private tutor dispensation and an associated assessment schedule. The academy have already acknowledged this," he said in his over effusive manner. "In short, I am pleased to tell you that this boy has considerable potential which, while well evident, is mostly untapped yet. He is of mixed heritage, being unusual in claiming blood of the Blue Folk. I will be his main sponsor and also the supervising tutor. I propose he undergoes only two cycles of three-phase classical instruction. I consider he has so much potential that I will call upon my privilege to set these phases at three weeks, with only one week review between; a compaction of education that is entirely unheard of I am told. Within this I would be most grateful if you would act as his first reviewer, and therefore a co-sponsor."

"Ah, Master Calm, ever have I heard that you court interest and excitement. Needless to say my personal disregard for tradition is well demonstrated. If you wish this I accept your belief and agree. Flouting the academy thus is something even I had not intended. I feel I know a little of your charge and assume that, as Marvellous is in attendance, this young chap is the drummer of Master Smee's youth band. If this all goes wrong then I may still benefit from his service in my club."

"Jeffers, may I call you so?" Master Calm added, happily smiling back at Jeffer's nod. "I am most pleased. I would ask an additional favour. Blue Boy's training will begin immediately. I am also grooming a specialist team and ask that you wait the three weeks of his first period and spend the time helping to train this group."

Jeffers looked at the shorter man thoughtfully, "That, Master Calm, is more difficult. Whilst I can remain in the area, I am here waiting certain guidance shall we say. As soon as my instructions are imparted it could be that I will be expected to deploy elsewhere immediately. If you will agree to petition my err... contact, then I am sure some agreement can be reached." As Calm nodded knowingly Jeffers realised that the master probably knew more of his future than he did, but he continued anyway. "The rendezvous is not until month end and is fairly close to here."

"Ah yes, Jeffers, that is good sooth. I will have your contact redirected," Master Calm finished emphatically.

Chapter Twelve

The running battle in the streets, that had lasted for six parts around the club, took all of that quarter day until dawn before Changworth was completely happy that that district was secured, went on much longer in the northeast of the town. As with all battles Changworth found it difficult to keep track of time and it was full morning, a total of fourteen day-parts after the first alert, before the exhausted general announced to the forward command post that the siege of the Fleet HQ was sufficiently broken and that the efficient patrolling of the forward docks could begin.

Only as Changworth and his guards surveyed the streets themselves could they begin to appreciate the true scale of the attack, rather than measuring it in terms of their own exhaustion or personal number of kills. All around were the broken bodies of various species, and further horrors were yet in store.

Changworth was taken to buildings near the club. Here it had been revealed that when the Roke had discovered the rooftop communication lines, they had started to slaughter any children they found. Changworth had to deal with these poor little victims, horribly strung up near the scene of several roof top watch posts. Reports that Changworth had received of town citizens readily entering the fighting now began to make sense, for this barbarism had only served to rile the population. Many times the Roke attack on the Admiral's Fleet HQ complex had been halted with the invaders having to fight off hit and run locals, so angry that they disregarded the general orders to stay in their homes until specifically called up.

One of the reasons that Changworth had held back on a full call up was so that the Roke would encourage signals to their troops landing outside the town. Initially he had thought that quickly retaking the town was a low priority had and intended to use only a small number of the Iron Islanders hidden in the hills.

Subtlety was first priority, so that any Roke reinforcements would be taken by surprise rather than encouraged to counter attack.

However, even with all the available standing troops committed, it had already proved a lengthy exercise to retake the town. Even with the enemy reduced to isolated pockets of resistance Changworth was pushed to come up with an effective ongoing strategy; due especially to the appearance of the huge tethered assault platform moored to the north. The wall tower, near where the Bigatrons were reported to have breached, had no doubt been taken by treachery. Message birds recorded that the tower itself and surrounding walls had actually been torn down. So smoothly had the landing happened that the Collector, and his troops, as captured Roke scouts had revealed, could afford the luxury of using the strength of these particularly massive monsters for simple demolition work, before sending them further up the wall and pushing his regular troops into the interior.

The local admiralty command remained in turmoil and Changworth had no choice but to leave his standard raised over the whole town, managing the politics as they sought him out, for he was one of the Iron Isles' council of generals, Charles Changworth. He finally announced a full war alert at around noon and committed a third of the populace to battle duty on the streets of Buccaneer Town. Despite still being under attack from the sea, admiralty ships began to drop heavily armed marines further along the coast, before continuing to fight the Roke fleet. These troops soon arrived at the town and organisation was restored; the last remnants of the traitor force needed to be drawn out of their holes.

Outside the sea gates the first ships that arrived, within a couple of parts of Midst, were drawn straight into the battle as the Roke vessels spilling over from the landings made their way to spread havoc along the coast. Through the night and into the day the odds swung dramatically: sometimes with the Roke vastly superior, at other times comfortably outnumbered. Just before dawn the odds had swung dramatically in the favour of the Roke again, at 20 to 8, but within the next part the fleet moved back to 30 to 20, all fifty ships battling furiously.

As the day lengthened, fresh admiralty ships, hastily despatched on news of the attacks, began arriving and pushed the odds down. Finally, with the numbers consistently level, the sea-wall defenders saw the admiralty tighten its grip and many more Roke vessels were sunk in proportion to local ships lost. Throughout the day the admiralty struggled to hold off the continually arriving Roke fleet. Finally 100 ships converged to break a second wave of Roke battleships, much further off shore, and as the number of human manned ships increased the fighting moved away from the sea wall and the danger of assault tailed off.

*****

Back at the beginning of the attack, just after leaving Lauren and Millie, Taverner ran carefully up the steps to the pigeon loft. He, more than anyone, knew the importance of careful planning. He had numbers of coded messages already prepared for instant attachment to a bird. Within moments he had selected several, and pausing only to fill in a few date and time spaces he let 15 birds loose.

"Good luck, my friends," he murmured absently to the departing shapes, already out of view in the darkness, some with considerable distances to travel.

Next he hurried to his room where he selected a carefully prepared kitbag before returning to the private eating room, where only the Admiral and an aide remained. After a few moments discussion he hurried down to the kitchens.

"Right Millie, shut down the club, combat operations only – its your command now, Major. I'll be absent for a considerable period as we discussed. Good Luck!"

Without giving Millie a chance to reply he was off, trotting towards the stables.

"Kint lad, we need the closed coach to get the Admiral back to the compound. Quick as you can, please!" Taverner called out to the yard before retracing his steps through the lantern-lit service corridors to the private room with the guard on the door.

Moments later there was a knock on that same door and Millie arrived with the other three members of the Admiral's honour guard. The door opened and the Admiral swept through, his greatcoat already on and firmly done up, cap of office pulled down, obviously forewarned as to the murky weather waiting for him outside. Still, he bobbed his head to his guard as usual and his jutting jaw and trademark salt-and-pepper beard flashed through the corridors. The two larger of his guards struggled to get ahead of the old fleet commander, who drove them on before him like a sled driver with his team.

With the guards in front to open the doors scant time passed before he was at the coach. Settled quickly inside the plush velvet interior, the guards mounted, his carriage was away, bouncing through the streets towards the Admiral's Fleet HQ. Surging past the loose knot of attackers who were approaching Changworth, the coach was safely past; one of the out riders was off and away covering the distance to the Admiralty as quickly as he could. They were hardly half way before he was back with the news that Fleet HQ was under attack. As the coach stopped for a conference to be held it became apparent that the highly visible, mounted officer, in his admiralty uniform, had attracted the attention of the brigands. The noise of pursuit ran through the street ahead of the attackers as they hurried to intercept the coach.

Quickly the Admiral was out of the coach door. He took a palomino offered by one of his officers, who moved to join the coach driver. As the admiral checked the gear on the big war horse the officer and the coachman turned the carriage to block the street. Reaching into the chest that formed the base of the driver's seat, each pulled out an arblast and began winding. Two of the mounted guards also drew horn bows and rode to the barricade to join the defence.

The Admiral called some brief words of encouragement back to the female warrior and the coach driver at the temporary road block and, with the other two men riding ahead, he turned his horse to race towards the western town gates, nearest the main road. As they raced back towards the club they saw a number of familiar armed and mounted shapes leaving its rear stable and race off ahead of them. On reaching the western gates the Admiral found the scene one of turmoil. The foremost of his guards pulled up suddenly and in a mighty voice bellowed,

"Protect the Admiral! Make way for the Admiral!" Taverner smiled beneath the fake beard. Very soon the whole town would know that the Admiral had fled the city by this route. As he rode under the gate's arch the Admirals two guards paused to join the fight and then he was out and away, on his own with barely a pause.

Taverner caught fleeting images as he passed: one which stuck and troubled him was a glimpse of Millie, battling furiously against a figure who, as it turned to look at him, was clearly holding her at bay.

It had never been part of the plan for Millie to become so involved with the fighting, she was too valuable in terms of organising the defence. Millie had obviously decided to take the bit between her teeth and echo Changworth's method of leading from the front. Fully committed to his own plan all Taverner could do was grind his teeth in frustration; knowing that Millie was tough and resourceful. Still, as the wind whipped his long grey hair back, he indulged in a few moments of concern, for despite her being a superb fighter he knew that a few of the Roke agents were better skilled and more deadly. As he spurred his horse down the road he looked back to see a party of dark, cloaked figures mounting outside the gate. He felt rather than saw that the dark figure he was worried about was one of that party. Taverner could only hope that he had disengaged and had not had time to finish Millie.

As a key part of the Roke party broke off, and quickly rode off to pursue the rapidly departing figure of the Admiral, Millie was able to pause and look out through the gate. Despite being out of breath Millie was unharmed and had never felt more alive. Initially she had been concerned at the skill of some of the Roke: the one she had fought, in particular, had cut through the gate guards like a scythe through wheat, which was why she had plunged into the fight contrary to her orders. He had been a truly talented opponent but she felt they had both held a little back in their engagement and now she would never know the outcome. At least she had prevented him from claiming any more kills and now, thank the Battler, he was outside the town. If anyone could survive being hunted by him, she felt it was Taverner.

"Major," one of the Admiral's guards rushed over. "There

are 12 in pursuit and, despite their head start, Giles and I could possibly catch their tail and even the odds some," the guard suggested selflessly.

"No, let's stick to the plan. You help us to get this gate secure and then we need to have a look at Fleet HQ," Millie replied firmly.

"Yes Ma'am," he replied as the pair turned back. Millie jogged over to help a struggling comrade fight. Even this far into the conflict Millie found herself about to hang back and watch Katie fight so that she could offer training tips later, but instead she lanced the Roke from behind, freeing the grateful girl from the conflict.

"Come on, Kate, let's get into the gate house and get that iron down," Millie bellowed, starting up the gatehouse steps. Within moments they were at the gatehouse door and Millie engaged the Roke agent defending the narrow opening. Committed to the plan, she was in a hurry and unleashed a full and blistering attack which had her opponent's throat open within an instant. Almost as the man was falling she stepped over the body and engaged the other two room occupants. They looked at her with disbelief as she spun under her own over-head block to backhand a dagger into the chest of the nearest. She completed a classic turning lunge to pierce the eye of the second even as his sword scrapped across the belly of her mail, just a measured fraction from opening her guts. Katie looked no less amazed as she barrelled into the room after her.

"OK, Kate, get the gate down and keep it down until somebody gives you appropriately coded orders. And bar the door behind me," with that Millie triggered the gate and portcullis mechanism and, waiting only to see them descend, ran out of the room.

Katie followed her exact instructions and immediately barred the entrance and searched for the hidden release that dropped the mini-cullis behind the guardroom door. Then she dragged the corpses into a corner, pulled up a chair and sat down to wait.

Millie paused at the bottom of the steps watching in satisfaction as both sets of wood and iron dropped into place. Then, after finishing another nearby fight, she called to Cat to continue the fight to mop up the defenders. Millie then mounted her horse and rode back towards the club. As she headed off she was completely unaware of the large number of Roke re-enforcements heading up the nearby streets from the opposite direction.

✳✳✳✳✳

Taverner only remained on the main road for about a league and then, as if trying to trick his pursuers, took a track that lead off gently towards the northern hills. Despite their appearing unsuitable and ill planned he had long ago explored and memorised all the roads and tracks within the area; this was part of a predetermined route that he had picked. He slowed Windrider for a short spell, knowing that the pursuit would need to be a bit closer if he were to keep them following. Looking back he had seen one of the Roke in pursuit free a tiny message bird. Taverner was pleased that news of the Admiral being hunted in the hills was being spread so effectively.

By now the Admiral should be safely on his chosen vessel and ready to co-ordinate the seaborne defence to the Roke threat. Hearing the sounds of a closer pursuit he spurred his horse gently and rode hard along the sloping track. Within the part, with the sounds of the pursuit firmly behind him, he rode across a high valley meadow. Had he been another day-part later his plan would have come apart as he would have been wading through the bulk of the Collector's landed force, a fact he was only to learn much later that day. At that time, though, he was unaware that the coast walls were breached and the Bigatrons, having torn out a large section, were smashing their way through the stockade complex at the mouth of the valley. The complex was a facility that served to house the defence force reserve and protect the route to the interior against any invading army.

Now though, with the ground opening up, he waited until he was sure that the pursuers could gain a clear sight of him in the gentle light of the full moon, before giving Windrider his full head. Taverner was well pleased with this horse, it had been many years since he had had a mount of this quality and he could feel the animals powerful muscles bunch beneath him as

244

he urged the mount on. For this section of his route it was crucial that he gained as much distance he could. Once across the meadow the track they would take would limit the speed of his mount as it began to wind its way up into the mountain foot hills.

He was fairly confident that the opposition wouldn't have mounts of the same quality, and he was right; although more to the point was the fact that the Roke were being careful to ride as a group, keeping the pace of the slowest. If Taverner had known this fact he might have been interested in this unusual display of professional behaviour.

*****

Mandibles had been pacing the room, back and forth, back and forth, fighting the feeling nothing mattered now the lad was gone. For the last twelve years, he had hidden his hope for the future in the young sponsored boy. The lad had grown up strong and not simply survived but flourished in these difficult times. All who knew Piker had welcomed his smile and strong arm. Several times it had been said that he had pulled other warriors out of difficult situations, despite his own youth.

"Oh my lad, oh Piker. Goodbye," Mandibles moaned wearily, his head in his hands.

The door creaked open and Changworth strode in. He looked worn. "Bout time boss. Need to get busy you know!" Mandibles called as soon as his friend came in.

"You look tired, Mandi. I am sorry about your boy. He died like a warrior. He was a credit to you." Changworth barely waited for any response. "Business goes on for now though. It seems up to us to hold the town." Changworth wearily pulled over a chair and sat heavily in it. "I've heard that if that envoy, with his bodyguard, hadn't been taking a bit of free sport himself you would have come up short earlier. I desperately need you good friend, don't go throwing yourself away." As if stiffening his resolve he returned to a more formal manner. "Mandibles, you will command the front line support troops and I order you not to put either yourself or your men in undue danger. Is that understood, Major?" So saying Changworth pushed a parchment of defence notes under Mandible's nose.

As he finished a knock came at the door. "Enter!" he called hoarsely.

Barney stuck his head round the door. "Commander Studos, the Caballeros envoy is here, sir. Can I see him in?"

"Yes Barney, straight away lad," Changworth replied.

The envoy almost bounded through the door and swaggered straight to the window, where looking, out he pursed his lips and stroked his moustache, nodding at the general and then glaring at Mandibles.

"Ah! Commander Studos, about your request to help with the defence of the town. Due to your heroic efforts earlier I have decided to grant your request. I would be most grateful if you would take joint command of the seafront defences with Major Mandibles here," Changworth said in a no nonsense tone, gesturing at Mandibles.

"General, your praise is most welcome to me but I fear that co-operation with this man, such as you propose, would not work. He is greatly careless and his style is erratic. Maybe you have another more refined leader with whom I may work, the envoy replied, casually gazing out of the window, not even bothering to face those to whom he was speaking.

Changworth's expression darkened visibly but he continued in a level voice. "Commander Studos, I am sorry, but that is your task. By all means take a few moments for the two of you to confer but you will be fully deployed in two day-parts I expect the battle to re-commence in four and you must be ready to plug any breach. Good luck to you both," Changworth almost shouted, and getting up left by the door, which he almost tore from its frame.

This demonstration of power, rather than the words, attracted the envoy's attention and he looked quizzically at Mandibles who, rising from his chair, walked over and patted the younger man on the shoulder. "Well, it seems you are landed with me, son. Come," Mandibles said soothingly, "I agree that I allowed my heart to rule my head earlier. But I had just lost a boy who was like a son to me. But let us put that aside. You're needed to rescue me like a green cadet." Taking the envoy's silence as agreement Mandibles suggested, "We need to collect

70 warriors and, I believe, split them into four rough groups. Each of us will lead one, with the others for relief rotation. What do you say to that plan?" He asked the young Caballeros duke earnestly.

"Fine Mandi," said Lauren standing in the open doorway. "Changworth has assigned me to the back-up squads. Although my command was all but wiped out this morning, and I have only 8 able-bodied troopers available, can I join one of your reserve teams?"

Mandibles looked to Commander Studos who, with a shrug, gave in and grinning at Lauren he replied for them both, "Certainly, Miss Marshall. I hope your men resist the urge for vengeance and fight to our orders."

"They will commander, I shall ensure it. They are highly trained," Lauren replied formally with a smile.

"Well, good enough," said Mandibles. "Including my assigned northerners we have some 30 troops, the barest minimum, with no possibility of rotation. Let us hurry with all speed to the citizen commander, he should have reserved us the same number of citizen fighters."

An eighth later they were standing near the remains of a dock-front warehouse. "Well, commander, a motley ragtag of men and women these. A couple look no better than whores, excuse my language, Captain," the duke commented, a bit too loudly for Mandibles' liking.

Before he could respond the Marine Captain replied in defence of his, albeit inherited, troops. "You are quick to judge Duke Studos, but I know your men were frequent visitors to the bonded brothels and despite their mix of civilian professions, all our citizens are trained and willing. So no offence, sir, but these are your allocated troops and frankly, sir, you can like it." So saying the officer walked off to supervise another allocation.

"Well that sorts that out," Lauren whispered at Mandibles who just shook his head in despair.

*****

Chill winds blew up from the choppy waters of the bay, making the lamp flame flicker behind the glass. The sparse light only emphasised the face of Lauren's companion and subordinate with his moustache, that dropped like a clump from below his much bent snout, er nose, Lauren corrected herself, with one of her rare, fleeting grins. A young man, who rather resembled an adolescent black bear as he stumped along powerfully, despite his slight limp, behind her long legged and panther-smooth gait. Already the fighting had proved the worth of his powerful frame, despite his lack of mobility on the sea wall. With a light voice Lauren called out encouragingly to her command, a voice which was, like her, small, neat, spare and yet strong enough to prevail. Lauren was prowling the ramparts, relieving Studos during a lull in the fighting, offering what she could in words and help to professionals and citizens alike. As the night dragged on and those on the wall waited for more Roke vessels to come in and challenge their position.

Suddenly a familiar female voice called out from the darkness with an offer of a couple of troops to join the defence. Lauren weighed her answer for a moment, as if picking her words carefully. Rumour had it in the club that Millie had once been a weapons instructor herself, but had joined Star's employ for a minor partnership when he had asked her. "Millie we do have enough troops to hold, thank you, but you and Kint are welcome to join us," she replied. Millie, her head cut and looking extremely tired, had arrived suddenly out of the darkness offering herself and Kint to reinforce the wall defenders. It appeared, Lauren thought, that all the espionage work had dried up in Buccaneer Town and now the only priority was to hold the walls.

*****

Night had fallen again by the time Changworth felt, rather than heard, the messenger approach. She was younger than he expected, at most 25. Her black hair curled thickly around her face, damp at the edges from her exertions and only now loosing from the compression caused by her war helm, evidently recently removed. Full lips, deep set, wine coloured eyes. A real beauty and tall for a woman as well. Stella Trim was the brave young under-officer who, despite loosing her senior officer and much of the wall command to early treachery, had fought on desperately to hold successfully the sea defences all through the preceding night and into the afternoon, until relieved by Mandibles and Studos. Even then she had fought on rather than resting and had come to report directly to the town commander when Studos had finally forced her to take a break. Her report was quick and precise.

Running out into the night on the greasy sea wall Stella had been in time to see the schooner, *Selfridge,* heading towards the sea gate, signalling that it be allowed through for forward defence. At that point it was easy, the gate was still down and the walls clear. The wall commander, Stella's leader, was missing and all his team dead, dying or in the water around the internal gate ladders which were still in place and had been successfully defended, with the Roke ship that had tied up to land an attack force burning below. The *Selfridge* swept past and Stella and her team began raising the gate, whilst a couple of her squad sheared the ladder bolts, causing the two iron cage ladders to crash down on the burning ship below. A Roke vessel, that had been struggling to turn under flame arrow fire from a number of brave little boats, was picking up speed to pursue the schooner, and at this rate it looked as if it might simply ram the gate. Stella's squad however was strong and, well practiced and moreover, angry, and the gate rose rapidly. On the other side of the wall the schooner began slewing dramatically as it sought to out-guess the four further Roke ships it was running towards and get safe side of only one. Fortunately, the nearest Roke vessel must have been sticking to its plan of assaulting the battery and was too committed to that manoeuvre to contribute to boxing the schooner in. The *Selfridge* was a renowned warship, Blighe Shaw, its Captain, was young but capable and partnered with Joonrer, the famous helmsman.

On board the tight-sailed vessel as it shot through the closing gates and out into the ocean, a shuttered lantern had been raised and signalled towards the gate house. Stella had missed the message as the twin guard towers shook with the force of the impact, as the Roke ship, speeding to block the entrance, hit the sea chain, and rising out of the water smashed into the upper part of the wall. Turning back to look outwards as the splintered shards fell back into the raging waves, Joonrer, the helmsman, turned his vessel and signalling his crew for more sail he smashed angled prow-ram against the flank of an approaching Roke ship. The schooner was turning away from the gate area and struggling to avoid the damaged vessel's fate as the holed rear end collapsed and it was sucked down under the waves.

Whether Joonrer prayed to the legends of the Ocean or the Battle God, Stella didn't know, but further signals showed he was concerned as he knew that more Roke ships were likely to be arriving at any time: he had seen at least four Roke battle cutters in the inner harbour. If the patrol ships were sunk the *Sea Spray* could well be the only Northern ship under sail within 50 leagues and, having left several parts earlier, there was no way of recalling the schooner's sister ship.

Torn away from Joonrer's concerns out in the bay, Stella had been hard pressed and was only able to report certain highlights of the sea battle to General Changworth. That the *Selfridge* had been able to hold off the four Roke vessels damaging two seriously, until reinforcements had begun to arrive for both sides was of key importance. But as the battle had ebbed and flowed Roke ships had at times been able to close with the wall. Then her team had been forced not only to defend the battery but also repel Roke marines who, with grapnels and ropes, had tried to climb the outer walls. Frequently she had lost track of time and very quickly did not know what had happened to the heroic schooner and its crew. Possibly it was now fighting further out or had been holed and sunk. Nor had she been sufficiently knowledgeable to identify specific vessels only giving the General a rough impression of how many Roke and Northern vessels she felt had been destroyed.

Finally, with only a hand full of able-bodied warriors remaining in her command, she had been relieved around noon. She felt the need to report to General Changworth at his forward headquarters near the docks.

*****

Taverner had instructed that the Roke should be allowed to send a number of positive signals before the serious efforts to retake the town began. The large number of Iron Islanders camped nearby, in secret transit to the Battle Lands, had been drawn fully into the town's defence, called for deployment by Taverner's messenger birds. As they arrived either Millie or Changworth had managed to get messages to direct them but by the first night they were spread all over the area. Stella had revealed it was some of these troops who were to break through eventually to relieve the battery and sea wall.

Even with the town mostly retaken, General Changworth felt pushed to come up with an effective counter attack against the huge tethered platforms to the north. With the nearest tower and costal defence wall ruined by the devastating strike from the Collector's army, and harassed by the strong residual force that the Roke commander had left behind, all that Changworth could do, whilst he fought for control of the area, was despatch some fighting troops with engineering experience. The nearby roads also needed protection but the vast numbers of enemy landed and the presence of Reptoids caused any patrols or barricades to be swept aside. Despite heroic and bitter defence, whether he sent small or large companies out relative to the scant resources he had at hand, it would be impossible to engage the vast Horde army reported, should it turn on Buccaneer Town.

As Changworth began taking official reports he became more worried on finding the scope of the force that had reached the interior. Logistically complex, the assault was clearly an attack meant to hold, rather than a strike and retreat operation – which is what they had believed the treachery was about.

The Iron Island's attack force had been due to continue onwards to the front under its senior battle leader, whilst Changworth was to begin staging the Iron forces for their movement into the less defended areas of the Battle Lands through to Trade Town. He, however, had now deployed his entire detachment of assault commandos and sent word to the Marshall, promising that he would not require reinforcements if his detachment could remain in Buccaneer Town.

The numbers of the Horde who had landed meant that Changworth was caught up in a full scale land war. The reports of his men fighting in the town also revealed a frightening number of Siblants. The count had already reached, perhaps, as many as he might have expected to find along the whole Battle Lands wall in a quiet season's campaign.

He had also lost key and valuable men in the heavy fighting. Squeeze, a hugely muscled team leader, squat and powerful and about as tough as the Iron Island forces had, had been tasked with entering and aiding the defence of a southern side-gate. But the small squad of 20 had apparently run into 60 Roke and 20 Siblant defenders in the process of securing the gate and both groups had proceeded to tear the other to pieces.

20 elite men dead. The first Iron forces on the scene had reported this as a dispatch making engagement. The backup teams found masses of bodies and only three Roke and six Siblants remaining to put to the spear. Still, even a 5 to 1 ratio would avail the Northerners little if such massive numbers of the Horde could be landed. Certainly, three particularly large Bigatrons had made it to land. There were other reports of heavy fighting further up, possibly right to the mountain bastion, which marked where the mountains ended the need for coastal walls.

If the Roke followed their standard practice, possibly a further two times as many ships might be waiting to land at various points. If these arrived where the Roke held, then enough additional troops, could be brought ashore quickly so that plugging the gap might become impossible. These would be both assault and also land campaign troops Changworth now understood.

The Iron fleet would need to be cautious, obviously it could slow and possibly even halt the ships, as had been the plan for this attack. But what if similar landings were also being attempted against the Iron Isles themselves, especially with the current delicate situation that had required his trip to Buccaneer Town in the first place. Also worrying was the fact that this number of ships had passed them at all. 'Could the northern Fleet already be sunk?' Changworth asked himself with dread.

Certainly, for once, the Northern and Iron fleets could be the smaller of the battling naval powers. Pushing these thoughts aside Changworth moved to improve his headquarters, both back at the club and also with key staging posts and protected lines of communication near the dock front. Heavy and light field weapons were being hastily assembled: the good news was that stocks of these were plentiful, both the official armoury and the secret one in the Chandlery having been kept in tact.

By the time further Horde assaults were likely Changworth estimated that eleven hundred harp and shrapnel throwers could be assembled along the town and sea walls. A call-out of the forty percent of the town's citizenry with defence training would serve to augment his own ballistic specialists. Of the rest of the town's inhabitants a small fraction would stay, limited to a ten percent support force. The remaining half of the town's population were being herded out into the hills and picked up and organised by the now fully deployed partisan commanders. Despite a meeting with a couple of senior partisan commanders early in the afternoon Changworth was pleased at how well that infrastructure seemed to be working, and also secretly at how little he was being asked to contribute.

As Midst-night approached reports from arriving ships began coming in. It appeared that the Iron fleet was indeed engaged by a Horde attack force of an equivalent size to the first. The good news being that they had held the advance offshore at the chained rocks. Deployment of anchorable, chained, barges now held the enemy under both the Iron Isle's land and sea co ordinated bombardment.

This good news from his homeland contrasted with that finally in from the coastal defence force, which had been breached again further north. A force of 2,000 Roke plus several Red Masters and numbers of Siblants were holding the breach. The fleet, however, had arrived in time to drive off or sink other landing craft that were attempting to follow the first flotilla in.

A couple of parts later Changworth received a report from some marines who had landed on the flotilla islands and made their way back to Buccaneer Town clearing away remaining Roke and Reptoids.

"Well sir, it looks like those Bigatrons that breached the wall, well, they were used to power the massive barge that the other ships are now chained to, them and some other big Reptoids. We have found spaces where the ships have big water-wheel like contraptions, connected by shafts to other wheels inside, that may have had Bigatrons harnessed in to turn them. One of our techs reckon they could have displaced enough water to move even the platform against the tide." The scarred marine captain scratched his shoulder. "We've never heard of any of the packs working together as cleverly as that before Human captives seem to have been kept as food, although we have not found survivors yet. Could be we've got some nasty new breeds."

"Right enough, Captain," Changworth broke in. "We have seen more evidence of Siblants fighting together in Buccaneer Town than I've ever heard, so I reason you are right. Maybe there were Siblants used to keep order on these ships as well as Roke, which is a pretty frightening thought. We've also had reports of the traitors feeding humans to some kind of strange water beast kept caged off the coast. I've a couple of teams looking into it but the influx of Roke ships was concentrated in the same area where it was reported, preventing us from having a good look round." Working away whilst he considered the report Changworth motioned an aide over and sent him out with a newly sealed packet of hastily scrawled commands.

"Captain, the numbers you have mentioned seem to indicate that all the Bigatrons that breached the walls have been killed. Do you have any numbers for the Reptoid masters that might also be loose?" Changworth asked the captain, as he walked over to consider a map on the wall of his hastily constructed command post.

"Well sir, the harness we've found suggests up to sixty," the Captain returned without hesitation.

"Battler be summoned! We've only dealt with a fraction of that number here and that shook us bad enough. Someone or somewhere is in for a nasty shock; as we haven't seen them here yet I suspect they have moved inland."

Changworth hurried to the doorway where he motioned in one of his men who had been wolfing down some food in the brief respite. "Slider, get the partisans to spread the word back in country, 60 Reptoid masters, type unknown, possibly in one group." He turned back as his man dashed off. "That number will be able to overrun smaller settlements easily where even large numbers of Roke could have been held off. I hope that is the extent of your bad news Captain?"

"Beg your pardon, sir," the Captain said, eyeing the door,

clearly ready to salute and leave but with one last awkward question. "I keep getting asked if there is anymore news in from the Iron Fleet. They would sure be handy with most of our scoops battle locked."

"I'm afraid we do have Captain. Two more flotilla packs are being held off the coast of Dark Spire and a fifth is being attacked further out to sea by the rest of the fleet. Therefore we are not going to receive any immediate help, but on the bright side, there are no immediate reinforcements coming for the Horde." Changworth looked steadily at the Marine Captain trying to hide his concern but offering the man the chance to pursue his concerns as far as he wished. Seeing no further questions were coming he was relieved to hurry on. "Captain, before you go, any estimate of losses from the fleet?"

"Well General, last I heard over 1,000 were engaged in battles of various sizes. Definite losses in the early fighting total about the same number either lost, de-crewed or limping for shore. Mopping up the first wave and holding off the second we have may be a total two and a half thousand vessels – the entire remaining coastal defence force. Whether the fleet triumphs all depends on how many ships the second wave of Roke brings. I reckon that some more will make it through to Buccaneer Town, just through weight of numbers. At the breach we are about to start sinking every third tethered ship to stop the Horde from crossing it easily, currently it makes a pretty effective walk-way to get to land. We shall avoid lighting it up as long as possible as that amount of wood, well, it would be a big fire indeed." The Captain hastily conferred with his aide. "We have also got some engineers out on the edges, sir, but its slow going separating the ships and towing them away. They are all packed so tight."

"Right then, Captain, do what you can and keep me informed."

"General, Captain can I interrupt?" Barney asked from the doorway. "Major Munroe is back from the coastal defences, shall I send him through."

"Yes, send him in, Barney," Changworth answered turning to the door expectantly. "Monty you have made good time. Can we hear how the repairs to the sea defences are progressing?" Changworth asked the dirt-covered officer, his face fully camouflaged. "Well sir, we have basic wood and dirt skirmish walls covering all the breach points but it's not going to stop large beasts or numbers of attackers. The main breach is still being attacked from the land side and that is really slowing progress and preventing decent materials from reaching the engineers."

*****

Sitting on the edge of the battlements in a lull in the fighting, Mandibles could reflect on the day's events. Not only had Piker gone on, but in the following tussle in the square Snibs had been cut up pretty bad and six of the local customers with them had also died. With Chang separated and on his way to the western gate and Mandibles in a battle frenzy beyond reach, Snibs had lead the remaining locals across town to the west gate. Now Snibs was dead and whilst that wasn't Mandibles' own doing, even had he been coherent, he would probably have sent Snibs there anyway. Looking back he felt uncomfortable that the rage had returned and that he had lost control of his senses, even temporarily, which he had struggled so long to keep in check.

*****

Three day-parts after crossing the mountain pasture, on the night of the initial attack, Taverner rode on through the forest. With the whisper of the wind behind him, the darkness began to give way before the warming light of the rising sun. This ancient forest was familiar to him and he loved it, for it was here he had ridden when first arrived in the North. Many years had past since he had been taught the art of war, and the past day had drawn him back like a toddler reeled in by his father. Training had made his body strong and quick, but battle always seemed to tire him mentally. Here though, he had lain through whole days, watching the small animals that inhabited the forest. Now he felt this former peace sink back within him. As the light finally rose he slid from the saddle and leading the horse he set off down the steep bank drawing the horse down, slipping and sliding on its hindquarters.

At times they slithered out of control down through the green grass, dirt or leaf mulch, branches pulling at harness and cloak. Suddenly they emerged into the clear of a smaller valley and as they punched out of the under-growth Taverner heaved himself upright and suddenly catching the saddle's cantle he sprang onto his horse and raced towards the nearby road.

A league later he came upon the small deserted roadside hut and checking in the leaning shed that served as a stable he found the light mountain-horse that he had requested. With a brief apology to Windrider, who had performed wonderfully, he tethered the mount and transferring his saddle bags mounted the fresh and spirited mare, of a breed more suited to the mountains than the large war horse. He rode on without hesitation.

In a nearby tree old Tiggs sat perched comfortably on a limb. His instructions had been to furnish the horse and wait for a period of his own discretion, allowing any pursuit to pass, before collecting Taverner's original horse and returning it eventually to the club in Buccaneer Town.

Tiggs' patience had improved as he passed from old to ancient and he settled back to wait for signs of the pursuit. He certainly didn't intend to collect the horse early and fall foul of whatever trouble Taverner had got himself into this time.

****

Well into day two of the battle for Buccaneer Town news finally arrived that all the breaches had been closed. The cost totalled some 3,000 troops lost, with the remaining 700 active coastal defence troops from that command spread thinly. Many were now racing further north to replace the garrison of the seventeenth, and final, coast fort, which itself had fallen to a host of strange imp-like Reptoids.

More and more Changworth was aware that not only had he seen the first time in a millennium when Reptoid masters, imps, or in fact any type of Reptoids, had been landed in any numbers on the continent, but that disturbing changes in their assumed behaviour and capabilities were also being observed. With the state of emergency already raised to the highest possible level he was finally forced to use his only remaining option and issue a full military call-up to everybody in the area.

That the early intelligence reports, which had suggested seven to eight thousand Roke with some Siblant support, launching a short raid in an attempt to burn Buccaneer Town down had been a clever piece of misinformation was now patently clear. With the aim not simply being to weaken the admiralty, the use of the Night Fort club as an intelligence station, had clearly failed. Although the accidental fact that it was packed with well organised, combat-ready troops who could act as a control and liaison base for an Iron Islander General was clearly a factor that had allowed the town to be saved thus far. Changworth silently vowed to redouble his efforts to preserve the facility and secure the surrounding area. Glaring at the wall map his staff a bustle of activity around him, he fought on more determined than ever.

Chapter Thirteen

The Roke captain, Karl, was desperate to regain some standing from the opportunity to kill the Buccaneer Town admiral. Since his failure to find the old woman in the woods the tasks he had been given had proven even more demeaning. His failure to injure the young militia commander in the warehouse fights was positively life threatening. All the sneaking around was undoubtedly blunting his carefully honed fighting skills, and even now, whilst he was practising his favourite hobby of hunting humans, the glory of the battle for Buccaneer Town was denied him.

'Finally the admiral has made his second and final mistake,' he thought to himself and ordered that their last message bird be released to confirm an imminent kill. The admiral's first mistake had clearly been that he had left the main road. Quite how he had appropriated the second horse remained a mystery that the Roke commander didn't really have time to resolve. Now his prey had erred for the last time, riding into what was clearly a high mountain valley that had only one entry or exit.

Karl decided that it was the time for caution and he paired up his six-man command. They were making their way stealthily towards the far end of the valley where there appeared to be a cabin. It was news of this, from his forward scout, that had prompted his cautious approach, for it was not impossible that the admiral had, in fact, found some isolated habitation.

Karl was aware that a number of mountain peasants might actually live in the area; it was possible that the admiral would be able to convince them to fight for him. That was why Karl and his number two man, Dirtch, rode slowly up what served for a track as his other men proceeded on foot, in pairs, through the trees parallel both to the road and the narrow valley walls as they wound towards the open grass in front of the shack. There was no way that Karl was risking being ambushed.

As they reached the edge of the clearing unchallenged Karl began to feel more confident again. He rode out into the open and was considering shouting some kind of derogatory challenge, to try and lure his prey into a stand up fight, but it seemed that he did not need to. From around the side of the shack rode a warrior in full crimson armour. It did, indeed, look as if the admiral had found some kind of champion and was hiding himself in the shack awaiting the outcome.

That the warrior looked professional and even carried a short lance and shield didn't particularly worry Karl. He called his men forward, out of the undergrowth, shouting his instructions to them in a rough, almost unintelligible, Roke dialect. His plan, he decided, was for himself and Dirtch to ride out as if to meet the charge of the warrior, whilst actually pulling up short so that the four archers could shoot him out of his saddle with plenty of room to spare.

He signalled to his men to advance and the two horsemen began to ride slowly forwards. Suddenly the crimson warrior spurred his powerful warhorse and it set off at tremendous pace. The well trained horse began weaving and the first two arrows flew narrowly past the rider, whose speed had surprised the archers. The crimson knight, angling across the riders with an arrow thudding into his shield and one grazing his leg, rode down the furthest archer to the left. His battle-bred horse seemed to pause, prancing on the body, destroying all chance that the archer could survive, and then was off again bearing down on the second archer who, with reasonable skill, threw down his bow and had a long sword out to meet the attack. He had little chance on foot, though, and he was skewered by the horseman's lance. The crimson clad man, with an impressive display of strength, couched the lance normally, transporting the twitching and impaled archer as if he was as light as air. With surprising speed the mounted knight and his victim closed the distance to where Dirtch had turned his horse and was riding in to attack what he thought would be a distracted horseman, his lance fouled by the unfortunate archer.

Karl could only watch as, instead of coming in cleanly, Dirtch was forced into colliding with the lance and body, which the rider released at the last moment directly into his path. It wasn't until his horse had ridden on for 20 more spans that Dirtch collapsed from his saddle, obviously injured in some way that Karl had not been able to see.

Karl began to back his horse away, conscious of wanting to give the remaining two archers a chance, and indeed, as the crimson warrior turned two more arrows sped in to strike his shield, which with three imbedded, was becoming a less useful article. Again the horse surged forwards, and this time the distance was shorter. The warrior had a morning star out and whirling it a couple of times around his head he released it in a dramatic throw, narrowly avoiding another speeding arrow, now able to disregard the archer diagonally behind Karl as he drew a blade. Having assumed his opponent was going to repeat his initial tactics, Karl had barely raised his sword to defend himself when the warrior rode in. A powerful man, the Roke Captain was shocked, as meeting the blows rocked him back in his saddle and he was glad when he was clear of the charge and turning to face the horse man.

The sight he met when he had completed his turn was bad. Both the remaining archers were down, one dropped with the chain of the morning star wrapped around his neck, the other on one knee coughing up blood from a dagger which the crimson warrior had hurled into his chest.

Glancing behind him Dirtch lay still on the ground, his horse pacing beside the body and Karl could only assume the same had happened to him. Turning back the crimson warrior seemed to have tired of his shield and the tangle of arrow shafts protruding from it. As he cast this aside Karl spurred his horse but now, instead of towards his opponent, he used his position nearer the shack. He dashed towards it intending to take the admiral hostage or at least kill the old fool before having to deal with this skilled opponent.

Slipping gracefully from his horse as it was still slowing, he came to the ground running and putting his shoulder to the door smashed his way into the dingy interior of the shack. The admiral, however, was nowhere to be seen and Karl literally howled in fury, realising that the old man had hidden in the trees on the far side of the clearing. Looking back through the door the crimson warrior had dropped from his own horse, which now stood stationary in the clearing, and was walking steadily through the grass towards the shack.

Karl decided that the man was too good to risk a fair fight with. Still in the darkness he broke a phial of fast acting poison into his sword scabbard, before sheathing the blade to give it a thorough coating. Thus, apparently unconcerned, he too strolled out through the grass to face his opponent, all the while knowing that all he had to do was score one flesh wound and then avoid the warrior for a few moments while the poison took effect.

As he closed with the warrior he drew his sword and with a complicated series of sweeps cut the air before the warrior in a move calculated to raise his guard and allow the Roke Captain a cut at his thigh or legs. Instead, Karl's cut was powerfully blocked and he drew back to cut at the crimson helmet, only to find that the move had been pre-empted. The crimson knight, having stepped in as he moved back, caught his sword hand in a powerful grip, crushing his fingers and stabbing his own sword down like a dagger, deep into the flesh and bone of Karl's leg. Screaming in pain Karl had time to register that the warrior had released his grip on his own sword, leaving it standing out from the wound, its weight dragging it painfully down through the flesh towards the floor. The warrior then transferred both hands to his grip on Karl's sword arm, the free hand twisting Karl's locked arm, turning his whole body down into the ground as waves of agony shot down his shoulder blade into his back. The powerful move threatened to tear his arm from its socket. It was almost in relief that Karl lost his grip on his own sword for this signalled a relaxing of the pressure on his shoulder. That the knight simply turned and using Karl's own sword, poison and all, lopped his head from his shoulders was perceived by the injured Roke as a blurred motion and then perpetual darkness.

Freeing his own sword from the Roke the crimson warrior turned and walked back to where his horse was waiting patiently, he took its bridle and led it back around the far side of the cabin.

*****

The band had completed their final song in a triumphant end to the opening night's concert. People were beginning to drift away casually from the hillside. However, Blue Boy's party seemed happy to stay around their campfire enjoying the communal spirit of the gathering in the seasonably warm night air. Master Calm was talking to a man and a woman who had appeared from the darkness, he seemed to be interested in introducing them to Marv.

As the two newcomers started up a conversation with his mentor, Master Calm moved round the fire to sit next to Blue Boy. "Perhaps you could introduce me to some of the band members while they are packing up their equipment, Blue Boy?" the Master asked the boy quietly.

"Certainly sir, it would be a pleasure. Do you want to go now?" Blue Boy replied, pleased that his early encounters with the celebrity appeared to be on an almost equal basis.

"Now would be a most excellent time, young fellow," Master Calm grinned back, and the two of them rose and moved off.

If Blue Boy had had eyes in the back of his head he would have seen that almost as soon as the pair of them left the fireside, the remainder of the group around the campfire began to cover the fire quickly and thoroughly and head off towards their own particular camping areas.

As they worked their way steadily down the hill, through the mass of people, Blue Boy was impressed, as always, at the inherent order that the citizens of the nation always managed to bring to their arrangements. Despite the large number of people entertained by the band, the careful way that the sections of hillside had been laid out meant that it was easy to move between the fire pits, but without the distances being too great and reducing the feeling of companionship.

As they neared the stage Blue Boy looked to Master Calm, who smiled back humming to himself a quiet but unfamiliar tune. Blue Boy was checking the older man's expression, for his keen eyes had picked out that Stonebrow was standing holding two sleek, fast looking horses. Starling was there too, as was Knuckles.

"Well Blue, this is it I am afraid. Our turn to say good bye,"

Stonebrow ventured. He offered the boy a warriors grip and then pulled him into a hug. "Good luck to you, lad. I am sure you will do us all proud."

"Take care of everyone, Stonebrow. I, well I, er," Blue Boy was searching and searching for the words.

"We know, Blue," Starling offered quietly. "Get on your horse now," she said firmly, her own voice thick with emotion. Master Calm was blowing in his own horse's nostrils to calm the beast and then smoothly climbed into the saddle.

"OK, my new pupil. Let us see if you can ride as well as you play," the Master said with a slight wave to Stonebrow and with that he cantered off leaving Blue Boy no more time with his friends. As he rode away from the fayre the tears streamed down his face.

Two whole days of non-stop riding and six changes of horse later, Master Calm finally let the exhausted ex-band-member drop from his saddle at their destination. Boy Blue fell straight into a kind, dreamless, slumber without a thought or emotion left in his body.

*****

Each settlement in the territory had a representative set of quartermaster offices. Working for the Quartermaster General these officials supervised a number of people and functions. Webbing, harness and scabbards were all recycled by the outfitters, with the pickers supplying as much as they could sensibly collect without impacting their more essential search for iron and weapons. Standard social convention permitted each citizen to be outfitted in a simple military manner, free of charge. In contrast the successful fighting companies with their wealthier individuals were often noted more for their ornate attire than the skills that actually allowed them to be so successful. Social fashion ran parallel to the fitness-conscious environment and looking good and dressing well had become a goal towards which many, many teenagers aimed.

Lawrence sat on a damp rooftop trying to secure his harness with needle and thread from his kit, wondering if the expense had been worth it. Night was beginning to fall at the end of a very long day. He concentrated on his kit despite being on lookout duty on the edge of the last portion of town to be occupied by the enemy. The watchers were in pairs. He was using his break to try and rejoin the bottom of his harness so that he could temporarily reattach a quiver. Like most archers he was quickest and most accurate when he felt comfortable and a hip quiver was his preferred arrangement. A green nasty had torn right down the side of his mail and through his harnessing earlier in the day and having lost his bow in the same attack he had fought hand-to-hand for the majority of the afternoon. Barf had eventually found him and filled him in on the teams losses. When he had found out about his father he had declined the opportunity to return to the Club to rearm and volunteered for the attack on the Roke stronghold. Now, perhaps, he wished he had taken the chance to pick up some new gear. Seeing the club again so soon wouldn't have exaggerated his loss any more. Still 'make do and mend' had always been an Iron Island motto and so, in the failing twilight, he tried to rethread his needle and put aside his troubles by focusing on the chore.

While he was mending his kit Lawrence was worrying about the activity he could hear within the two water towers, adjacent from his position within the compound. He was fairly sure that the traitors were working to convert them into weapons' platforms as periodically bolts were dropping from the tanks. He was calculating how long it would take to open some firing ports. It was difficult to know, as he couldn't tell if the construction of the tanks had included ease of conversion as a feature. The type of weapons that would be brought to bear, he guessed, were bows and arblast. A contraption that looked like a standard, heavy, four-shot-arblast-like spear thrower been carried up inside tower one about a day-part earlier. As Laurence worked away the final bolt was removed and a large oblong plate fell away from the first tank; noises from the second recorded the same thing happening there. Fortunately the rooftop that he had chosen had a high wall-ledge together with a number of chimney breasts and until combat actually commenced it was unlikely that, as a pair of silent lookouts, he or the kid would come under fire.

Unknown to Lawrence, as he kept his vigil the Roke

compound defences were desperately behind schedule in priming the key features that the concealed fortification offered. Secrecy being essential, the guards had been afforded little opportunity to train in organising the defence. The command had also suffered desperate misfortune when the commander of the camp guard, also a product of the new sophisticated Roke training camps, and the second most dangerous and clever man in the organisation, had been killed by a freak accident. He had been supervising the token defence of the outer, wire fenced compound, penetrated earlier by Lauren and Barf, from the safety of one of the warehouses. Being the last to leave he was walking to the covered exit when a stray arrow had, by chance, shattered a glass skylight, causing a mass of fragments that had knocked him down and opened a leg artery of the now unconscious warrior. Therefore he had died quickly, no one else aware of his wounding.

The next in the command chain continued with his prescribed duties not knowing that he had, effectively, been promoted. He continued assuming that his commander, who should have left the warehouse in perfect safety, was out and about arranging the other defences which only he had particularly good knowledge about. When the discovery was finally made that the guard commander had either deserted or was missing, vital time had been lost and the fluctuating morale plunged although the basic defence continued in reasonable order.

Across the street, Barf was becoming more and more frustrated. Twice now his troops had approached the enemy across open ground, already littered with bodies, and each time they had met unacceptably high arrow and quarrel fire and now the tanks offered the threat of ballistae. Finally he searched out the rooftop where Lawrence and the sea cadet partnered with him were keeping watch.

"Laddo, scoot back to the Fort will you and bring me one of your converted harps, a cable set and ten sliders. We'll use a cable slide to get me over the wall. Get Chubby to bring out some two-inch hollows with steel springs and six rings of namptha in porcelain or something similar, as a distraction – you choose as you'll be operation director. I'll stay and spot your mate till you get back." Barf fired at Lawrence when he crouched safely behind the chimneystack.

Thirty counts later, Barf was back down on the street organising the rest of his crew as Lawrence winched his equipment up to the roof. "Scars, have you got your set of gear?" Barf asked anxiously. "Good, take Breeder and six marines. You two on the cutter, the others with the turtle shields. Take it in and rip open that side door," Barf instructed his comrade, pointing carefully at a deceptively innocent looking wooden side-door and trying to ignore Scar's eyebrow, raised in unspoken irony. "Lawrence and I will be creating a distraction on the wall further round and we've 16 archers to try and keep you dry." With no reply other than a quiet cough from Breeder he continued quickly. "OK, go in six counts. Good luck." With that he rushed over to the building where the other six marines were helping with the hoist to get the heavier parts up to the roof.

Climbing up himself, Lawrence was waiting for him calmly assembling the powerful steel 'harp' crossbow.

"Barf, I tested the doors with shafts earlier, both are definitely wood over metal. Good luck to the lads with the cutters," Lawrence had commented when Barf had first outlined his entire plan. "I've swapped the coils for a two-funnel flame blast. I reckon that will clear the wall enough to get most of you over before the Roke are ready to react. I assume the marines are going as well?" Barf grunted as he checked his knives. "Now here is my proposed timing. Half of a count to get the cable taut, if it grips at all, and up to another half before you are away. At one and seven tenths the spreader fires about ten spans in front of you and you should clear the wall with only slight singeing. You'll be down within the second count and another count and you'll have six large marines landing on you. As for cover, we'll have the two towers alight by the time you are in the dirt and there are three Roke silhouettes that I have marked with arblast, that could puncture you, so me and the kid will try for them. After the count you're on your own otherwise we could pin you ourselves. Sound like a plan?" Barf said nothing, smiling at the other man's complete professionalism despite the recent chaos.

"OK, on my count," Lawrence continued, clapping his friend on the shoulder and resisting the urge to beg him to come back safe.

"Hell, yeh," Barf replied, finally beginning to work himself up for the almost idiotically dangerous plan he was about to attempt, in order to break the deadlock and carry out his orders.

Lawrence then moved to the tripod and settling himself in the shoulder brace took careful aim. With a loud screaming twang the weapon fired and almost instantly a thud marked the projectile's impact. Reckless of the steel cable tearing at his gloved hands the young officer then clipped the restraint into the tensioner mechanism, frantically jacking the lever. As he felt the cable tighten he said in a low voice, "Little Salt, on a count of ten light me the left tower, like I said."

The pulleys on the tensioner finished their job a few moments later with the cable running good and tight. "OK Boss, clipping on the spreader. Now you. Right, it's on the edge. On a count of five push it off, count three, then go yourself, count six and you'll feel the spreader-tether buck and shout its hello. Close your baby blues for three and then give them hell."

"Start your count, marines," Lawrence called more loudly. "Little Salt, good," as Lawrence glanced at the burning oil running down the first tower targeted. "Ready heavies. One to six clip on now!" he barked at the marines. "Little Salt, give them another," he said as he fumbled at his feet for his own bow. He heard Barf's whoosh as he slid away down the cable and quickly fired one and then a second oil splash fire arrow at the right hand tower, both catching. He heard the explosion and instinctively looked up as the wire attached to the spreader pulled tight and mixed the pressurised oil with the burning wicks, spraying a cone of fire 20 spans in length across the path of the slide wire.

Praying to the Battler still seeing the outline of the fire burst, he quickly glanced to the left tower where the young cadet had fired four flame arrows by the look of it, and hit with three. With no time to evaluate the effects of the fire cone, or even look to see how Barf had fared crossing the perimeter, all Lawrence could do was finish enforcing the timing that he had outlined. "Heavies go now, now, now, now, now, now!" And all the marines were away on the slide.

With an arrow knocked on his longbow, Lawrence peered

into the night-time gloom. The remains of the spreader lit up the immediate area and several traitors could be heard screaming. He was looking for movement, where he had spotted two arblast men earlier, and sending two arrows in quick succession felt happy that he had winged at least one when he heard a cry of pain.

Down below he could hear the cutter engaging in the door and checked to see if his angle gave him a shot over the parapet. Barf had said that the team would have 16 archers for cover. The air in that direction seemed to burn every few moments with flare arrows mixed in, one in four he estimated. Back on his station, more heavily shielded marines were following through with ladders, charging across towards the blackened wall where Barf had crossed and also towards the next nearest door. Lawrence slid off a four-way lantern, down the slide cable which caught on its tether line just over the wall as he had intended, and stood waiting to see if defenders regained the ramparts so that he could pick off a few. All the light picked up, though, was one of the marines crouched on the wall behind his shield working his way cautiously towards the right hand tower's covered stairway. Lawrence was impressed that he had made the wall at all, especially as it would still have been burning when he landed. He couldn't tell how the marine's other comrades were doing but relied on the fact that, in the dark, Barf was known as one of the nastiest men around.

Lawrence's attention was drawn quickly to the enemy activity. The Roke weren't content to allow the local troops to just climb over the walls unopposed. Belatedly metal on metal sounded as a set of multiple, crude but large arblasts, known as bolt throwers, were manoeuvred in the right hand tower to bear on the marines, who were now almost at the top of the ladder.

Almost at the instant that Lawrence released an oil-pot arrow from his bow did the one shot by Little Salt, who had also seen the danger, impact on the brutal weapon's shielding. Both projectiles sprayed harmlessly off. In fact it was only the small namptha grenade that the solitary marine on the wall threw that smashed above the framework, dowsing the crew's enclosure momentarily in flame. Suddenly the Marine cried out. His positioning to get a good throw had exposed him to archers in the other tower and he sank down writhing in agony, pulling his shield over him preventing further hits.

"Get down son," Lawrence urged his cadet partner as the newly arrived Roke archers to their left turned their attention to his own rooftop. Despite his warning Lawrence took a gamble himself, stepping to the cable shooter and winching the springy steel arms back to firing position. He loaded in the spare cable harpoon and sighting on the bolt thrower itself, fired off the shot to plunge solidly into the armoured plates of the covered weapon. Ignoring his commander's instructions the cadet had come to stand behind him, covering them both with a raised shield and Lawrence was glad as his new friend grunted under the impact of several projectiles on the shield's face. Ducking down the cadet continued to provide cover as Lawrence pumped frantically on the tensioner as gradually the cable began to tighten.

Because of the light nature of the enemy weapon's construction, despite the bulky looking shielding, the bolt thrower was designed to rotate round a central pivot to cover a maximum area and the effect of the tensioned cable was to pull it round to face only the rooftop. This, in itself, protected the marines, several of whom had now reached the parapet and were covering the left hand tower with a spray from their flame pump which, whilst running off the metal cladding, was in turn forcing the archers to keep under cover, allowing more and more local troops to gain access to the compound in support of Barf's attack.

Infuriated at not being able to target the bolt thrower on the parapet the remaining handlers clearly decided that as it was pointing at Lawrence's roof they might as well fire on their tormentors. Belatedly, Lawrence realised this. The cadet continued to kneel over him as he fought to increase the tension and topple the weapon over on its stand. Unfortunately it fired just too early, although in a slightly depressed state so that only the top two of the four bolts hit as high as the roof. One of these was enough and on striking the cadet square in the shield he was immolated by its tip and the fragments of the shield it drove into him. The young cadet was carried straight over Lawrence, lying prone working the lever with all his might, and plunged, already

270

dead, to the street below. The second bolt did, in fact, hit the tensioning rack by fluke. Rather than relieving the tension, it was this extra inertia, in combination with the final desperate surge by Lawrence, that saw the bolt-thrower torn from its footing and dragged out to crash at the foot of the tower below.

Lawrence lay back gasping with effort and shaking with emotion, forcing himself to expel the air from his lungs, his heart hammering at his ribs at the loss of his comrade. He could not help but drag himself to the furthest edge of the roof and look down on the broken body, heedless of the danger of enemy archers. As Lawrence gradually came back to himself he realised that fighting could now be heard from a number of locations within the compound. A brief glance from a covered position, towards the enemy, confirmed that both doors were now open and that further numbers of marines were gaining access all the time.

Having checked that there was nothing he could do for his companion, he realised that the enemy archers in the towers were now busy fighting for their lives against the heavily armed marines. A sudden recklessness struck Lawrence and so, looping his bow over his back and grasping the dead cadet's spear, he snapped a spare runner over the original cable and leapt out onto the slide. He, too, released his grip to land lightly on the ramparts and proceeding slowly began making his way around the camp walls in search of the enemy.

*****

Barf's breathing was erratic and Lawrence's was sounding positively ragged as they, and the remaining two marines, crouched back in the shadows of the doorway a day-part later. Lawrence had soon caught up with three of the marines, one now dead, and an eighth ago they had helped Barf finish six more defenders. The defences of this smaller, inner compound were murderous and finally Barf was at a loss as to how to advance. All the underground doors seemed too well defended and the closed, windowless building offered none of the elevated access that they had exploited in their initial crossing of the wall.

Behind them came the noise of running armoured men and

Barf relaxed when he heard an Ironer call out a code word. Killing each other would have been all too easy in this nasty complex. Barf was shocked when he recognised his reinforcements. "Commander!" he saluted.

"At ease, Major," the commander of the Iron assault brigades replied. Commander Jenks was a big man and a well known fighter.

"I didn't even know you were green side, sir," Barf offered.

"Yep. We are staging in the quarry, or at least were until this mess kicked off. Been a while since I earned my coin so hard with the iron," he commented, brandishing his notched and bloody sword. "Chang sent us when we had finished at the battery. Some of these Roke scum are getting pretty good. Did you see the Reptoids? We were the last to arrive. Only sent half initially but when we heard what had happened to Squeeze we all mustered over – and a good job too," he commented, wiping the streaming sweat from his brow. "What's holding you back here, son?" he asked Barf directly. Barf just pointed round the corner in reply. Sliding carefully to the wall the older man used the offered mirror stick to look around.

"Hmmmm. Underground entrances with bolt throwers. OK. Chambers, light up the doorway will you?" the commander asked one of his newly arrived men.

From the back of the team a pair of tough looking men rushed forwards with what looked like three black drain pipes fused together. One holding it steady and the other using his weight, they set three stubby-armed spring mechanisms to tension, one for each tube. They carefully loaded three large egg-shaped porcelain oil reservoirs and set a burning glob of pitch on the end of each. The larger of the two men, Chambers, Barf assumed, then attached the firing tubes to a harness contraption that allowed him to carry its weight, whilst keeping the tubes pointing forwards. His companion was handed a large iron plate and the two scuttled off into the darkness, rushing straight round the corner. Several counts and lots of crashes and smashes later Chambers scurried back.

"Now then, boss. The door is well fixed, plate armour, floor to ceiling. Standard thrower, four shots every six counts."

"Barf, my lads can handle the doors. Why don't you head

back to our holding areas and get your head down for a couple of shouts, we need to fetch kit up from the club. I'll let you know when we are through. You as well son," the weathered old man clapped Lawrence on the shoulder and pushed him off in Barf's direction.

No sooner had Lawrence slumped exhausted on a roll, tossed to him by one of the waitresses from a cart back at one of the outer compounds shattered doors, now secured as a holding area, than someone was shaking him by the shoulder. He dragged himself up, aware only of his rest as a feverish time, when his mind had reminded him over and over of the loss of his dad, like a dog worrying a bone, or a child who knows only one word. When he reached the tunnel entry he found Barf and the commander crouched behind a shield wall. He joined them there clutching an assault shield that he had scrounged and with his harness replaced by his own full set of armour and matching equipment. Even in confined assaults he favoured a light bow rather than the more penetrating arblast. Justine had clearly returned to the club whilst he slept and specifically had sought out his kit once she had recognised him from the back of the cart.

She had even left him a packet containing some fruit and a sealed field pasty. He munched on some of this as Barf filled him in on what he had missed. Chambers and his mate apparently hadn't liked what they had seen down the tunnel and they had used some extra time to bring down a full tunnel bridge. Essentially, this was a metal tube that could be altered easily in its height, depth and breath so that it would fill a tunnel and offer troops inside protection in all four directions. Operationally it was rushed in after a team of four men had charged the face panel right up to the armoured door. The face panel was a complex set of plates and doors, made cleverly from heavy treated steel. It allowed combinations of the plates to be removed so that soldiers could work on any section of a door, protected at all times.

Chambers had chosen this because of a suspicion about murder holes in the roof or walls, or even pits beneath the floor. The speed with which it was forced into position was the real key to its usefulness. Although the four men on the face panel were badly bruised when the bolt throwers opened up at close range the kit was placed and locked before the defenders could react and this saved the attackers considerable difficulty. During the time they had worked and Lawrence had slept, concealed attacks of burning oil and some kind of acid from above, and someone trying to pierce the floor from below, were noted but the men worked on with no further fear of harm. The 'rat' tube, as it was nicknamed, also had clever screw devices and these had been engaged further anchoring the tube in place, even should the floor be dropped entirely which, at one stage, it apparently had felt and sounded as if it was.

All this evidence convinced the Irons not to use an open-geared drill, which although quicker and more effective would have allowed flame pumps or acid tubes to be directed through at their men. Instead, a drill mechanism, using angled shafts and sealed pistons, had taken longer than the two-part gap envisaged and Lawrence soon found out that he had been asleep for four.

Somehow the Roke had managed to foul one of the gear bits, or the door's armour had conspired to prove extra troublesome. Regardless, though, a foot-wide breach had been made and several rounds of flame pump, steel ball discharge and disk spinners had been blasted through into the area behind the door. Now a sealed set of lanterns and mirrors showed only corpses and debris beyond the door. Moments ago the drilling had finished to weaken the edges and a large 'door ripper' was being inserted. Four men, in skin capes treated against fire and strange springy armour, were about to engage the final machine and tear out and drop the door. Four pairs of advance troops similarly attired, with double arblast and slotted full body shields, would then advance carefully inside to secure the position.

Volunteers and brave men all, these men would be walking into potentially lethal traps. Six squads of six assault troops waited with Barf and the others beyond the mouth of the tunnel, many with spot focused lanterns, ready to follow up the advance party or rush in and attempt to drag their comrades out. The entry, though, proved relatively safe. A final barricade had been erected round the corner and though projectiles initially pinned down the advance troops, the first wave of six assaulters carried the fight past the barrier. Barf's squad, however, was held up for another two parts as more booby traps were discovered further in. In all it was four parts after Lawrence had returned, at the start of the entry, before the final 16 Roke and two Siblants were killed and the whole area finally declared secure. Incredibly, from the start of Barf's initial approach it had taken almost a whole day to storm and secure the compound and only the prepared equipment and training had prevented the attackers from suffering crippling losses in the brutally fortified underground complex.

This was the final circular corridor, secured with three other entrances off it, all leading to the surface, an estimated one hundred defenders had been killed when the final body count was done. The Ironlanders had lost a total of four men in the inner compound, with three more wounded in the final attack. This was not the end of the investigation, for in the midst of the final corridor stood a circular room with a single ornate door. Other troops on the surface had reported taking underground weapons, food and poison stores and even some make shift prison cages. No one had so far had captured or killed the Master Baker though. This heavily defended area focused around one room, the only one with more than practical decoration seemed to be his final hiding place.

*****

Master Calm clambered high into the branches of the great tree. Perching there he bade Blue Boy join him and within moments his young apprentice had scuttled up through the boughs, balancing carefully next to him.

"We will meditate here today," announced Calm and promptly quested inwards to achieve the communion trance. Blue Boy relaxed as well as he could, perched so high. He felt Calm's soothing thoughts wash over him. It was only the second day on which Blue Boy had experienced the trance-like process of mental thought exchange. The previous day, as soon as he began to rouse from his exhausted slumber after the mammoth ride, his new teacher had begun to school him in the art of gaining a trance like state that would enable Master Calm to impose the thought transfer process. Apparently, in the coming months and years, the student would develop his mind to allow him to perform the same process fully conscious, but until then the trance was necessary. Too tired to give the issue much thought, after about ten attempts Blue Boy had found the activity comfortable if not natural.

This lesson involved an understanding of the tree's wooden texture, expanding out to consider the quiet relationship between all the life within the surrounding area. Master Calm usually began his lessons by focusing on a surrounding object or objects. He coupled this with a lengthy discourse on the importance of angle perception and relative positioning of terrain height when engaging on uneven ground. Downward angles, views of terrain and use of gravity and inertia he discussed, expounding on topics ranging from tree-based ambush to cliff path assaults and cavalry charges up and down hill. All these were added to the theme that the tree climb had triggered.

Blue Boy finally returned to himself long past the sun's zenith, whilst Master Calm enthused that he was well pleased with all that his student had been able to assimilate. He had learnt a couple of month's worth of terrain tactics in just one sitting.

Calm suddenly exploded into motion, leaping dramatically downwards to swing one handed on a lower branch and then onwards to one yet lower on the next available tree, calling for Blue Boy to meet him on the ground. Not to be out done by Master Calm's grace, Blue Boy followed exactly, although at each branch performing a number of complex gymnastic and acrobatic feats typical of a high wire performer. As he dropped lower the flips and twists became more and more extreme until he finally landed with a complex somersaulting dismount on the ground. With a quizzical eyebrow lifted, Calm promptly tripped him and with his foot planted firmly on Blue Boy's forehead he chided the young lad, informing him that exhibition and pride often excluded good tactics. In this case his lead could have disguised the fact that one of the branches was less than sturdy, thereby causing Blue Boy to slip and fall. "Even friends can often disguise danger whether wittingly or not," was his final comment on the matter.

Calm then questioned Blue Boy at length to determine all he could concerning the relative position of the tree they has just evacuated. Over many years of memory tests Blue Boy had become much accustomed to such random tests of memory and observation. Calm was pleased, observing that despite the many times he had sat in the tree he could add little to Blue Boy's observations. Immediately switching the topic he started discussing the relative merits of forestry, concerning tree thinning and rejuvenation. Blue Boy became unsettled as he realised that this was a precursor to cutting down the majestic tree.

Even as he understood that the removal of the tree would allow two young trees, struggling to grow up towards the light, to reach their full potential, he still felt uncomfortable that such a task should fall to him. Calm, however, was firm and produced two small but heavy hatchets, explaining quickly but thoroughly the sequences of precise cuts that Blue Boy was to make in order to prepare the tree for felling. As Blue Boy began the complex series of spinning movements and leaps to cut and chop away at the tree he, was unaware of Calm's retreat to the nearby shade as he began to count and repeat the motions in order to fulfil his assignment. As the chips of wood began to fly more quickly Blue Boy realised the enormity of the task that Calm had set and the pure physical effort that it would take to keep up the routine to completion. Counts became day-parts as he kept up his chipping and slicing cuts and thrusts. Finally the cuts began to take shape and he was able to use the back of one hatchet to tap in the holding wedges that Calm occasionally tossed into Blue Boy's routine for the purpose of rendering the tree stable.

When it was finally done Blue Boy allowed himself to collapse exhausted to the ground. Calm sauntered over dropping a long-handled felling axe and a number of coils of rope that he had somehow managed to acquire whilst Blue Boy had been occupied. Carefully directed by Master Calm, Blue Boy attached the ropes here and there around the trunk and then, with a number of blows of the felling axe and an amount of heaving and tugging, pulling and straining, finally Blue boy and Calm guided the collapse of the tree down to the ground.

Having camped overnight in a bivouac at the tree site, the

pair were up early the next morning. They shared the task of rendering the tree into useable building products of planks and bark tiles, sap for caulking and collecting the leaves and other sundry products. Two days went by as the pair laboured non-stop to complete the task.

Next on the agenda, Calm announced, was Blue Boy's task of constructing a cabin. The design was detailed verbally and required that a three-room structure, fully roofed and resembling a tavern, including a walled bar area, to be constructed in a clearing near the stream, three miles to the south. A quick map was sketched on the ground with a stick.

The explanation of the required construction ran onto a discussion on how campaign fort construction techniques could be tailored to suit residential construction. Although a rather brief lesson by Master Calm's normal standards, it still left Blue Boy starting the task near dusk. Calm began preparing his own supper fire as Blue Boy munched his hard, trail rations, and considered this task. He was required to move all the building materials to the construction location before dawn. Wincing, Blue Boy used the remains of the daylight to prepare and memorise a paced route, fairly obstruction free, from one site to the other.

He then shouldered small but substantial amounts of building materials and, at a jogging pace, ferried these loads back and forth through the dark forest night. He was grateful for the care with which Master Calm had organised and stacked the materials as they had been finished. A couple of parts before dawn an almost identical mirror-image of the site had been created, and Blue Boy slept.

Up again at dawn Blue Boy solidly struggled for the next two days, but despite laying out the rooms, erecting the external walls and roofing the building, he was still a long way short of the target that Calm had set. Blue Boy was resolute but uncomfortable when he challenged Master Calm over the impossibility of the task; the first one, Blue Boy was pleased to say, of the first few days that he had failed. Calm quietly listened as Blue Boy made his report and indicated that he had indeed set a task that was anticipated to be overly lengthy for the time available, but was pleased that Blue Boy had, persevered and had in fact, defined and completed the key aspects of the construction that Calm required at this point in time.

Calm bade Blue Boy wash in the stream and relax for the rest of the evening, whilst he prepared a freshly killed buck and a couple of partridge for the evening meal. The pair, student and teacher, sat comfortably by the fire before Calm suggested that Blue Boy retire and be up and ready at dawn.

Chapter Fourteen

Walrus climbed the winding path through the damp hillside. The sun had yet to rise enough to burn off the dew and every fern he passed added slightly to the moisture soaking into his clothing.

The old warrior ignored the slight discomfort, for he was nearing home. That he had met and been taken into the household of Master Calm and his lady were no small things and every day he gave silent thanks for their help and companionship. Ten years before, Walrus had come to a watershed in his life. He had fought almost constantly for nigh on 15 years, rising at one point to command his own company. He had struggled all through that time to find a meaning or purpose; he had taken the comradeship of a group of warriors and their part in the struggle against the Horde as his purpose. Only when his company was slaughtered, and he was looking deep within himself for answers, had he realised that it was not truly his responsibility, for the same thing had happened over and over through the long years of war. That his friends had died without really achieving anything, and that he was in danger of following them, had shocked him to the core.

The hillside levelled and as he was making good time he took a seat on a stump close to the path and looked back over the wooded hills through which he had passed. One reason he had become so distracted from the real meaning of life, he now realised, was that like so many fighters he had fought and lived solely in the Grand Forts. He had spent the better part of ten years moving back and forth between the two, only spending short periods back in the North and then only in the port towns that served the escorted ferries.

Huge places the Forts, and a wonder of civil engineering capability. Had they not been packed to bursting, full of provisions, weapons and soldiers, their arched ceilings and grand construction would have been well worth a visit. But month after month packed in the overcrowded barrack quarters the grey walls began to dominate. The rest of the world was reduced to the patches of sky that could be seen from the parade and training squares or to the grim view of the Bloody League filled by row after row of enemy battlements.

The time gongs regulated the day, and not the sun and moon, themselves replaced by smoky torches and lanterns. Having large underground training rooms, the roster sometimes only detailed a crew out to the external training areas one shift in ten. Training, exercising, eating and drinking became the focus of living in the huge, grey, granite battle forts. On reflection, Walrus had decided that the generations of fort commanders actually worked miracles, keeping up morale for so long. The working environment of the troops stationed there was actually very carefully managed indeed.

Still, eventually, Walrus had become jaded. He had fought that feeling because of his responsibility to his crew, but after their slaughter he had searched in vain, for meaning and purpose, doing volunteer shifts with the pickers. He had even considered taking the vows of a knightly order. Nothing had helped, and even when he shipped back to Clearwater Port with everything being geared to support the war effort, he had sat listless in the dockside taverns nursing drinks and had finally decided on the enders. He had intended to visit the enders office the next day, with his small pack, and complete the ritual ceremony that, for the benefit of friends and family, bade farewell to the veteran. At the end of the farewell ritual the ender would enter the rear of the building, through the symbolic door, and would leave immediately for the ender staging posts, where the small companies were formed and sent to the most dangerous fighting fronts, never to be seen again.

That same decisive afternoon he had met a small fellow who sat at his table with a jug of juice and beamed a smile. They had engaged in small-talk and suddenly Walrus realised they had discussed many things, and one of the never-ending afternoons had become late evening.

Occupation had come up in the course of their conversation and he had freely admitted to feeling bereft of direction. As they ordered some food the chap, and it was then that Walrus realised they hadn't even traded names, suggested, "My friend, I have contacts way back in the hills who are recruiting men of varied talents. It would be demanding but honest work. Why don't you travel with me and check it out? It seems that you have some free time and not much to lose."

Walrus had promised he would think it over and they had eaten. On parting the chap had given him a time and departure point and an open invitation for him to come along, or not, at his convenience and then simply wandered off.

The next morning, with all his worldly possessions in his kit bag, Walrus had turned up at the rendezvous and was formally introduced to Master Calm, which seemed more natural now than it had been at the time.

After days of travel they had arrived at a location not too distant from where he sat now and he had met the second most impressive, and soon important, person in his life: Master Calm's wife, Lady Green. He had been amazed by the way that she worked in partnership with Master Calm. It was she he now worked for on a daily basis, and the nature of that work was constantly changing. She had striven to break his ingrained military manner, although she now claimed that some of the habits he had picked up would have been better left as they were. He loved the fact that he could pick, make and mend his own clothes. Not that even now if he found something comfortable he would necessarily change it until it was soiled beyond repair.

He had worked hard to pick up mountain skills and soon had become accepted by the ragged trappers, the boot leggers and mountain tribesmen. He worked hard for the partisan chain of command, which was far more active than he had realised. Travelling vast distances, to the north to the tundra, to the Legion, and south to the ragged parts of the Battle Lands he performed many tasks. Some were simple, like distributing messages or food, others were more complicated, terminations, resistance organisation or even Reptoid-hunting trips.

Soon he had come to realise how small a part of the war was concentrated at the front, though even he still worried now about the problem of maintaining the Forts without instilling the feelings of institutionalisation, that he had come to hold into the young troopers. Lady Green had helped him realise that his experiences were exceptionally personal, his circumstances drawing out his service far more than for the average person. She often joked that this was why he now went to extremes, revelling, as she called it, in the freedom of dirtiness and lack of personal hygiene.

Whenever she said this, though, she made it clear that he was always welcome. Currently the Calm residence occupied a grand multi-level cabin at the top of the hillside that Walrus was in the process of climbing. Built on a slope, with two terraces dug into the soft ground, it offered the Calm family residence on the upper floor and a small, compact, independent guest bunk-room below in the space left by the stilts that supported the upper level.

In these later years Walrus was very content to be part of Master Calm's extended family. Life in the country suited him and he had taken on many traits of the nearby mountain folk with whom Calm worked, traded and who formed the body of his command.

Over the years Walrus had discovered that the Calm family came together, separated and moved location frequently. Rather than being challenging the gentle order that Lady Green applied to this seemingly continually process, seemed to soothe the spirits of all those involved. Walrus loved the fact that he always felt at home, but that the scenery and the views would constantly change. He also found that this mechanism left behind a number of comfortable, and usually discrete, places to which he could return, either as part of his travels within the area or just if he needed some space.

Sometimes he would arrive at one location to find that another traveller had had the same idea: usually that worked out just fine. The Calms organised a huge, if diverse, network of loosely affiliated folk, many from the surrounding area but also people from great distances away. There were almost always people coming and going discreetly, bringing news or seeking information. Walrus got the impression that Master Calm seldom allowed members of his network to be completely free from tasks. Quite how the two of them managed to juggle all their interests and resources Walrus had no idea.

"Walrus dear, are you coming to breakfast?" The gentle,

cool voice of Lady Green brought Walrus back to the present. He immediately jumped up and bowed respectfully to the slender figure standing quietly behind him.

"Yes ma'am, I was just enjoying the view," he replied with the grin of a naughty school boy caught at mischief.

"As was I my friend, as was I," she replied, taking his arm as they strolled quietly up the hill.

*****

On the final morning of the fayre the band were beginning to pack up when the herald approached their camping area. Stonebrow and Marv had been standing together, Marv working his way round to finally saying goodbye to his friend of long standing when the announcement was made.

It was long but delivered quickly and precisely. In essence it gave the news that upwards of eight tenths of the establish crews assembled had been recruited, and that they were all to report immediately to one of three coastal staging ports for direct transportation to the Grand Forts.

Whilst many of the companies knew they had been selected for a duty, few had expected to be dirt-side within a week, let alone in the numbers the announcement heralded. This announcement was also accompanied by the news that the local partisans were to ring the fayre site. Any support personnel not linked to a company were to remain at the fayre site for an additional three days, effectively under guard as an additional act of security.

Furthermore the companies were to split into the three groups and travel each to their allocated ports, escorted by a regular military escort. It appeared to Stonebrow that the high command was aware of Roke spy resources and was making an attempt to delay news of this unprecedented activity from reaching the Roke command dirt-side for as long as possible.

Finishing the announcement the herald visited briefly first with Marv, who was simply given papers exempting his party from the general voluntary internment, Stonebrow was also instructed to move out immediately and avoid being caught up in the more complicated logistics of the companies who were also scheduled to use the same port for their crossing.

With their departure pre-empted in this way Marv moved quickly through the band exchanging hugs, kisses and good natured insults before taking his leave.

He then hurried over to his small company. He explained their orders and quickly his five companions, Jeffers, Heron, Mother and the two lads, moved their gear beyond the ring of partisan perimeter sentries who had already formed around the camp. Marv knew the importance of the flexibility in their later departure this would give them once they had chosen their route.

*****

Several parts later, lounging against the tavern wall, Marv watched as Mother and Jeffers Star left the independent weavers' store in Riding Dale, loaded down with a couple of bales of cloth, and headed over to the outfitters department of the General Quartermaster for the region.

Marv had been surprised by the list of tasks that Master Calm had supplied him with for completion before the small company were to meet up at the rendezvous. One was the provision of two new uniforms for each of the company members. Although Mother had offered to make these, time and facilities were pressing and so the group had decided to spend a day in Riding Dale, in order for the batch cutting and basic stitching to be completed by the outfitter personnel. This would cut down their available journey time but the work that it would save Mother was, in Marv's view, worth the risk.

Despite having met Mother casually before, initially Marv had been surprised when Master Calm had told him of her inclusion in the detail. Still, four seemed to be an unusually small number of people to make up a company, especially as two were green recruits direct from their first tour of service.

As he had watched both Jeffers and Mother with the youngsters he realised that the pair were to have one to one tuition from expert teachers, certainly for the training period. The experience that Jeffers Star offered also seemed to compliment Marv's own textbook approach and Mother's firm, but motherly, ways. Marv reflected that he should long since have given up questioning the decisions of people like Master Calm and Master Smee.

Only a few parts into his new assignment and already the group appeared to be bonding and Marv was surprised at how quickly the hurt of leaving the band was fading. He felt deep concern for all the students he took on and, even though Blue Boy was absent, the two young lads gave him a focus for his activities in a way he had not been expecting.

Initially he had felt a tinge of jealousy when Master Calm had announced that he, Blue Boy and Heron would be the ones to head off for the first period of training and that the others should rendezvous with them a week later, having completed their list of errands.

Unusually, although he had entered the town, Jeffers volunteered to head back early to the camp where the two boys were doing weapons training. Marv was happy to be left to help Mother arrange the provisions they needed but he thought that Jeffers, the entrepreneur and club owner, would have wanted to have spent as much time in a sizeable town as possible. Marv wondered about the emptiness that Jeffers' possibly felt now that he was separated from his wards. In all the stories of Jeffers' battles, the one subtle point that came across was that he had always done his best for those who served with or under him. Maybe now he too would fill the gap he felt by working more closely with the two young recruits.

Where would we all be if there was no war Marv wondered, deciding that he might need to revise his opinion of Jeffers Star away from the image of playboy warrior and mercenary entrepreneur.

*****

Over the next days Changworth suffered more from organising logistics than he did from the rigours of defending the town. That wasn't to say that numbers of Roke attack ships, some carrying Reptoids, didn't make it past the naval cordon. Many of these ships attacked Buccaneer Town directly as it was the most obvious target, and although his manpower available fell far short of what, in normal times, he would have considered the bare minimum, he had talented soldiers, well armed, who fought ferociously, managing their problems locally and simply reporting the outcome.

His more serious problems were the areas out of town, especially to the north where the enemy had smashed through the coastal wall. Repeatedly Reptoids came out of the countryside to attack the temporary fortifications and the troops working on them where the breach had been. It was as if they had been set the task of keeping the hole open.

Reports had also come in that it was proving difficult to cut apart and separate the cluster of ships that the Horde had built for the first wave of landings. Unusually, the Roke had shown a high degree of sophistication in developing chains which, when locked and tensioned, could only be separated by physical cutting.

Saw blades capable of cutting the medium-grade iron, and occasional steel, soon became in short supply. It was very difficult to set up foundry conditions that would allow these chains to be cut in other ways, given that the floating wooden platform was sensitive to fire and extreme heat.

Because of the way the ships were packed together the technique of sinking every other one also proved unsuccessful. It soon became apparent that even when holed, the tightly packed ships wouldn't necessarily take on enough water for the weight to tear them free of the pack and sink.

In the end the engineers compromised by cutting the decking from numbers of strategic or suitable vessels. This wood was then transported back to the breached wall where it could be used in constructing the stockades and replacing supplies that were frequently lost to raids by the Roke and Reptoids, who still seemed to be working unbelievably closely together.

Whilst Changworth struggled with all this regular campaign business he also worried away at other problems in the back of his mind. The most challenging of which was what to make of the rooms that Barf had finally broken into that had belonged to the Master Baker. Chubby, with Barf's help, had finished clearing seventeen traps, of varying degrees of nastiness, before Barf had decided it was safe to enter the suite of underground rooms.

A few parts earlier Barf had insisted that Changworth see for himself and refused to explain further. Initially, when Changworth had entered the first room, he had wondered what the fuss was about, it was clearly a reception room cum office. The walls were filled with detailed maps of the North. On closer inspection Changworth was impressed by exactly how recent and how detailed these maps were. The desk was covered with a variety of oddments, including quills and red ink that bore a striking similarity to the colour of fresh blood, pots of assorted teeth, some human and many clearly not, and a nasty selection of strangely shaped, sharpened instruments, probably devised for some sickening kind of torture. Shelves around the room contained arrays of books, many up to date technical works, some arcane and decrepit. Overall it was the room of a sophisticated yet dangerous and dark individual.

The term 'dark' was swapped for 'evil' when Changworth entered the inner room. Here there were blocks and devices created to inflict great suffering on the human body. At the far end of the room the wall was covered with numbers of grisly trophies, some too awful to describe. Tearing himself away from the polished bones, jars of preserved body parts and other ritualistic items that he felt sure he didn't want to inspect too closely, he followed Barf to a door. The final room was little more than an arm's span in width. As soon as Barf opened the door a sickeningly sweet smell assailed Changworth's nostrils. Here a number of corpses were draped carefully across the floor, partially buried in a mound of manure and soil. Each of the corpses varied in age, size and state of decay; but the one thing they had in common was that each had the ribcage cut open and pinned back and from which now grew small numbers of large ornate fungi.

Changworth had backed out quickly and hurried back towards the sunlight, the world and the sanctuary of his command post. Not only was the Master Baker a traitor of the worst kind, but now it appeared he was also some kind of inhuman monster. His lair had triggered fears in Changworth that rational thought alone could not overcome.

The arrival of Commander Jenks broke his dark reverie. "General Changworth, what are your orders now, sir?" the second most senior Iron Isle solider in the team asked.

"Commander, I ask a difficult thing of you. I need you to take the 300 most rested of our command and reinforce the wall breach. A few marines and engineers are dug in and trying to construct stockades to deny easy access from the beach, but are coming under heavy attack from the tail end of the Horde force that landed. That force seems satisfied to keep the defences weak, so that if a second wave arrives it will be an easy task to storm the defences from the landing craft. I need you to provide the workers, with enough space to build a secure defence."

As his friend saluted and turned to move away General Changworth bit his lip in frustration and continued, "It is a badly dangerous mission, the partisan forces report numbers of the most dangerous Reptoids, including Masters and Siblants. The partisans themselves have been thrown back three times already, although they have not had the single weight of numbers or power you will. There will be some 100 partisans to support you. Take whatever weapons you need. Good luck my friend." Commander Jenks once again moved to take his leave when Changworth remembered and called after him. "Oh, before you go, the news from home is that the Isles are still fighting at sea but remain un-assaulted on land. May that news help preserve you as well."

*****

Upon taking command of the scene at sea, Admiral Pentak was pleased to receive the following message which he forwarded on a squadron wide basis.

Buccaneer Town: The Roke ships within the harbour are sunk or are still burning. Town sea-gate defences tightened, early heavy fighting becoming more sporadic. Sea gate not to be reopened. Heroic actions of a handful of ships saved sea defences. Admiral's sea force just about keeping the outer limit clear with only a few non-tethered Roke ships coming about for battle. The second wave ships, heading in the town's direction, are to be pushed and committed against the most heavily defended of the two landing sites. Disregard Roke standards flying in Buccaneer Town and accept coded bunting.

289

The reports in from the naval engineering teams at the breach point were not so good. As more barges arrived at the breach point the crews initially found themselves spending more time landing wood to reinforce the temporary stockades plugging the breach. But gradually as more vessels were dispatched from the naval stock yards to attempt to tow the platform further off shore, including several of the scarce recovery galleys, it was discovered that the Roke had installed no retraction system for the huge anchors and time was spent waiting for another pickers barge with a windlass pulley system.

The Admiral, therefore, needed to distract Roke fleet attack vessels from sinking the engineering ships. Desperately short of men, Admiral Pentak ordered that any small ships taken should be carefully holed, sunk and the position buoyed for later recovery, rather than fired, so as not to split crews any further but also to preserve a certain amount of collateral. But out of necessity heavy resistance should, however, be met with fire, as a last resort.

As time passed Admiral Pentak finally received more comprehensive reports. He became fully confident of the situation on the third day after the attack on Buccaneer Town and the mass landings. In some ways he was reassured that after the initial landings of 20,000 on the continent only another 8,000 estimated, had successfully made the land, and certainly less than half that number had made it inland. He was also pleased to have received reports that not a single ship had reached land on the Iron Isles. That was about the extent of the good news.

He estimated that some 80,000 creatures had been landed north of the Serpents Tongue. Those estimates were based solely on the number of ships reported sunk by his fleets, not including the numbers that had made it back to deep ocean waters.

In terms of the remaining fleet, well, he could hardly apply the name any more. The Iron Islands kept a sea going force of about 7,000 fighting ships which had been reduced to two and a half thousand. On the face of things at least he could take comfort that their losses paled against some 10,000 Roke vessels of various sizes sent to the bottom. These included further large landing platforms and it certainly consigned hundreds of thousands of Roke sailors and uncounted numbers of Reptoid beasts to a watery grave. The North's own ships had also suffered terribly and the coastal defence force was reduced from 3,000 active vessels to 1,000 in total, of which probably 300 remained in an acceptable condition.

What the Admiral feared most was a sixth fleet of Roke ready to attack and appear within parts or days. Any one of the five groups already faced contained more ships than the Admiralty had been aware the Roke could crew – if they could have four more then why not five?

Together with the Iron Fleet he was working to deploy longer range, supported patrols and he was confident that given a day, possibly two at the most, he would be able to rest, confident of no more surprises. In the meantime he had already received permission to reclaim up to half of the ships that had been scrabbled together to meet the Marshall's transport needs. Within the week he planned to have them refitted and back at sea as part of the patrol rotation, although quite where he would find additional combat-qualified seamen was another matter entirely. If only there had not been major combat actions on both continents, then possibly the marine assault teams could have been squeezed for a good number of competent mariners. As it was he could only really count on his own naval academies.

A further complication was how he would respond to the southern fleet commanders who, within a matter of day-parts of the conflict beginning, had sent notice that the southern fleet and their counterparts from the other human nations were being challenged and tested by Roke ships as never before. Once the news of the massive flotillas had reached their ears, those commanders had refused point blank to send relief ships, for fear of meeting the same scale of opposition. Admiral Pentak was, therefore, in the short term, on his own. And he liked not at all the way in which his requests for help had been refused before he had even made them.

*****

As Lady Green entered the clearing she called softly, "Still as difficult to locate as ever, Fury. Every time I meet you I am sure I will be able to trace you when you leave, and every time you fade like a ghost until you show yourself again."

"Ah, my lady, it is pleasant to know that I still have some secrets from you and your husband for even in my realm I sense your activities," the large man was sitting stock still, he and his mount more like a statue than a horse and its rider.

"You even manage to pass your traits to your mount, sir. I warn you I will have the secret of it in time!" she laughed, admitting to herself that the master of the far north was more than a match for her renowned powers of persuasion.

"If only those were the kind of issues we could dedicate ourselves, to my lady," the big man answered as he swung himself smoothly from his saddle. Crossing the clearing took her hand and kissed it gently. Almost sniffing the air his gaze narrowed and he listened more intently. "Mistress, you should not go about without protection, even here deep in your own environment. The Horde reveals more and more advanced creatures capable of amazing feats all the time. Should they want you dead, all your immediate retainers would be hard pushed to defeat some of the creatures that could make it here undetected. Our continent is no longer free of the threat."

"Stop your scolding, Master Fury. I am well enough equipped to spend a few moments on my own, especially as your message alluded to the need for secrecy. How secret would this be if I had brought all my household. Now can we please get down to business. I take it you won't be staying tonight," the lady answered like a school mistress to a talented but unruly child.

"Fair enough, mistress. I have come to ask if you would take responsibility for Jeffers Star's ward children. The Marshall has confirmed that Jeffers will be joining my command, but the work and the journey will be too dangerous for any dependents. Jeffers has served the nation long and well and in a different time would be a householder and caring family man. That, I believe, is what has allowed his talent to have been so well used. Unfortunately, in this time my needs are greater." Fury paused for a moment, looking around the clearing. "The Marshall and I felt this would be a safe place and that Jeffers would accept you as a fitting substitute to look after the children. Will you do this for me? It will be vital that no one can exert pressure on Jeffers because of ties to relations, blood or otherwise." Hesitating uncharacteristically for just an instant Fury continued, "I would also appreciate it if you could keep a watch on my father," Fury asked, as meek as Lady Green had ever seen him.

"Very well, Legion Lord," she agreed. "Is there any time scale within which Star is likely to return?" Lady Green asked.

"Our mission is such that it is more likely we will never return. I must warn you, lady, that this could well be more than just a temporary request." Fury finished, his voice as cold and firm as stone.

*****

One full day after they had left the fayre site had Stonebrow and his troupe well on the way to their assigned coastal destination. Perhaps it was the dramatic news of the call up that had changed his people's perspective or perhaps it was a factor of the distance from the protection of Master Smee's camp or even the exposure of seeing the capabilities of other companies of professional soldiers. Whatever it was Stonebrow was already seeing a change in their outlook and he liked the air of cool and business like professional competence that had settled about them like a familiar cloak. He reflected that they had probably always had this and it was he who was simply learning to look more carefully. Either way he had a sense of competence around him that, for the first time since he had received his dramatic orders, made him feel as if he had a chance of completing his mission successfully.

Nathan and Dave were relaxing more into their roles and he felt that gradually they were throwing off the shadows of Master Smee, Bart and, to a degree, Marvellous. Many men had also expressed their reluctance at leaving him until they were reminded that his orders had come from a high and unquestionable source. A surprising number of people had also expressed regret that Blue Boy would not continue with them and Stonebrow detected that in some ways he had been accepted as the troupe's mascot and symbol of youthful good fortune. Whatever the outcome of the separation, Stonebrow was keen to put some distance between them and the fayre site. With no more animal problems, and a high degree of self control, the band were speeding across the countryside and currently ahead of schedule for their assigned check-in time with the coastal transport corps.

As they moved closer to the coast, the mostly flat centre of the plains began once again to give way to a more rugged terrain. Once more Stonebrow signalled that the band should slow up, and even went as far as sending some musicians out to practice precision riding whilst performing; so with sets of individuals alternating out front the band gradually wound its way through the hillocks of the coastal mountain foothills.

*****

"Bishop Vesper, Marshall Sarpayne. Commanders, I have called you here to discuss the current crisis," Ewgene started the meeting politely when all the command structure remaining in the High Fort had been assembled. "As you all know," he continued quickly, "through your various communication channels, we are under threat of invasion. No, I suggest a threat of annihilation. I ask that the command vote through war status and invasion alert, and I ask that article 16-12 of the war manual be invoked, giving myself, Bishop Vesper and Marshall Sarpayne full military command status in order to counter the threat."

When silence was the only reply to a motion which, most of the room must have understood, was a key reason for the summons, Ewgene continued, "I invite the Marshall to complete a summary briefing so that everybody has the same level of knowledge before the vote is cast."

Taking the War Chamberlain's invitation the Marshall stood up. Drawing a dagger to use as a pointer he moved to the detailed map on the wall. "Gentlemen, lady. Here is the situation as currently confirmed. Three days ago the attack started. We have reports now in, that this occurred on our eastern coastline and all along the coast of the southern command simultaneously. At present we have lost communication with the Caballeros Nation and also northwards with the Legion. I believe it is safe to assume that they, too, are under serious coastal attack." The

Marshall paused as he moved back across the map and pointed to Buccaneer Town.

"Our intelligence suggests that discounting the ships deployed with the High Marshall, every other naval resource in the three nations I have mentioned is deployed against the Horde, and specifically, Roke, naval attack. This suggests that the Horde have ten times the seaborne power that our most generous estimates have ever concluded. The number of additional sea trained Roke is over one hundred times the total number we believed living in the Battle Lands. It points to the existence of Horde resources bordering on the total number of humans living in the known free world – a staggering discovery."

The room sat quietly absorbing the news that not only did they face the vast enemy of the Horde but in addition subjugated enemy humans rivalling the numbers of free humans. "In terms of the defences the southern command report only ship-based raiding. Our eastern coasts are the only ones to have been targeted by the landing platforms, with the Legion being the possible exception." The Marshall looked to Ewgene invitingly but was left to continue. "Our coastal defences are now holding despite the army that has already been landed. The defence of the initial breach and neighbouring Buccaneer Town hangs in the balance as the navy struggles to hold back further equivalent-sized Horde assaults."

"What of the Horde army in the interior?" asked Jules Brightleaf, the partisan commander assigned to the High Fort.

Both the Marshall and the Chamberlain looked to the third of the proposed senior commanders. "Well Jules, there have been three points of incursion," Bishop Vesper began, "Although only two have landed significant numbers of troops. We certainly face a single army of between 20 and 30,000 warriors. This combined with reports of considerable advancement in capability, organisation and tactical ability within this force, is beyond our recent experience. In short, with the crusade deployed we are already facing a force that our contingency defences will be challenged to defeat; only the grade one strongholds are certain to be defensible. If they land another 10,000 troops in the northern command even the High

Fort could fall," Bishop Vesper answered, his almost albino-pale face a cold and stern mask.

*****

Four days after Lady Green had received Fury, Claphand, Mags and the children arrived. When she had learned that they would be travelling with two rough and ready legionnaires, relative strangers to them, she had been worried as to what emotional state they would be in when they arrived. She was pleased to have worried for nothing; they both arrived laughing and joking, each riding properly in the saddle in front of a legionnaire.

Lady Green walked out onto the upper storey veranda so that the children could observe her and make comments to their companions freely, without fear of offending her. Nothing of any significance appeared to be discussed and after only the barest of instants the little girl, Sophie, raised her hand to wave vigorously up at her.

Throwing all caution to the wind she walked steadily down the outer stairs to where Walrus had appeared; Lady Green just wished he would stay down wind until the children had settled. It was not that he smelled badly, it was just that he seemed to carry an odour of musky male sweat and vegetation that was all his own.

By the time she had descended the stairs the adults and children were down from the horses. While Claphand led the animals back a few paces away from the house, Mags fussed with the buttons on little Liam's coat and gently pushed Sophie's ribbon-tied hair back to make the children completely presentable to their new host. Looking at the two legionnaires, who seemed to be dressed by the same tailor that Walrus used, Lady Green was happy to assume that it was the children who had requested the extra help with their appearance rather than it being forced on them by the adults. Lady Green had heard some comments on the extent to which Jeffers Star had recently paid attention to his wardrobe and she had been sure that, to some extent, this would have rubbed off on the children.

"Pleased to meet you, Lady Green," spoke out Sophie curtseying prettily.

"Pleased to meet you, Lady Green," mumbled Liam shyly as his big sister prompted him with a dig of her thumb in his back.

"And certainly pleased to meet you, children, and your kind companions also," Lady Green replied bowing in the way of the green folk to each of her four guests.

"Ma'am," both of the legionnaires saluted back in their most formal manner.

"Walrus, I believe you have acquaintance with our older guests. Could you perhaps show them around? Oh, and Walrus try not to give them any of your bad habits, I don't think Fury would like that!" Lady Green called over her shoulder as she took the children hand in hand, one on either side, and led them up the stairs.

"Would you like to see my house?" she asked them. "You need to watch out for Walrus, he's a bit of a rascal you see," she called out loudly, in an impish manner.

"Oh, we will be very careful, Lady Green. You should meet some of Uncle Jeffer's friends, they can be a right nuisance on occasion," the little girl answered, keeping such a straight face that Lady Green couldn't tell whether she was joining in with the joke or not.

"Now here is the main part of the house," Lady Green explained as they reached the doorway where the veranda met the steps and the house. These tall wooden legs you see supporting the house are stilts. We use them to keep the building level and so that we didn't have to chop out too much of the hill side to make it flat for us to live here. Do you like the view?" she asked, leading them to sit at the table fixed next to the window where, with the shutters thrown back, a glorious view of the whole valley through which they had travelled was spread out in the haze of the evening sun.

"Lady Green, it is truly beautiful, did you build the house yourself?" Sophie asked all excited.

"No, dear. For years my husband has planned to build a house here and finally, this past spring, with a lot of help from our friends we managed to build this cabin. I think it was worth the wait though, don't you?"

"Oh yes, lady," Sophie replied.

"Scars helped me build a wooden gate once but it wasn't as good as this," Liam added respectfully.

"My dear boy, one day when you are bigger we will all work together to build something just as grand, I promise," Lady Green replied, pleased that the young boy had already picked up the courage to join in the conversation unprompted. 'Things are going to work out nicely,' she thought.

*****

Despite the delay detouring and staying overnight in Riding Dale for the uniforms, Marv, Jeffers and the group found that a comfortable pace soon had them well on their way to the rendezvous. Master Calm had yet again factored in their detour. Well, Marv supposed it made sense as he must have known what his orders had entailed. As they rode through the countryside and it rose slowly to meet the mountains the small company were in good spirits. The standard of the two youngest, already good and clearly tempered by seeing combat service, was coming on in leaps and bounds under the one-on-one tuition that the party size offered.

Marv was happy to leave most of the training to Jeffers Star, who had already built a natural and friendly relationship with the other three. His leadership style, though gradual and almost applied at a subconscious level, was as effective as Marv had heard. He had no doubt that if Jeffers had led the group into a fire they would have followed.

Jeffers himself was operating day to day. It had been far harder than he had expected parting from the children and he was deliberately immersing himself in the task of welding the group into an operational unit as a way of avoiding his own concerns and uncertainties. The team was looking promising. Marv was an old-hand campaigner and Jeffers recognised that he would be a good and thorough leader, although he often wondered just how good the famous swordsman's skills would prove today. He managed to avoid the obvious one-on-one training session despite his interest though.

Mother was a different issue. She was a good, solid all-rounder and he suspected that in the heat of battle she carried her cool professional demeanour with her and would prove an effective partner, with the magical qualities he could only describe as being a 'survivor'.

How long Master Calm had taken selecting the two young lads was a question that Jeffers found interesting. The more the two were trained the more their quality began to come through. They seemed to take it in turns to leap ahead in the training and sometimes it was almost as if they learned from each other. In service they had served at different locations, in different units, and it seemed as if they had met by chance, striking up an instant friendship. Jeffers picked up a hint in talking to them that possibly Heron, as he was called now, had somehow been involved in their chance meeting, for they seemed to have arrived at the fayre in his company. Still, they believed they had met by chance and, for whatever the reason, Jeffers believed they would come to make a formidable team, either together or partnered with Mother or Marv.

As for Jeffers' own instructions he had little choice but to wait for Fury to arrive and had decided there was little point in speculating on what his action would be.

They arrived at the partially built cabin, about 120 leagues from where they had started, on the afternoon of the fifth day, having made excellent progress. Master Calm had ensured that the company received the best horse flesh and all the team were, or were about to become, accomplished horsemen and horsewomen.

Marv, Mother and Jeffers had regularly reviewed the list of competences that Master Calm had requested and which, by any stretch of the imagination, was as complete a list of techniques and environment and terrain skills as Jeffers could have detailed himself. Whilst they had so far only scratched the surface of most of them, progress was good. Jeffers had been worrying about how to manage the boat and marine-based training so far in land, he being the most qualified to take those areas on. Close to their camp site he found a sizeable lake and here he decided he could probably engineer the situation so as to cover almost all the aspects he could expect to, with the possible exception of the effects of waves.

Chapter 15

Stonebrow stood on the sea wall above the massive cement quayside of the Grand North fort, looking out across the channel that now separated him from his homeland. With the sun rising from the other side of the fort, the sea was shadowed for a great distance, suddenly becoming a gleaming mirror as the hazy sun rose to light it.

They had disembarked late the previous evening after a crossing that had taken the best part of the day. Several times their vessel had anchored to allow higher priority shipping to move past. The amount of security patrol boats that could be seen in either direction was impressive. Stonebrow wondered at who or what was on the ships that were receiving higher priority than the band.

Reaching the port terminal late at night, instead of being allocated lodging as he had expected, they were taken to a secure dockside compound and entered into a queue of both troops and freight that were to be loaded as soon as possible. Already the port facility appeared to be operating at maximum capacity and Stonebrow could appreciate why they had been urged to take a head start over the other section of the central fayre recruits due to use the same crossing. The added several thousand troops and their support infrastructure and equipment would have made quite a queue.

Stonebrow's control contact, Milton, had waited calmly with them until they were in the holding queue, which Stonebrow observed also acted to fence off the different companies from each other, and certainly didn't encourage inter-company communication. Milton then casually detached himself and hurried off through the stolid security personnel with no trouble at all. He was back within a quarter-part and instructed Stonebrow that although the band as a whole would travel together across to the fort, preparations should be made to separate off the special projects team who, numbering 60 men and women, would end up housed within a different area of Grand North.

Thus it was here that Stonebrow announced the realities of the band's final disposition. Starling would be the bandleader for the traditional activities within the fort and Stonebrow and his team would be completely separated from them for the duration of the campaign. His squad were allowed to keep their own customised wagons and horses, whilst the official band's kit was transferred to the special 'fort designed' carts which could be hand, pony or cable transported and which packed easily into the transport ships that all regular fort transfers made use of.

It was at this point that Stonebrow felt the nerves begin to return. He, Nathan, Dave and Milton were the squad commanders making up the four teams of 15 attached to the mission.

The exercise to move the kit had gone well and port staff had appeared to remove the other wagons and animals for the majority of the band. They provided Starling with the appropriate chits and paperwork to recover whatever was needed from the storage facilities around the port once the band finished their duties. Equivalent equipment could also be claimed should another port facility be used for their return.

The two groups of band had waited the couple of parts until dawn, which was when they were told by Milton to expect their crossing to together to be scheduled. Night traffic was apparently a prime transport period under a 'what can't be seen can't be talked about' kind of idea. Stonebrow got the impression that there were other channels within the port where traffic literally rolled up to the dock and was loaded straight onto waiting ships.

The crossing itself had been uneventful. After the shock of the size of the transport operation had worn off, the troupe were treated to a calm crossing with the grey clouds in the sky only threatening sullenly from above.

The main troupe disembarked first and were sent off along the rampways that led to the upper portion of the fort. Stonebrow and his unit were directed to what amounted to little more than a large hangar space off to the side of the docks. Here the band

301

members met the rest of their combat team. Quiet, thoughtful and resolute the battle-hardened men seemed to fall into two groups. The first, about 80 in number, wore dark brown fatigues and were described to Stonebrow as combat miners from the Iron Islands. Certainly the powerful arm grips offered as he was introduced to the officers reminded him of the old saying, 'Grip of Iron from the land of Iron'.

The other group were all attired in a variety of combat camouflage colours. Stonebrow was told that this was a special outfit, recruited a few months ago, for the purposes of land warfare beyond the wall. Young and old alike they had a variety of officers, a few of whom Stonebrow had acquaintance with, and several others Stonebrow had heard of by reputation, including a couple of tribesmen from areas near where he himself had been born.

Stonebrow was quietly impressed that he had been provided with a force of 1,000 such warriors. He felt much better about his mission seeing his fighting force first hand.

Milton was moving comfortably between the groups. He had spent some time with each of the three parts of the team and was the official liaison man. The rest of the evening had been spent with all three groups mixed randomly around three cook centres within the hangar, coming to know their comrades.

It had not been until the morning that Stonebrow had got dispensation from Milton to leave the area and visit with the official band. Stonebrow was aware that the schedule for his mission could be changed at any time and was keen to check that the band were settled appropriately.

First, though, he felt the need to spend a few moments looking back across the water, coming to terms with his situation. He stood quietly at the sea-wall rail looking out over the waters and the ships constantly ferrying back and forth to his homeland.

*****

"Has Liam always been able to perform water magic?" Lady Green asked.

"Oh yes," replied Sophie, "we have always had our

powers."

"What else can he do?" Lady Green probed carefully.

"Mostly he plays with sprites when he can find them in running water, otherwise he just creates a play one for fun. Yes, copies that perform but have no life," Sophie answered, considering the correctness of her reply carefully.

"Is it water magic you can do as well, Sophie?" asked the slender woman as she moved to the window, as if to check on Liam, out by the lake.

"Oh no. I wish mine was fun or useful like that," Sophie fired back without hesitation.

"Well, what can you do?"

"I just dream that I am a god, and see little glimpses of what she can see. That's all. Just stuff like that," the little girl replied casually.

"Why is that magic?" Lady Green dangled temptingly.

The little girl hesitated for a moment, forming her reply. "Let me put it this way. About three weeks ago the god, she was flying over your cabin and looked down, your man Walrus out there was having a bath, it was a sunny day."

"Why would a god, female or otherwise, be watching Walrus take a bath?" Lady Green commented almost to herself, clearly a bit confused by the twist in the conversation.

"Oh, she wasn't watching Walrus. She just looked down from high up and happened to see him, didn't really know who he was. Neither did I till I met him here, I can always remember what I have dreamed. She was really on her way to watch a meeting between Fury and someone else. Some big man in a huge stone room."

"Do you know what was discussed?" Lady Green asked, feeling more at ease with the coherence of the answer if not the content.

"It was about the war but I woke up before they really got into it. Oh, and the man had a bad scar over his eye. Can I go and find Liam now? He is bound to be up to mischief without me. He is always getting into trouble."

"Yes, of course dear. If you see Walrus on the way can you send him in here, please?"

*****

Ten days after they had slipped through the sea wall at Buccaneer Town the *Selfridge* was still at sea fighting the Horde armada. Lucky to have survived the first few day-parts, Captain Shaw and Joonrer had begun to drive the specially equipped ship further towards the tethered platform, once other fleet vessels arrived who could protect the sea gates. The *Selfridge* was equipped with newly engineered adjustable trajectory projectors, to fire lead and stone projectiles through wooden ship hulls at or below the water line. The schooner had been designed as a vessel for attacking Roke ports in order to sink or cripple as many opposition boats as rapidly as possible.

With six projectors capable of firing accurately from ten to one seventy spans the idea was to run the *Selfridge* in at high speed, and turning to a parallel course fire the six weapons supposedly capable of sinking three anchored ships in one pass.

Once out at sea Captain Shaw found that if he kept to the edge of the battle, approaching and passing one ship, careful to avoid being caught by a grapnel and boarded, the six weapons configured to a variety of ranges had a devastating effect, regardless of the size of the Roke opposition. One day after their departure and with 20 damaged or sunk vessels to their credit they ran out of ammunition for the prime weapons. The second ship they attempted to ram resulted in hand to hand fighting. Crewed with specially trained marines the conflict had not lasted long. Leaving the enemy ship burning they fought for another two days in a series of battles, sometimes alone and sometimes supporting packs of admiralty deep-ocean hunters, that had arrived for the fighting.

For the last few days Blighe Shaw had managed to rest the crew somewhat. Joining a section of the outer-cordon patrol roster they were included in well co-ordinated shifts by the admiralty command boats that were now working the area. The *Selfridge* had even been supplied by a small fishing boat that was doing the rounds with fresh water and biscuits. All in all Blighe had managed to leave Buccaneer Town with 60 of the 80 strong compliment on board and now had 48 able bodied men available to crew. Judging from the carnage they had witnessed and heard about, his ship had got off incredibly lightly, despite the crew being on the verge of exhaustion and pretty strung out.

Calmly Captain Shaw raised his eye lens and surveyed the horizon, looking for more Roke vessels foolish enough to attempt to pass by his section of the cordon.

*****

As they consumed a moderate breakfast of fruit and thin, oat porridge Master Calm announced that the next week of the stage would be a trek into the mountains. Mountain warfare would be the subject. Blue Boy would start on his own with a mapped scramble up into the nearby foothills against a tight deadline. Trekking had always been one of Blue Boy's favourites and he welcomed the chance to put complex and dextrous activities aside for a while.

This time Blue Boy was actually given a map, although he was bidden to memorise it as soon as possible. Then he was passed a pack craftily prepared by Master Calm and out he set at a carefully paced ground-eating lope. His destination was a cave high in the foothills and the sun was shining as he passed up through the sloping forest landscape towards the tree line break. The journey became more difficult as the day passed noon for the terrain changed to shallow scree slopes with few easy tracks. As dusk fell Blue Boy dropped wearily to his knees to unpack the low single-man mountain tent.

He awoke just before dawn to the sounds of gusting wind and driving rain. Quickly packing the tent away he discovered just why he had needed to memorise the map, for as the rain beat down it became evident that the ink used on it was not water resistant. Blue Boy cursed as he struggled onwards wondering whether Calm had intended for this to happen as an extra part of the test. Struggling to make up time Blue Boy battled gamely on through the worsening weather and was soon unable to see back down the mountain through the swirling mist. The second night was well fallen by the time he staggered, dripping and gasping into the cavern, discovering a switch back protecting Master Calm from the weather in front of his comfy fire. Instantly on his feet he had his curved sickle out and jammed under Blue Boy's

305

chin, rebuking him for not properly scouting the cave before plunging straight in and for not hailing the camp, something that could have got him killed as well by his friends as his enemies.

Despite the pair of 16-part days of constant journeying Master Calm forced Blue Boy back out into the weather until he could adequately report the key strategic factors concerning the cave's position. Blue Boy finally collapsed into sleep after gratefully accepting a warm meal of rabbit and mountain goat. He passed into slumber wondering on the apparently easy route by which Master Calm had managed to beat him up the foothills and still find time to hunt for game, of which Blue Boy had seen no sign since the weather had worsened. Calm's gear hadn't even seemed to be particularly weather stained.

The usual early start the next morning saw Blue Boy and Calm perched on a small ledge near the cave with Blue Boy rapidly using a mind report to paint the journey up through the foothills. Calm seemed more amused than surprised when Blue Boy flashed him the ink running on the map, his only comment being that Blue should re-draw the map using more permanent ink at his convenience.

The mind lecture following the report was based on the terrain described, during which Blue was posed a number of scenarios concerning a fighting retreat by a group of partisans under hot pursuit. The situation required great care on Blue Boy's part, not simply because of the urgency of the pursuit that the enemy displayed but also because the partisans were painted as a group of heavy cavalry, forced on foot from the scene of a demoralising defeat. Poorly equipped and provisioned for any kind of campaign within the mountains, with all pavilions lost, and heavily armoured with maces, war hammers, shriven lances and heavy armour, Blue Boy directed successfully a number of ambushes. The supposedly lightly armoured skirmishers of the pursuing forces were cleverly held off in a fighting retreat that satisfied all of Master Calm's rigorous requirements.

*****

Sophie would have been pleased, if surprised, at how seriously Lady Green took their conversation about magic. Several times over the next day Calm's wife had arranged to watch the boy play with water, her own mental talents gently probing the boy as he was absorbed with his play. Whilst it became clear to her that much, if not all, the girl had spoken of was true, she detected another more alien presence sitting over the boy.

Breaking her contact immediately she began to worry and finally came to the realisation that Reptoids, now aware of such power and finding it interesting, were not only watching the famous and obvious candidate of the Green Lady herself, but also subjects like the boy.

Carefully she shifted her focus to the girl who appeared to be subconsciously defending herself from the crude Reptoid surveillance. Lady Green's mind eye watched the girl as she dreamed of the shattering, last major invasion of the Battle Lands 1,000 years ago, in precise and graphic detail: of flying at high altitude in the cold air of the tundra wastes.

Lady Green was still inside her head when the girl came to an astonishing realisation: her current dreams had a more recent theme, a likely Horde invasion was being prepared, her dreams were of the god inspecting the plans for a host crossing.

The next day, shortly before Fury reappeared, Lady Green arranged for a number of messages to be sent but also received further news of the Horde landings at the coast. Although the influx had been stopped. the force moving into the interior was causing chaos, destroying a number of significant facilities and defeating the troops thrown hastily against the army. All the news she received from her varied sources, with their different perspectives, told her that the invasion force was definitely around to stay. Despite this dramatic news, or because of it, she sought out the girl for a further careful discussion.

"Sophie, do you know anything else about the people here from dreaming of the god?" the woman asked the child.

"No, no. I dream I am the god; well, her awake when I sleep and sometimes vivid flashes when she dreams and I am awake," the girl replied as if this was a common mistake people made.

"How do you know she is dreaming in those flashes?" Lady Green pushed.

"Well, it seems gods dream funny. You know she can't be

awake because the things, some happened a long time ago, and sometimes more than one thing is happening at once and at different times."

Pausing the girl did not seem inclined to continue, instead peering out of the window lost in thought. "Does any of that relate to people you have met here?" Lady Green demanded, not wanting the flow of the conversation to fail.

"Yes, a month ago. She dreamed about Fury in an ice cave. I think Claphand was there too, although I only saw him briefly having forgotten about him until I saw him again at the fayre. They were battling a large red-backed Reptoid monster and having some trouble I should say. Many of their companions were wounded all around. Anyway, at the same time she was also dreaming about when Fury and Walrus were fighting on a beach, with a few other soldiers against, well, lots of different Reptoids. Except Fury was very young, dressed all in dark green he was, and Walrus had some dark in his hair. It must have been a dream as I know I can't think of two things at once, especially when the same people appear but with different ages."

"Oh, can't you," said Lady Green dryly. "If you remember all the dreams as well as these your little head must be very full."

"No, Lady, it is easy. In the god's mind there are little crystals of colour which you can store things in. I described them to Uncle Tav and he explained how I could use them. He calls it a mosaic memory. That's also why Uncle Tav says I dream about *being* a god, not *about* a god because I can use her memory. Also, when I see the people it triggers memories that I have dreamt but not realised I had stored."

"Tell me about Uncle Tav then, girl," Lady Green asked, interested in someone who clearly had a lot of useful knowledge.

"He isn't really my Uncle. He is just the restaurant manager at Uncle Jeffer's club. Uncle Jeffers sponsors me and Liam, so he's not my real Uncle either."

"So Taverner is the only one who knows about the dreams?" Lady Green broke in, before the little girl headed off at a tangent.

"Well, yes. Liam also knows, but you three are the only ones. I know I can trust you as well. Can't I?"

"How do you know that? You seem pretty sure, but didn't Uncle Tav advise you not to share your secret?" Master Calm's wife asked, taking a chance.

"Oh, I know because I can trust Fury and his men with us here because the god watches over them, so they must be all right. They all trust you a lot, I can tell. Mind you, the god watches over the scarred man as well, even though he looks more sinister. Fury doesn't laugh much but he's not as rigid as most people say. I've never seen Fury do anything bad in the dreams, not like the other man although, he sometimes cries afterwards. Still, please keep it a secret. I didn't even tell Uncle Tav." Sophie mumbled herself to a halt, as if she were running out of conviction. After a few moments she had her head up again and continued. "Liam likes you, he asked the water sprites at the lake and the whole land loves you very much," the girl finished clearly having thought the whole issue of who to trust through to her own satisfaction. "Can I go and check on Liam? You know how he gets into trouble."

"Yes, certainly, and call in that oaf Walrus, on your way will you please," the woman replied gently.

Moments passed with the Lady lost in thought, only returning to the present when Walrus coughed, standing at the door with a look of amusement on his face.

"Walrus have you ever fought along side Fury?"

"Oh, yes Mam, well not quite alongside, but on the same beach years ago. We came pretty close up, Reptoids were swarming in on us but remnants from both our teams managed to pull clear," Walrus replied with a questioning furrow to his brow.

"Is it true that Fury wears clothes the colour of Reptoid blood to fight in?" his patron asked, shrugging aside the unasked question.

"Yes Mam, and he certainly did that day. Even as young as he was then."

*****

Torag, proud, tall, raw-boned and second in command of the Roke army glanced up from cleaning the grime of battle from his war gear, the camp was ringing with the sounds of victory. He was using gilt edged, expensive paper, just to clean his sword, plundered from a town the day before. His command raged around him partying after another easy fight, only loose order kept by his blood chilling directive – torture and then death to any who directly disobeyed him.

In the north many soldiers' sole extravagance was their drinking cup. Often carved or decorated in expensive fashions, he had received a good few more, a couple bordering on the exquisite, and he decided to start his own collection.

Despite the continued string of easy victories Torag was somewhat cautious. The leader of a large Roke battle company he had not survived the years of manoeuvring without developing a highly tuned sense of danger. For the past couple of days he had been seeing signs that worried him. Whilst not a natural supporter of the Collector, he had found serving in an army led by a human easier than past campaigns of mixed Roke and Reptoid command. He figured therefore that if anything happened to the Collector either it would also happen to him or the consequences would, at the very minimum, cause him concern.

Torag had found that the set of Siblant sent along as the Collector's bodyguards were quite different from those he had dealt with in the past, especially in terms of willingness to work together. What had not changed was the nature of their body language and manner of holding council. In the past 20 parts alone, all the seniors from the bodyguard unit and several others spread amongst the command, had met three times with no prompting by the Collector or his direct chain of command. It was as if they were discussing matters in a separate council and this worried Torag.

Several leagues distant, Stilith shoved her sword back into its sheath and wiped her fingers on a rag. A battle commander's ability at collecting and storing information should appear uncanny, but today she stood helpless. Cursing her inability to do anything other than follow behind the enemy, picking up the pieces, whilst her scouts were all forced to stay close to the main corps, she could only assume that the smoke on the horizon meant another settlement lost.

Stilith O Chas ran a renowned battle school, known for its quality, and often captains would approach her to bring entire crews up to fayre standards. Now her battle banner flew over 6,000 troops. She had brought all the remaining crews in her area, plus secured a high, extra, proportion of the citizenry from the partisan groups, to mount a central army. Unfortunately she still did not have enough to cause the Collector concern, especially if units kept throwing themselves into battle like the scene a few leagues distant where a town had just fallen. At least now, though, the traitor would no longer be able to split his forces to take multiple towns at once, for fear that this larger force shadowing him would fall upon them and crack his troops against the locations under attack.

*****

Admiral Pentak and his flagship, the *White Swan,* docked at Buccaneer Town 12 days after the treacherous attack had begun. He was interested to take General Changworth's report and was surprised at the limited number of town folk who had actually been involved in the plot, despite it having ripped the town apart. Those that had been traitorous had been mainly been induced to it through mind-altering drug dependency and psychological pressure. The final few parts had also seen attempted inducement through hostage taking and death threats, although in the majority of these cases the individuals targeted had sacrificed their loved ones rather than acceding to the demands.

Able to look at the evidence in retrospect the Admiral was shocked at the sophistication that had allowed the plan to come within moments of completion. It was the restricted number of key individuals and locations that showed the real cleverness of the mind behind the scheme. The Admiral knew he would be pushed to name anyone in the northern army that he was sure could pull off an equivalent operation; that the Roke had such people literally gave him chills. The main bulk of the gangs that had fought against the town defences, seemed to have been cleverly smuggled into the town over a considerable period and kept hidden away until released for the final attack.

Had it not been for the facility at the nightclub the town

would almost certainly have fallen. If the enemy had successfully taken a defendable port then the consequences would have been disastrous. He was, therefore, in two minds concerning General Changworth and Major Millie Benge. On one hand they had succeeded in fighting off the attempt, having gathered just enough information to stall and then defeat the enemy units. Certainly his own command had been outwitted and penetrated to such an extent that he could expect a much shorter career than he had anticipated. On the other hand, this specialist facility, which he might have expected to have uncovered the plot earlier and avoided the whole sorry episode, had only escaped by the skin of their teeth.

Even now, as he toured the streets enforcing the message that he had not fled the town but left it prudently to successfully defeat the largest Horde armada ever assembled, he was dismayed by the scale of the destruction.

*****

"Come in, come in Fury. Walrus is most disgruntled that you got so close so easily," Lady Green greeted the big man as he was about to knock on the cabin door.

"Oh, it wasn't easy Mistress Calm. Master Calm trains his men well. Unless you trained him yourself," Fury replied with a wink, taking a seat in the corner opposite the cabin door. "I was passing for the final time before I head off back over the mountains and thought I would see how you are getting along with the children. I can also stay tonight and collect any messages the kids have for Jeffers. I was wondering, er… is your guest room available for the night? These past weeks haven't exactly allowed much in the way of creature comforts."

"The quarters are yours Fury, but first I think we need to talk about the female child. She knows things that she should not and I am not sure she will be safe here," Lady Green replied awkwardly.

"Well, I did promise Star specifically. What does she know? Not that I doubt you, but is it important enough to change the arrangements?" Fury asked, interested to see her looking nervous.

"Yes Fury, it is. I wouldn't deny your rest over nothing. She knows about a day on the beach years ago when you fought the Horde. Walrus was there too."

"Well, I've fought Reptoids on a lot of beaches but I suppose she refers to a battle on Carcass Reef during the Summer of Retreat. I have heard others recount the tale, could she not have picked it up from hearing it?"

"I don't think so, not in the amount of detail she told it to me," Lady Green replied.

"Hmmm, possibly. I must say I wouldn't necessarily have remembered Walrus was there but then it was ten years ago. I think he was named differently then. What other details?" Fury asked, his attitude one of attempting to humour the woman.

"Well, you were wearing the blood green," the green woman added, brushing her long green-black hair back over her ears in a deceptively youthful manner.

"Easy! I always wear that on campaign," Fury replied without hesitation.

"Oh, and fighting Purple nasties," his verbal sparing partner added.

"Well, that is more specific," he grunted disdainfully, but entering into the spirit a bit more.

"Ok, look, come outside," Lady Green said motioning towards the veranda. "That is just the start. The girl claims she dreams she is someone with special powers and then sees what that one sees. Sophie also dreamt, a few weeks ago, that she flew a route that took her roughly over this cabin. Apparently she was flying to follow you to a meeting."

Fury looked back carefully, his eyes narrowing with interest. "Ah, and who was this meeting with then?"

"Why, the High Marshall, of course. She can't name somebody unless she has actually met them or knows them by description. She could only describe the scar," Lady Green informed him.

"Well, that is interesting. Only, of course, if I did meet the Marshall," the Legion Lord replied vaguely. "Still, I did pass by on another errand and I must admit I was riding hard as a matter of course. So possibly we should look into this more," Fury admitted a bit too casually. Clearly unwilling to give a hint of his secret agenda even to this woman whom he trusted completely.

"I should think you would want to, if the third tale about you fighting more purple nasties, red backs, siblants and various other Reptoids in an ice cavern in the last few months also bears a hint of truth. I certainly believed that no red masters had made it near our shores this century."

"Just a moment, Lady Green," Fury said, leaning over the balcony and bellowing into the night air. "Oy! Claphand! Get over here!"

Moments later his trooper appeared at a run. "Claphand, Mistress Green here seems to know plenty of gossip about our recent adventures in the ice box. Have you or your girl been gossiping about our business."

"No, boss. If there is one thing we ain't gonna do it's, that." Claphand replied, looking Fury levelly in the eye.

"Oh. Well, keep a spare and close eye on the kids please." Fury said shooing his man away with a curious gesture. "Lady, did the kid recognise anybody else from the cavern?"

"Well, Claphand was in there, but Mags was minding the yaks apparently," the lady of the house replied, pleased that she had drawn Fury carefully into the discussion.

"OK Mistress, enough of your fun at my expense. What do you propose we do? I can't believe you don't already have a plan." Fury asked. He was clearly aware that Lady Green had deliberately spun out the conversation keeping the conclusive evidence until the end.

"Well yes, Fury, I do. Not least because the war is already here. I suggest we send the children, with Walrus, Claphand and Mags as protection, through the pass to winter with my viner cousins on the south slopes until I have time to investigate the extent of their powers. The boy has some kind of water magic as far as I can tell. Both of their talents are much rarer than, say, the simple telepathic abilities that crop up from time to time like my own," Lady Green finished seriously. "Walrus can arrange the passage."

"Do you really suspect the girl is so important?" Fury asked directly. "I take it you have chosen the vinners who are not the closest, nor the safest, but who are rumoured to share your own particular skills," Fury said, displaying knowledge about areas that among her close-mouth kin were particularly secret.

"Oh yes, I do." Lady Green replied, as close to indignation as Fury had seen her. "In fact if I would also ask you to accompany them if I didn't suspect how busy you are about to be," Master Calm's wife said. "The Horde can detect powers of this kind now and I have felt their interest in these children," she added matter of factly.

"I am sorry, but you are right, I can't help in this but why don't you keep them here? Calm should see her certainly. Plus out of the way here you should be safe enough."

"Safe here, I am not so sure and Calm is busy enough. I think that the Reptoids are becoming more aware each season that passes and a war party that could reach here might already be underway."

It was clear that the mistress of the house had made up her mind so Fury changed tack slightly. "What about the boy? You were saying he has water magic. Does his talent appear in a similar manner to the visions of the girl?"

"Oh, sorry. No Fury, I forgot to explain he has power 'over' water. To him the water has a life of its own which manifests itself as miniature figures of men, animals or fish." Switching the topic she moved quickly on. "Fury, I know you are acquainted with Battle Masters. Think not of the brutes you have seen recently but the legends of large and intelligent beings, warlike but clever. I feel we are now facing one far more aware than ever before. This has not escaped its attention. I am expecting company soon, possibly under cover of the invasion."

The lady paused as Fury took his time reconciling what he was being told. "What about you mistress. I am not answering to Calm if you get hurt. Mainly because I wouldn't live long enough to speak if he found out that I knew and he did not."

"Shame on you, Fury! I am no shrinking violet. I am a plain's woman and I have certain other talents as you well know."

*****

Ronnie Chung ground his teeth and swam on. He judged he had less than a part if he was to be at the rendezvous point and guide

315

the ship in through the reef. Being a double agent had been a manageable proposition so far, especially as he was known within the Roke navy as one of the few men who could guide large boats through the Grey Reef off the Ragged Land coast. Such skill had made him a prime choice as the commander of a coastal patrol boat and, in fact, all the boats operating around that part of the coast. Certain of his crews had even encouraged him to allow them to undertake smuggling activities. He had worked the situation to his and the Northern army's benefit over the past couple of years.

These last few weeks though the whole Roke routine had been turned on its head. The usual compliment of sailors had been depleted to extremely low levels in all the facilities where he stopped. The majority of the support and associated military personnel, such as they could be described, had all been marched off into the interior on bizarre exercises.

All the recent developments had pointed to the fact that the disloyal Roke sailor should consider giving up his position and disappear to the North. He had, therefore, decided on the next operation being his last. In the end the orders had come through an obscure and unusual channel and offered no scope for query. The fact that he would almost certainly have to kill the majority of the crew he used to man his patrol boat offered him few chances to remain undetected in the exercise anyway.

The day before would have proved a shock even had the state of his nerves not already been stretched. He had returned early morning to find that for his next night patrol three of his fighting crew would be replaced by siblant warriors. This was unheard of. For a start Siblants, as everybody knew, made poor sailors and usually only travelled on board a ship as a last resort, and then only as passengers, never as crew. He might, in fact, have called off his enterprise if he hadn't been confident that the Siblants would be easier to deal with when out on the water. Only when the night patrol finally got underway had he found that the Siblants he had been assigned were unusual in their ability to remain upstanding as the boat pulled away from the quay. This gave him a serious problem. Certainly these beasts were different from any he had encountered before.

As he was the experienced navigator the three additional

Reptoid warriors seemed happy to allow Ronnie to run the patrol. However, two stood at the prow of the 20 span boat as if they were on board especially to spot out and attack an expected incursion. All three were armed with dangerous looking harpoon-like spears, the complexity of which again revealed that these weren't typical siblant warriors. Siblants usually used simple weapons, relying on their great strength and natural speed. The third of the beasts stood quietly beside him as he sailed carefully towards the reef instructing his crew as normal.

The fact that tonight he was to meet a boat of indeterminate size and guide it safely to beach in the Ragged Lands certainly wasn't something he felt they would welcome. He had several parts early in the voyage to formulate a plan and eventually only came up with one of the most extreme desperation. Running his boat in quickly, under full sail, to make up some time, he had eventually slowed as he approached the reef and rapidly made his way near to the rendezvous point, but in this case inside the outer reef limits. Here the night tides plucked at the rock and swirled in dangerous eddies which began to cause signs of alarm in the crew.

Suddenly, stabbing the nearest siblant deliberately through the head, he had stepped off the boat as he rammed it soundly into the reef, jumping to a nearby section of shallow rock where he was protected from the worst of the wave action. He began to wade along the reef as the holed boat, crew, Siblants and all were sucked down by the deadly undertow.

All of the boat's occupants appeared to have been taken unawares by the cruel nature of his plan and he assumed them all drowned, as soon the spray of the waves revealed only fragments of the stricken boat, pounded to pulp. A full part later he was sometimes wading and sometimes swimming over the familiar reef as best he could towards the rendezvous. At every moment conscious that if he missed the ship he would himself be left marooned to die at the hands of the sea, his mistress for the past 20 years.

*****

Before Blue Boy's first evaluation, and the same night that he was sent into the hills, Master Calm, Marv and Jeffers were all sat round a camp fire. Marv had just returned from an errand to the nearest village.

"Well, Master Calm, it sounds pretty serious. Coastal defences have been breached intermittently although effectively they still hold. An army, possibly above 20,000 strong are loose in the middle plains winning, emphatic victories at a number of medium-sized installations. The Roke commander is the traitor Craig 'Collector' Millis who is said to be displaying a frightening degree of confidence and competence."

"Any positive news at all, old man?" Jeffers joked.

"Well, the plus side is that the admirals are holding the bulk of the Roke armada away, by what is being described as an offshore picket line and, with amazing timing, Ironhead General Charles Changworth has appeared on our coast to save your own little town. He was the man responsible for burning those six Roke forage dumps the season before last, mentioned in the Marshall's year end dispatches. Now with the Roke army dirt side and cut off from predictable reinforcement, the High Fort and other major besieged towns are tying up their troops and the considerable Roke force is becoming stretched a little. In fact the way they overwhelmed River Ford en-masse early on sounds beyond them as far as the large fortresses are concerned, every partisan brigade is now fully active and it looks as if none of the Marshall's assault troops need to be recalled from the front at this point," Marv replied in comprehensive answer to Jeffer's flippant remark.

"What say you to that then, Jeffers?" Master Calm beamed at Jeffers.

"Well, Master, I am somewhat embarrassed to find that an Iron Island's general was hiding under my bed without me realising. Changworth and a set of his better assault troops were stationed green side as a contingency against a Reptoid raid before being forwarded for action in the Battle Lands. Masquerading at my club as staff." Jeffers whistled at the sky and laughed. Remembering the invasion his brow furrowed quickly enough and he continued." Those are the details of the largest Roke offensive I have ever heard of. Marvellous, how fares Buccaneer Town?"

"Well lad, it was the first attacked and the first held. I believe the Roke were duped into a second landing there and became involved in a second attack. This too was thrown back but the losses were doubtless high. After the fleet intervened the battle moved on although the mêlée allowed some groups of Roke ships to break loose and attack the nearest coastal wall, to breach again for another landing. I would guess that the artillery chiefs will be tearing the buildings down for casting stone; the town will be pretty jumbled by now. Your club is probably gone. I'm sorry."

Jeffers didn't seem too downcast though, "Take heart Marv, she has a stout girth that girl and if Buccaneer Town stands then I would bet she does. You may play there yet my friend."

Marv was not cheered at all and plunged on to get all his difficult news out. "Well, speaking of such things, Calm, I'm afraid the Roke army is heading to the west plains, possibly even towards Camp Smee and it is assumed they will pass onwards and attempt to take the gulley. Your own home may come into the conflict."

"Thank you Marv, that may yet come to pass, though I pity the Collector if he disturbs my wife. I believe this season we are all destined to fight. I also have certain sources of information. I can confirm what you have heard. This high on the hillside we are not likely to be disturbed – for a while at least." Calm beamed out. "The raiding force has not yet fallen on Smee's camp and it will likely be a hard fought week before it falls. I have arranged some partisan cover both for us and Smee's Camp. Byron Jacques is currently a guest there so, depending on numbers and luck, it may even hold. I suggest, therefore, my companions, that we see out the next few days as we had intended. My friends are searching for your courier Jeffers, though I suspect he will endure and arrive pretty much when he said he would. We will say no more of him until later." Master Calm looked meaningfully at both men. "Will you both stay with our unit and forsake vengeance for a time? You can see I am unwilling to deviate even in this time of war. We have important work here my friends, you and I."

The others hesitated, clearly attracted by the idea of joining the fighting and taking some measure of revenge.

Calm continued as if he had not noticed their hesitation. "Marvellous, you and Jeffers, I propose, travel together with the unit for a ways once we have completed this part of the training. I suspect your paths will be similar for a couple of weeks. The boy and myself will be headed on a different path and we too will soon part, though we also go to war."

Hauling himself to his feet like a rope falling upwards, Calm suddenly stood over them and looking down he finished, "Waste not a moment with the boy, he will need all your knowledge to survive the year. Right then. My great thanks, we are back on schedule. Marvellous has the details for your next activities. I will see you again soon. Agrik's men will pass from time to time to relay news. Decide as you must and pass word through his team. You have my thanks. Oh, and whilst I am up the hill with the boy could you work together on the planning and the house?" And with that Calm was off again into the night.

For quite a time after Master Calm's abrupt departure Marv and Jeffers sat together silently. "Do you really think that Calm meant he would be going to war?" Jeffers finally asked.

"Oh yes, he has not quite the calm about him that he has managed these last few years," Marv replied sadly. "I believe the training of this boy may have stirred his blood. We may even come to pity his Roke prey. The final battles before his marriage make a harrowing tale. One might think that other whirlwind, Fury, inherited all the fervour when it left Calm, though his is not as relentless or pitiless as the Shark once was. But no, I think that what was will come again."

"Well, if it is fervour you are about old chap I too might claim a bit of the old boy's inheritance, but I know what you mean. Fury is as intense a fellow as this chancer is ever likely to meet." Jeffers joked, pointing to himself and trying to lighten their mood.

Neither of them seemed to be able to loose their train of thought and moments later Jeffers himself returned to the topic of war. "Now that this invasion is on, do you really think that training this boy is a worthwhile exercise?" He frowned as Marv shook his head. "Don't disregard me out of hand, you old bag of bones, it's just that we three together could cause the Roke a riotous amount of strife, not including the unit, who are looking pretty good."

"Well lad, I will not prejudice your view. Let us talk again after a few days with the boy." Marv laughed, finally finding something that raised his spirits but only served to confuse the unsettled Jeffers even more.

*****

Changworth finally entered the main bar. He had recalled all the surviving and mobile members of the club staff. He fought back a wince as he saw how few of his command and the other club workers had survived.

"Right then, ladies and gentlemen," Changworth started, forcing good humour through, "It is a relief to see so many of you here today. Please convey my regards to your wounded comrades should you see them before I can manage to." Changworth motioned to Barney who unceremoniously dumped a folded standard on the table. "As you may know, Admiral Pentak arrived earlier this morning to take up his command once again, so the luxury of fighting under my banner is once again, denied you scallys."

Changworth waited for the few groans, cheers and whistles to subside. "What I would say, however, is that I have been incredibly proud of all the people who have fought with me to defend the Buccaneer Town area. Especially the people here within this room and all the other club personnel, whether currently wounded or who have gone on before us. Over the past days almost everyone in this facility has performed deeds that in normal times would earn mentions and awards. Too many, in fact, for them actually to be awarded and so, for now, my thanks will have to do."

Changworth walked to the door where Barney had turned and they both helped Millie to limp through on her crutches. It seemed that all those who had any chance of getting to the meeting had made the effort. "Thank you for coming Millie. I'll let the others fill you in later. What I have to announce now is that our facility is down graded but not, you may or may not be happy to hear, closed, as I certainly expected it would be. I have been asked to head up this facility for the next few weeks and would ask you all to transfer to this command. Permission for which I already have. My task is simple. Commander Jenks has the main body of the original command and he will continue to remain attached to the Coastal Defence Force with those troopers. We, however, have one mission to accomplish. The job for those who remain with me is simply this, to hunt down and capture or kill, the man known as Master Baker Pearson."

Changworth, surprised at the strength of hatred that just naming the son of a bitch caused him, soon found that the rest of the room echoed his sentiments, as all those who could rose to their feet, everyone shouting their acceptance.

Chapter 16

Starling, Martin and Knuckles stood in the early dawn chill and looked out over their first dawn together at Grand North. Knuckles shuddered, and it wasn't exactly from the cold. This was a massive defensive facility, the scale of it boggled his mind. Up at this height he could only just make out the enemy moving about behind their lines. Knuckles would be the first to admit that his grasp of learning had been haphazard, poor even, but despite that he was well aware that for the past 1,000 years the Northern armies had struggled to hold the two massive fortresses. He could even remember tales of the Forts' walls described as literally stained green with Reptoid bodies and blood. The number of the Horde was what he shivered at, not the cold. Looking out over the 20 walls of the Bloody League and the Horde controlled territory and settlements spreading off as far as the eye could see, it was as if worrying fingers plucked at the edges of his courage.

Starling stood huddled in a large sheepskin coat, one arm across her front, as if trying to hold in her body heat, and one hand firmly on the hilt of her sword. Knuckles knew that Starling was a veteran of many conflicts and had served at one or both of the Grand Forts for a spell. The way she was staring out into the distance he could not tell if she was sharing his feeling of concern or if she was trying to pierce the horizon and see far away into the lost continents, from where her dark skinned ancestors had originated.

Whatever her train of thought her grim expression acted to discourage Knuckles from breaking the silence. Only Martin appeared mostly unconcerned, although he scowled down at the Horde lines as if he could scour the walls clean of the enemy by the very power of his gaze. It was only when Martin had been announced as the deputy band leader of the members who would be staying as the official war band at the fort, that Knuckles had given Martin's seniority any thought.

Knuckles, and in fact every other cadet, had been subject to Martin as the senior instructor for music on the move. Since the early age that Knuckles and his cadet peers had been accepted for training they had spent at least one third of their time practicing travelling musicianship, whether it be marching on foot or riding on horse. After all, by necessity a war band on campaign spent much of their its time moving about. As such Martin had been the cadets' closest senior. It had only been Blue Boy who had not come to view Martin as their main mentor.

When not overseeing training, Martin was a quiet character. He valued his own privacy and, as far as Knuckles could remember, Martin had never competed in competition, nor had he ever heard either musicians or cadets tease him about this, as they did, say, for Marv. Quite simply his inclusion in the troupe had been taken for granted, and his exclusion from the leadership as easily overlooked.

Seeing him there in his dark brown, long, leather coat, which from the irregular bulges already looked to be worn over full battle harness, he was clearly undaunted by the Horde. This look of steel-will prompted Knuckles to forget his own concerns and true to his nature he sauntered over to Martin and casually looking out over the view asked, "Been here before, Boss?"

As he turned to face Martin, who seemed to be considering his answer thoroughly, he caught sight of Starling who, despite still looking into the distance, now had the hint of a wry grin on her face.

"Knuckles, lad, I was born here." The answer was given and Martin was walking away before the reality of his answer hit Knuckles. If he had lived here as a child, maybe for ten years, Martin would have lived beneath the high grey ceilings and slept, eaten and learnt to walk to the sounds of the battle front. No wonder he stood unbowed on the ramparts where he had learnt to breathe air. Suddenly, Knuckles, who had drifted off into a day dream over Martin's childhood, was jerked towards the gaping arch of the nearest exit as Starling grabbed the neck of his thick green cloak and dragged him towards the stairs, down to the platform on which they were billeted.

When Stonebrow finally reached the appropriate level, or platform as the levels within Grand Fort North were known, he discovered that Starling and Martin had been taking in the view to the front of the building as he had at the rear. He spent a few moments wandering among his fellows, soaking up the comradeship as if he would be able to hold it to his heart through the hardships he knew he faced ahead.

Since he had accepted his command and mission he had, in a way, switched off from the normal band members who he knew would not be campaigning. These friends would be helping within the fort, instead working to keep the morale high for those other warriors who would be passing through. It was only when he had made the announcement of the final split of his mission team, housed separately within the fort complex, that he had begun to reflect on the members of the troupe that he would no longer lead. The silence, when he and all the band members had stood quietly reflecting on his briefing and gazing at the fortress, finally brought home the enormity of the struggle. From far off the stronghold appeared nothing so much as a large monolith, showing them the path to the lands that their ancestors had fought for and eventually lost.

Even after he had left the highest of the dockside ramps, some four storeys above the sea wall, it had taken him half a part to reach the central gallery complex and another part to take the spiral way to the platform on which the Band had their partition. Fort tradition worked so that companies were housed together. An area of a platform, usually a series of large rooms, with one or many arched segments for partitioning, was capable of housing teams of specific sizes. Once a team was allocated a section they were provided with further materials, mainly lumber, so that they could construct smaller temporary partitions as appropriate.

The band would no doubt complete this in time, as Martin and Starling saw fit. Martin was a native of the fort, his early ancestors having been enrolled in service to the former royal families who had taken stewardship of the forts as the Shattering came to its conclusion. Stonebrow was one of the few who knew that Martin had a mother and three brothers, or half brothers, still living within Grand North as part of the steward fellowship.

The steward fellowships equated to a life-long commitment in much the same way as the Knightly Orders. The fellowships, however, were much more relaxed and informal, allowing people to enter and leave periods of service by arrangement. Despite this, the two fellowships, one at each fort, often saw people serving all their lives with other people who never left their complex at any time, from birth until the end of their lives. Martin was the only one of his siblings who had left the Fort for an extended period as far as Stonebrow was aware. Whether one day he would return to take service in the fellowship was a question that Stonebrow had never been keen to explore, even though it was a logical query.

Stonebrow wondered whether Martin was aware that one of his brothers would temporarily take his place in the outside world, as part of the team accompanying Stonebrow on his mission. As it was highly classified Stonebrow guessed not, and wasn't at all happy about the prospect of discussing this inclusion on the 'away team', as the mission was now blandly described, should Martin come to find out.

*****

Lauren Marshall drew her scarf more tightly around her face as she and Barf attempted to crawl silently through the thorn infested undergrowth to take a look at the enemy patrol, camped in the nearby clearing. Scars was back with the horses, tending the wounded partisan woodsman who had informed them of the danger before collapsing in pain.

Lauren had learned much about the Iron Isles' men during the rebellion in Buccaneer Town. She had also learnt much about herself during and since those few days which had turned her life on its head. At first she had been reluctant to admit to herself that Barf had been her guardian angel for so many weeks. She had struggled to throw off the image of the scruffy club worker and accept the description that he was one of the most talented young officers in the Iron Isles' army.

Well, only in the times when she wasn't reliving the battles around the town after she had mustered out with the club staff to fight the rebels. Lauren had always known how talented her instructors were and that she had learnt a great deal from them to make herself a talent too. No doubt it was the pride that they had instilled in her that had encouraged her to fight in the warehouse as the Whip. Only after she had seen first Millie and then Barf, Mandibles, even young Barney and particularly General Changworth himself, had she come to realise that fighting talent was only a very small part in the reality of being an officer fighting in action.

The fighting part she had picked up quickly. She now had a healthy dose of respect for everyone she met and was not as cocky or self focused. She would never, never forget the first few moments when she and Barf had inspected the courtyard scene where Piker had taken down the Master, or the following part as she and Barney had laboured to stay with Mandibles as his grief rage, (Barf's description,) took him into suicidal encounters. He was so out numbered at times as to appear to be cut off in a sea of Roke and minor Reptoids. Lauren and Barney had struggled to limit the insane risks he was taking and keep up with him.

Later, on the sea wall, when he was fully composed, Mandibles was even more impressive. He performed many of the same incredible moves and feats she had initially assumed to be the mad acts of a man close to breaking, nevertheless, all the time aware of, and working to protect his fellow fighters.

In a break in the fighting she had said as much to Mandibles, who had turned out to be a very easy fellow to get along with. Changworth had agreed with her when she talked to him about Mandibles and Millie, who he had only seen fighting when she had volunteered to take a spell on the wall. He had advised her, the one to watch, though, is Barf. I don't think anyone, least of all Barf himself, understands quite how dangerous he can be. If I had to describe his talent I would say it is simply the ability to be slightly better than his opponent, which always allows him to win. He never seems to try one ounce harder than is necessary and as such his battles always look very close. The truth is, though, that he can just keep on doing it for much longer times than the rest of us. That, I have heard included, his weapons instructors, when a youngster, after he joined the Iron Isles' cadet force, every training partner he has ever had and a good number of Reptoids, however dangerous."

Lauren, with her new found seriousness, had taken this to heart and had watched him like a hawk ever since Changworth had informed her of her new posting and that Barf and Scars would be accompanying her for part of her journey. She could not fault the description of Barf and despite its vague and imprecise nature, she was unable to shed any further insight into Barf or his capabilities. The one thing she had confirmed was that his apparent sloppiness and rough exterior were entirely engineered to suit his current responsibility and mask his true talents.

That Barf had found the wounded woodsman had been an incredible feat, or pure fluke, except that Barf could demonstrate tracking and in country skills far beyond the levels that Lauren had ever been privileged to see at the training academies. Now she and Barf were worming their way on their bellies through the damp brush, ignoring the unpleasant drizzle that found its way either through the trees or was caught and concentrated into huge droplets that the trees then hurled down on the camouflaged interlopers.

The woodsman had been feverish and sick and his information had been vague and difficult to understand. It seemed to involve Reptoids and refugees and that both were nearby or close to each other. Consequently Barf had decided to take the initiative and seek out the Horde force with a view to preventing a massacre of refugees incapable of effectively defending themselves.

Finally the undergrowth seemed to be clearing and the two slowed even further, until first Barf, in the lead, and then Lauren, came to a halt, staring fixedly at the hellish scene they had pushed themselves towards.

*****

Seventy leagues northeast from Lauren and Barth, Changworth was even closer to a couple of Reptoids. Having quit Buccaneer

Town he, Chubby and Barney were another team attempting to track down the Master Baker, whoever or whatever that person might prove to be. Now for the third time they had come across Reptoids informally known as Purple Nasties. Like their cousins, the Green Nasties, that had been seen in Buccaneer Town Purple Nasties were common in the Battle Lands. They had only single digestive stomachs and very, very short periods of hibernation, irrespective of the climatic conditions and seasonal cycles in which they found themselves. The colour that gave rise to their name being one physical difference from the Green Nasties; the other being that whilst the Green Nasties could stand upright and balance on two legs and, therefore, to some extent could jump and climb the purple species only ever scuttled on all four legs. They were about the size of a small pony and although a bit heavier they were moderately speedy when encountered in the open.

Mounted on his warhorse Changworth was, therefore, once more acting as bait. He had attracted the attention of the Nasties, that the trio had managed to spot through a lens, without being observed, despite the annoying drizzle that reduced visibility to a bare minimum. Now he had led the three beasts in a wide loop. This being the third time of the day that the trio had worked this ruse he was a bit more confident with the plan. As he crested the rise he could make out the two hunched forms that were Chubby and Barney and their small tripod-mounted harp. His path took him directly between the two men giving them about a 50 degree arc of fire to target and bring down, the pursuing monsters. Once he was beyond the trap he slowed his horse and dismounted. He grabbed spear and axe from where he had placed them atop a rock earlier and raced back to where he would meet the third beast.

Changworth had heard a twang and a scream that indicated that at least one beast had been hit. As he topped the first hillock he had time enough to spot one beast, less its head, down and dead, and a second staggering and screaming and being approached by Chubby and his heavy arblast. It was all Changworth could do to wipe the rain from his eyes and point his spear towards the charging Reptoid, placing his foot firmly over the grounded butt to brace against the creatures weight.

Even as the beast impaled itself on his weapon, Changworth was bowled over. As he rolled over his hip he smashed up with his axe into the Reptoids belly. Changworth felt it buck from another impact and guessed that Barney had pre-empted his task as back up to hammer his own attack into the beast's flank. As he pulled his bruised form from the mud he did indeed see Barney lance the creature heavily in the weakest part of its head carapace, delivering the death blow. His own broken spear still protruded from the beast's side.

Barney walked over to his Boss and wordlessly slapped him on the back and they both turned to watch Chubby stump back up the hillock. Looking down at the beast he hawked and spat. "Two spears between three men," Chubby commented matter of factly, kicking at the shattered haft of Changworth's weapon. "If we see anymore mass Reptoid landings, that will be why we lose." Chubby continued. "It's not that a man can't kill a good few of the bastids, it's that he can't easily carry enough weapons to keep on fighting." Looking at the ground and using the sleeve of his already drenched cloak to wipe his face he turned and prodded Barney playfully, "Well lad, we had best get the harp packed and dried lest we are only left with my breath and your pimples as our major weapons."

As the two men trudged off Changworth wiped his own weapon and cut into the fallen Reptoid to recover the spearhead at least. Taking that and the iron-butt cap, as a pair, back to his saddlebags, where his horse waited patiently, he reflected on the team's lack of progress. Despite supposedly hurrying towards the High Fort to locate and tackle the escaped Master Baker, should he be trying to rejoin the Horde army units there, all they had achieved in the couple of days so far was avoiding several large bands of Reptoids and Roke. That they had also spent weapons to kill several smaller groups of Reptoids, apparently set loose to harry partisan forces, showed that the enemy tactics were working all too well.

As cold as the trail of the Master Baker already was this added delay could only serve to prevent them from ever tracking him down. Whilst Changworth wasn't overly concerned at the short term prospects for the mission, he was worried about the number of Reptoid packs they were finding. So far their ambush scenario had worked faultlessly. Despite this, the most useful weapons in fighting the larger beasts, the harp bolts and the spears, were being used up rapidly. This meant that future confrontation at closer quarters would prove much more dangerous. The other fear was that sooner or later a second band would come along in the midst of another attack and then they really would be up the spout without a cleaning rod.

*****

Starling waited for a couple of parts after Stonebrow had departed before beginning the final and official briefing. It had been held back until the band was finally settled and Stonebrow and his team were completely severed.

"OK, ladies and gentlemen," she began informally when everybody was assembled, seated in a semi-circle around her. "Now we have arrived at our destination I can confirm our exact deployment and likely operational status." Looking around the room she checked for immediate questions before continuing. "We all know that Marvellous and Blue Boy were the first to leave the party. You should all know that not only are they separated from us but also that they are no longer officially band members. Blue Boy is now a personal student of Master Calm." She paused before continuing as a number of younger members nudged each other, exchanging nods and winks, frowns and smirks. "If we take a moment to think about that fact we will see how it not only confirms what many of us have felt, in that Blue Boy was an extraordinarily talented student cadet, but also that the band members share in the rare honour of having a comrade placed as a personal student of a Master. I hope that you will spare him some thought from time to time and remember that a band should always support its comrades, should you ever be able to aid our friend in the future." This time as she paused the nodding was almost uniform across the whole troupe, even the more sceptical members who had viewed Blue Boy's unorthodox tuition as inappropriate, succumbed to the family feeling of the band.

"We should also take a moment to honour Martin Marvellous who as a band member of 30 years was, along with

331

Master Smee, a founding member of our band and a man who has upheld every virtue that we strive for. Such is the band council's faith in the young drummer that Marv has left just to continue as his mentor and, in the war torn future of our nation, his guide and protector. I raise a salute for Marv."

"Hurrah!" came back the unanimous shout from the band.

"Right then. Secondly, I will speak a few words about our position here at Grand North and this time, finally, I do mean all the members gathered here who form the official war band. We are here to serve two functions. The first is the traditional musical position of a war band through which we will work to raise morale and perform the official and traditional responsibilities throughout the campaign centred at Grand North. If you come across other band groups while we are here, know that they will be present only as combat teams and part of the offensive. Our secondary role is on the reserve list." Starling's face settled as the murmur of the troupe matched her own personal reservations.

"If you hear me out you will come to understand the reasons for this. As you are aware Stonebrow is taking a command of our fellows plus some other specialist troops. At this time his mission will be considered as the honorary combat duties rightfully performed by the war band. Some might ask why, if we have been separated from our fellows so completely, can we not be considered separate and put onto the active duty roster. There are two reasons for that. First, is that we are one of three companies held in reserve to attempt the contingency action should Stonebrow's command fail to meet their minimum objective. Second, is the nature of this campaign. Basically the goal of the crusade is to retake the Battle Lands and in doing so the primary tactic will be to storm the Bloody League. Impossible as that sounds, especially to those who have viewed the defences, there is a realistic plan in place. The plan will be such that losses will roll forwards. Each of the assault units will be committed in their turn with no rotation, retreat or regrouping until the objective is completed or the assault moves on. There would be no place in the starting plan for the band such that it would be preserved past the initial few day-parts. We will, therefore, move slowly in behind the assault lines along with the command unit."

Barf waved the others back. It had taken nearly two parts since he and Lauren had scouted the Horde patrol to circle their camp and locate the position of the refugees. Barf had been shocked to find the two positions so close and only with excessive caution had he been able to locate the two Siblant sentries stalking the perimeter of the human camp.

Clearly the Horde patrol felt they were in control and were in no hurry to finish the refugee camp, their pantry well stocked with fresh meat. Barf, Scars and Lauren had discussed the situation thoroughly, crouched behind a tree in the damp undergrowth. The partisan, Rocks, was failing fast and despite being in peril the refugee camp was well placed and had more facilities that would give Rocks a fighting chance of survival. The outcome was that the three warriors had decided to enter the group of tents and help arrange the defence. There seemed to be numbers of fighters with the refugees who had formed a fighting perimeter and Barf was hoping that together the three of them might tip the balance.

Barf's difficulty now was to get the four of them safely into the camp, preferably undetected. The siblants on patrol were proving too effective to allow this. Barf decided that his best chance would be to kill one in silence, which would at least allow unobserved entry to the camp even if the subsequent discovery tripped the alarm.

In the end, balanced precariously on the limb of a tree he dropped down onto the chosen siblant passing beneath. Mouthing a silent prayer as he fell he was brought short by the length of rope that secured his right ankle to the branch. Halted at the height of the Siblant's head he jabbed forward with his left dagger as he smashed his right weapon, up to the guard, into the monster's mouth area.

As Barth hung, his right leg screaming under the stress, the siblant died, twitching and thrashing in his arms, grinding its jaws on the front most dagger and unable to emit anything other than a slight whine as Barf chopped through its rear brain portion. Twisting and driving his blade relentlessly through to the most sensitive areas he finally pushed the siblant into oblivion as its brain sacks collapsed.

Dropping the dead weight Barf dragged his body to 90 degrees to slice the rope and earned a face full of limey bark shavings disturbed by the rope's progress over the tree limb. With the rope cut Barf plunged to the floor, rolling upright casually but into the path of a second siblant who had approached him silently. Cursing his misfortune Barf reacted in an instant, plunging first one and then another of his daggers into the chest and neck of the siblant. Despite his speed the siblant still succeeded in wrapping its arms around his and tensing against the pain with effort it drew Barfs head and neck slowly into biting distance.

His arms pinned awkwardly against the beast Barf managed somehow to draw his dagger through the creature's carapace into the lung cavity. Despite these wounds which he didn't doubt would kill the creature, he knew one bite would sheer off his face and he would die. Whatever he thought his actions caused the monster to draw back its head and filling its damaged lungs prepared to roar. As it opened its mouth, though, its head exploded in a spray of green bloody mush and the beast was hammered sideways, dropping Barf to the soft mossy ground. Wiping his eyes clear of the mush and putrid ichors Barf realised that, simultaneously, Scars had shot the siblant through the head with his arblast, the stopper bolt and close range causing a massive wound, whilst Lauren had lanced the beast through its chest, slamming it backwards as the spear cross-guard met the tough carapace.

Clasping Lauren's arm he dragged himself to his feet as Scars reappeared from the damp darkness leading the horses. The three were soon in their saddles riding for the camp, unaware that their encounter had passed off without further Horde pack members becoming aware of them.

Lauren rode to the front waving a white cloth in an attempt to stop the sentries from shooting the riders out of hand. As it was the sentries proved to be nothing more than a couple of young girls, who Barf doubted could have hit them with the powerful but demanding arblast that they carried.

In the next half part before the raiding party discovered their dead sentries and summarily attacked, Barf discovered that the partisan guards assigned to the refugees were mostly dead or wounded. It was revealed that the raiders had been herding stray refugees towards the camp, for some obscure reason without making any further attempt to enter and simply preventing the women, children and oldsters from leaving.

Barf found that much of the camp organisation had, in lieu of partisan officers, been organised by two people he knew, a former customer and colleague at the club. Mary Standu, sometime companion of Jeffers Star and sister of the naval envoy was so pleased to see Lauren and Barf that she rushed to hug them both regardless of Barf's filthy state. She and Melanie, a bubbly and cute little thing who had worked the club as a kitchen helper for Millie, had taken over the running of the camp by default and seemed to have done an excellent job. Barf assumed that Jeffers Star or Millie or both had assigned Melanie to Mary, and possibly other refugees, for close protection. Now the slender girl looked much more the part dressed in combat fatigues and armed to the teeth. Whether Mary had realised Melanie's status Barf left well alone.

Barf and Scars knew they only had a short time to prepare as the siblant scouts were sure to be missed. That two had been killed silently would no doubt be taken as a serious threat and the Master and the other Reptoids would surely attempt to overrun the camp, whatever their strange prison warder status.

Scars quickly deposited Rock with the other wounded troops and informed Barf, incidentally, that Mistress Skillet was running the first aid tent. Then the two of them were struggling to build the two junior harps on their tripods as quickly as possible. They were both aware that at least one direct belly hit would be needed to slow the Red Master, but with only two weapons they were limited to being able to cover only one third of the camp perimeter. Despite a lack of warriors the camp seemed provisioned well with weapons and equipment. The now dead and injured partisans had at some point brought in a number of the wagons with base platforms filled with weapons and stores.

Scars was able to lock and load four arblast, placing them

within range of his position. They quickly imposed a plan. Scars would take the north side, facing the Reptoid camp, with Melanie east, Lauren west and Mary on the south side, each with instructions to support the others should the attack concentrate on only one place. Each team was assigned a group of oldsters or women, armed as was their preference, and each would fight as a pack or team. In all the 30 major Reptoids and ten Roke were facing about 60 armed refugees. Barf pilfered two bandoliers of assorted equipment and with a short horn bow, two quivers and spear slipped away into the night to take the battle to the enemy, as was his way.

Lauren shrugged at his preferred guerrilla tactics but threw him a smart salute as he passed by, the flash of his pale teeth his only acknowledgement. She gripped her spear tightly and drove it into the ground; unslinging her arblast and priming it she stood stroking the smooth wooden stock as she waited.

Indistinct shouting, cries and screams soon drifted in from the direction of the Horde pack. Lauren gulped in air slowly to regulate her breathing and steady her nerves as she had been taught. In many ways standing in the dark forest, with only an overturned handcart of fragile wood for a defence, and with the enemy coming across level, ground seemed much, much worse than waiting on the walls of Buccaneer Town. Suddenly hooves were pounding and five Roke riders appeared from the gloom. All thoughts left her and she barely acknowledged that one plunged from his saddle at the rear as they rode in to attack. Several of her group loosed their weapons too early and only one grazed a horse sufficiently to make it falter and, as it reared in pain, Lauren calmly shot the rider from the saddle. Grabbing her spear she ran to the side of the barricade and stood ready to attack one of the two remaining horsemen. One of her team seemed to have dropped another, whether by luck or intention Lauren would never know. As a rider rode in brandishing a stabbing sword in her direction, she side stepped the horse's path and rolled the razor sharp leaf head of the spear across the arm and front of the raider allowing him to ride past. Whatever his state she had cut him deep, for as she drew back her arm to throw the spear towards his back her nostrils detected the spray of blood coming from the spearhead. Ignoring this disconcerting effect she hammered the spear forwards to where the Roke sat slumped in his saddle, struggling to turn his horse. The spear sped straight and true to plunge into his side and slam him from his saddle.

Cries behind her warned of more attackers and several of her team muttered weakly as they spotted a Green and two Purple Nasties scuttling on all fours towards their section of the barricade. With a couple of moments grace, but foolishly bereft of her spear, Lauren checked that the horsemen were all accounted for and called to her closet team members to form a loose fighting wedge behind her. One old timer still retained a spear and took a position on her left side, clearly an old professional who would balance her right handed sword arm.

Then the first Purple was upon them and Lauren's world went mad. Afterwards she recalled that the oldster had stepped forwards and expertly stabbed the beast, locking the spears cross piece and forcing the beast down and to the left in classic manner, allowing her standing in front to lance the beast in its head with her sword. The weight of the beast smashed the old man's arm, breaking it cruelly under the intense force of the animal's charge. That he drew a dagger with the other hand and rushed selflessly into the path of the second beast Lauren only found out later, for immediately she and a couple of others were fencing with the green creature, the third to arrive. The beast barrelled one woman over to her right and then stamped her body on the ground. Lauren took the opportunity to stab the beast in an arm joint, only to be hurled from her feet as it twisted its thorax back towards her spinning, her through the air like a sack of bones, to crash stunned into a wagon positioned further behind. She lay there stunned for a few moments. Staggering off the wagon she barely had time to scoop a sword from the ground as a small pack of dog-size Reptoids lunged and snapped at her, trying to bite into her flesh. The rest of the battle became a blur. She dimly recalled loosing that sword fighting a large Reptoid with her dagger. She finally reclaimed her spear from the body of the Roke horseman, but the rest of the battle was just a blur of fire, smoke, blood, pain and screaming.

Some time later Barf pulled Lauren to her feet, from where she had collapsed in exhaustion, and poured a canteen of water over her head and into her face. Supporting her arm he helped her check on her squad, as a good officer should. Most were dead and Barf informed her that her section had been the second most heavily hit. The old timer with the spear was barely recognisable but one of the survivors confirmed that his sacrifice had lead to the death of the second beast. Several of the younger women had survived, with a variety of wounds, and Lauren's area was littered with the bodies of tens of the dog-sized Reptoids.

Regaining her composure she asked Barf who else had survived. Barf shook his head, "About 40 are dead, including Melanie. Mary and Madam Skillet aren't hurt too bad, they fought hard near the infirmary and saved the injured from certain death. Melanie joined with Scars in the centre and faced two dozers and three siblants. Scars' cabled arblast shots worked like a treat on the dozers and his axe claimed them two. Melanie did brilliant but three siblant was too many and although she took two, the third killed her and six of her squad. Killing the last dozer saw Scars cracked in the ribs, and a Reptoid puppy chewed his leg up pretty bad," Barf tailed off.

"What about the other three siblant we saw, and the Master?" Lauren asked looking around anxiously.

"Err… the siblants never made it into the camp, along with a few Roke riders. The Red Master also sort of burst into flame as he reached the barrier and it was hit by both harp as it slowed up," Barf replied vaguely. "Look, Lauren, I think we need to move out of here, but I don't know where, and we have plenty of wounded."

*****

The Collector sat in his camp priming a new pair of ears for his collection. Life was going well. After the North had abandoned him following his capture, when somehow news of his double dealing had emerged, he thought he was finished. The Horde commander, instead of killing him as they often did to exposed agents, took him to the south coast of the Battle Lands. There he was subjected to some very weird underwater experimentation whilst under the influence of powerful drugs. After each of the many sessions he could seldom remember much more than the sensation of swimming with a grey shape and a lingering of tickling sensation around his nostrils.

Since then they had awarded him a spacious estate where he spent leave and where he was provided with a staff of the most perverse men and women he had ever encountered. They encouraged him to practice his rituals of taking body-part souvenirs from his victims and gave him authority to hunt humans in the Ragged Lands as much as he pleased, or his free time would allow. It soon became apparent, though, that he was primarily required to lead a force of troops into the central plains of the North, where he had grown up. Fuelled with drugs he had been endlessly questioned and worked to produce a plan that he could execute to cause the North the most pain. Initially it had been separated into two phases.

His controllers, one quiet tattooed Roke and one amazingly attentive siblant-like Reptoid had started on the second part first. They had worked long and hard on tactics that could be used to prevent the Nation from raising one large army and eradicating any invasion force within days. Secondly, and for the longest time, they had worked on what the collector considered to be the single biggest factor, the ability to penetrate the sea defences and transport a significant body of troops inland within parts of the first attack commencing.

That was where he felt he had first truly tapped what he knew was his inherent genius. His knowledge of the central plains had played only a small part in the success of his mission. It was his idea to make the floating platform. It had emerged from one of his drugged swimming sessions and had been the key to the recent success.

Even the disruption caused within neighbouring Buccaneer Town by his main rival operative, mysteriously known only as the Blood Ghost, had been insignificant compared to the part his plan had played.

Now established deep within the heart of the central plains the Collector was delighted to be able to wreak his revenge on the town where that bitch had first spurned his teenage advances. This many years later there was no way to be sure she still lived in Riding Dale, but then that didn't really matter. Under his expert tuition all his playmates eventually transformed into Julie and the best thing about it was that she would spend the rest of his life paying for her rejection again and again. Certainly within the town there would be her relatives and friends, many of whom he would call to pay her price.

*****

Violet sat by the cooking pot at the main fire stirring the stew reflectively. The partisan commander had been with her when he had been brought the awful news. Whilst it was common knowledge that all major towns had been ordered to hold at all costs, the theory was that reported intelligence on the position of the raiders would allow the dependants and selected individuals to be safely evacuated beforehand. In this case, however, there had only been a warning a part before a small but powerful force of siblants had sped across the countryside. There had only been time for as many children to be mounted as possible and rushed from the town before the gates were closed just as the encircling force appeared. Even then most of the mounted guard protecting the children had been killed as one after another had turned to fight the band of siblants who were determined to run the party down. Many children had been double mounted with the guards and those poor infants had also been victims. It was only when a partisan force had reached the fugitives blocking the remaining eight Siblants that some youngsters' safety had been assured.

The partisan force pushed south rapidly but had only arrived in time to find the town burning. Incredibly, in a matter of parts, three of the four gates had been reduced by rams and 1,600 people slaughtered or worse, for there was clear indication that many had been taken captive and marched out of the town. The partisan outriders had begun to give chase but had ridden into the vanguard of a large section of the Collector's army, which appeared to be almost all the mounted raiders in his force.

The mounted partisans had no choice but to fade into the countryside, those that escaped at all. Those scouting the town brought further disturbing news. It appeared that tracks and a couple of hastily scribbled witness reports, discovered unburnt, recorded that the town had been attacked by a force composed almost entirely of sibilant, numbering in the hundreds. These Siblants had carried, and then effectively used, complicated teamwork-based siege equipment to smash through the town gates so effectively as to destroy the defences within a part.

Violet worked on, tasting and seasoning the vat of food and trying to ignore the pair of off duty partisan guards sitting nearby speculating on the horrors awaiting the 100 poor souls carried away into the midst of the Collector's evil force.

*****

The Collector stalked his camp heading for the prison stockade. He had just defended the Riding Dale action from another of the siblant commanders, angry that he had snatched away their troops for the attack and exposed his bodyguard for the sake of spiriting away his play slaves, as the Siblants limited vocabulary described the captives.

"That I chose to test the troops and officers in my command is clearly beyond your pathetic grasp. Now leave me," had been his insulting reply. Paying the siblant leaders no further heed he had stormed out into the night. There was no way he was listening to their pathetic complaints when he had so much entertainment awaiting him.

Had the Collector been quite as smart as he believed then he might have noticed that his remarks to the siblant commanders produced none of the irritation that he would have expected from the vain race of warriors. If a siblant could be said to shrug, then that was as close to their reaction as humans can come. The majority of the leaders left and stepping to the mouth of the commander's tent Torag saw them send for the rest of the now obligatory sub-council. Instead, the Collector bumbled his way through the campaign considering himself safe under the protection of one of the highest Reptoid commanders in the known world: the giant siblant like-beast known as First Claw from which all others holding that title now derived their instruction. With such patronage there was no fear of betrayal by the treacherous self-seeking Roke commanders.

Eighty seven captives were chained in a ring near his tent and it was to this location that he hurried, knowing by the time he had made his selection the siblant would have left his tent to return to their own part of the camp.

He cast his mind back to his youth and creating a mental list of preferred victims began to inspect the captives to choose the first few to suffer. No point in rationing himself though, he thought, salivating at the fun he would have.

*****

The Watcher folded its wings and sat perched in the hills high above the position of the Collector's camp. It still felt drowsy and weak but was glad that it had been able to throw off its recent lethargy and inspect the human continent.

She had been remiss not to have inspected the humans more recently and it had only been by chance that the flight had passed over the scene of the battle for the plains town. Never before had the Watcher seen Reptoids fight like humans, working in teams and using complicated equipment. Now she was disturbed. How could the race have evolved so quickly and efficiently, appearing to take steps in a period of a month, when the past ten centuries had shown such behaviour only infrequently?

Could the changes that the Watcher had been hoping and waiting for actually be about to happen? The trouble was that she had detected the right kind of changes in the humans of recent centuries and it had been her view that the humans offered the most promising developments. Now it looked as if both species were about to enter a similar phase of new capability. That thought was worrying. With both species independently launching major simultaneous offensives there was a danger that they would eradicate each other, and both the potentially interesting evolutionary strains might be lost.

To top it off the Watcher, now free of lethargy, was reluctant to return to her base until she had identified what was causing her problem. However, until she did she would be unable to contact the Gatekeeper.

Chapter Seventeen

Barf's problem concerning moving the injured but rescued members of the camp only lasted for the rest of the night. Just before dawn the tired sentries roused him and he was taken to meet a partisan commander who had hurried to the area to relieve the suffering that the roaming bands of Reptoids were inflicting. The commander turned out to be Agrik Wainright, formerly retired and now reactivated as the acting general for the central plains militia forces.

Scars and Lauren were introduced to him separately for it appeared he had a passing acquaintance with Barf.

"So, city girl, I hear you got a good look at the Roke back in Salt City. Reckon you'll be up for a bit of our relaxed country living?" He joked within moments of being introduced to Lauren.

"General Agrik, I can assure you that my land skills are current. I had a secondment year from the academy with the third ranger battalion trainers down in the Stoss lowlands," Lauren replied indignantly.

The big 'country type' just looked down on her and smiled. "Fine then, Lauren Marshall. Although I'd appreciate it if you called me Agrik. Or Big A if you prefer, as it seems my old nick name has returned now that my retirement has been revoked."

As Lauren looked at his wiry frame, sizing him up trying to put an age to his athletic form, doubting he had been retired, he continued. "Voice any concerns if I detail an activity outside your third battalion training. I doubt Makram will let me off returning anything less than his whole daughter. But otherwise I will consider you blooded and country wise. Stammer will be your second and you now have 30 mixed calibre warden staff you can view as rangers and 100 more country folk, all with wood skills and capable of partisan activities in your command. Meet 'em, know 'em, but don't waste 'em."

A tall woodsman made his way over to the pair, nodding to the general and viewing Lauren as if she were a snake about to bite him, not knowing if she was poisonous. "Stammer, here, will introduce you to your relay messengers. Your first duty will be as one of many crews sent to support Lady Green, but I will require the remainder of your unit in the Scale foot hills for partisan duties three weeks from today, should her defences look solid. How high is your light bow rating?" He finished abruptly.

"Three to three gen… er… Agrik," Lauren replied immediately, proud of her good score.

"Fine, that is a good start, have Stammer work on the theory with you and I will hope for an improvement when you next report," he said turning on his heel and motioning Barf from where he was skulking to walk with him.

*****

Barney dismounted to examine the ground churned by the hooves. "Bloody well moving fast, Boss. If it was the same scum who moved between this point and the last place we stopped."

"We will catch them," Changworth said grimly, "whoever they are."

For the last day the partisan guide had taken them over the remains of the tracks that had been found several weeks earlier. Changworth had received a message passed on by the partisan scout who had also volunteered to act as a guide. Taverner appeared to be the source of the information as he had sent the message hinting that Changworth's operation had come to his attention whilst he was occupied helping with the coastal defences to the north of Buccaneer Town. What the defence force needed a part-time spy cum restaurant manager for Changworth wasn't sure, but the note had gone on to explain that a tracker had followed the path of a lone horseman who had made some extraordinary kills, blazing a path directly away from the hills north of Buccaneer Town heading for the mountains.

The route chosen by the Roke never came close to any encampments. Eventually Changworth realized that the horses could not keep on as they were going. Chubby heard muttered curses, and looked up from the tracks as Chang pounded his thigh with a gauntleted fist. Finally he ordered everyone to dismount. They led their horses on foot, up hill and down for a couple of miles and then proceeded at a trot. Trot a mile, then ride hard for a mile. Walk then trot then ride. Finally they reached the lip of the rise that marked the start of the mountain foothills, a great wooded valley leading up into the mountains.

Changworth threw back his head and laughed, at first a bitter sound that carried his realisation that to hunt just one man into the vast mountains was an expedition for which they were not equipped, but gradually coming to tell of his delight at the splendid view and his joy to be alive. Chubby and Barney joined him there looking up into the majestic mountains before they eventually turned to return to Buccaneer Town and re-equip.

*****

The Tallway village on the road to River Ford was in such a state of total devastation that only a mound of rubble marked where the road entered the village. Though the rubble showed where the wall had been no attempt had been made to clear the path and it looked as though the Roke forces, having destroyed it simply went around it. The village, though, was not completely deserted and a few Roke jackers were killed by the scouts before Agrik led the rangers across jagged bits of broken stone, past mounds of rubbish and piles of stinking corpses.

The Collector's war plans only ever paid the enemy in destruction, the convenience of fall-back positions or secured food stocks were factors to which he paid no heed whatsoever. From what Lauren knew, this attitude of remorseless expansion typified the Reptoid and, therefore, Roke persona. Once inside the wall, there was little immediate improvement in their surroundings. On either side of the road stood nothing but ruins. The villagers had clearly fought at every step. Whether the buildings had been torched in the taking, or once the village was secured, was unclear.

Gaping holes half filled with rubble showed where cellars had been, and sometimes it appeared that the Roke, probably the stay behinds, the 'jackers', had investigated them. Where the fires left off the Roke had apparently continued, smashing down stonewalls so that the uneven remains of brick and plaster work spilled many buildings into each other.

Certain wooden buildings that had had no cellars showed as bare earth rings as they progressed along the main street. "Hardly an awesome fortress to start with but it still shames our ancestors that we have allowed even a single village to fall." Lauren was interested to hear from Agrik's speech that he clearly followed the old ancestral religious views. With the marks only slightly hidden by the early morning rain, Ince Coluc rode in from scouting to announce that the considerable Roke cavalry force had staged in and around this village, pretty much all the reported number in one company. News which cheered the Rangers at least.

The rest of the day was spent with Lauren checking her men and Agrik, off to one side, receiving partisan intelligence. Since she had first met the enigmatic general she had not been able to get him out of her thoughts. Whilst he came across as a bit of a backwater yokel, she knew from lectures at the academy that he was a respected and talented soldier who had won many awards, both for his personal bravery and also his ability with tactics. That he was older than her father served not to blunt the sexuality he seemed to exude. It was almost as if he carried the strength of the land and its fertility about his person. 'I've got to stop thinking like this,' Lauren berated herself once more. But even so he was soon back in her thoughts.

Another old ranger famous for his achievements, Erorn Quesr, also arrived as they set up early evening camp. His had been the task of skipping the town and scouting as far ahead as the partisans could pass him safely.

The pale light softened the deep scars on his forehead but emphasised the lines around his eyes. The tough old man seemed greatly worn by his exertions. He reported that for the next 100 leagues town castles and other facilities had been levelled in a similar fashion. Whilst this seemed bad news on first inspection, he confirmed that the Horde's raiding army had split finally into two main sections.

The remaining Northern forces were too scattered to merge into one great army to act as a rock on which a single Reptoid force would break itself. Erorn's news, therefore, was well received. Two medium-size forces would give any location a better chance to resist, and possibly make it easier to tear one section apart and defeat it.

Lost in thought Lauren wandered from the shattered village beside a path down which rode numbers of arriving northern troops. As her mind worked over the tactical options she trudged steadily. When finally she raised her head she realised that passing through the reinforcements, she had wandered a considerable distance from the town. She finally turned and used the now well-worn track following after the last group who had passed her some minutes before.

Mingling with these troops, though, were a number of spies and Roke assassins. Unknown to Lauren, as she walked through the deadening mist she came into great danger. Almost as if she could sense her mistake Lauren sped up and began to silently but quickly retrace her steps, slightly off the track itself, back towards the camp. She was too late, she had been recognised and targeted. Out of the mist reared an ugly man with a pair of nasty looking knives. Lauren stepped back and drawing her sword she took a classic defensive position, only to see him leer at her in distain. Only then did she realise a second man had approached silently from behind.

Agrik was a silent ghost-like vision as he in turn emerged from the mist; his greens and greys seemed tinged with black liquid splashes. He shot the second assassin through the side of the head from only a couple of spans as Lauren attacked the first assailant. He fought desperately for a few moments and then broke free, attempting to run into the night, but took an arrow through the knee from Agrik's bow. Stammer appeared from the gloom and without appearing to hesitate, trussed the wounded man to stop him from taking his own life.

"Lauren, come walk with me for a while," Agrik said, carefully not mentioning the episode.

Lauren shivered as he placed an arm across her shoulders, not from the mist, nor from the fright of the attack. Agrik turned her face up with a finger nudging gently under her chin and with her face turned up to his he told her gently, "I know, Lauren," he told her. When she failed to reply he mumbled, "I love you, too.

I don't know why here why now. I just suddenly knew when we met a few days ago that I do."

As Lauren worked to form an answer, flattered but unsure of her own feelings, the moment for challenging his thinking passed and they walked on into the night.

The pink rays of the distant, hidden sunrise peered out like a ship emerging from beyond a rock out at sea. Cloaked by a faint idle mist, the river could be heard lapping at the nearby bank. On the shore Lauren and Agrik lay entwined in their oiled cloaks. A carpet of sweet-smelling pine needles and the leaves from nearby birches covered the forest floor. Close by a wren began to sing, and was answered by the croak of a rook. Agrik was suddenly on his feet, indicating for Lauren to stay silent. Motioning her back into the undergrowth he disappeared, reappearing moments later with Stammer.

"I must leave immediately," Agrik told her, already half turned away as if to leave. "Needs must. I go to relieve a force that has become surrounded by an evil type of Reptoid. I had hoped never to see the pack hunters on this continent," Agrik muttered, as if reluctantly acknowledging a new responsibility to explain things to her. He motioned Lauren to hurry. Stammer followed along seemingly oblivious to Lauren's new relationship with the older general.

*****

Fury was also south of the mountains to pick up some extra rangers who included the youngest non-committed northern commander. This fact had effectively forced Agrik out of retirement, once the current general, Ranger John, was seconded by Heron.

There were also lecturers from the military academy accompanying Fury. Both groups had left the High Fort separately for security reasons. The academics were taking a more direct route to the rendezvous at the Fayre site. Planning to take just as long, because of a detour via one of the university depots for research materials, they then needed a partisan escort through the countryside affected by the Collector's army and had a hard time making the rendezvous on schedule. They were eventually found by Master Calm's messenger who diverted them to an alternative rendezvous point, of which the travellers were so far unaware.

One of the lecturers, an aged, although still fit lady historian, complained almost all the time, but not about anything in particular. The other historian, a younger man, said little and watched everything and gave the impression of being a planner or intelligence officer even when dressed as a common woodsman.

Fury finally got his band all together, except for Jeffers Star, six leagues from where Master Calm had his party camped. He left his new recruits getting to know one another whilst he sought out his flamboyant replacement.

*****

Although the Northerners talked about the Roke army being under the control of a single general, the Collector, most knew that really Roke armies were just a collection of war chiefs. The usual case was that the most powerful, mainly due to being in favour with the Reptoid command structure, carried his wishes forward through threat and violence, bribe and persuasion. The famous renegade, the Collector, was in this case, having such an easy time that he actually felt more like a general. In fact had he not fallen into the dubious pleasures of money, power and a vicious need to prove the twisted view of his own superiority, he had enough real talent that he might have risen to the equivalent rank in the Northern army.

Not long into the invasion he was bitterly disappointed because had the landings occurred perfectly he would have had an unstoppable army of 100,000 fighters. As it was the primary goals he had been given in exchange for command of the army, had begun to fail long before he could know, with the faltering of the secondary beach landings and the survival of Buccaneer Town. The primary task he had been set, to take and hold the lowlands long enough to allow a force to reach and capture the route into the mountains, passed beyond his reach as the forces failed to arrive.

Playing on his own perceived cleverness he still hoped to

achieve a certain amount of success. At the back of his mind he felt a plan force its way from the vagueness of his subconscious and take its place as if he had always intended it. Just for a moment he was uneasy because the idea felt alien and out of place but then the feeling was gone. Instantly he decided to split his force and personally set out with the fastest portion of the army to take the Gulley.

With that pass controlled, the only one in the mountain chain clear enough to move numbers of troops easily, the ability of the brutish greens to aid the Northerners would diminish. At the same time it would allow those of the Horde army that had been pushed to land beyond the Serpent's Tongue, to pass around the far side of the mountains and pour past his command centre, while he remained safely blockaded in the defensible, natural high ground. More than that, every northerner knew that the treaty with the Greens meant that they controlled the pass, insisting it remained unfortified, and the current Greener in charge of the defence was that fraud, Master Clam's wife. The Collector firmly believed that no woman would be his equal.

Obviously, that was why he had moved first to take less strategic lowland towns in the central region, the plan must have been with him all along. Now, making his campaign successful, even with the moderate portion of his troops landed, was secondary to his need to be in the Gulley as quickly as possible. Initially, even as it became clear that the second wave of troops were not forthcoming, he found that major bodies of northern troops had been sent overseas and he had relaxed, but now he was re-invigorated and began formulating his way through this new backup strategy.

Within the day, despite the standing army being absent, he received word that the citizenry had become organized more quickly than he had anticipated. They had smashed his smaller raiding bands rapidly once they got into the fighting and he had little time to further test his planning. Behind his outward calm he was becoming increasingly desperate but knew that he should in no way show this in front of the other war captains, especially as they were mainly Siblants, products of the secret camps restricted even to him. Contrary to all his intelligence he still clung to the hope of the landings becoming more successful again, cut off from the real fact that the majority of the fleet had already been sunk. The rumoured burning of the floating platform as an act of northern desperation, actually a hoax message sent inland by Admiral Pentak, made it sound as if the armada was stalled and it finally convinced him that he would need to press on with what he had in hand.

At the back of his planning he also knew the northern army's own landing craft were battle ready. Those later in the schedule, retaining a few extra troops, which would allow them to return and enter the fight immediately. Whilst small they would begin hunting in packs, slowing things down further. The exact nature of the Marshall's plans seemed strangely obscure and the Collector was wary that the increasing attacks might signify an organised trap.

Knowing that if he could at least reach the pass quickly enough, he could remain safe until the Reptoids on the tundra were able to trek around and reinforce him, the Collector, normally a lazy individual, was seen rushing around his force, arms waving, as he exhorted his troops to greater speed.

*****

Back in the mountains Blue Boy sat hunched on the cliff edge, feet dangling over, eating a strip of dried pork rind. Master Calm was off to the side finishing his own fruit breakfast. The young teenager relished any spare time which he could take in the view: in part because it gave him a chance to reflect on what he had learnt since the intensive training had begun. He had learnt many, many things from Master Calm in the mountains, and down in the lowlands with Jeffers Star over the past days.

Distracted by his discomfort Blue Boy could still feel his arms throbbing. Although used to climbing exercises, Master Calm had put him across the underneath of a cave bridge six times already since dawn. The climb required hand and toe jamming and periods hanging solely from one hand to another. The cave was an ideal training ground for such activities, with the rock bridge only some twelve spans above the ground so that Master Calm could walk below the boy instructing him as to where to place his hands. Blue Boy suspected that up future climbs would not be so protected.

Indeed, when Master Calm had finished his breakfast he tied a rope loosely around both their waists and led Blue Boy on a precarious route around the mountains. They paused periodically for Master Calm to repeat a certain point of weapons instruction. Circling around they were back to their camp by late afternoon.

Calm then deliberately fetched Blue Boy's full pack. "Now, my lad, we only have about three parts until dusk, we will repeat this mornings route. You will lead and we had best double our pace or better," Calm motioned Blue Boy forward.

A conscientious student, Blue Boy tightened his straps and was immediately back out on the trail. He had taken great care in examining Master Calm's movements out across the rock, but the climb had been long and he soon began struggling to follow the exact route whilst maintaining a hectic pace.

At about the halfway mark Blue Boy called over his shoulder, "Master Calm, we are but halfway and yet barely a part from dusk. I fear that we will not complete the route, may we detour to another camp place?"

"No, this is a deliberate route, boy, please continue. You should be pleased. Thus far we have sustained a significant pace." Whether this report was meant to encourage or mollify him Blue Boy was not sure. However, he redoubled his efforts and managed to move across the face of the rock smoothly and quickly with deliberation.

Dusk came and Blue Boy estimated that he was still some day-parts from the camp position. Master Calm called over his shoulder, "Pause for a moment, lad. You have done well. Now we must continue into the darkness. Hold here and recall for me your memories of the next few feet of the climb. In this way, with Blue Boy pausing occasionally and the two men discussing his recollection of the rock face, they very slowly inched their way back to the camp ledge.

"Good lad, very good, you have excellent powers of observation," Master Calm commented as Blue Boy finally staggered onto the rock ledge. "I am well pleased. You must be terribly tired but if you could demonstrate to me the middle 40 moves of the defence of an unarmoured man against a multipledmounted assailant I would be delighted. Retain the pack. You may begin."

So Blue Boy, fighting cramps in his neck, shoulders, calves and thighs, finished the night with rigorous day-parts of stance taking. Master Calm seemed to feel some need to check each posture slowly with his cane in the dark, running the stick over Blue Boys torso to judge the correctness of the position. Blue Boy was forced to repeat two sections three times, because of incorrect knee bend, and finally, with a grunt of satisfaction, Master Calm allowed him a couple of parts of sleep before they began a partial descent.

This descent, though, had Blue Boy carrying two packs and required him to fight off Calm from above, who tickled at him with his cane as if imitating a number of assailants making pursuit. Soon Blue Boy became tense and actually considered attempting to throw his master away down the mountain or find some way to use his training sword to break Calms cane.

"Blue Boy, wait! I sense your tension, halt at the next sizeable ledge." There Calm led them in a lengthy period of relaxation therapy, towards the end instructing Blue Boy to continue in position eyes closed for a sixth before continuing the descent until he caught up with his teacher. When Blue Boy opened his eyes Master Calm was nowhere to be seen on the slopes below. Despite descending rapidly to the foothills and maintaining a fast loping run, back out of the rough terrain, stopping only to slow in the darkest of night when the clouds obscured the moon, he could not catch the man.

It was well into the next day when the exhausted student rounded a stream bend to meet an armoured man upon a horse. A strong voice rang out, barely muffled by the full helm. "Time for your testing young man. Prepare to defend yourself!"

*****

"Damn it, Vesper! I feel so helpless!" Ewgene Candwell spat, not for the first time that day.

"Patience, my friend," the Bishop soothed, taking on a rare tone of conciliation. "We are secure here and all the folk from the surrounding area are safe within the fortress. Food supplies are excellent and, despite the Reptoids loose in the countryside, we still have communication lines open to the coastal defences, which are holding. One way or another, the Nation will survive Ewgene," the bishop finished.

"Well, impregnability didn't help, but isolated, the twin forts over in the Battle Lands, so just sitting here safe behind our walls doesn't seem like a very attractive option long-term. It has been a month since that wretched traitor landed and in that time he has devastated great tracts of our land and destroyed countless communities of varying size. We, in turn, have hardly damaged him at all. This morning I found out that Stilith O Chas is, herself, stuck behind the walls of a stockade surrounded by a brutal type of pack Reptoid that Turling referred to as Dragondogs. With her out of the game the threat hanging over the Collector is weakened and he will be much freer to act as he wishes," Ewgene bemoaned, tugging at his ear lobe. "If the reports of him splitting his force are true then we have two significant armies to deal with. There will be much less chance that we can anticipate his true agenda, especially as he will now realise that any further troops are denied him."

"I can confirm those reports, Ewgene, but you neglect to mention that both Master Calm and Agrik are likely to be within striking distance, with considerable bodies of men, very soon. We also have confirmation by bird that the Bishop of Stoss has acceded to my request and has sent Philos and a mounted brigade from the southern City," Vesper replied, uncertain as to whether Ewgene's personal sources could match the Churche's own.

"God's teeth Bishop!" You have sent for the Black Monk and expect me to be thankful for the help!" Ewgene spat out the words as if offended. "Recent reports suggest that his sermons make even your own pale into liberality. The last thing we need is the citizenry fearing a purge like the south saw in the last two centuries," Ewgene fretted.

"I can assure you, Adjutant, that our population are appropriately pious and I resent the insinuation that Arch Deacon Philos would have anything to find fault over," Bishop Vesper snapped back; bowing slightly to his opposite number he took his leave in a swirl of black robes and clinking armour.

Ewgene Candwell waited until he was sure the bishop had truly taken his leave before letting out a sigh of relief. He found this constant politicking so much less satisfying than the arcane but complex negotiations of the Desert Kingdoms. That he had a complete and full picture of troop movements within the Northern Realm, and significant information sources courtesy of Agrik, Calm and Fury, was something that he felt Bishop Vesper didn't really need to know.

By God, though, that Arch Deacon Philos was a right pompous windbag. Still his 450 heavy mounted cavalry would certainly make quite a dent in whichever part of the Collector's army they could first locate, Ewgene had no doubt. If anybody hated a traitor more than the Black Monk then Ewgene had yet to meet them.

*****

Starling waited patiently for the meeting to grow quiet. It was the third weekly review meet that the band had held since arriving in the fort. It offered a forum for discussion and a social break from the routine of practice that had been formulated whilst they waited for the campaign to start.

The bland opening item had been that the band were going to invite other companies, in rotation, to attend nightly concerts. Then one of the cadets had raised the issue of the Horde invasion.

"Well Tawny, I can confirm that the Horde force, at least two thirds Roke and numbering above 20,000 fighters, is currently loose in the central plains. The only definite intelligence we have is that they have not yet reached the western plains and so, although our camp is likely to be on combat alert, I cannot confirm if we will have to engage the enemy." Starling found that, unusually, her statement was met with shocked silence. Whilst they had all heard rumours and official news since the invasion, life changing news of their home was a two edged sword.

Stewie Lancer, one of the support staff, raised her hand. "Yes Stewie," Starling invited the quiet, shy girl to speak.

"Star, with the number of troops we have packed in here at

the Fort, can we assume that there won't be enough regular troops green side to raise an equivalent army?"

"I believe the partisan brigades are all fully operational and that some troops reserved for the later stages of our attack were still in port across the channel, so the Nation is not entirely defenceless. There are semi-official reports of a large force shadowing the enemy army, waiting for the appropriate time to act. I think the situation is that we are cutting it pretty fine but are hopeful." Starling answered. With no more useful questions to be asked the meeting soon broke up into small groups, all discussing aspects of the news.

Martin wandered over to Starling and led her aside, "Star, Riding Dale has fallen and if Camp Smee is not already engaged by half the Horde force then it is either near or over. I heard it on the fort gossip web just before you started."

"Battler help the Boss, Martin; Battler help him, for someone will need to."

*****

Hundreds of leagues away Ewgene Candwell was sitting back in his red-leather padded chair contemplating the news he had just received. There was a pounding on the door and Marshall Sarpayne rushed into the room. Deciding that etiquette was already thoroughly sundered, Ewgene didn't even bother to get up. He motioned the big man to the adjacent chair. He did, however, open the conversation. "Well big man, what can I do for you?"

"Gene, good news. No, great news! We finally have the break we need. The Collector has erred and split his force. Now we have the chance to tear him down, like packs of dogs on two bears. One force of about 15,000 is continuing towards the Gulley and will have no choice but to take Camp Smee which, when I last visited, looks to be no mean feat. Even if he passes it by Smee and Agrik can combine and catch him as he tries to take the Greener's defences. The other 10,000 are headed this way, apparently with the bulk of the Reptoids. Stilith and Master Calm should be in a position to help us shortly," the Marshall reported, his level-headed style unusually pumped with excitement.

Ewgene hesitated some moments, having been aware of the news himself for several parts, before hinting at his concerns. "After all this time and all his considerable display of talent in the campaign so far, do you believe the Collector would make an un-pressured mistake at this stage?"

"Oh, sure Gene. I know that you have met the traitor but I think he believes the misinformation we have been feeding him and has sent the 10,000 to be near where he, incorrectly thinks his relief forces are breaking through our defences." The big soldier paused allowing the War Chamberlain the opportunity to contradict him. "Shall I contact the individual commanders to formulate the final strategies?" the Marshall asked.

"You are right, big man, we should not delay." Ewgene replied. "Find Bishop Vesper first though. You know how he insists on being involved. Thanks Sar," he finished, offering his hand in friendship and dismissal.

After the Marshall had left Ewgene sat for a long time gazing at a small parchment map of the northern region worrying at what the real tactics were behind the enemy split.

Chapter Eighteen

The defence of Smee's band hall was conducted perfectly. It fell because all fortifications will, given the right amount of time and attrition.

When he had been first asked, Byron Jaques had wondered why his old friend had invited him to stay, somehow it had felt more like a summons than a request. Still he hadn't needed too much encouragement, and the music and the company had kept him there for two weeks, ostensibly on manoeuvres. His company of mounted horse had accompanied him, for as well as the entertainment it was known that Smee's training was top notch. Byron wondered whether Smee had something to do with his band's non-selection. Independent companies of mounted horse were, after all, quite rare. Still, his men were able to have some entertainment and stay sharp.

Once the news of landings came in it had made sense to stay at Smee Hall, as many referred to the camp, which was a pretty good fortress located in a defensible position. Even the small town outside the fortifications would stand on its own for a short time, and where better to stand than with friends anyway.

General orders soon came round that all settlements of class two and above should hold at all costs. This dramatic sounding order was, as expected, tempered with a preservation order for people termed dependents, to ensure the next generation would survive. In effect this meant bating Roke forces at every turn, giving them the option of taking the towns or leaving behind rebel strongholds.

Towns fully populated with adults would take some overwhelming. Youngsters and eligible mothers would be moved back in country to specially defended locations, from where, if the worst happened and the Horde gained a permanent foothold, following generations would continue, to ensure resistance. To Byron it seemed pretty bad timing that the Roke offensive had come so early on in the Marshall's campaign, before he had been able to exert any level of pressure. Surely now the Marshall would need to retreat to avoid being caught between two sections of the enemy.

News was, however, soon sent out that the campaign would continue unaltered and that the defences would need to prevail as they currently stood. After several weeks of tense waiting Master Smee had received a report that Riding Dale, only some 80 leagues south east and recent host to the Campaign Fayre, had fallen with no survivors after a hard fought defence. The loss of every man and woman of fighting age had been compounded by the fact that raiders had swooped early managing to catch the tail end of the evacuation column and that only a selfless sacrifice by the escort had allowed any youngsters to escape.

To avoid the same kind of problem Smee, therefore, petitioned Byron for 75 percent of his riders to accompany the evacuation until it reached guaranteed safety. A plan was soon formed that allowed the riders to return and begin raiding the enemy as soon as they were able. Sixty percent of the band town's dependents were then moved to the safety of the mountains. A rendezvous plan was activated for those youngsters remaining temporarily with Smee, all of whom were almost of fighting age.

Byron declined the leadership of the escort, preferring to stay with his old battle comrade to the end. He had also enjoyed renewing a former relationship with Judy, one of the band members. Red Rufus, one of Smee's younger talents and an accomplished horse raider, took the company off instead.

When the Roke arrived they were in large numbers, but even so the effort it had required to take Riding Dale and the other towns was visibly apparent, with men and equipment looking worse for wear even from the distance of the walls. Three thousand troops and a few Reptoids arrived initially, probably double the number that it ought to have needed to take such a small settlement. The defenders took heart in reports that the sea and coastal defences were holding and that all other landings were being pushed north, beyond the Serpent's Tongue. Thus, deprived of regular reinforcements, every lost fighter whittled away the Horde's chances of gaining a strong foothold.

News also suggested that relatively few Reptoids had made it on to land so far. Still, Byron judged that Smee's 600 mixed-age defence force was up against it, whichever way they looked at their immediate foe.

As usual the Roke command seemed steady rather than gifted. Attacks began immediately they soon faltered under the defenders' heavy bow fire. Nearly 400 of Smee's people could claim to be competent archers and this allowed both sites to be defended effectively in the early stages of the fight. Remaining teens acted as loaders and fletchers, and stocks of arrows were high. Two harps, six spreading ballistae and three light catapults were also available to disrupt the Roke's own field preparations. The town buildings were generally built of stone, except for the music hall in the bailey, and early on fire proved only a minor threat.

Initially the outcome looked like a positive result with losses in the tens for several hundred Roke, killed as they struggled abortively to reach the walls. Smee saved the field weapons long enough for them to have a more concentrated effect, but the real success, however, came when the Roke brought up their heavy bombardment artillery, eight pieces in all. A sortie from the camp combined with one from a partisan force that had spread itself in the surrounding country, was able to reach the mangonels just at the final point before they became useable. The Roke paid a heavy price as they had pooled all the spare ropes and engine gear in one spot, in order to speed the construction process. One well placed nampha casket, and all the spares, were gone in a dramatic conflagration. That the partisan light-horse sortie also managed to disguise the fact that in their midst they had a very basic pair of flame spreading pumps on small chariots, meant that all eight targets suffered sufficient damage to be rendered unusable.

The town battle party themselves escaped reasonably unscathed, whilst the daring partisans suffered the consequences of what had effectively constituted a suicide mission: almost all their lives and equipment were lost, to the tune of about 50 warriors.

As the troops involved in the strike on the artillery raced

back to the town pursued by the Roke vanguard, the second phase of Master Smee's planning was effected. The 100 heavy horse who had remained with Byran Jaques, but who had been left outside the keep just for such an action, rode forth. These men were to ride down as many Roke as could safely be engaged; hopes being that a furious but disorganised pursuit would be mounted. Then they deposited their heavy gear and any remaining lances and joined the partisan actions until recalled by Byron. At the point of burning the artillery, and, had the horse returned for a second pass and Smee's entire force sortied the siege could have ended with the Roke routed, and that order was so nearly given.

With moments to spare, however, Smee's remaining local intelligence managed to deliver a last ditch message that the Collector had raced up unseen. The rogue general's unexpected pace had been effective, with the majority of Smee's scouts in that direction taken and killed without warning. Signals were quickly sent and all remaining forces retreated to positions of maximum safety. Now all hope of dispatching a second set of young evacuees vanished as the surrounding siege force, augmented by a ten thousand-strong battle force, turned a loose cordon into an impassable wall.

That afternoon only 700 able warriors, of varying capability, remained behind the walls and a heroic defence now looked to turn into a rapid slaughter. Still Master Smee appeared to remain confident that the defence would remain practical and that the cost to the turncoat Collector could be made unacceptably high.

The Roke plan from this time on was singularly simple: one massive, overwhelming, attack. Master Smee, true to his orders, was ready to stand to the last, not that the Collector offered any choice. In order to offset the disturbing enemy numbers the band leader delivered a rousing talk about their brush with victory and told his people that if they held on for long enough a relief force would be sent. Secretly Smee was pleased that the enemy was prepared to risk its head start to take the camp, in reality a fairly insignificant facility.

Despite the enthusiastic bravado, Byron looked around him during the early part of the battle, sure that nearly 13,000 attackers would prove just too many. The fact that it was the traitor, the Collector, also proved an unfortunate distraction. Long had a massive glory bounty been placed on the renegade's head, and Byron's remaining men, both inside and out, conspired through signals to perform one more sortie. Smee eventually gave grudging permission to the warriors, only loosely under his command. From two directions the horsemen sallied forth with one objective, to kill the wily commander and render the Roke command once more ineffective.

Master Smee also allowed two of his own specialist horsemen to try their luck. The Collector's position certainly looked hurried and ideal for the attack, but it soon proved that not only had the action been anticipated but also encouraged. Normal Roke troops broke more easily than expected at the fore, whilst at the side the charge was easily thrown back. Both charges faltered at the point where they ran into blocks of siblants wielding pikes, a tactic so far unseen according to records. These highly drilled siblant Reptoids, one of the species that had been considered so independent as to be untrainable, appeared to make up the Collector's personal guard. Thus, whilst either charge may have penetrated the 400 bodyguard had they been Roke, the heavy horsemen were soon either down and dying or stationary and fighting for their lives. In this way the band master was served a hard warning that not only was the Collector now a very, very powerful man, but also that he was capable of new tactics previously thought impossible.

Byron looked on, no longer wondering how or why Riding Dale had fallen so completely or so quickly. The only positive note that the Camp could take was that between 30 and 50 siblants had been killed or wounded, a very impressive toll for the dead horsemen. Witnesses using an eye glass had managed to record that both of Smee's men, and at least three of Byron's who had remained fighting long enough had been seen to dispatch a number of siblant and, therefore, gain a posthumous mention. The impact of the charge had been almost enough to cause the Roke on the periphery to spiral closer to the camp. A long range cask spreader was able to deliver its fiery load into the massed ranks of the Roke, who had reformed to watch the end of the slaughter, burning tens of them quite badly.

Whilst the killing of the siblants helped reverse the initial shock of their new organisational skills, and was cause for some cheer, they never again ventured into the battle. The early loss of the one 150 men proved more costly than their charge had achieved. In short, the Roke died in their hundreds, taking the outer town first and then trying to reach the bailey walls. Smee's defence was remarkable and his camp had been prepared so carefully that even the surrounding terrain had been reworked to prove as difficult as possible to fight across. Fire trenches, concealed pits and sections of the road fired to reveal collapsing wooden bridges all delayed the enemy advance and the night was over and the sun high overhead before the town was considered lost.

Once the town wall was taken groups of warriors continued resisting, fighting an organised retreat, house by house, back through the town. Concealed tunnels, to be collapsed after use, allowed the defenders to be moved between locations, until the town was finally abandoned mid-afternoon. When Byron had fallen back to fight from the bailey he had had time to watch comrades close at hand. The last defenders down in the town and many of the actions he had seen would stand out in his memory long afterwards. Next to him, Split, a female band archer, was seen regularly to put two arrows into flight simultaneously. Matt the barber had command of the outer wall defences and he certainly killed eight Roke as he remained the last man defending the town walls. With shouts of encouragement from the keep defenders his only support, he stood for an eighth part with his back to the battlements and the best archers working to keep him from being surrounded as he stood against the tide of enemy soldiers. Finally he was swept away by a surge of the attackers, whipped on mob-like by their superiors.

With the core of hardened warriors depleted to some 250 Smee made only a token defence of the intervening ground. Archers were set to pick off targets as they crossed from the town and trade fire with the Roke archers and arblast men now stationed on the captured town walls.

The Roke soon got a shock as a final run of the tunnel system was collapsed and a fair chunk of town wall facing the keep collapsed inwards. Smee's keep had been deliberately designed so that the high rear walls and lower front walls would tempt any enemy to attack, mainly at the front gates. The gap between the two walls was filled with a disguised stack of oiled wood to create a fierce burning firewall. For a day part, that evening after it was lit, both sides waited for it to die down. Timed to perfection many Roke soldiers caught in the crossing lost their lives in the awful inferno.

As soon as it burnt itself down the Roke resumed the attack, now driven on more forcefully by their commanders who had taken advantage of the brief enforced respite to give incentive to their men. Using crossing ladders they attempted to bridge the gap, only to find, a number of short-range shrapnel throwers had been set up on the bailey, which quickly scoured the near-wall area clean once more. Crouched behind the ramparts Byron wound his arblast, the third of the day, totting up numbers like any good commander. He figured that at this stage the Roke could easily have lost four or five thousand men, dead or wounded, unable to fight on. How the enemy general would deal with his seriously wounded had been an open discussion point for weeks.

The next tactic the Roke employed was to attempt bombardment and the new force had brought forward and assembled 12 heavy catapults. For three parts Smee's troops had to sit tight as the night-time bombardment kept up unabated. Whilst the Roke bombardiers struggled to find the range it soon became apparent that what they lacked in skill they made up for in power. Soon large chunks were being blasted out of the rear and front walls, sweeping away many of the fixed weapons and great areas of the ramparts as well.

The going was slow for the Roke, however, as they soon used up their transported stock of stone, needing to tear down parts of the town walls for further ammunition. Once they had range over the bailey walls many barrels of oil were fired over, but even here Smee was prepared. Wire nets and skins over the music hall protected the only building particularly susceptible to fire. Realising that the town wall rock, when torn down, was relatively soft, the Roke commanders scaled down the bombardment and began to send in their assault troops once more.

As dawn approached and Byron became heavily involved in fighting for the walls and his life, Heat, the smith, was working hard down in the bailey to clear the armoury. His team had set up wheeled sleds which pulleys could move from the armoury to the well-courtyard. After four parts of work they had nearly finished stripping the store of weapons. Already kept separated into sets based on quality, the prime weapons had been lowered by another set of geared pulleys down the side of the well shaft, and stored carefully in cases or wrapped in waxed skins. They were carried off manually into a side shaft cunningly cut into the wall of the well.

Fully briefed recovery teams had been sent out as part of the evacuation and would return at a later time, safe in the knowledge that large numbers of quality weapons could be recovered behind the back of the Roke army after it had left the area. The well being dry, the final step was to lower the massed bundles of middle quality weapons to the bottom, and this had taken them majority of the time. Nearly 1,000 weapons had meant many trips with the sled and Big Tar and Bill fought exhaustion manning the winch. After the weapons were stacked and braced a heavy metal cap and fire bricks followed before 300 bundles of mixed arrows were lowered on top. When the team came to the end of these, Heat was faced with his final big job, fitting the tank tray. He liked to call this part his large metal mixing bowl which, when caulked, gave a watertight seal being coated on the inside with hard baked clay. It representing a false bottom. Fully fitted it was filled to a depth of six feet with water to give the appearance of a real well.

The fitting of this cap and addition of the water, even with all three men on the pulley rig, was timed at about a full day-part. Towards the end Master Smee visited the well to check on progress. He congratulated them on their job and warned that the street fighting would soon begin. Big Tar completed pouring in the water and casting rubble around the courtyard, before finally pushing over an old bucket winch which had been designed to look as if it had been struck by falling masonry.

Heat was busy back in the armoury forge, bending lower grade weapons to look as if they had been attempting to destroy the remaining armoury and removing his tools. Casting a friendly farewell glance to Bill and patting Big Tar on the back he made his way to his appointed escape tunnel. Dressed as a partisan peasant warrior he headed off regretfully out of the camp to take up his posting at one of the temporary cave-based partisan armouries.

Big Tar quickly dressed as an armourer and taking two large hammers made his way to his appointed street and, gripping his friend's wrist, disappeared into the joke of the street. Bill, no mean archer, swung his arblast and light bows over his shoulder and clambered up to the platform that protected the street from above. Atop the platform two defenders were firing rapidly at the barricades and the higher buildings beyond the killing break. Twister lay dead, an arrow through his throat and Slaps, the arrow boy, had taken his place. Bill patted Stacie on the shoulder as she continued firing, asking how she saw the situation and then slipped into her spot as she slumped down for a rest, filling another shallow, fast-draw quiver from the arrow bucket behind them as she sat on the floor. Bill could vaguely make out Big Tar tucked into a sealed doorway watching for any Roke attempt to clamber over the barricade. The street smoke pan behind him was still effective and all any Roke coming over the barricade could see would be the smoke. The small spreading ballista had been moved to another avenue, but had been used here at least twice judging from the speared Roke bodies at the end of the street. By moving the multi-shot weapon randomly between several streets, the Roke had become reluctant to risk any of the alley ways, although some leader was always in the background whipping them forwards.

*****

"Calm, well, I mean, is he deranged? He comes across well enough; polite, friendly, if a bit overly enthusiastic, but the stories people tell, of how he is supposed to change into this killing machine. A shark that walks on land! It seems a bit over the top. Yet I heard him discussing his condition as if he believes it," Jeffers asked Fury as they sat around the camp fire.

"Jeffers, you are a brave man and well respected, but you have yet to see the world as it really is. As a nation our teaching is excellent. We have embraced a total-body approach in our training: developing our whole person, body and intellect, from a very early age. But what we see here in the Northern army, though, is precious little of what the world knows or has seen. What we believe impossible for us is entirely different to views elsewhere, especially in matters of the spirit. I know more than many the feeling that, whilst I have worked hard to develop my body and intellect, I lack a certain something spiritually." Fury paused moderating what was becoming a lecture with a sigh. Seeing Jeffers shrug noncommittally he continued in a conversational tone.

"Calm grew up in a shamanistic environment where the elders, they related all of human life and talent back to the animal world. Every child is awarded a 'mirror creature' at some time from birth to adolescence. From a very young age they are urged to study their mirror beast and understand its true nature. Many of the people, twinned with dogs, for example, would take them as constant companions. Calm's childhood must have been difficult, remaining untwinned to an adult age, even though he was probably attached to the shark all the time. Nobody appeared to know or help explain his strange mannerisms. As I understand – it links with non-mammals are very rare and a shark had never before been awarded almost impossible for the boy to relate to, him living inland. For many years he lived an isolated life, withdrawn from his people due to his strange bond. Yes, he studied for an answer but this proved little enough use, and eventually he made his way here to the Northern armies, a young 13-year-old scamp. Alone in the world he enlisted, and pretty much everyone knew he had lied about his age. By this stage, though, his extreme metabolism was displaying itself and he seldom slept more than two parts per night. He was displaying very high nervous tension and his accelerated reflexes were making him very dangerous. The army trainers almost couldn't keep up with him. His mind proved equally as quick as his body," here Fury paused in his tale to stretch and fetch a meal from the sentry tending the fire.

Settling back down he slurped down his broth and started talking again around bites of his cutlet. "My father was one of the recruits who followed soon after Calm. The instructors were still somewhat subdued, and otherwise-sensible men were naming him freak or worse, so little could they understand him."

"Fury, are you saying that Calm is older than your father, he looks not much older than us?" Jeffers asked suddenly.

"Why, yes Jeffers, I am saying they are roughly the same age. Calm was graduated from the academy in only one year. He was so energetic and unruly that they sent him as a regular grunt to all the worst spots. A period I am sure you can relate to. Eight years he served in a row, outliving whole battalions and raising holy terror amongst the Roke." Fury lent back and stretched his arms before fishing out a dagger and skimming the blade over a small sharps stone.

"When Calm finished his last signed tour and left the Battle Lands he had a crew of some ten survivors who went with him. They sailed round our coast to the Caballeros nation and, fighting as mercenaries, they paid their way round warmer continental waters. It was there that Calm met his beast symbol. Five years later eight of the crew, including Calm, returned to the North. They enlisted in a rag-tag company and got assigned to hunting Roke and Reptoids in the wastes. The Legion accepted their next commission and their exploits pushed further into the western reaches of the continent where a certain band of Green Folk took to this motley group of outcasts. Jack Grip and Marsy Tout went along, plus Steel Nose and Cut Joy Jones. I have to say, a group the likes of which we may never see again."

Jeffers stopped Fury with the universal sign for a toilet break but was back from the tree line momentarily.

"The Land Shark transformation was understood and frequent, but still uncontrolled at that time. Many of the stories were of the band serving to constrain the Shark rather than as his crew. Finally the hunt wound down and the Shark met the Lady. A woman as fine and as noble as the Greens might hope. Her family had followed their traditions of matched marriage, supposedly based on a strange rite of fortune telling. The problem came when her match was revealed as a brute. Unusual for a plainsman, and also unusually huge and powerful, certainly beyond any man the North has seen excepting Master Kroll. The Shark, though, had learnt of love but was not ready when the renegade whisked the Lady away into the deep interior."

Fury paused as Jeffers lent forwards to stir up the camp fire. "Fury, please continue."

"More Shark than Calm, he and the crew pursued the green brute who, by now, had broken his own race's peculiar laws and been declared fully renegade, although mainly by her family. Whatever the circumstances much diplomacy was required to smooth a Northern war band pursuing a green noble into the interior. In the end a surprising number of greens, who themselves follow a kind of shamanistic path, having met Calm pledged to his cause in this matter, some of them powerful far beyond the lady's own family. A right of trial by combat was decreed as each was facing a number of legal charges from various green factions presented to their highest court, the Council of the Plains."

Fury grimaced as he continued telling his tale, as if he could see it in his head. "Victor innocent, dead one guilty, that type of thing, based on ancient green customs and part of their law. Our ambassador was needed to find this acceptable in interpretation to our laws, for Calm himself had powerful Northern army supporters, having served for so long and so well, and this was acceded. Against an over grown, battle hardened plainsman few of either kind actually expected Calm to survive. In this, though, he again proved resilient. It is said that the Shark hacked the green bulker apart mercilessly, piece by piece. The trial was over and despite his cold, relentless, display in combat, many more greens took to him. For reasons known only to herself the green Lady pledged to a betrothal with Calm and returning to our borders waited two long years, companioned by the majority of the crew, whilst the tormented man and a few greens and humans travelled deep into the interior, to find for him some kind of peace. Finally it was Calm who returned, he had travelled far beyond our bounds of knowledge and there, amongst a party rumoured to be of all the colours, he had worked and studied to control his mirror personality."

"So Calm returned cured of his inner demons then?" Jeffers asked gently, surprised at the bitterness that Fury had shown telling of the trial.

"From then until now some have described him as cured, whilst others have thought he has spent more energy restraining his alternate persona than ever he did in actual combat or living as the Shark. Certainly he still sleeps little and is known to wander around vast swathes of country for leagues and leagues. He also talks quite openly, mentioning that if he ever faces more combat he expects the Shark to prowl again, though next time, he says with a controlled and more human side. Both Calm and beast together, or so he plans. Deranged or mad you say, a hero beyond our race I say." Fury then stood and took his leave of Jeffers as if wearied greatly of human company by the telling of the tale.

*****

Big Tar stood in the shelter of the doorway as the smoke billowed down the street off the burning pan behind him. From the clash of arms that could be heard in the adjacent streets he knew that the streets of the bailey would soon be overwhelmed. He knew that if he was to survive it was time to take his fight to the enemy. He waited until the first sign of Roke at the wall and then ran forward, sparing only a quick thought of the danger of being shot in the back by his own support archers.

Bill, up in the tower saw him go. He was too busy firing into the next, parallel, street, where Roke had swarmed over the wall and all three in the tower were firing down as quickly as they could, to pay much heed. It was like shooting fish in a barrel. Still, he sent a wish for good fortune in his friend's direction instead.

Big Tar clambered up the footholds on his side of the barricade and, letting a hammer dangle from its wrist strap, he pulled a spike from his belt and stabbed the first Roke to top the wall through the eye. Without waiting he heaved himself up and over the wall to land, both hammers swinging in vicious arcs amongst the shocked Roke party as he began to systematically spread them around the street. Big Tar was outnumbered but certainly not cowed.

*****

Ewgene Candwell met his contact at the bird coop with a flask of brandy juice in one hand and a cloth full of meats and cheese in the other. A distant relation, Jiggy was the reason that Ewgene always received the update reports before the other military commanders.

Jiggy controlled the bird coops for the network referred to as the 'Voice at the top of the world' or simply the 'Voice'. This was a network that used birds to transmit coded messages up into the mountains where, weather permitting, a relay of isolated mountain-top lantern points were used to pass messages up and down the whole line of the mountains. The nearest mountain point would then either user lanterns themselves, on exceptionally clear days or, more usually, birds to carry the message the last leg to the High Fort. These secured locations and a handful of 'dependent' shelters had been deeded back to the human nation by the Grey Folk in return for regular food drops and the promise of 'non interference'.

As Ewgene laid out the lunch; Jiggy, needed to keep working as birds arrived and messages were brought up to be relayed. Ewgene mulled over the message that had arrived shortly before he had reached the bird platform. Master Smee was fully engaged with the entire 13,000-strong army commanded by the Collector. The report detailed destruction of much siege equipment and indicated that heavy losses had been inflicted on the attackers.

The Chamberlain allowed his attention to wander slightly, imagining that the second Horde army had arrived, in fact, it was still two days south and slowing down, and the High Fort itself was the one besieged. Well the news confirmed that Camp Smee would certainly fall, a real loss to be sure, and the Collector would get his attempt at the Gulley where, Ewgene suspected, he would build himself a nice stockade and dig in to wait while the vast numbers of Reptoids beached north of the Serpents Toungue peninsula attempted to make their way overland around the natural barrier that the mountains formed.

Whilst this was undesirable, the pass being relatively defensible even for the poorly organised Roke, he knew that the defences arrayed against the Collector would probably stop him before he gained a suitable vantage point. The Collector was far from stupid, so why had he not realised that himself and kept the army together, even if it had slowed him down? It was as if there was some timetable of which the northerners were not aware.

*****

Once the battle in Smee's bailey came to hand fighting the defenders were soon pushed back through the streets. The Roke sensed a victory and, frustrated by the drawn out battle to take a fairly insignificant town, they pushed hard for the end. The design of the streets, however, funnelled the troops towards the hall, with carefully placed barricades, and field weapons were again used to devastating effect upon the packed Roke troops. Cobbled streets were sown with caltrops, porcelain shards sprayed from the roof tops and gulleys filled with oil used to deter the few Reptoids who had been deployed once the walls were suitably breached.

Arrows remained available and the remaining battlements had been greased where key points couldn't be pulled down. The defenders were at their strength's end, however, after almost three days of continuous fighting. Archers began to find their arms failing from cramps or had torn and bloody fingers too damaged to be used.

The music hall was a beautiful building created from panels of hand-carved hardwoods and the Roke were delighted as the defenders finally began falling back to this building, knowing that the final fight could be avoided by causing one large pyre. The screens that had been erected to protect it had been pulled away by the defenders. Standing in its own courtyard Roke were able to see it from rooftops long before they had displaced the defenders still fighting in front of it.

With the defenders pulling back, the barricades were over run and Byron's team used the rooftops to escape back towards the hall. As he was about to drop down from the final one he looked back and saw a small group of defenders become surrounded. The hall's head chef, Stallic, and three stable hands it was, but rather than going under the chef cried something and the four actually managed to fight their way back up the street a creditable distance before they were overrun and slaughtered.

In all the surrounding streets, small groups and individuals mirrored the chef's squad's defiant display of courage, skill and training and, for a short period, still the Roke were held back. Music struck up from the hall and the Roke finally came to surround it as small sorties tried in vain to prevent entry to the three main doors. The Collector himself and a smaller group of his bodyguards moved up inside the bailey walls to witness the final end.

To his surprise it soon became apparent that the hall had been torched from within, but still the music continued to play. This irritated and intrigued the Collector. How could the musicians display such calm as the hall around them burned at their own hands? He redoubled his attacker's efforts to dislodge the defenders, although now this became more difficult as sturdy iron gates had been dropped and the hand-held rams were having surprisingly little effect. Belatedly he ordered his Roke to torch the outside and found that even with oil it was difficult to get the wood to burn. Why, then, was so much smoke coming from the eaves?

Smoke pans, the Collector realised quickly. He issued orders that his troops surrounding the keep should expand their perimeter, searching for a tunnel exit. He was relieved when news came back that they had soon found it and were battling a few guards who had been hiding there. It was much later that they discovered that it was actually a deliberate blind. Unfortunately a short time later they also stumbled on the real exit.

Back at the hall one of the Roke teams succeeded in tearing out one of the gates and his men entered the hall just as the four ancient volunteers finished setting fire to a huge pile of pressured oil cans. Simultaneously the tunnel collapse system, having been burning for the required quarter-part, kicked in as these final brave men were put to the sword fighting to the last. The chained tunnel supports gave in all six directions at once, even as the last defender died. Once the first toppled, helped by a cunning weight assembly over two wells, six tunnels in wheel formation collapsed simultaneously, destroying 80 percent of the bailey walls, which collapsed inwards, and levelling over half the town.

The Collector, however, had tired of the smoky town and

returned to a nearby hillside. Thus when the dust cleared the Collector found himself, alive, if filthy, but with nearly 7,000 warriors dead, injured or buried for the loss of only about 1,000 locals. At this rate of attrition he knew he was doomed unless the fleets began landing troops again in the south.

Of the brave 12 who had left the hall last most survived, including Master Smee, to emerge into the dusty aftermath. They managed a significant killing spree among the Roke guards left at the tunnel mouth in the confusion of the town collapse. As the wooden wall supports continued to collapse they fought their way past, taking horses as they could.

Indeed Master Smee had been most particular when designing his camp in the beginning; all his top men had been employed in planning its defence. No fool, the Collector instructed his men to continue searching for further escape tunnel exits, even at the expense of helping his men buried in the rubble. The Roke began searching frantically, if not in a particularly sophisticated manner, and reaching the first exits already captured found the guards dead or dying and raised the alarm.

Thus the last escape party, including Byron and Master Smee, were spotted leading their horses through a concealed culvert to the north. The majority were near enough to its mouth to be mounted and away before any Roke could prevent them.

The nearby Roke became frantic and raced towards the dip. One of the Collector's prime objectives was known to be the death or capture of the northern commanders. Few Roke were therefore keen on being blamed for the escape of any defenders, however few in number. Now people were known to have escaped the Collector would be enraged, especially as they could join the partisan bands being raised against his campaign.

Roke commanders were, therefore, quick to react and hound any fugitives, relentlessly tracking them down, even at the expense of men and horses. Byron, Judy and Split, the third from last group, were able to reach the wooded hills safely. They were surprised to meet partisans quite quickly who whisked them away, shortly before the Roke reached the woods in numbers themselves. The more Byron saw the more he was convinced that the whole exercise was much better planned than even he had realised. Whilst they had lost the position the Roke had been delayed and had suffered telling losses, without gaining anything really significant. Certainly the Northern army troops lost had cost the Roke up to ten times the number and the siege gear used up would not be easily replaced.

Byron wondered how many other exercises had been or were being carried out in a similar manner, and how quickly the initially large Roke force was being whittled away, despite the standing armies over the channel.

Byron knew bad luck could still prevail and all too soon news reached him that his was the last party to make the woods in safety: Smee's horse had been seen taking an arrow. Witnesses said that his escorts had turned intending to double mount him but the Roke had proved too close. Indeed none had made it before the partisans were forced to withdraw. Lame and hunted in occupied lands, the outcome for Smee looked hopeless and Byron was desolate that at the last he had not been at his friend's side. The only hope was that he had died cleanly and not been captured and delivered to the evil Collector's twisted hands for a horrible tortured fate. Master Smee would be certain to know a fair amount and the Collector was said to be able to extract every detail.

*****

Moffet had been told by Master Smee to depart with local partisans, but decided he would rather watch out for his friends at the camp. He had snuck carefully to the edge of the woods and seen the success of the first charge against the artillery. Dismay soon followed when all the Roke reinforcements came into view. Outer perimeter scouts had soon begun to comb the woods to check for any more Northern partisans.

Moffet was, therefore, sitting high amongst the branches of a towering tree and spent the remainder of the fighting either watching or dozing as the battle for the town raged. He could see that the vast numbers of the enemy would swarm over the camp although for a long period it seemed they could not. The collapse of the town walls terrified him and he began to sob quietly as the smoke began to rise from the centre where the hall had been.

Even braving capture to watch out for his friends he felt torn with guilt. Master Smee had asked him to take a wagon of precious instruments away with him but, because he wanted to stay, he had just wrapped them in sacking and buried them in his vegetable patch. Moffet loved the sight of instruments but also knew it was the people he cared for more. With his snaring and tracking skills the young farmer was sure that he could easily avoid the Roke, especially because of their strange odour. Even the ones who had some wood skill could be seen missing obvious signs left by the partisans who were still dotted around the area.

Moffet's position allowed him to see the culvert and as dusk was falling he was excited to see groups of people quietly leaving from what could only be the camp.

The instant he saw Master Smee he started to descend the tree. Halfway down he glimpsed Split make the trees but also saw Call and Fingers shot out of their saddles just behind her. The pursuing riders stopped at the bodies and began hacking at them; a mistake, as Bart and some others were riding hard into them from behind. Moffet was only a few spans up when he saw Master Smee's horse go down and once on the ground he could make out little more through the twilight. Crouched low he began a zigzagging run towards the commotion where the two small groups were battling. With the responsibility of leadership Master Smee had insisted on remaining until last: his group of five were among the most formidable warriors to afford him maximum protection.

As Smee felt his horse begin to go down he kicked free and, despite his bad leg, was coming to his feet as his left-hand man turned into the approaching Roke to offer protection. Despite this a riderless horse smashed the band leader from his feet and into unconsciousness. The brave warrior ploughed into the approaching Roke, Master Smee disappearing from view. Lythe Kyle, as the women called him, had been an early training partner of Stonebrow. Only the position in Master Smee's honour guard had blunted his disappointment at not being in the war band. Barrelling into the nearest Roke squad, his cavalry sabre a blur in the fading light, he reared his horse, stabbing one opponent. Kyle killed the horse of the next and finally lashed out to cave in the face of the squad's leader. A fourth Roke slammed into the rearing animal and tumbled it over, barely allowing Kyle time to slip safely out of the saddle. Rolling smoothly to his feet Kyle found himself being buffeted in the midst of the remaining Roke, brought to a halt by the collisions. Sheathing his sword he quickly whipped the short spear off his back and stabbed it into the belly of the nearest horse, jumping over it as it collapsed in agony. Spotting another target he snapped his arm back to cast the spear twenty-odd lengths into the side of a Roke trying to turn his horse past Kyle's, which was now prancing and kicking as trained to do shortly after loosing its rider in battle. The Roke pitched from the saddle and Kyle was just in time to use his small round shield to fend a blow from another mounted attacker. He quickly hammered his shield against the horse's flank, shattering the Roke's ankle and driving the shield spike deep into the mount's lung.

More and more Roke were closing in, surrounding him, and Kyle knew his time was running out. Spinning round, with luck on his side, Kyle performed a spectacular draw of his sabre, whirling it in a great arc as he twisted 360 degrees, shearing through any horse and human flesh within four spans of him in all directions and finally coming to rest caving in shield armour and chest of the closest Roke. Stepping back into a textbook stance Kyle was delighted to find that Bart had also broken left to cover the second party of Roke, riding at high speed to meet them. Although a larger group their desperate dash had spread them more and he was unable to halt the group with his charge.

Around Master Smee the battle was chaotic. Behind Bart, Tucre had also spun his horse, with Starris hard on his shoulder racing back to collect the band leader. Tucre, in the lead, rode straight into the arblast bolts from the pursuing Roke and was blasted out of his saddle ten lengths away from Smee and 60 from the main pursuit. Of the six Roke only two had arbasts and a third, with his light bow, wasn't skilled enough to hit Starris, now weaving his course. Nor was he a skilled enough horseman to prevent Starris's morning star from removing him from the saddle permanently, and neither were his two comrades close behind. The final two Roke soldiers proved luckier, one avoided Starris the other lunged and whilst missing his human target managed to stick six inches of steel into his horse. The horse, caught kicking out at the assailant, missed its footing and ploughed bottom first into the ground.

Starris managed to stumble, free knowing the poor creature had broken something, and watched in disgust as both Roke slashed at the horse trying to finish it off, maybe figuring it would deny him any possibility of escape and that they could finish him at their leisure. Starris flung his morning star expertly at the nearest horse stabber and was satisfied as it whipped him out of his saddle crushing his neck. Drawing his blade he easily fended off the final Roke's attack but as he moved to finish him he stumbled in a rabbit hole and was pierced in the shoulder. A swift thrust of his own, while the enemy blade was still in him, had the Roke dead, though, and instants later he was in the saddle of the enemy's flea-bitten nag. As he raced back towards where he estimated Master Smee lay, he could hear Bart singing and rode up in time to see him dispatch another adversary. Obvious enough though, was the blood from numerous wounds to both Bart and his magnificent steed, Nightsfall. Both were reeling a bit and there were still some ten or so Roke circling for attack with sounds of others approaching.

Moffet found himself on the ground and running through the dusk towards Master Smee's body. As he came close he could hear Bart the Magnificent singing and Roke voices raised and shrill, screaming at each other. As he got nearer and Bart fought on, Moffet could detect the pain and the tiredness as he sang. Accelerating, the country farmer ran as fast as his young legs could take him to help his friends. Suddenly Bart's note tightened and his voice stopped, the music fading off into the night. Slightly further out Moffet heard a bellow and sounds of combat continue, and once he heard a voice cry out, calling Master Smee's first name.

Moffet's luck held. He had managed to keep a straight line to where Master Smee lay. All around lay debris and the ground was cut up by hoof marks. Unaware of his good fortune he never realised that 27 dead Roke lay within a stones throw nor that 20 more were hurrying through the night distracted by the near dead Starris and Kyle, who, on horse again, was wreaking bloody slaughter. As he worked Smee out from under a dead body, he dragged him a few feet away and then hoisting him over his shoulder started to run further on in his straight line, out onto the plain.

Moffet ran quickly past a number of corpses and in the darkness failed to see Bart, lying on his back, a look of calm on his face staring up at the sky, nor the Roke whose throat Bart had crushed whilst dying, struggling to finish the last stanza of his favourite piece. Over by the woods, where Moffet had started, the Roke patrols had gained a degree of organisation. Moffet passed by just before a mounted group had ridden up only to be shot from their horses in a hail of arrows from the partisans, hoping more defenders would appear. Two more mounted patrols perished before the partisans withdrew; one set of Roke even riding full pelt into the trees in order to avoid the arrows, only to find sturdy fetlock-height trip wires and spiked pits waiting. The other set were simply shot down in the fading light. Moffet missed the significance of the horn blasts signalling the partisan retreat and Starris, dying of at least three critical wounds, in Kyle's arms after the pair had failed to find Smee's body and, Kyle hopelessly outnumbered, eventually riding for the trees in the hope of finding him there.

One full part later, exhausted but having made the high ground on the far side of the plain away from the woods, Moffet stopped briefly to tend Master Smee. Fairly quickly the band leader was taking water but at this point he did not really regain proper consciousness and Moffet was almost wild with worry, for he knew little of healing battle wounds. From what he could tell their pursuers had run into some interference or were just slow and inept.

Unknown to Moffet the Northern army's territory defence plan always included external partisan troops who would move in towards a besieged town as it looked likely to fall, running interference for weary troops attempting to escape after the defences had collapsed. In this way defenders were encouraged to hold for as long as possible and even after defeat lives could be preserved. Large numbers of casualties could also be inflicted on an enemy torn between holding the cordon around strongholds, to prevent significant numbers of escapees, and facing partisan raids attacking the Roke perimeter itself.

Deciding he was still too close and that even the setting of a low smokeless fire could prove unwise Moffet settled on walking for the night, carrying his friend. Fleeing the battle site, risking some rest occasionally but only when he couldn't go on, his progress, even carrying his burden, was excellent, taking them high into the scrublands to the north east of Camp Smee.

Chapter Nineteen

"We must come down from the mountains," the Land Shark said.

The big mountain clansman, Grand, shook his head. "That would play our hand early don't you think? Any extra time we stay unseen leaves us with more of a surprise. The odds'll be bad enough as it is."

"Surprise is not our only weapon. The Moose are mighty and not a foe that the Roke have faced for many generations." The Land Shark paced determinedly away, the words barely uttered, peering off down the slope as if he could sense his enemies or see through the mists.

Grand looked to his son who shrugged, as did Mooseman and his lad.

"If that is what you wish, Fin, then we'll put our Moose down the hill." Grand reluctantly addressed the Land Shark's armoured back. "I suggest we charge from the outcrop by the stream, as we discussed, in a part. Send the foot first to silence any sentry scum and then the Moose masters, charging in formation," he added for the benefit of the new arrivals and stragglers.

As the message and a map of the terrain and route of the charge, to avoid the riders crushing those on foot, was passed around many older fighters turned and raised their fists to salute the mountains. The Shark did likewise and left without a word. Unbidden, some of the older, more grizzled woodsmen followed to help him clear a path.

Grand sighed at the change in his friend's behaviour who, not so long ago, would have spoken on further in encouragement. Clapping his son on the shoulder he gave the official sign to form up and he, too, turned and left the clearing. He assumed that now the plan was set the Shark, and anybody on foot crazy enough, would begin their approach, slithering on their bellies as close as possible to the fortification. Throughout the preparatory planning it seemed clear that the chosen strategy had been previously considered by the Shark most likely, as Calm. Prepared as one of a number of contingencies, determined more by the weather than the placement of the enemy, he had seen the Shark's gauntletted hand choose from a selection of battle maps that his aide offered. Once chosen the old guy had hurried away, his stash of intelligence surrounded by a number of mean looking escorts. They were on the brink of a suicidal charge, a few hundred warriors against many times the number, not forgetting that the enemy were already dug in for an extended siege. Still the eccentric veteran was acting as if he was conducting the first part of a full scale campaign.

With a casual glance to his son, Grand mounted White Snout and they both nudged their moose over to their closest kin. Mooseman was Grand's brother by marriage. His wife, Grand's sister, was off with the herd as it was moved back through the mountains in an attempt to preserve some of the breeding stock. Seven young animals were all they could spare. As dawn began to break they joined the rest of the tribe and when all 63 were finally mounted up they each quaffed a swig of moonshine, in one communal bending of the law, and then they were off on the final ride to glory.

As they began to move Grand thought that despite all the discussion, leading up to this moment, on the two week journey to answer Calm's summons, nothing had quite prepared him for the reality of the situation. Firstly the clans were solitary and extended social contact seemed to chafe like ill-fitting boots. On top of that was the transformation of their leader. Whilst everybody had heard the story of Master Calm's battle ego, the reality of the Land Shark persona and the way it had so completely transformed his friend, was unnerving. Add in the last straw, the fact that Calm's command was heading to relieve the besieged town of Mid Vale, a lowlands settlement well known for its contempt towards the free-spirited mountain dwellers, and Grand was nonplussed to say the least.

As they picked their way down slope they saw a couple of dead Roke pinned to trees. Periodically they were guided or halted by woodsmen who were silently terminating the enemy scouts. The tree line finished barely half a league from the gently rolling hills where the town was situated, and the Roke were being careful to patrol it. So far none of the many sentries had been able to sound any kind of warning. Quite what the effect of the charge would be in the heavy mist he wasn't sure.

Suddenly, Grand's son flinched at the sound of a horn close by. Grand leaned forward and patted his son's arm reassuringly and whispered to the boy that certain calls were also required to verify that the sentries were still in place. Grand just hoped that the code was a match.

All too soon they were bunched at the edge of the trees and a final woodsman signed that three markers would guide their route, and roughly which direction would take them first to the dips that would serve to partly mask the charge. Grand and his son were going first, their moose young, fit, fairly fast and agile. Mooseman would bring up the rear guard. The woodsman paused and listened and something he detected in the air caused him to begin a ten finger count down. The moose charged. As the riders followed the hollows the route seemed too vague to trace but at about one third the distance, a mountain man with a bow appeared smoothly as if from the ground and pointed the way. They were just past halfway when a second rose up to indicate the final turn and Grand, clinging to his saddle, wondered how many they had passed unseen.

About this point they were so close that either the mist didn't fully conceal their outlines or the sound of the heavy harness and weapons gave them away to the Roke, who once warned used horns and rang bells which began sounding all around the siege camp. The small hillocks through which they sped could not cover the huge moose and soon they too could make out the target. Finally reaching completely open ground the mist cleared and Grand spotted the Shark rise up, barely 70 lengths from the rear of the camp, and in a blur of speed launched several arrows and proceeded to sprint at the enemy in a weaving run. Periodically other green-mottled shapes would also spring up and these warriors also began firing rapidly into the enemy camp, a pair close together managing a fire pot and doubtless attempting to set part of the camp ablaze.

Whether the moose or the Shark reached the camp first,

Grand never knew as he turned from several other neck and neck front riders and pealed off to one side, riding directly through a horse picket. Bucking his moose into a war frenzy to scatter the picketed animals, those that didn't collapse under the great beast's antlers or flailing hooves, he swept to either side, his axe a blur.

Unfortunately for Grand his turn had brought him into the heavy cavalry area, probably the most intelligent and, therefore, elite of all Roke troops. The Roke, not being much in favour of discipline, arranged their horse troops around one main type, generally managing only to train useful numbers of light skirmishers, expected only to attack as a pack and not hold a line in a charge. These were proper cavalry, though, equipped with heavy lances. As soon as it became clear that their normal tactic of 'mount up and ride the enemy down' would not defeat a war moose in close combat they heaved up the lances. Using them as pikes, 20 or so began advancing on Grand on foot.

This in itself didn't prove too bad as his boy came charging in from the side bowling over and trampling many of the main body of the men. Seeing the tactic though, a number of other Roke began copying and, more worryingly still, a number of archers formed behind this second line of lances. Fearing things would only worsen if he waited, Grand ploughed White Snout through the nearby tents, and whirling his axe he began hacking the lances to smithereens. He managed to break through with only an arrow in his thigh and a bloody gouge to White Snout's front left leg. He was quickly able to angle his ride away through one side of the lance line, dispersing the Roke archers in a sudden panic as he approached. Unfortunately, of the arrows that had missed him, one had pierced the eye of a following moose.

The broken arrow head, deflected by her tough eye socket, failed to kill the beast outright. Irrespective of training the noble mount literally went mad with the pain, breaking what little formation was left in the five moose riders who had followed Grand, and bellowing frantically charged straight into the nearest Roke. Smashing them and then her rider as she went down on top of the bloody heap, snapping a leg as a result of her frenzied prancing, she died rolling around in the wreckage of the camp, threshing in agony, beset by the enemy.

"So the Horde are, again, unpredictable," Bishop Vesper pronounced in his stiff, formal manner.

"It would seem that way, Sir Bishop," Ewgene replied. "The town of Mid Vale captured intact could be quite strategic for the enemy. Not only is it in striking distance of the High Fort but it also lies at the base of the foothills in the part of the mountain chain where the peaks are the lowest. There, if anywhere is the spot that I would choose if I intended to attempt a mountain crossing from either direction." Ewgene jabbed his finger at the section of the map pinned to the wall. "Even if crossing the range isn't the goal then there are numbers of caves in that part of the mountains that could serve to house a fair number of the Reptoid beasts. If taken intact Mid Vale's prime defensive position would mean it could take years to ferret all the beasts out once they gain a suitable hold in the mountains if we are delayed. I suspect there are plenty capable of breeding in that section of the army, unless I miss my guess." Ewgene finished, a bitter smile crossing his cherubic face as he rearranged the array of writing pens in his jacket pocket.

Detecting grim humour in the Chamberlain's voice the Bishop cast the smaller man a withering stare and again considered the odd little man who had once been ranked in the ten most dangerous competition fighters in either the Northern or Southern sections of the Nation. "Why are you amused, Sir Chamberlain?" the Bishop asked irritably, annoyed at his counterpart taking this disastrous news so well.

"Oh, Vesper, it just sounds as if I might get a slice of the action after all and I find it so dull being cooped up here," he chuckled deliberately. "Anyway we have good news as well. The sacrifice at Camp Smee cost the Collector almost half his force for the loss of under a 1,000 people, many not even on the combat register," Ewgene added. With a brief pause, his face becoming more solemn, he continued. "Smee, who is incidentally missing, presumed dead, certainly fought one of the classic defences of modern times, as I hear it, and will be long remembered for inflicting such heavy casualties." Back on more positive news the Chamberlain quickened his tone. "I can also tell you that Calm, or the Land Shark now, by all reports, is in the Mid Vale area with a force of mountain folk including some heavy moose cavalry, the Rough Riders. He reports that he will be able to hit the siege in its early stages and also that the slower portion of the enemy army, have yet, to arrive in the area. So, things aren't as black as they might be."

*****

Leaving the long yard Taverner shouldered his kit and laughed, contemplating that the service on an assault galley he was seeking with their shallow draft and front line landings was usually to be avoided. He was aware that the light ships were made mostly at a yard on a forested headland far away in the southern command but that recently the Marshall had no desire for the Roke to be made aware of his planning by seeing hundreds of the craft sailed round the coast. Therefore an arrangement was made for wood to be transported to a secret site just south of Buccaneer Town, transported inland or by ships passing by on their usual business just yards away offshore. The Roke spies, favouring long distance observation, were themselves monitored through this time. The intelligence service passed them as much misinformation concerning new construction work as possible. The Roke even managed to acquire blueprints for new settlements and in some places academy surveyors laid out large site footings to support the fiction.

Had the Roke managed to penetrate the scheme or been able to inspect the output of certain formerly commercial engineering works they would have discovered that the construction of the galleys had been refined into several stages of prefabrication. The nautical engineer, Pithrake, used cutting templates to speed up the first stage of construction and even basic yards could now construct craft suitable for fair-weather sailing. Landing galleys needed a shallow draught, fundamentally opposed to a displacement which is necessarily quite large. A vessel which would be used in all weathers and winds, sometimes with shortened sails, but more often under fire and of manual propulsion, was a challenge unsuited to mass prefabrication, but Pithrake had solved it with new design techniques.

Formerly, traditional longships had been used for raiding and landing duties. Clinker built, constructed of overlapping planks, caulked and then fitted with plugs and further pitch seals, these shallow-draft longboats provided small numbers of men sturdy, all weather attack craft. Indeed, Taverner was far more experienced in the use of such craft and it was for one of those vessels particularly that he was searching.

Over time, though, the admirals in charge of naval development had invested in the newer designs and commonly only outer-island coastal forces and specific marine-based combat crews would use the traditional vessels. Painted grey and black with irregular stripes and patterns these ships became invisible at night, although in daylight distinct designs depicting crews and owners, through elaborate characters blended in with the camouflage.

Shadowswell, for example, was the most recently famous raider's ship of the old style. Even though clinker-built she had been known to sail for hundreds of leagues in varied weathers free of leakage. She carried attack crews on missions all around the further coasts of the Battle Lands and, if the braggarts of the crew were to have been believed even far beyond. Recently she had been reported sunk in a fierce night fight with Roke coastal patrol ships not far from the Hook of the Change, a promontory at the eastern end of the Battle Lands.

Taverner soon spotted the vessel he was searching for. The *No Regrets* was a battered-looking ship, once proud in the traditions of raiding, but now with flaking paint work and a refitted mast yet unstained to match the dark hue of the remainder of the boat's camouflage. He jumped blithely onto the decking, stepping from the quay across one of the rows of trunk benches. This vessel was deployed in the classic longship style. Small in ratio to the number of crew who worked, fought, ate and slept on the space of the decks; they stored their possessions in long chests doubling as their oar benches. This cleverly constructed seating could be detached easily and moved around the deck in a number of different configurations.

Taverner was pleased to see an arrangement with which he was familiar. The deck hand responsible for the ship called a belated challenge. He was obviously on double duty and had been checking the action of the mast fixture to ensure that the base of the mast could be levered up and dropped flat along the deck easily. He scooped up a notched, heavy cutlass and hastened over to where Taverner was standing.

"Seaman Cutster reporting for duty mate, is Captain Roebuck here abouts? He arranged for my service and I was asked to deliver him his final tenure when I made my way over. Shouldn't really hand it over to no one else," Taverner explained casually.

The mate cast his eyes over his new crew member, carefully noting the dirt ingrained beneath his nails. Lank hair tied back beneath a grimy head scarf and wearing a heavy oil-soaked woollen jumper beneath a waxed, leather sleeveless waistcoat the stranger looked a bit of a state, even for this rag-tag crew. Well, he talked competent enough. No weapons were visible except possibly the underarm bulge of a knife and a pair of battered cases, one for a bow and one a four-span blade case.

"OK mate, you'd better wait here until the skipper returns. The *Regrets* sails with the tide, until then take a look at the drag anchor, some of the stitching needs checking." Saying that the mate reached into his frill-fronted shirt and pulled out a soft leather wallet. "Here's a stitch kit. Get yourself to work."

"Sure," Taverner sketched the mate a bow and a wink as he snatched the kit out of the air and turned directly to the stern of the ship to start work.

Propping his gear within reach he sat himself cross legged and began the taxing task of checking the drag anchor. A drag anchor is a complex funnel of oiled leather, carefully stitched, into a framework of steel bars. Jointed so that it folds up into a tight bundle but which, when tossed or lowered correctly into the sea, forms a large funnel that fills with water and acts to oppose the motion of the vessel, holding it steady in calm seas and making drift more manageable in heavier waters.

Checking the stitching itself required basic knowledge but actually replacing it was a tough task. The heavy leather was almost always baked and scoured hard by a combination of weather and salt. Inserting the stitches, even with the heaviest of needles, proved very hard on the hands. Taverner, or Seaman Cutster as he was now known, was soon into the work. From the mast area the mate could tell enough to know that he was progressing with the work at a steady pace.

Not wanting to cast attention on himself Taverner, was in fact, working at a much slower speed than he was capable.

*****

Heading through the woods, which were now being searched by Roke with lit torches to dispel the gloom of the tree shadow, Moffet ran full pelt away to the east. The early dawn was alive with the sounds of searching troops. Frequently he was forced to stop, ducking down or back tracking, and it took, him two long parts to heave Smee's body two leagues further north-east of the battlefield, once the sun had risen. Moffet was skating right across the top of the ring of Roke besiegers moving in to secure the town and receive fresh orders.

Despite his burden he flitted past the more distant patrols just as they were receiving their instructions about escapees. Over to the west a horn was relaying orders from the Roke command. False ones they were, not that Moffet ever knew, urging the Roke to converge on the town from all directions. There were many partisans working and performing simple pieces of deception on the outer edge of the Horde army as it paused at the wrecked settlement like an injured animal licking its wounds.

By noon Moffet was 11 leagues away and Master Smee was beginning to regain consciousness. Moffet made it to a thicker stand of trees and placed the twitching form gently on the ground, belatedly looking to see if Smee had open wounds to be tended. Not that Moffett was confident of what he would do if he found any. If anything Master Smee seemed to be breathing better. Moffett cleaned blood from a cut on his forehead, the only wound he could find, careful to apply a bandage of torn shirt and not to restart the bleeding. The cover in the area was fair and although exhausted, Moffet set some snares out near where they had stopped, to make noise if anyone approached.

*****

Overall things could have been going better Mooseman reflected. As his second wave of moose attacked, Cleft had sped out in front and showed his comrades his best moon, starting the fun. He also delivered it to the Roke who seemed less amused. This spurred the mounted men on and their initial attack, down hill towards a relatively weakly defended part of the siege, hammered into the Roke.

Mid Vale was a square-plan settlement, built on a gentle rise in the undulating foothills. Being so far from the sea, at the base of the mountains, it had only high inner walls, leaving the bulk of the settlement free to grow outwards, unconstrained but also unprotected. A lower grade fortification, its defence strategy was simply to move the population into the strong fortified section and abandon the outer town if attacked.

Despite not pulling down the building shells of the outer town properly the Roke had proven well, if haphazardly, dug in amongst the ruined houses. Had it not been for the brute strength of the moose, using cable and grapnel to pull down temporary barricades, and the wicked accuracy of the trapper bow men, their small number would have been comfortably repulsed.

Obviously the Roke had been expecting an attempt on their siege, but once inside the perimeter the battle became a free for all, to which the mountain folk were well suited. The Shark and his standard had immediately turned, as planned, to fight towards the town's main gates: for a while he was even able to do this along the Roke fence-line. The green warrior, Bryce, had obviously handed off the standard and could be seen sweeping away with a massive broadsword. Towering above the enemy he attracted the majority of missile fire, although this often caused Roke to over shoot and hit Roke as they misjudged his speed.

Shortly after, Bryce disappeared from view, with Mooseman battling more slowly behind. Additional Roke disruption had followed a disturbance further towards the town gates. Mooseman assumed this to be a sortie from one of the town gates, but how many troops had ridden out and how successful the manoeuvre had been the moose rider could not now tell. Looking back he had certainly not been aware of fighting beside any town defenders around that time, but then the Mooseman's progress had not taken him far round the wall. Whatever the cause the enemy repositioning had relieved the pressure in his part of the battle, for which he was unreservedly thankful.

Quite where his marriage brother, who had lead the first wave, had disappeared to Mooseman was unsure, although in the chaos of fighting through the haphazard Roke encampment they could have passed each other a number of times and still remained unaware.

*****

At the end of the first day of the training assessment, Jeffers Star had retreated to his billet and went about disarming as if nothing unusual had happened. He had forced himself upright as he passed Marv, who had smiled in an annoyingly smug manner, as if totally confident that the boy had done well. It had taken a considerable effort to mask his body's distress and Jeffers had fumed all the way back to the camp, about how casual he had been in his approach to the review.

It wasn't that he hadn't prepared the scenarios carefully enough, it was more the fact that he hadn't felt totally in control for much of the assessment. That the kid had reacted so unexpectedly was overall a good thing, and Jeffers could probably trace his ill humour back to the point, right at the start, when the boy had unhorsed him. The power and timing it had shown was incredible. Although he had watched as much of the lad's training with the others as possible he hadn't seen such an indication of skill.

As he rolled his battered body into bed Jeffers wondered whether it had been a good idea to test the boy after he had been pushed so hard in the mountains. Quickly rejecting that idea, Jeffers homed in on the thought that Calm had probably counted on the fact that the weary boy was more likely to react by reflex, and that the wily Master had intended Jeffers to see the true inherent talent that the teenager displayed.

In fact as Jeffers thought on he became more and more

pleased with his own performance. From the moment that the lad had managed to smash his blunted cleaver irretrievably into the small horseman's shield and, pushing the horse one way and dragging Jeffers' arm directly down in the other and tumbled him from the saddle he had managed, through quick wits and reflex, to continue the appraisal. Jeffers had released his hold on the shield and, rolling smoothly to his feet, had continued the fight scoring several potentially disabilitating strikes. Even when the youth had used his remaining cleaver to shatter Jeffer's training sword, a prodigious display of strength, the instructor had moved straight into the unarmed combat section. For several minutes he had held the upper hand until the boy, with a subtle twist, had turned boxing into wrestling and dragging his instructor down had done his best to beat the older man black and blue.

Even then Jeffers had performed professionally, shrugging off the boy's disregard for etiquette. The two had competed closely through archery and spear throwing, as a competing pair rather than teacher and student. Finally, in the combat tactics section based around the event of storming the (now constructed) cabin, the lad had first scored full marks on the theory section and then, disregarding all his answers, stormed the room with pure physical talent leaving Mother winded and Jeffers, hit by a flying table, even more bruised.

Knowing that Master Calm had left the camp when the appraisal started, without even a quick goodbye for the boy, Jeffers had felt worried as to how the youth would perform when he discovered his absence. Now, at the end of the testing, he was pleased to note that his fears had been unfounded. Blue Boy was back in the hands of Marv, who insisted that the young student retire until the next morning, performing no debriefing either that night or the following two, before the morning of the formal announcement. That the boy had been exhausted before the testing began, and that it had dragged on for three unrelenting days, would probably cause it to sit in his memory only as a blur of attack and defence, action and reaction.

Those present at the short ceremony, who now included the mysterious Heron and the enigmatic Legion Lord Fury, all took part in a semi-official presentation. The words spoken of his transition to adulthood brought colour to Blue Boy's cheeks and almost a tear to his eye as Fury pinned a small sword-shaped clasp to his dishevelled band uniform. Jeffers handed him his own well-used sword as an unofficial sign of his approval and friendship.

When the ceremony passed off and the witnesses had signed the two credits into a document, given into partisan keeping for return to academy records the party split up. Fury, Marv, Jeffers and Heron, plus a new arrival named Agrik, had taken secret council much to Blue Boy's obvious disappointment.

Agrik, fully briefed by his rounds amongst the partisan network started. "News has come in that there is little likelihood now of the predicted High Fort siege which, I think you will agree, is positive. Also of interest is what is being termed as 'the march of Master Kroll'. He has taken up arms and, true to his word, is leading both his students and the Host Guard, with dramatic effect, through the Horde raiding parties that split off around the coastal ports early on. Although starting from the middle of the region he should be at the coast by tomorrow evening. Ships are being re-routed to carry him across as we speak. Just to be on the safe side." Agrik paused with eyebrows raised.

Looking directly at Marv he continued, "But I am sorry to inform you that Camp Smee, has fallen with high casualties."

"Oh Battler, what is this?" Marv mumbled through his anguish.

Agrik looked to Fury for guidance but the normally energetic man also looked pale and glum. He motioned to his friend that he should continue, hardly pausing to look at Marv, with his eyes closed and wringing his hands. Agrik turned to the other pair and gently continued, "Fury, what are the plans for yourself and Mister Jeffers?"

"Jeffers and I will head up directly into the High Mountains where we will cross to the tundra and execute our orders. Jeffers, I will brief you exactly as to your mission whilst we travel on our not inconsiderable journey," Fury replied. "And yourselves Agrik, Heron, Marv? Marv, what do you intend to do now? I am sorry for your loss, you are welcome to join us," Fury offered kindly.

"No, I am sorry, Fury," Heron broke in. "For all the importance of your task and the help Marv could offer he is not finished here yet. He has unfinished orders from his Master which now become mine to supervise. Blue Boy, the team and myself will travel together, skirting round the promontories and across the track through to the Gulley. We will split at an appropriate time when further instructions will be given. Whilst our tasks will be much simpler than your own, my friend, they are privy to only some few and you will all have to accept my apologies for being so vague." It was the longest single dialogue any of them had heard from Heron in years.

Early the next morning Blue Boy and Marv had taken some time together to grieve for the destruction of their home, and in many ways their family. Although Marvellous was vague about the scale of the losses, and Blue Boy had enough etiquette not to push too hard, the young lad was sure it had been quite a serious defeat. The one concession he managed to get from Marv was that Master Smee was still missing; Blue Boy took more comfort from that than Marv seemed to.

As they left the training camp the young cadet had time to collect his thoughts for the first time in many days. Blue Boy realised he had assumed that Master Calm would peel off to help his wife. Instead, when they passed partisan patrols, he heard that the first battle had commenced in the Gulley area and that Master Calm had gone on to lead the fight against the second Roke army.

A small force was waiting for them near the track leading to the Gulley, lead by Ranger John. His was a name Blue Boy had heard frequently as he grew up. Being a ranger was a role that, because of their far flung, and by implication secretive missions, was often discussed with a degree of envy by the younger cadets back at the camp. Not quite as desirable as being a war musician, of course, but a close second. As with the High Marshall taking his title as a last name, so by tradition the commander of the rangers took 'Ranger' for his first name and lost his last name somewhere in the process. Despite many attempts to quiz his instructors Blue Boy had never got the hang of the name changes that seemed to flow through certain people's careers.

Aware of the use of the numbers which were imprinted on every soldier's dog tags, and which, used with ink blocks, allowed military paperwork to be quickly and uniquely personalised, Blue Boy had only ever seen the process with his own eyes when he had pressed his numbers on his review document alongside Jeffers Star's. Blue Boy liked to imagine the name changes were a secret tactic to confuse enemy spies although deep down inside admitted it worked for celebrities because the fatalities during compulsory military service kept the population numbers so low.

Ranger John and Agrik spent some time in discussion. Finally Blue Boy discovered that the older man was being formally handed the ranger command for the entire central plains region, and that John, Blue Boy and Heron were headed for the coast south of Buccaneer Town.

*****

The moose had been dying all morning and soon the splendid beasts would be gone. Mooseman had lost his beloved Twelvetimes quite early on, and had since then been fighting on foot, savaging all who came within reach. His boy, Clyde, had ridden Rougharse magnificently. It was but a quarter part ago that he had glimpsed the pair locked in a heavy tussle with a couple of minor Reptoid and a pack of Roke savages. The tide of the battle had pushed him away, losing sight of his son. When a little later he could catch his breath, he had glanced round and failing to see them knew they must have been pulled down. He saw Canker Phil in trouble away to the left and he surged into the fray, swearing and heaving himself onwards, clearing enemy from his path using sweeps of his hook-billed axe. He was too late, though, and the old tinker was coughing his last, smashed through the ribs, but still glaring in his hateful way at the bodies of his mostly dead foe.

Mooseman soon settled the survivors and barely had time to turn and split one of the Roke that had spun from his path earlier, obviously as a ruse. He was definitely dead this time though. Again the antagonists had thinned and the enemy in view were scarce. Twice, at least, the town had sallied and the second time horsemen had made it to the east quarter where Mooseman was fighting. Whilst they had not lasted long against the concentration of Reptoids they had split the enemy enough to allow the mountain-foot to penetrate further into the ruined buildings of the outer town, which the Roke had failed to level.

This environment for hand-to-hand fighting favoured the mountainers and levelled the odds against the monsters. In amongst the buildings Mooseman had survived because he had been able to take short rests, at one point sitting amongst three dead Roke in an upper-story room. Below, he had seen the Land Shark fight his way down the street. Mooseman, a rough, uncouth and very powerful warrior himself was still shocked to see the Shark in action. He did indeed tend to glide like his namesake, but when he attacked it was frightful: sudden lunges hacked off hands and limbs, mandibles and carapace. Twisting and snapping he slaughtered Roke and Reptoid alike, his serrated swords making a clashing noise as they sheared through flesh and bone.

It was hard to reconcile the bloody, armoured figure with the peaceful, happy chap Calm, who had lived in the nearby mountains for ten years now. Mooseman could certainly see how he had gained his name, his movement seemed almost lethargic until he closed with the enemy, when lightning bursts of savage movement would see them pulled under and put down, torn and broken.

Watching the Shark's progress towards the end of the street the press of bodies became greater and his sinuous movement sped up. His twin blades flicking out, snapping, almost grabbing and shaking those nearest had a visibly traumatic effect on those around. The following hesitation or momentary fear, prevented opponents from attacking, leaving enough of an instant for the Shark to counter the next: no movement wasted, turning frequently, using the closest enemy to shield him until he was ready to face another.

On foot and alone Mooseman planned to spend his time doubling back and forth, picking off all the separated Roke he could find. At one point a cry arose from the wall that some rangers were attacking the enemy from the north, but again Mooseman had seen no sign. 'A good 1,000 would be a well granted wish,' he thought. Whilst his mountain folk had obviously dealt the Horde a fierce blow, Mooseman had seen a significant number of his fellows pulled down and killed. He had seen fewer and fewer about, almost none since entering the buildings. Now he waited, recouping his strength, as the Shark disappeared into the distance.

Almost time to leave, Mooseman reached above the door frame and felt for a hidden mark; it pointed him to the cupboard and pulling it open he ripped out the floor to reveal some dried food and a clay flask of water. Tepid even there, it still washed the dust from his throat. Munching on the dried pork and beef and some apple rings he glanced over to the three dead Roke. Tempted by the wine left visible on a dresser Mooseman thought. He tucked the waxed paper in his belt pouch and finished the water. The poison had no doubt taken them quickly as they fought to gulp it down. 'Never trust the obvious in a conquered town,' Mooseman reflected. Climbing gently back over the table he made his way to the door. It was about the sixth house he had used. Evidence stood out that a number of 'stay behinders' or 'jackers' had been causing plenty of murder amongst the Roke, killing by night and planting traps no doubt. He had seen many murdered Roke but no sign yet of any behinders caught and strung up.

As he waited in the doorway some of his men came round the corner and he left the house to join them, stepping smoothly out to match the pace of his comrades as they carefully picked their way further round the wall, looking for fresh Horde units to engage. This part of the siege, whilst littered with bodies seemed picked clean of the enemy and soon they were picking up their pace to rejoin the attack.

He would have admitted to mild surprise regarding his new companions. Whilst he had known Tiggs was a tough old bird he wouldn't have expected him to last this long, the 60-year-old coot. Rumour had him as former special forces. His son, Slicker, was also old to be around this far into the fight. Although bloodied and scratched both raised three fingers to him in salute and to signify 30 kills each. The old trappers had followed the charge in on foot and no doubt holed up as soon as possible to deal out as the battle raged in the streets around them. The

Brawn was also still going, although he was so covered in cuts and bruises it looked as if he had been fighting the Roke bare handed all day. He also carried Jayne Gold's scimitar in one hand and the Prince of Weeds' elaborate hand axe in the other.

He shook his head for both when Mooseman threw each weapon a look. Two individuals Mooseman didn't know were also in the group. One, dressed all in dark grey, Mooseman took to be a stay-behinder; His smooth, confident movement and short, wicked, black-steel sword matched his demeanour. He offered no name but nodded in recognition. The other Mooseman took to be a townie from one of the sorties, – heavy horse or infantry. He had heavy a breastplate and a wicked, three-quarter thickened broadsword carried lightly in powerful arms. He was the youngest of all; his curly black hair and infectious grin would no doubt have had Jayne panting if she were still around. He sketched a bow and when he announced his name, Nikos, his thick accent placed him from the Caballeros south.

Tiggs had assumed command of the motley band and quickly relayed that the Shark and his troop had suddenly doubled back to the north to clear a break for arriving rangers to begin to re-supply the town. The Land Shark's runner had asked Tiggs, and all others, to push round towards the gates where a force of Roke had dug in, attempting to keep the main entry to the town closed even though the siege was mainly broken.

Rangers from the east had apparently started arriving in groups of about 30, and finding that the mountain men were attacking the first lot had thrown themselves straight in, regardless of orders. It had been a nightmare at the start, but a group of townies had lowered themselves over in the disruption and given the rangers enough leeway not to be swamped immediately. As soon as three more sets had arrived, the battle had really begun to turn.

Finally, rounding the corner, the comrades came upon the last part of the battle. Two or three moose and about 20 horse were still skirmishing with Roke troops who had thrown up a ringed, shield-wall on the main road. Scores and scores of dead horses and infantry showed that the town's sorties had been full on battles and that they had managed to shatter the Roke gate-force, though at considerable cost. Clearly a party of horse had been tasked with breaking loose to start harrying the rear and it was the remainder of these that was still fighting.

Tiggs, Slicker and the quiet chap called up to the walls and received replacement bows and quivers from the battlement guards. The party took up a loose skirmish-line as they ducked and weaved towards the Roke, who themselves were still firing off missiles. The three archers in the group soon found their range and the two oldsters proved game, one using an arrow to try and disturb a shield bearer, the other one waiting to take advantage. 'Sly,' as Mooseman labelled their mysterious comrade, immediately picked up the scheme and with all three showing wicked accuracy they had soon claimed several victims.

Suddenly one of the moose charged the loosening part and hefting what shields they had, Mooseman's group raced to support the attack. As they reached half way an armoured horse sped past them and smashed into the shield wall further down, bowling over the Roke. Rearing his mount, the rider slashed once and then twice before angling his horse to burst back out again further along. Whether it was intended or a lucky weave, his horse skipped sideways about 20 spans out and the two Roke archers trying to shoot at his back both missed narrowly.

Whooping out a cry the daring rider twirled his sword about his head and reared his horse out of bowshot. Vixen and her moose ploughed into the empty gap. Again. Although the mighty beast had lost much of its plate, she heeled Olebones around and he gave a mighty kick to rear. His savage hooves sprayed a pulp of bone shards out over other nearby Roke as their two nearest comrades lost helmet, head and life. Carrying on, Olebones' antlers sliced into the Roke line to the front and it looked for a moment as if Vixen intended to ride him all the way around the path of the shield wall.

*****

Although they could see the enemy army's tracks, the trees spread an even canopy over the valley floor cutting off the line of sight and muffling travelling sounds. Stammer muttered, staring at the dense forest, but Lauren was gazing thoughtfully out over the lush green view. With a smile she signalled that her force should continue.

Lauren was beginning to feel out her troops. She picked up a sense of trust from the majority for their leaders, herself included. Not that this dispersed the barely controlled anger that the hard-bitten mixture of displaced soldiers assimilated into the troop displayed as they chased the tail of the Roke, or stop them from expressing their opinions vocally. Whatever their motives or level of anger, though, her crew had performed solidly ever since she had been handed command and sent to shadow the section of the Roke army reported to be led by the Collector.

They had made good time, riding hard but carefully, and soon began to reel in the lead that the enemy had. Lauren and most of her crew found out that they were within two days of the army when they reached the battle site that had formerly been Camp Smee, home of the famous war band. The few local survivors had slipped back into town after the enemy moved on and were toiling over burying the town's people who had died. They were even in the process of digging a mass grave for the enemy, to avoid the risk of disease.

Lauren allowed herself a brief moment to approach the ruined walls. It looked as if the town had been scoured with flame and then been smashed down by the very fist of the Battle God. Lauren was partially relieved when a partisan commander met her outside the main gates and explained that it had been Smee's own tactics, and not weapons carried by the Horde army, that had created such devastation.

Not wanting to dwell on the loss of life, especially with the battle ahead of them, Lauren soon had her command back in the saddle. Once again as they rode through the countryside they came across a number of places where the enemy had been attacked.

Many freelance crews and bands of citizens, displaced from the smaller, undefendable, towns, had arranged ambushes and running fights to attempt to delay the Horde army. At one place Lauren's trackers determined that a group of several hundred fighters, mainly women, had fought a pitched battle, further delaying the Roke. Losses had been high but the tracks revealed that the enemy had been unable to outflank the troops.

About a league further on Stammer picked a campsite and they stopped that night, just inside the woodland that marked the start of the foothills, off the trail and with heavy perimeter sentries and many scouts out. Partisan runners were ferrying back and forth and Stammer chattered with them, thoughtfully, around mouthfuls of rich stew: information was forthcoming once they had established her group's credentials.

Each new group of partisans carried additional intelligence. Apparently a pitched battle was being prepared some 15 leagues north where it was reported that General Agrik was using delaying tactics to bunch up the Roke raiders into an area where a large ambush had been planned. The relay messengers urged the troops to mount up and follow them that very night so that they could make progress and reach the area in time to join the start of the battle. To help get the troops to the proposed site the partisans switched out the weariest third of the horses and 60 percent of the Lauren's command rode on through the darkness; The remainder leaving at dawn with the baggage and supplies.

When they arrived at the next staging point the partisans there were able to fill in some more details. The site of the smaller battle they had passed had been needed for the final delay to the Collector's army. Troops including the Second Highland Light Cavalry, the Mountain Ranger Skirmishers and three freebooter companies were now deployed to stand with Lady Green's Gulley defences and give no ground. Lauren was again told to continue towards the Gulley and stopped only to pick up a handful of other partisan archers. They had only retreated from smaller encounters when they had fired their last arrows. As they passed one campfire an ancient, ex-company captain, Long Tall Brogue, was telling loudly how he would fight his way into the Roke lines with his closest comrades and put an end to one group of Roke head-men, at least, before going down.

Lauren found that as the time came for the final showdown her fellow men and women became happier and more positive despite the approaching danger. With a force approaching the size of the enemy army reported in the area, everyone was ready to play their own part and people she had never met were coming over to wish her luck in the 'big one'. Lauren supposed that the fear of the Horde gaining a foothold on the continent, the last preserve of humanity, was receding with every enemy killed in the interior.

Partisan confidence was so high that large open-cook fires had been sanctioned. The support people, who were only going to fight as a last resort, helped bolster morale further with decent food and an almost festival atmosphere.

At the final the station, as each hidden partisan camp was called, the station leader, Lars, was telling that a lady archer, Jenny, had shot the Roke second-in-command while waiting in a tree for the Roke to enter the woods, as Lauren's squad arrived for instruction. Carried away by the recent lighter mood, one of Lauren's crew snorted loudly, but Lars went on unperturbed to describe how his sister's headless body had been found a mass of arrows, when the furious Roke had finally passed on.

Embarrassed by her trooper, Lauren had mumbled her support somewhat sheepishly, and quickly herded them out into the night back to where the bulk of her command were taking their ease. Despite feeling that the squad needed to catch some rest, however short, before the next afternoon, Lauren had been keen to push on. Noon the next day was the general estimate of when the Collector's army would engage the Green Lady as she moved to attack them, entering the final approaches to the Gulley. Spurred on by the incident Lauren decided to reach the main body of troops and spoke her concerns over lax behaviour in no uncertain terms.

*****

Mooseman sat down on the bank of a grassy hill where the earth had been disturbed only slightly by the fighting. He pulled loose his dented helm and dropped it off to one side. With a weary sigh he placed his head in his hands and leaning forward to his knees he began to shake. The sound of more troops arriving and rangers being sent off to scout the countryside faded and his body, racked with tension and grief, trembled beyond his control. He had fought and won, but he had lost his son and Gill, his son's partner, was also dead, along with his brother by marriage, Grand. For two of his nephews, whom he had not seen since the dawn he also suspected the worst.

Mooseman also mourned the moose that had been his life. Near 20 of the great beasts that he had personally tended had come to fight today, and only one remained, generations of breeding lines cut off abruptly. He could only hope the remaining herd would be able to recover.

A hand clutched his shoulder and Sly, he still didn't know his real name, knelt before him urging a dented cup of brandy into his hands. He shrugged off part of his grief and lurched upright, grasping the goblet and forcing down the spirit, surprised to find it smooth. He looked into the man's eyes and noting the concern there he nodded to him and grunting thanks clapped him on the shoulder. As he glanced around he realised a small circle had formed. The Shark was there with a surprising number of his guard still alive, Bryce the greener, some townies and rangers and a handful of his friends and distant kin. Without a word they all raised their weapons to him in a silent salute for all the mountain people who had fought and died. Pausing only a moment to silently name those he would honour Mooseman raised his own weapon. There they all stood for some considerable time, each with weapon raised, lost in their own thoughts and goodbyes.

Chapter Twenty

It was late, a part before midst night, when the Collector received a group of his commanders. He was working on a map of the Gulley, preparing his plan. He knew the battle would be close as his intelligence on the precise defences that he might find was sketchy at best. He was also aware that a sizeable force was approaching from the rear and whilst he was confident he had superior numbers he knew his troop's discipline was as weak as their camp defences. That was why he had a double ring of conscripts on the unpopular task of night-watch duty. Unrelieved night-watch was almost certainly a death warrant for the exhausted troopers having missed out on sleep, should full battle be entered the next day. Still, several hundred troopers dead was the least of his concerns.

Once his army was marching he figured they should be in good shape. The supplies were protected in the middle of the army and a large section of Roke and some few siblants acted as a rear-guard. The power of his siblant bodyguard could finally be unleashed and he knew they could breach any defence. Yes, he decided, that was the planning taken care of for they only had some eight leagues to travel before they would construct the first stockade structure to fence themselves inside the pass through the mountains.

He was somewhat irritated as not one but six of his Siblant guard entered the tent without summons. "Well?" He snapped, signalling that his human slave guards, conditioned to complete obedience, should stand easy. 'Reptoids can be so ill mannered,' he thought. His own First Claw walked forwards at the head of the group and uttered in its halting approximation of the Roke language. "There is a problem."

"Oh, and what might that be?" the Collector replied arrogantly, deliberately returning his attention to the map, rudely and unnecessarily keeping the Siblants waiting. As the human commander looked up his Roke guards were already dying.

"You are alive," the Siblant hissed in return, and with a flick of his hatchet caved in the Collector's face.

The other five Siblants turned to leave hurrying, as agreed, to where all the Siblant force had been gathered. The last one stopped to thrust the nearest surviving camp guard towards the tent entrance, where the First Claw stood blocking the way. "Fetch me the Roke commanders," the siblant leader hissed.

The guard rushed away and in moments came back with two Roke war leaders. Torag, with a man watching the Collector's tent continually, was forewarned, and had limped, his wounded leg throbbing, through the shadows and witnessed the instructions from the safety of a dark, tent doorway.

"The enemy are in the camp, they have murdered the general. My warriors are pursuing the cowardly flesh responsible. You must communicate the final orders to the other commanders. As First Claw I decree that any Roke commander who makes it through the Gulley will become a free warlord, able to run his own kingdom and raid the lush grasslands as he desires. Thus I speak. Charge the enemy, break through and become kings. I demand it!" the First Claw commanded in an unusually long speech.

The siblant turned and moved away and the Roke commanders waited for but a moment and then, each intent on being the first through the Gulley, hurried off. Soon each had their own troops pushing through the camp, instantly turning it into a scene of utter chaos.

*****

The Green Lady's Uncle, Mulch, was one of two full-grown green plainsmen come to hold the pass until more of their clan could arrive. Those others arriving in time for the battle were groups of youngsters sent ahead in response to Mulch's call. These giants, though smaller than his ten-span high, eight-span wide frame, still represented the difference between the sexes with the females on average between six and seven spans tall, and strong. but slender. The males, however, were all eight spans and massively muscled.

Whilst the majority of the green folk arrived in simple clothes and harness, Mulch was very rare in that he had trained to fight in armour and carried with him an enormous pack. Lauren later learned that 30 green folk were left at the pass and the remainder split into two teams, to attack the head of the Horde army from opposite sides.

The ranger and partisan force in which Lauren became enrolled numbered about 1,500 troops, some being juniors or cadets. Informed of the ambush but unaware of the size of the green folk presence, Agrik, who had yet to appear near Lauren, circulated details of the required troop formation as a loose crescent, to fall upon the Collector from the rear when the trap was sprung.

Lauren, hearing news described as coming directly to her from Agrik once again felt her confusion rise. It was not that they had even done anything that night other than lie in each other's arms and talk. Lauren had had a few proper lovers before but it was his immediate declaration of love, following on from her own powerful sense of attraction, that had managed to get beneath her skin. Since that night he had never been far from her thoughts or, she believed, her own heart, which she knew was coming to match his declared feelings. When she had heard that he was racing with a body of men attempting to cut across the front of the Collector's army and reinforce Lady Green she had found herself worrying more for him than herself.

As it happened Lauren's section had barely reached their allotted billet position when the battle was joined. Mulch, it was later told, had pre-empted the attack by bounding in great leaps through the front of the enemy, smashing a short but direct path and roaring at the top of his lungs before bounding off. A good 30 Roke were left dead or stunned, some alive but physically broken by his charge. For some reason the Horde force had given up all pretence of an orderly attack and picking up their weapons had hurled themselves directly for the Gulley entrance; this occurrence had caused the green giant to act precipitously. Whatever the state of the Horde mind, to provoke the ragged charge, the effect of the appearance of an armoured green giant soon dented their confidence, although not their bravado as they still continued to approach, screaming insults.

Lauren signalled her men to approach carefully. The Roke camp seemed to relax after the shock news about the fighting at the front had been relayed through their ranks, if such a muddled mass could be so called. Confident she was correctly positioned Lauren's signal caused her first 60 archers to advance. Pausing only to kill the sentries they opened up with their over size bows which, using stoppers, simply blasted Roke off their feet all over their camp. Immediately the attack had those enemy not advancing milling about in chaos as other groups performed the same tactic from different directions. Noise from the front and the lack of progress of the Roke waiting in the rear ranks to move forward, soon made Lauren suspect that the Green Lady was having a similar effect at the front.

Almost as if she had performed a mental summoning, a slender green form appeared, tugging at Lauren's sleeve, drawing her back from her position in the forward archers. "Lauren Marshall, I am Meadowrunner, assistant to the Lady Green. I need to brief you on the current situation. The reason for the haphazard enemy behaviour, and the Lady's Uncle's dramatic attack before time, is because the Collector is already dead within the camp. Whatever has happened we don't yet know but the Lady has ways of knowing he is dead. Be aware that his entire bodyguard force of Siblants is missing from the camp, having smashed through the cordon north-east of here and is now unaccounted for. So sentries and rear defences are essential." With that the lightly-armoured form of the green woman was gone like smoke on the breeze.

Lauren arranged for perimeter guards to fall back and comprehensively cover the rear of the force. She brought up a second set of archers to begin their attack, using the approach of firing their arrows over the front troops to drop in arcs into the now stationary body of Horde warriors, desperately short on tactics and now huddling under whatever shields they could find. Some sections managed to break loose, although whether as an attack or to try and surrender it would never be known. The arrow fire was now quite heavy and deadly with more northern reinforcements arriving all the time. Alternate flights of mixed arrows – needle points, leaf and stoppers often meaning that Roke were hit by two or three kinds in quick succession.

Messages circulating had it that at the front of the enemy advance, green warriors were fighting hand-to-hand, and that the plan previously circulated was back in effect. The news from the front reported the green men and women smashing down brutally row after row of Roke. Because of the lack of enemy tactics, the attackers were only lightly affected by projectile weapons which could have exploited their unarmoured forms.

In concert with the planning the green giants suddenly pulled back, as if stung. Spotting this obvious retreat the Roke momentum returned and the enemy surged forward again only to find that they had passed over boarded trenches where groups of two or three plainsmen lay lightly covered, only to surge up suddenly, using massive swords to scythe down the surrounding Roke troops.

Instead of retreating, the Roke, unfamiliar with the terrain, were struggling to bring up their few heavier armoured, mounted troops from the camp. These mounted warriors were sent riding into the trees to attempt to cut the opposition lines. Whilst their losses at the front were almost total their weight of numbers allowed this tactic to be partially successful to the sides and in the middle of the army. Here the rangers were forced back until they moved to a skirmish mode with big oval shields firmly planted and staggered pairs of archers cross firing, each supported by spear-carrying soldiers.

Using a mixture of pikes and, where time permitted, tree limbs sharpened or strung between trees and swung towards the enemy, the middle expansion was broken up just before the ranger force as a whole withdrew further back into the tree line.

Deliberately this allowed the Roke to regain a degree of formation and lured them into continuing outwards, in the middle sections, believing themselves to be gaining the upper hand. The valley leading up to the entrance to the Gulley, although being a giant funnel in shape, remained broad enough and so heavily forested that the Roke had remained clustered around the central pathway through the trees. In fact the defence tactics had left the pathway usable to encourage the advancing army to stay close. The point where the valley actually entered the Gulley was, however, only several hundred spans across and, despite the fearsome physical power of the green warriors, the defence planners were keen to reduce the pressure that enemy weight of numbers could apply.

About a third of a league further up, the Roke were happy to revert to their usual loose formation with horse and a few scouts at the front. Suddenly rangers shot down the scouts and 16 medium-size harps began to sing as one, exploding through the front rank of the horse. The smell of the blood and the screaming of the horses, as those beside them were torn apart, caused chaos in the Roke cavalry ranks. Surrounded by covered pits and heavy groups of archers the harp were lifted off their tripods and hurried away behind steel shields, with the wooden tripods torched or left behind.

Trackers were reporting that the Siblant party had headed straight for the mountains, With time now on his side Agrik once more used the tactic of drawing back for a while. The Roke reorganised and had time to consider their options, finding that upwards of 40 percent of their number had been slaughtered already.

With the enemy capability to fight back plummeting, Lauren found that more and more she needed to direct her troops from a safe position, so she could easily receive the increasingly frequent runners. From a passing relay Lauren learnt that the Greens had lost only a handful of their company dead, and several withdrawn with a range of wounds, and the Gulley defences remained well manned. Performing a quick count Lauren and the other teams between them had lost only 108 fighters, mainly from the rear and mid-forces, with about another 100 out of combat through injury. Lauren had been impressed with the archery skills of the green ladies; a number had taken their powerful bows to several different locations to help keep an even net around the enemy army.

With no message to return the runner sat down. When Lauren asked after Calm she was told that he had called for his armour and had led a successful battle, his standard raised, the day before. Calm had with him Bryce, the son of Mulch, as his standard bearer. The clans of the mountain folk had joined his ranks, including the Rough Riders and their 50 armoured war-moose the remainder of the clan on foot.

Now more a slaughter than a battle, and with her officers

operating efficiently, Lauren relaxed and had more time to reflect. Discussing the situation at one point with Meadowrunner she was told that Lady Green was clearly saddened because the war had proved the end of many ancient mountain clans, including the infamous, self-styled, Sir Fox and his band of trappers.

Lauren, however, was buoyant. The breaking of the siege of Mid Vale meant that the second Horde force had at least been sundered, as had this section after the battle at Camp Smee. Rumours even began to run around the ring of the northern army that the Collector had been murdered by his own troops, who could see that their depleted numbers and split force no longer had the capability to survive.

The frequent relay messengers also had news from the south. Master Kroll, his Host Guard and former students who were rallying to his standard, had waylaid the only additional band of Roke of any size that had managed to breach the coastal defences after the initial landing. This news, more than anything, was perceived as the cause for the Horde's confidence beginning to fail. That Master Kroll had stripped the force of arms, speed marching towards the central plateau, destroying all Roke in his path, had been news that the Collector had been allowed to pick up, and certainly had only served to strengthen the defending army's morale at his expense.

Master Kroll appeared determined to end his banishment and cause as much damage as possible by charging straight through the small area of territory near the coast, the only captured settlements that the Roke had made any effort to keep. Lauren knew that his legend had as its backbone the 50-day period as the basis of his sworn oath to return to his birth place, even across enemy held territory, once he picked up arms to fight. With the whole enemy occupied Battle Lands to cross she wasn't surprised he was heading for the coast with all haste.

Lauren ventured an opinion on Master Kroll the next time the well informed green runner passed round the perimeter. "But Meadowrunner, would he not be better off helping here first before crossing the channel?" asked Lauren.

"Yes Lauren, but he has an ancient oath and once he picked up arms he faced becoming forsworn should he prolong his departure. Did you know he caught Roke cooking live children for eating? Anyway, he is always described as saying that the best way to stop the Roke doing to us what they did to his home would be to retake his homeland." Meadowrunner paused squinting into the grey pre-dawn as the breeze carried sounds of fighting over from the Gulley entrance. "Apparently it was only he and his six guards scouting alone that came on the scene. He personally killed 38 Roke before picking up a weapon, and each died in a different way. The remaining children were saved but he had already used steel. A 100 Roke were destroyed though and 300 more when the full honour guard arrived. Master Kroll's flute standard was soon raised after the Host Guard performed the ceremony to free him from his service to us. Commander Shield and the rest of the guards pretty much kept up, but turned north past Life Rock to try and reach the coast and get Kroll some boat transportation as he attacked the Roke-held settlements towards the coast."

The green scout paused before continuing, "I don't know if you knew him, but it has been confirmed that those killed in the battle for camp Smee included the Magnificent Bart, with Master Smee still missing presumed dead."

Lauren paused only a moment to reflect that, despite the imminent victory, the loss of key talents within the nation that this invasion had caused would last the rest of her lifetime. Then she was hurrying back to the perimeter where the archers were keeping up an unrelenting barrage slowly cutting down the remaining body of the enemy one by one.

*****

Moffet followed the band of scrub that he knew led down to the river, where it carried along the bank for a couple of leagues. Any search party, especially with horses or trackers, would not take long to find them but the cover would help.

Hearing the dogs Moffet therefore decided to risk the stream bed as it rose into the hills and, draping the semi-conscious and unintelligible Master Smee over his shoulders, began wading through the shallows. He could judge where to walk pretty well as he had spent years tickling trout along these

411

waterways, especially where the water undercut the bank and where there were shallows. After about a part Smee came to again and this time managed to groan. "Is that you, Moffet lad, find a dry place to put me down will you?"

From back down the stream came the sounds that their trail had been spotted again but this time Moffet was too exhausted to continue and agreed to the band leader's request. They sat on dry gravel under an overhang listening as the Roke followed the tracks up to the point where they had entered the water, the noise of the pursuit carrying easily through the thin, clean mountain air. The search party leader seemed to have split his squad, some up hill and some down, the men and horses finding it slow going to parallel the stream exactly. Master Smee gave Moffet's hand a weak squeeze and winked encouragingly with one bloodshot eye as they sat, both lacking the physical capacity to continue, and waited for capture, torture, death.

*****

Although a good distance into the fortified pass, the clear mountain air brought the sounds of the fighting below up to where the children waited for the dawn to light the skies. Lady Green had told Sophie that she would join them for the journey into the Great Plains once the outcome of the battle looked sure. She then sent them up whilst she remained with her relatives to arrange the defence as per the human/green folk treaty concerning the Gulley.

The party had left Lady Green's home three days earlier, riding as hard for the pass as the presence of the children would allow, and had arrived at the gap to find the area a hive of activity. Many woodsmen were carefully digging trenches and according to Sophie's count, 100 plainsmen and plainswomen were sat around a giant figure who was rumbling out instructions and answering questions in the chant-like language of the Green People.

Both Sophie and Liam had stopped in surprise at the sight of the giant, hulking figure. "That is my Uncle Mulch," Lady Green had explained. "He has come to perform his duty as the guardian of this entrance to the Green Lands. So far only these

100 youths, his students, have arrived but many more of my people will come here to join the fight over the next few days."

"Lady, your Uncle is huge. I thought that Brother Stream at the fayre was big," said Sophie, before turning with a serious expression to Liam. "Mind you don't cause any trouble with the green folk or cause one to step on you," the girl told the little boy, his eyes still wide with wonder.

The morning after they had arrived saw many other new arrivals, mainly human, from the mountains either side of the Gulley also a couple more mean-looking green men. Suddenly a stir had run through the camp. Scouts had reported that the enemy was approaching.

Walrus, Liam, Sophie and the Legionnaires had been sent hurriedly to begin their journey up the Gulley itself; Lady Green firm in her instructions that they should wait for her only when they had reached the halfway staging point. Sophie and Liam led their ponies silently along with the others who, dressed in a variety of well used armour and each with weapons readily available, looked serious and scary. Even Liam had carried a determined air as they climbed and Sophie observed from the white at his knuckles that he was gripping tightly the miniature spear Eamon Sombers had given him.

The climb was slow going as they frequently had to pass through stockade fences that only allowed single file traffic, and which caused the travellers to double back frequently on themselves to make progress. Human and Green warriors were also making their own way down and periodically the party stopped to let these troops hurry down the trail. Climbing with Walrus, he informed the children in a quiet voice that for weeks now Lady Green had been sending work parties to the pass to build these temporary obstacles in case the fighting could not be held in the lowlands. Judging by the numbers of sharpened wooden stakes used Sophie could see that many people had worked very hard.

Little seemed to happen below during the day, with faint sounds carrying up the hint of a few light skirmishes. When they stopped at the quarter-point to shelter in a wooden shed for the night, sat amongst bundles of arrows, looking back down into the valley the group they could see a myriad of fire-lights between the trees. Claphand had explained these were where the enemy had made its camp. Throughout the day Walrus had become more and more tense. It was Mags who had taken Liam aside when he had asked if Walrus was angry with him. "Little lad," the scarred woman started, "Walrus is just upset that he will not be able to help his friends or protect the Green Lady when the fighting starts. He is especially uncomfortable as he is also secretly glad to be here keeping you safe with us. When you grow up you will come to know this sort of situation as a conflict of interests, they really can be most upsetting."

Now that the enemy was visible in this way the tension seemed to double and nobody, with the exception of Liam, was able to sleep much. Off to the side, on the nearby trail, numbers of the large plainsmen could be heard making their way down through the defences. Old timers were stationed at various points to direct them in the darkness and so played their part in the defence as best they could.

It had been the middle of the night when the combat had suddenly begun for real. Walrus and Mags had exchanged shrugs. Sophie sat cuddled in Claphand's arms watching the fire arrows fall by the score and hearing the screams of the humans, the melodious chanting of the plainswomen and the terrifying bellows of the plainsmen as the battle was joined.

*****

The Land Shark stood facing the mountains with Stilith O Chas and Habgood, one of the partisan captains in the area north of Mid Vale. Stilith was finishing her report and Habgood had only just arrived.

"So, Shark, we have seen a few bands of 20 to 50 Reptoids as we pushed up. We were using a wide front of scouts though and I cannot see that we have missed or passed any bands of Reptoids in the numbers that you are talking of."

"That is what I expected, Stilith. You have done well to maintain your fighting force throughout this difficult campaign. As you saw on the battlefield only a relatively small number of Reptoids were slain in the breaking of the siege. Come, give us your report, Habgood, you have the answer I am sure."

Hadgood sketched an old style bow to each of his audience before he began. "It is as you suggested, Fin. The tracks led to the lumberyard. Despite the fact that they displayed dead Reptoids nailed to the stockade since the Horde first reached this area, some two weeks past, it is definitely an enemy facility."

His face turning a mask of distaste Habgood continued, "We have detained one of the partisan team responsible for the security in that area and he is a traitor. He admits only to falsifying reports and claims no part in the murder of those of his comrades who remained loyal. Two others remain unaccounted for but are suspect. So far we have not approached too closely lest we give up what element of surprise we may yet retain. The yard stockade has been enlarged to cover the significant portion of the valley mouth and we suspect it has been additionally fortified. From the tracks we estimate that at least a 1,000 Reptoids of mixed type have passed through the gates, although in places the ground has been dragged and so we cannot be precise without more investigation."

The Shark was clenching and unclenching his fists as the report progressed, anxious to be moving about, burning off nervous energy, but he remained stationary. "Habgood, are the guardians in place?" he asked the captain.

"I passed on your communication to the grey ones, Fin, but there was no immediate answer. We have since received an encoded map location which matches your general request. I suspect in their quiet way, their hatred for the Horde far exceeds our own. I would be surprised if their goals differed greatly from your own." Habgood paused awkwardly, passing over the location code on a scrap of the soft leather parchment used in place of paper by the Greys. "It is rare that any activity on the mountain borders goes unnoticed, and yet we have received no indication of the lumber yard activities through normal contacts. It makes me worry, Fin. Will you not take more men?"

The Shark looked up from his message to his man and shook his head, almost grinning. Instead of answering the question he turned to the female veteran. "Stilith, I take it you have the core of the situation from this news. Put an official report out on general alert, but only after you decide to assault the yard. Will you work with Habgood to secure the town and then surround the traitors' nest?" Taking her nod as complete acceptance he turned to look up into the mountains. The Shark finished in a voice almost too soft to carry. "I go up the hill to hunt the beasts with my brothers," and in a couple of strides was hurrying away at a ground-eating pace.

*****

The same early dawn light that revealed the Gulley defences squeezing the remains of the invasion force saw Stonebrow standing at the end of the mission hangar that led down to the docks. He was, therefore, the first to meet the fort command team as it raced up the equipment ramp.

"Stonebrow, good to finally meet you. I am sorry we have kept you here waiting on permanent readiness for so long. You were scheduled to leave after you completed the final integration ten days ago, but the Horde invasion caught and destroyed some of the ordnance essential to our own assault and we have had to wait for replacement supplies," the Marshall told the smaller man without loosening his greeting grip.

Spinning to point a circle at the entire hangar, the energetic leader of the northern army continued without waiting for a reply. "I am happy to say that tonight the weather will be perfect for the entry operation. You need to be embarked and away within three parts, for the crossing will be tonight and, Battler help us, we begin our assault just before dawn tomorrow," the High Marshall informed him bluntly.

Even without his fearsome helm the Marshall cut an impressive figure, especially with a savage scar down the right side of his face only newly healed. He carried his armoured bulk as if his form was as light as a feather.

Still without giving Stonebrow a chance to reply Makram Marshall clapped him on the shoulder as if forcing some of his own vigorous energy into the man he was sending out. "I won't keep you. Rest assured we will fight to reach you as soon as we can. Now I must have a quick word with Milton. Fare you well young musician, and remember you must not fail in, this whatever it takes. In your hands lies the power to free us of a great terror." Then the big man was gone, his arm drawing

Milton in close, speaking quietly into his ear.

Stonebrow signed some instructions to his deputies and stood looking down the ramp fixedly at the departing figure as frantic, if well organised, activity spread through the hangar as the mission prepared to embark. Shrugging off his doubts and fears Stonebrow followed the line of equipment down to the assault ship. After 1,000 years it was time for the humans to take back their land.